Praise for *This Book Is Full of Spiders*

"Kevin Smith's *Clerks* meets H. P. Lovecraft in this exceptional thriller that makes zombies relevant again. . . . From the dialogue to the descriptions, lines are delivered with faultless timing and wit. Wong never has to reach for comedy, it flows naturally with nary a stumble . . . the most pertinent story of the genre since George Romero's *Dawn of the Dead* . . . a tighter, more concentrated read than *John Dies at the End*. . . . David Wong (Jason Pargin) is a fantastic author with a supernatural talent for humor. If you want a poignant, laugh-out-loud funny, disturbing, ridiculous, self-aware, socially relevant horror novel then *This Book Is Full of Spiders: Seriously, Dude, Don't Touch It* is the one and only book for you."　　　　　　　　　　　　　　　　　—*SF Signal*

"The comedic and crackling dialogue also brings a whimsical flair to the story, making it seem like an episode of AMC's *The Walking Dead* written by Douglas Adams of *The Hitchhiker's Guide to the Galaxy*. . . . Imagine a mentally ill narrator describing the zombie apocalypse while drunk, and the end result is unlike any other book of the genre. Seriously, dude, touch it and read it."　　　　　—*The Washington Post*

"[A] phantasmagoria of horror, humor—and even insight into the nature of paranoia, perception, and identity."
　　　　　　　　　　　　　　　—*Publishers Weekly* (starred review)

"Violence, soy sauce, and zombie survivalists abound in this clever and funny sequel to *John Dies at the End* (2009). One of the great things about discovering new writers, especially in the narrow range of hybrid-genre comedic novels, is realizing that they're having just as much fun making this stuff up as you are reading it. Sitting squarely with the likes of S. G. Browne and Christopher Moore, the pseudonymous Wong (*Cracked* editor Jason Pargin) must be pissing himself laughing at his own writing, even as he's giving fans an even funnier, tighter, and justifiably insane entry in the series. . . . The humor here is unforced and good-naturedly gory. Anyone who enjoyed the recent films *The Cabin in the Woods* or *Tucker & Dale vs. Evil* will find themselves right at home. A (cult?) film adaptation of *John Dies at the End* promises to lure new readers. A joyful return to the paroxysms of laughter lurking in the American Midwest." —*Kirkus Reviews*

Praise for *John Dies at the End*

"Sure to please the *Fangoria* set while appealing to a wider audience, the book's smart take on fear manages to tap into readers' existential dread on one page, then have them laughing the next." —*Publishers Weekly*

"Strikes enough of a balance between hilarity, horror, and surrealism here to keep anyone glued to the story." —*Booklist*

"You can (and will want to) read *John Dies at the End* in one sitting." —*BookReporter.com*

"Wong blends horror and suspense with comedy—a tricky combination— and pulls it off effortlessly." —*FashionAddict.com*

"It's interesting, compelling, engaging, arresting, and—yes—sometimes even horrifying. And when it's not being any of those things, it's funny. Very, very funny." —*January Magazine*

"This is one of the most entertaining and addictive novels I've ever read." —Jacob Kier, publisher, Permuted Press

"The rare genre novel that manages to keep its sense of humor strong without ever diminishing the scares; David is a consistently hilarious narrator whose one-liners and running commentary are sincere in a way that makes the horrors he confronts even more unsettling." —*A.V. Club*

"A loopy buddy-movie of a book with deadpan humor and great turns of phrase . . . Just plain fun." —*Library Journal*

ALSO BY DAVID WONG

John Dies at the End

THIS BOOK
IS FULL OF
SPIDERS

SERIOUSLY, DUDE, DON'T TOUCH IT

DAVID WONG

THOMAS DUNNE BOOKS ⚏ ST. MARTIN'S GRIFFIN   NEW YORK

THOMAS DUNNE BOOKS.
An imprint of St. Martin's Press.

THIS BOOK IS FULL OF SPIDERS. Copyright © 2012 by David Wong. All rights reserved. Printed in the United States of America. For information, address St. Martin's Press, 175 Fifth Avenue, New York, N.Y. 10010.

www.thomasdunnebooks.com
www.stmartins.com

Design by Steven Seighman

The Library of Congress has cataloged the hardcover edition as follows:

Wong, David, 1975–
    This book is full of spiders : seriously, dude, don't touch it /
David Wong. — 1st ed.
        p. cm.
    ISBN 978-0-312-54634-2 (hardcover)
    ISBN 978-1-250-01790-1 (e-book)
    1. Friends—Fiction.   2. Slackers—Fiction.   3. Zombies—Fiction.
I. Title.
    PS3623.O5975T47 2012
    813'.6—dc23
                                                    2012028299
        ISBN 978-1-250-03665-0 (trade paperback)

St. Martin's Griffin books may be purchased for educational, business, or promotional use. For information on bulk purchases, please contact Macmillan Corporate and Premium Sales Department at 1-800-221-7945, extension 5442, or write specialmarkets @macmillan.com.

20 19 18 17 16 15 14 13 12

*For Carley, who was a better person than I am
even though she was a dog*

WARNING: THE FOLLOWING ACCOUNT CONTAINS FRANK DESCRIPTIONS OF MONSTERS AND MALE NUDITY.

THIS BOOK IS FULL OF SPIDERS

PROLOGUE

You know how sometimes when you're drifting off to sleep you feel that jolt, like you were falling and caught yourself at the last second? It's nothing to be concerned about, it's usually just the parasite adjusting its grip.

I guess I should explain that a little further, but it will take a while. And you have to promise not to get mad. My name is David Wong, by the way. It's on the cover. If you don't know who I am, that's perfect. That means you didn't read the previous book in this saga which, to be frank, doesn't paint me in the best light. No, don't go read it now. It's better if we get a fresh start. So, hello, stranger! I'm pleased to have this fresh opportunity to try to convince you I'm not a shithead. Just skip the next paragraph.

If you do know who I am, presumably because you read the previous book, I know what you're thinking and in response I can only say, "No, fuck *you*." Stop sending me hate mail. Please note that all correspondence regarding the class action lawsuit resulting from the publication of that book should be directed to the publisher's legal department, not me. Go find the address yourself, you bunch of greedy fartsouls.

Now, on with our tale. Note: I apologize for the harsh language above, you'll find that is not typical of me.

EPIPROLOGUE

So here's how fucked up this town is. My friend John and I were out celebrating his birthday last summer. At the end of the night we were good and drunk and we headed outside of town to go climb up the water tower and piss off of it. This had been John's tradition for the last twenty years (if you do the math, you'll realize that goes back to when he turned five, which really says more about John's parents than John). This was a special year because they were in the process of tearing down that old water tower to build a new, more modern one and it didn't look like the new one was going to have the kind of platform that you could piss off of, because this is no longer a world of men.

Anyway, it's two in the morning and we're taking turns pissing off of the tower (rather than going at the same time, because we weren't raised by wolves). So it's my turn and I'm right at that transcendent moment when the long stream of urine connects me and the ground below, when I see headlights off in the distance. A row of them, out on the highway, about a quarter mile of cornfield away from where I was pissing. That was enough to get my attention, because that is not a busy stretch of highway at any hour, let alone in the wee hours of the morning on a weekday. As the headlights got closer, I saw they belonged to a row of black military transports.

I squinted and said, "Are we being . . . *invaded*? Because I'm too drunk to pull off a *Red Dawn*."

From behind me, John said, "Look at that one. In the back . . ." and my pissing immediately stopped because I sure as hell can't go while somebody is talking to me. I found the last set of headlights and saw that they were waving lazily back and forth—the truck swerving out of control. Then, with a faint *crunch*, the vehicle connected with a telephone pole.

The rest of the convoy moved on without it.

Before I could even get zipped up, John was already climbing down the ladder, over my slurred protests. He managed to somehow not tumble off and break his neck, and jumped into my rusting old Ford Bronco. I followed him down and barely made it into the passenger seat before we were speeding down the lane, rows of corn whipping past, John with the Bronco in stealth mode with the headlights off.

We found the wrecked truck (which was built like one of the armored cars banks use, only minus any markings) off the side of the highway, its steaming grille looking like it was caught in the act of trying to eat the wooden pole. We were alone with it—none of the rest of the trucks had doubled back to check on the crash, a fact that at the time I was too intoxicated to find odd. We cautiously approached the vehicle. John went right to the driver's side door, I guess to see if the driver was hurt. He peered into the window, yanked the door open, then just stood there, in silence.

I said, "What?"

Nothing from John.

I glanced nervously down the highway and said again, "*What?* Is he dead?"

Again, no answer.

I approached and reluctantly peered into the driver's seat. Now it was my turn to stand there slackjawed, breathing air that stank of leaking antifreeze. My first impression was that the driver's seat was empty, which wouldn't have been that odd—maybe the driver was dazed and had stumbled out before we arrived. But it wasn't empty. Sitting in the driver's seat was a six-inch-tall plastic GI Joe action figure. It was half obscured by the seat belt, which was clasped around it.

John and I stood there trying to puzzle through what we were seeing, the gears in our heads creaking against a thick vodka sludge. Not that it would have made sense in perfect sobriety, either—the driver, what, crashed his truck into a tree, then before leaving the scene of the accident, decided to position a toy in the driver's seat and buckle the seat belt around it? Why? So the first responders would think the *Toy Story* universe was real?

John pulled the keys from the ignition and closed the door. He glanced around outside, looking for the driver. Nobody in sight. Then he circled around to the back of the truck, to the windowless, locked rear doors. He banged on the door with his fist and said, "Hey, you guys all right in there? Looks like the accident turned the driver into a GI Joe."

No answer. If we'd been sober, we'd probably have realized that there was a great chance that if anybody was inside this sinister, black, unmarked armored vehicle, they'd more likely jump out with guns and kick the shit out of us than thank us for our concern. But that didn't happen, and John immediately went about figuring out which key on the key ring would open the door. After a dozen clumsy attempts, he found one that worked and slowly pulled it open.

No one was in the back of the truck.

Laying on the floor was a box. It was army olive green, and about the size of a toolbox, or a lunchbox for somebody who always got really hungry at work. It had a simple handle at the top. The sides were ribbed in a way that suggested it was reinforced or armored somehow. There was no visible latch or lock, and in fact there was no obvious place to try to wedge in a crowbar. Across the front, stenciled in yellow spray paint, were a series of markings that looked like Egyptian hieroglyphs.

John climbed into the truck and grabbed the box. I clumsily climbed in after him, banging my shin painfully off the bumper on the way, whispering, "John! No! Leave it!"

Inside, I realized that we weren't alone. The mystery box was being guarded by six more GI Joe action figures, each carrying a little plastic assault rifle. They were wearing tiny black suits with face masks. I guess more Cobra than GI Joe, then.

John grabbed the box and jumped out into the night, oblivious to my slurred demands to leave it behind.

If you're asking yourself what exactly John expected to find inside that truck, the easy guess would be, "a shitload of cash." But we're not criminals, if we had found a pile of white bags with big cartoon dollar signs on them, we'd have locked up the truck and called the cops. No, the answer is more complicated.

John didn't know what he would find inside that truck, *which is why he had to open the door.* There are two kinds of people in the world; the first see locks and warning signs and say, "If they're keeping it locked up so tight, that means it's both dangerous and none of my business." But the second type say, "If they want to keep it a secret so bad, then it must be worth seeing." That's John. That is, in fact, the only reason he hasn't moved far away from this fucked-up town. If you don't understand what I mean by "fucked-up," well, I ain't talking about the unemployment rate. This thing with the trucks, it wasn't exactly an isolated incident.

Six centuries ago, the pre-Columbian natives who settled here named this region with a word that in their language translates to, "The Mouth of the Shadow." Later, the Iroquois who showed up and inexplicably slaughtered every man, woman, and child in those first tribes renamed it a word that literally translates to, "Seriously, Fuck this Place." When French explorer Jacques Marquette explored the area in 1673, he marked it on his map with a crude drawing of what appeared to be a black blob falling out of Satan's butthole.

In 1881, a group of coal miners got trapped when an explosion caused the entrance of the mine to collapse. When rescuers showed up to the mouth of the mine, they found sitting in front of the rubble a coal-dusted kid, the youngest of the miners. His exact greeting to the men was, "Don't dig 'em out. They sent me out here to tell you that. Them boys blew it themselves. Caved it in on purpose, to keep what they found in there from gettin' out. So just leave it be. Now you there, with that pickax? I'd appreciate it if you'd go ahead and use that to cave in my skull, same as they did to that mine. Just maybe it'll gouge out that blue eyeball that's starin' back at me from inside my own head."

Things have only gone downhill from there.

Here, in this town, three friends will stroll into a dark alley, and only two will emerge from the other end. Those two will have no memory of the third. It's rumored that a year ago, a five-year-old kid went into surgery to have a brain tumor removed. When the surgeon sawed open his skull, the "tumor" jumped out, a ball of whipping tentacles that launched itself at the surgeon and burrowed into his eye socket. Two minutes later, he and two nurses lay dead in the OR, their craniums neatly cleaned from the inside. I say this incident was "rumored" because at this point in the story, men in suits showed up, flashed official-looking ID and took away the bodies. The story in the paper the next day was that everybody died due to an oxygen tank explosion.

But John and I know the truth. We know, because we were there. We usually are. Tourists show up here because they've heard the town is "haunted" but that word does nothing to convey the situation. "Infested" is better. John and I have made this stuff our hobby, in the way that an especially attractive prisoner makes a hobby out of not getting raped. Jesus, that's a terrible analogy. I apologize. What I'm saying is that it's self-preservation. We didn't choose this, we just have talents that makes us the equivalent of that new guy in the cell block who has a slim, hairless body and kind of looks like a woman from behind, and has an incredibly realistic tattoo of boobs on his back. He may have no desire at all to ever even touch a penis, but it's going to happen, even if it's just in the process of frantically slapping them away. Jesus, am I still talking about this? [*John—please delete the above paragraph before it goes off to the publisher*].

So anyway, that's why John looked inside the truck and that's why he took the box even though for all we knew, the contents were worth-less, or toxic, or radioactive, or all three. We did eventually get into the box, and considering what was inside it, they didn't have *nearly* enough security around the thing. But that story will have to wait for a bit. Oh, and if you're thinking that it was a huge coincidence that the truck happened to crash in the exact time and place where John and I were birthday tower pissing, don't worry. It wasn't. All of this will make sense with time. Or, maybe not.

Now let's fast-forward to November 3rd, about . . .

48 Hours Prior to Outbreak

"I'm not crazy," I said, crazily, to my court-appointed therapist.

He seemed bored with our session. That actually made me want to act crazy, to impress him. Maybe that was his tactic. I thought, *maybe I should tell him I'm the only person on Earth who has seen his entire skeleton.*

Or, I could make something up instead. The therapist, whose name I had already forgotten, said, "You believe your role here is to convince me you're not crazy?"

"Well . . . you know I'm not here by choice."

"You don't think you need the sessions."

"I understand why the judge ordered it. I mean it's better than jail."

He nodded. I guess that was my cue to keep talking. Man, psychiatry seems like a pretty easy job. I said, "A couple months ago I shot a pizza delivery guy with a crossbow. I was drunk."

Pause. Nothing from the doctor. He was in his fifties, but looked like he could still take me in a game of basketball, even though I was half his age. His gray hair was cut like a 1990's era George Clooney. Type of guy whose life had gone exactly as he'd expected it. I bet he'd never shot a delivery guy with a crossbow even once.

I said, "Okay, I wasn't drunk. I'd only had one beer. I thought the guy was threatening me and my girlfriend Amy. It was a misunderstanding."

"He said you accused him of being a monster."

"It was dark."

"The neighbors heard you shout to him, and I'm quoting from the police report, 'Go back to Hell you unholy abomination, and tell Korrok I have a lot more arrows where that came from.'"

"Well . . . that's out of context."

"So you do believe in monsters."

"No. Of course not. It was . . . a metaphor or something."

He had a nameplate on his desk: Dr. Bob Tennet. Next to it was a bobblehead of a St. Louis Cardinals baseball player. I glanced around the room, saw he had a leftover Halloween decoration still taped to his window, a cardboard jack-o'-lantern with a cartoon spider crawling out of its mouth. The doctor had only five books on the shelf behind him, which I thought was hilarious because I owned more books than that and I wasn't even a doctor. Then I realized they were all written by him. They had long titles like *The Madness of Crowds: Decoding the Dynamics of Group Paranoia* and *A Person Is Smart, People Are Stupid: An Analysis of Mass Hysteria and Groupthink*. Should I be flattered or insulted that I apparently got referred to a world-class expert in the subject of why people believe in stupid shit?

He said, "You understand, the court didn't order these sessions because you believe in monsters."

"Right, they want to make sure I won't shoot anyone else with a crossbow."

He laughed. That surprised me. I didn't think these guys were allowed to laugh. "They want to make sure you're not a danger to yourself or others. And while I know it's counterintuitive, that process will actually be easier if you don't think of it as a test you have to pass."

"But if I'd shot somebody over a girl or a stolen case of beer, I wouldn't be here. I'm here because of the monster thing. Because of who I am."

"Do you want to talk about your beliefs?"

I shrugged. "You know the stories that go around this town. People disappear here. Cops disappear. But I can tell the difference between reality and fantasy. I work, I have a girlfriend, I'm a productive citizen. Well, not *productive*, I mean if you add up what I bring to society and what I take out, society probably breaks even. And I'm not crazy. I mean, I know anybody can say that. But a crazy person can't fake sane, right? The whole point of being crazy is that you can't separate crazy ideas from normal ones. So, no, I don't believe the world is full of monsters disguised as people, or ghosts, or men made of shadows. I don't believe that the town of—

The name of the town where this story takes place will remain undisclosed so as not to add to the local tourism traffic.

—is a howling orgy of nightmares. I fully recognize that all of those are things only a mentally ill person believes. Therefore, I do not believe them."

Boom. Therapy accomplished.

No answer from Dr. Tennet. Fuck him. I'll sit like this forever. I'm great at not talking to people.

After a minute or so I said, "Just . . . to be clear, what's said in this room doesn't leave this room, right?"

"Unless I believe a crime is about to be committed, that's correct."

"Can I show you something? On my phone? It's a video clip. I recorded it myself."

"If it's important to you."

I pulled out the phone and dug through the menus until I found a thirty-second clip I'd recorded about a month ago. I held it up for him to see.

It was a nighttime scene, at an all-night burrito stand near my house. Out front was a faded picnic table, a rusted fifty-five-gallon drum for a trash can and a whiteboard with prices scrawled in dry erase marker. Without a doubt the best burritos you can possibly get within six blocks of my house at four in the morning.

The grainy shot (my phone's camera wasn't worth a damn in low light) caught the glare of headlights as a black SUV pulled up. Stepping out of it was a young Asian man in a shirt and tie. He casually walked around the tiny orange building, nodding to the kid at the counter. He went to a narrow door in the rear, opened it and stepped inside.

After about ten seconds, the shot shakily moved toward the door. A hand extended into frame—my hand—and pulled the door open. Inside were some cardboard boxes with labels like LARGE LIDS and MED. PAPER BAGS—WHITE along with a broom and a mop and bucket.

The Asian man was gone. There was no visible exit.

The clip ended.

I said, "You saw it, right? Guy goes in, guy doesn't come out. Guy's not in there. He's not in the burrito stand. He's just *gone*."

"You believe this is evidence of the supernatural."

"I've seen this guy since then. Around town. This isn't some burrito shop Bermuda Triangle, sucking in innocent passersby. The guy walked right toward it, on purpose. And he came out somewhere else. And I knew he was coming, because he did the same thing, every night, at the same time."

"You believe there was a secret passage or something of the sort?"

"Not a physical one. There's no hatch in the floor or anything. We checked. No, it's like a . . . wormhole or something. I don't know. But that's not even the point. It's not just that there was a, uh, magical burrito door there, or whatever it was, it's that *the guy knew what it was and how to use it*. There are people like that around town."

"And you believe these people are dangerous."

"Oh, Jesus Christ, *I am not going to shoot him with a crossbow.* How can you not be impressed by this?"

"It's important to you that I believe you."

I just realized he was phrasing all of his questions as statements. Wasn't there a character in *Alice in Wonderland* who did that? Did Alice punch him in the face?

"Okay. I could have faked the video. You have the option of believing that. And man, if I could have that option, like if I could buy it from you, I'd pay anything. If you told me you'd reach into my brain and turn off my belief in all of this stuff, and in exchange I just had to let you, say, shoot me in the balls with one of those riot control bean-bag guns, I'd sign the deal right now. But I can't."

"That must be very frustrating for you."

I snorted. I looked down at the floor between my knees. There was a faded brown stain on the carpet and I wondered if a patient had once taken a shit in here in the middle of a session. I ran my hands through my hair and felt my fingers tighten and twist it, pain radiating down my scalp.

Stop it.

He said, "I can see this is upsetting you. We can change the subject if you like."

I made myself sit up and take a deep breath.

"No. This is what we're here to talk about, right?"

He shrugged. "I think it's important to you."

Yes, in the way that the salt is important to the slug.

He said, "It's up to you."

I sighed, considered for a few beats, then said, "One time, early in the morning, I was getting ready for work. I go into the bathroom and . . ."

. . . *turned on the shower, but the water just stopped in midair.*

I don't mean the water hovered there, frozen in time. That would be crazy. No, the spray was pouring down about twelve inches from the nozzle, then spreading and splattering as if the stream was breaking against something solid. Like an invisible hand was held under the showerhead to test the temperature.

I stood there outside the shower stall, naked, squinting in dull confusion. Now, I'm not the smartest guy under normal circumstances but my 6 A.M. brain has an IQ of about 65. I vaguely thought it was some kind of plumbing problem. I stared stupidly at the interrupted umbrella-shaped spray of water, resisting the impulse to reach out and touch the space the water couldn't seem to pass through. Fear was slowly bubbling up into my brain. Hairs stood up on my back. I glanced down, blinking, as if I would find a note explaining all of this taped to my pubic hair. I didn't.

Then, I heard the spray change, the splattering on the tiles taking on a dif-

ferent tone. I glanced up and saw the part of the flow farthest from me slowly return to normal, the water shooting past the invisible obstruction in a gentle arc. The unseen thing was passing out of the stream. It wasn't until the spray looked completely normal again that I realized this meant the invisible thing that had been blocking the water was now moving toward me.

I jumped back, moving so quick that I thought the half-open shower curtain had blown back from the wind of my rapid movement. But that wasn't right, because the curtain didn't return to its normal shape right away. It stayed bulged outward, something unseen pushing against it. I backed up against the wall, feeling the towel bar pressing into my back. The shower curtain fell straight again and now there was nothing in the bathroom but the radio static sound of the shower splattering against tile. I stood there, frozen, heart pounding so hard I was getting dizzy. I slowly put a hand out, tentative, toward the curtain, through the space the unseen thing had passed . . .

Nothing.

I decided to forget about the shower. I cranked off the water, turned toward the door and—

I saw something. Or I almost did. Just out of the corner of my eye, a dark shape, a black figure whipping through the doorway just out of sight. Like a shadow without the person.

I couldn't have seen it for more than a tenth of a second, but I did see it, now imprinted in my brain from that flash of a glance. The form, black, in the shape of a man but then becoming formless, like a single drop of dark food coloring before it dissolves in a sink of running water.

I had seen it before.

". . . I thought I saw something in there. I don't know. Probably nothing."

I slumped in the chair and crossed my arms.

"This is a source of anxiety for you. Having these beliefs, and feeling like you can't talk about them without being dismissed."

I stared out of the window, at my Bronco rusting in the parking lot, the metal eager to get back to just being dirt. Life was probably easier for it back then.

I said, "Who's paying for these sessions again?"

"Payment is your responsibility. But we have a sliding scale."

"Awesome."

He considered for a moment and then said, "Would it put you more at ease if I told you that I believe in monsters?"

"It might put me at ease, but I can't speak for the people who hand out psychiatrist licenses."

"I'll tell you a story. Now, I understand that with your . . . hobbies, people contact you, correct? Believing they have ghosts or demons in their homes?"

"Sometimes."

"And I am going to make an assumption—if you arrive and tell them that the source of their anxiety is *not* in fact supernatural, they are anything but relieved. Correct? Meaning they *want* the banging in their attic to be a ghost, and not a squirrel trapped in the chimney."

"Yeah, I guess."

"So you see, fear is just another manifestation of insecurity. What humans want most of all, is to be *right*. Even if we're being right about our own doom. If we believe there are monsters around the next corner ready to tear us apart, we would literally prefer to be right about the monsters, than to be shown to be wrong in the eyes of others and made to look foolish."

I didn't answer. I glanced around for a clock. He didn't have one, the bastard.

"So, a few years ago, while I was presenting at a conference in Europe, my wife called and insisted that the walls of our laundry room were throbbing. That was the word she used. Pulsing, like the wall itself was alive. She described a hum, an energy, that she could feel as soon as she walked into the room. I suggested it was a wiring problem. She became . . . let's just say, agitated at that point. Three days later, just before I was due to come back, she called again. The problem was getting worse, she said. There was an audible hum now, from the wall. She couldn't sleep. She could hear it as soon as she walked in the house. She could *feel* it, the vibration, like something unnatural was ready to burst forth into our world. So, I flew home the next day, and found her extremely upset. I understood immediately why my suggestion of a wiring problem was so insulting—this was the sound of something *alive*. Something massive. So, even though I was exhausted, jet-lagged and just completely dead on my feet, I had no other thought than to go out to the garage, get my tools and peel off the siding. Guess what I found."

I didn't answer.

"Guess!"

"I'm not sure I want to know."

"Bees. They had built an entire hive in the wall, sprawling from floor to ceiling. Tens of thousands of them."

His face was lighting up with the telling of his amusing anecdote. Why not? He was getting paid to tell it.

"So I went and put on a hat and gloves and wrapped my wife's scarf around my face and sprayed the hive, I killed them by the thousands. Only later did I realize that the bees are quite valuable and a local bee-keeper actually came and carefully removed the hive itself at no charge. I think he'd have actually paid *me* if I hadn't killed so many of them at the start."

"Hmm."

"Do you understand?"

"Yeah, your wife thought it was a monster. Turned out to just be bees. So my little problem, probably just bees. It's all bees. Nothing to worry about."

"I'm afraid you misunderstood. That was the day that a very powerful, very dangerous monster turned out to be real. *Just ask the bees*."

36 Hours Prior to Outbreak

I said, "Can you see me?"

The freckled redhead on my laptop screen said, "Yep." Amy Sullivan had her hair in pigtails, which I like, and was wearing a huge, ironic T-shirt with a badly drawn eagle and American flag on it, which I hate. It was like a tent on her.

She asked, "How did your therapy go?"

"Jesus, Amy. You don't start a conversation with your boyfriend asking him how his court-ordered therapy went. You have to ease into that."

"Ah, sorry."

"It's a sensitive subject."

"Okay, forget it."

I said, "Are you coming home for Thanksgiving?"

"Yep. You miss me, don't you?"

"You know I can't function on my own."

After a beat and another sip of tea she said, "Are you going to be all right? Not just with the therapy but that whole . . . situation?"

"Your, uh, roommate isn't around, right?"

"No."

"Okay. Yeah, it's fine. Everything is quiet."

She said, "That scared me, that night."

"I know it did."

"Nothing had happened like that for a long time—"

"I know."

"If something like that happens again—"

"I'll shoot it with a crossbow again. I told you that."

"Did you talk to your therapist about that?"

"Subtle, Amy."

"Well, I'm curious."

"How did I find a girl who's worse at conversation than I am?"

She took a sip from a teacup she pulled from off camera. She had to balance the cup with her left wrist. That is, the stump where her left hand should be. She was in a car accident when she was a teenager, before I knew her. The crash took her hand and her parents, and left her with chronic back pain and an implanted titanium rod in her spine. She refused to get a prosthetic hand because she thought they were "creepy." But in my mind, between the titanium spine and a robot hand, she'd be like 10 percent of the way to a cyborg, an idea that I found more than mildly arousing.

Amy and I had "met" in high school, in a special ed classroom for kids with "behavior" disorders. Neither of us really belonged there, she was there because she had a bad reaction to pain medication and bit a teacher, I was there due to a misunderstanding (a bully kept fucking with me until I snapped and gouged out his eyes—you know how kids are). Our fairy-tale romance began by us completely ignoring each other for five years, during which I only knew her by a crude nickname some asshole had given her. Then one day, John and I were asked as a favor to look into her disappearance. It wasn't a big deal, and only took us a couple of days to get to the bottom of it (she had been kidnapped by monsters).

Setting aside her tea she said, "So what's he like? The psychiatrist?"

"It's just like you've seen in the movies, Amy. They get you talking and wait for you to announce you've had an epiphany." I thought for a moment, then said, "And the therapist was a she, not a he. She's about twenty-two. Busty. She kept turning everything into some kind of sexual innuendo. Like she said she believed therapy should be 'hands on' and grabbed my crotch. Then we porked on the desk for a while and the time was up." I shrugged. "Like I said, it's just like in that movie. *Anal Therapist VI*."

She sighed and sipped her tea. "So I guess you don't miss me after all."

"Wait . . . were we not supposed to be having sex with other people, Amy? I guess that was never made clear to me, sorry."

She didn't answer, or laugh, and I said, "Come on, you know if one of us wanted to sleep around you'd have a way easier time than I would. I'm the crazy guy who sees monsters and shoots delivery people. You're the adorable redhead. You could go down to the guys' floor of the dorm and say, 'I'm a woman. I want to have sex' and you'd have twenty guys lined up with roses and shit. I'd have to work at it."

"Why do guys always say that? It's just as hard for a girl."

"That's ridiculous. Every bar is full of guys desperate to get laid and girls desperate to fend off all the horny guys. It's just the way it is, it's biology. It's easier for girls."

"That's actually impossible. Heterosexual sex takes one man and one woman. That means guys and girls have the exact same amount of sex. *That* means there are an equal number of sluts and desperate people on both sides."

"That . . . can't be right."

She shrugged. "Do the math."

"And yes, just to settle the issue, I do miss you."

"I know."

"There's nobody here to ruin movies for me."

Amy had a superhuman ability to pick out the one flaw in a movie that would make it impossible to ever fully enjoy it again. During a single weekend's George Lucas marathon, she pointed out to me that if Indiana Jones had just stayed home, *Raiders of the Lost Ark* would have turned out exactly the same way—the Nazis would have opened the ark and gotten vaporized. Then, during *The Empire Strikes Back,* she paused the movie when a character referred to Luke's ship as an "X-Wing," which is impossible, she said, because there's no way that ship should be called an "X-Wing" based on it being physically shaped like the English letter "X" since an ancient race of people in a distant galaxy would never have seen that letter before. Jesus, I'm making her sound like a bitch.

To the webcam window I said, "How are the classes going? Have you gotten to the part where they teach you to make computer viruses? Because I have people I want to send them to."

"If by 'virus' you mean a program that accidentally freezes up your whole operating system when you try to execute it, then I think everything I've coded so far counts as one. Oh, did you know you could hack the phone system with a Cap'n Crunch whistle?"

"Uh, is that like hacker slang or . . ."

"No, the phones back in the seventies did everything by tones, the different frequencies and stuff told the system how to route the calls and all that. So there was a hacker named John Draper who figured out that the little plastic toy whistles they were putting in boxes of Cap'n Crunch had the exact same frequency and tone that the phone system was using to end charges on a call. He got free long distance for like two years just by blowing his toy whistle into the phone every time."

"Holy shit, I'm going to try that. See, this is the type of stuff colleges should be teaching."

"Well they've updated the phone system since then."

"Oh."

We sat in silence for a moment then she said, "Give me a second, I'm trying to think of a way to work the conversation back around to your therapy again."

I said, "I love you."

She said, "I know."

"Actually, tomorrow's a group session. I'll probably have to wax beforehand."

"Gross."

"Sorry."

"Though maybe I shouldn't talk, since I'm sitting here on a webcam without any pants on."

I said, "Oh, really?"

"Wanna see?"

"Yes. Yes I do."

30 Hours Prior to Outbreak

There exists in this world a spider the size of a dinner plate, a foot wide if you include the legs. It's called the Goliath Bird-Eating Spider, or the "Goliath *Fucking* Bird-Eating Spider" by those who have actually seen one.

It doesn't eat only birds—it mostly eats rats and insects—but they still call it the "Bird-Eating Spider" because the fact that it can eat a bird is the most important thing you need to know about it. If you run across one of these things, like in your closet or crawling out of your bowl of soup, the first thing somebody will say is, "Watch it, man, that thing can eat a goddamned *bird*."

I don't know how they catch the birds. I know the Goliath Fucking Bird-Eating Spider can't fly because if it could, it would have a different name entirely. We would call it "sir" because it would be the dominant species on the planet. None of us would leave the house unless a Goliath Fucking Flying Bird-Eating Spider said it was okay.

I've seen one of those things in person, at a zoo when I was in high school. I was fifteen, my face breaking out in acne and getting fatter by the day, staring open-mouthed at this monster pawing at the glass wall of its cage. Big as both of my hands. The guys around me were giggling and punching each other in the arm and some girl was squealing behind me. But I didn't make a sound. I couldn't. There was nothing but a pane of glass between me and that *thing*. For months after, I'd watch the dark corners of my bedroom at night, for hairy legs as thick as a finger poking out from behind a stack of comic books and video game magazines. I imagined—no, *expected*—to find strands of spiderweb as thick as fishing line in my closet, bulging with clumps of half-eaten sparrows. Or spider droppings in my shoes, the little turds laced with bits of feather. Or piles of pink eggs, yolked with baby spiders already the size of golf balls. And even now, ten years later and at the age of twenty-five, I still glance between the sheets at night before pushing my legs in, some part of my subconscious still looking for the huge spider crouching in the shadows.

I bring this up because the Goliath was the first thing that popped into my mind when I woke up with something in my bed, biting my leg.

I felt a pinch on my ankle, like digging needles. The Goliath Fucking Bird-Eating Spider leapt out of the fog of my sleepy imagination as I flung the blankets aside.

It was dark.

Lights were off. Clock off. Everything off.

I sat up and squinted down at my leg. Movement, down by the sheets. I swung my leg off the bed and I could feel the weight of something clinging to the ankle, heavy as a can of beer.

A spasm of panic ripped through me. I kicked out with the leg, grunting in the chill air of my dark bedroom, trying to shake off the little biting whatever-it-was. The thing went flying across the room, passing through a shaft of moonlight spilling in around my blinds. In that brief second I saw a flash of jointed legs—lots of legs—and a tail. Armored plates like a lobster. The whole thing was as long as a shoe. Black.

What in the name of—

The creature that my panicked mind was calling a "spider"—even though it clearly wasn't an arachnid or any other species native to planet Earth—flew across the bedroom and hit the wall, landing behind a basket of laundry. I bolted up out of the bed, squinting, edging around the room, feeling the wall with my hands. I blinked, trying to get my night vision, scanning for something to use as a weapon. I pawed around at the jumble of objects on my nightstand, saw something jutting out from under a copy of *Entertainment Weekly*. Round and slim, I thought it maybe was the hilt of a knife. I grabbed it and threw it, realizing only after it was airborne that it was my asthma inhaler. I reached again, grabbed for what looked like the heaviest object on the table—a jar of cheese sauce.

I spotted movement across the baseboard. I chucked the jar, grunting with the effort. A thud, a tinkle of broken glass. Silence. I grabbed the table lamp, a novelty item that consisted of a naked bulb jutting out of a stained-glass sculpture of a turkey. A birthday present from John. I yanked the cord from the wall and raised the turkey by the neck, holding it over my shoulder like a quarterback photographed in midthrow.

The spider(?) skittered across the floor, out the doorway, and into the living room. It had legs all over it, walking on half a dozen legs with another half dozen sticking up in the air like dreadlocks, like the thing was made to keep running even on its back. The sight of the thing froze me. That awful, primal, paralyzing terror that only accompanies an encounter with something completely alien. I lowered the lamp and forced myself to take a step forward. I tried to control my breathing. I risked a glance down at my leg and saw a crimson stripe leaking down from the bite.

That little bastard.

I felt a heat, and then a numbness, creeping its way up my leg. I didn't know if the little monster was poisonous, or if it was just the shock of getting bitten. I took three steps toward the doorway and had developed a serious limp by the fourth.

I slooooowly peered into the living room. Not quite as dark in here, the streetlamps outside spilling halfhearted ribbons of light on the floor, writhing among shadows of windblown tree branches. No sign of the spider. I heard a scratchy rustle from the kitchen tiles to my left and spun on it—

It was the dog.

Molly stepped sleepily toward me, a knee-high reddish shape topped by two eyes reflecting bluish moonlight. I caught the faint blur of a wagging tail behind her. She was looking right at me, wondering why I was up, wondering why I smelled like terror sweat, wondering if I had any snacks on me. I glanced toward the front door. Ten feet of carpet between me and it. I had half made up my mind to pack Molly into the car and flee to John's place, then regroup so that the two of us could come back here tomorrow with a shotgun and holy water.

My feet had never been so bare. Those little naked toes. That spider thing probably looks at those like the ears on a chocolate bunny. Where had I left my shoes? I brandished the turkey lamp and took a shaky step, my bitten left leg having fallen asleep. I willed it to hold up from here to the driveway.

A scream, from behind me.

I flinched and spun, then realized it was my phone. John had set my phone's text message ringtone to a sound clip of him screaming, "TEEEXXTT!! SSSSHHHIIIIITTTTT!" I never figured out how to change it back. I snatched the phone from the coffee table and saw it was a blank message with an attached photo. I opened the image . . .

A man's penis.

I quickly closed it. What the hell?

The phone sounded again in my hand. A call this time. I answered.

"Dave! Don't talk. Listen. You have a picture in your inbox. DO NOT OPEN IT. I sent it to the wrong number."

"Jesus Christ, John. Listen to me—"

"Man, you sound out of breath—"

"John, I—"

The phone slipped from my fingers, which were suddenly unable to grip it. I took a step toward the fallen phone, then another, and the room started wobbling in front of my eyes. Losing my balance—

NO NO YOU CANNOT FALL YOU CANNOT GO DOWN THERE WITH THAT THING!

I fell face-first on the carpet. My left leg was fifty pounds of dead weight dragging behind me. My right leg was tingling now, terror pumping the poison through my veins with horrible efficiency. I swung an arm around, finding the coffee table. I clawed at it, tried to raise myself. No grip with that hand.

Flat on the floor again. I didn't even feel the impact on the shoulder I landed on.

"HELP! SOMEBODY!" I squealed. I wished I knew the names of my neighbors. "HEEELLLLPP!"

The last cry ended in a croak.

The cell phone screamed again.

Mustering every last calorie of energy from my right arm, I reached out for a phone that seemed to be ten miles away. I got my dead fingers on top of it, then dragged it across the carpet toward my face. It was as heavy as a bag of concrete. Manipulating the hand was like trying to fish a stuffed animal out of one of those claw games at the carnival. I saw that the incoming message was from John.

"JOHN!" I screamed at the phone, stupidly. I slapped at the buttons with my clumsy carnival claw hand. I fought to lift my head from the floor.

The screen changed. An image appeared.

Penis.

My arm went dead. My head bounced off the floor. Spinal cord totally unplugged now. I was staring across an expanse of carpet, seeing tumbleweeds of dog hair that had gathered under the TV cabinet across the room. Couldn't look away—didn't even have that much muscle control. Couldn't close my eyes.

I could hear, though, and I detected the ever-so-faint rustling of carpet, many little feet stepping through the fibers. Hard, black, jointed legs shuffled into view. The spider completely filled my field of vision, no more than six inches from my eyes. Legs everywhere. A half dozen of them were coated in nacho cheese sauce.

The creature's mouth was as big as mine, surrounded by needle-thin mandibles. Two lips parted and I saw with revulsion that it had a pink tongue, exactly like a human's. It inched toward my face.

The spider was my world, its many glistening black legs extending past both ends of the horizon. I could count the taste buds on its lolling pink tongue, could see the wet ridges of the roof of its mouth. Its carapace glistened with some kind of slime. Two of its legs were touching my mouth. It tickled.

A huge, furry nose descended into my field of vision, like the fuzzy snout of God Himself. Molly had finally grown curious enough about the situation to wander in from the kitchen.

Her nose twitched as she detected the smell of nacho cheese. She licked the spider, discovered that her most ambitious doggy dream had finally come true: naturally cheese-coated prey. With a snap of her jaws and a quick twist of her head, she ripped off four of the monster's legs and buckled down to the hard work of chewing them.

The spider shrieked with a piercing noise that made my bones vibrate. It sped from view so fast I had no idea what direction it went.

David Wong

29 Hours Prior to Outbreak

Paralyzed.

Was this permanent? I pictured the venom turning my spinal column into mush. Molly glanced at me, quietly judging me for my laziness. She worked over her severed spider legs, realizing there wasn't much meat inside the crunchy outer shell. She settled in and pinned the legs under her front paws, then started carefully licking the cheese off of them.

I lay there for an interminable amount of time that in reality was about one hour. I eventually felt a tingling across my torso as I sleepily imagined I had landed on an anthill. It was, however, the feeling returning to my body. Twenty minutes or so later I found I could twitch my fingers, a half hour after that I was sitting upright on the sofa, cradling my throbbing head in my hands. I devoted all of my mental energy to blocking out any thoughts of what the spider had intended to do to my immobilized body.

Well, the first step would be to lay eggs . . .

Oh, wait. The spider. It could still be here. Shit.

Three seconds later I was on the porch, peering back through the front door into my own living room. No sign of the spider, but then again it was pitch dark inside and I had a streetlight behind me, so all I could see in the little window was a reflection of my own stupid face. My hair looked like I had combed it with an angry cat. I reached for my cell phone, then realized it was still on the floor in the living room.

I flung open the door, sprinted in, rolled, grabbed the phone, and sprinted back out, slamming the door behind me. I dialed John. Voice mail:

"This is John. If you're calling because you found the rest of my guitar, just bring it by the apartment. Sorry about the rug. Leave a message."

I didn't. Even on a Thursday night, the man was probably marinated and comatose by now. I glanced around the neighborhood, my nervous breaths barely visible in the November air. Why was mine the only house that didn't have power? I raised the phone, but didn't dial. The English language needs a word for that feeling you get when you badly need help, but there is no one who you can call because you're not popular enough to have friends, not rich enough to have employees, and not powerful enough to have lackeys. It's a very distinct cocktail of impotence, loneliness and a sudden stark assessment of your non-worth to society.

Enturdment?

There was a broom leaning by the front door, from when I had used it to knock a dead bird off the porch a few days ago. I clutched it in front of me like a spear and pushed through the door. Molly brushed past me in the opposite direction, presumably to find the perfect spot outside my car door to take a dump so that I'd be sure to step in it the next time I was in a hurry to get to work. I took one step inside, focusing on the floor to—

The spider thumped onto my head, twitchy legs tangling in my hair. I dropped the broom and threw my hands up as the monster climbed over my ear and onto my shoulder. Itchy little legs, all over my face and neck. I grabbed the spider around the body, rigid legs bending under my hands. I tried to pull it off. I couldn't, the feet were latched on somehow. My shirt—and my skin—stretched away from my shoulder as I pulled. I heard a screeching like steam from a teapot, and realized it was me.

Sharp mandibles filled the view in my right eye. A stab of pain seared through my skull. I lost vision in that eye and thought the bastard had plucked out my eyeball. I let out a scream of rage and grabbed bundles of legs with both hands, ripping them away from the skin. I felt wetness and realized the monster had left one leg behind, the foot still attached to my shoulder. But I was free of the creature now, the unholy thing thrashing around in my hands, twisting its mouth toward me, trying to bite.

That freaking tongue! Goddamn it!

I frantically looked around with my one good eye, trying to find a container I could cram the creature into.

Laundry basket! Bedroom floor!

Into the bedroom. I kicked over the plastic basket, dumping the clothes. I dunked the beast inside and turned the basket over, imprisoning it. I knocked the shit off my nightstand and laid it sideways on top of the basket. Good and heavy. There were vertical slots in the basket and the spider stuck a leg through. It couldn't crawl out but I suspected it could bite through the plastic eventually. Have to watch it.

I sat heavily on the bed, chest heaving. Face wet and sticky. Cringing, I lifted a tentative hand to the right side of my face, expecting to find a squishy eyeball laying on my cheek. I didn't. I winced as I felt around the eyelid, raw skin stinging at my touch. Everything felt torn and ragged up there. I blinked and tried looking through the eye, found I could a little bit. I looked down, intending to dig my cell phone from my pocket, and let out a disgusted hiss.

The spider's black leg, the one that broke off when I was pulling it off me, was still stuck to my shirt. I grabbed it and pulled it and it would *not* come free. It wasn't stuck to the shirt, it was stuck to *me*, pulling up the skin like a circus tent. The foot was hooked in somehow, dug in like a tick. I pulled apart the hole in the shirt and pinched the skin between two fingers and tried to get a close look at it. I couldn't tell the exact point where the severed leg ended and the patch of skin on my shoulder began. It was like the leg had fused to it somehow. I pulled and twisted. It was like trying to pull off one of my own fingers.

I was getting seriously pissed off at this point. I stomped out of the bedroom and into the kitchen. I yanked open several drawers until I found a utility knife, what some people call a box cutter. Molly came trotting in behind me, figuring maybe I was making a snack and she could get some scraps.

I pulled off my shirt, then grabbed a long wooden spoon and stuck it sideways in my mouth. I stabbed the tip of the utility knife's short blade in at the point where the monster's foot was fused with my skin, and started prying. I growled and cursed around the spoon, teeth denting into the wood. A thick drop of blood ran down my chest like candle wax.

It took twenty minutes. In the end I had the six-inch-long jointed leg in my hand, with a little dot of bloody skin and fat on the end that used to be part of me. I held a bundle of wet paper towels to the wound, smears of blood making my abdomen look like a finger painting. I put the monster's leg in a plastic container from my cabinet. I leaned against the counter, eyes closed, taking slow breaths.

I had taken one step back toward the bedroom when a knock came at the door. I froze, decided not to answer it, then realized it may be John.

I went into the bedroom to check on the caged beast. It had two legs through a slot in the plastic basket but had made no progress toward biting its way out. I made my way back across the living room, smacking my foot on the coffee table on the way. I yanked open the door—

It was a cop.

A young guy. I knew him, name was Franky something. Went to high school with me. I straightened up and said, "What can I do for you, officer?"

I saw his eyes go right to my torso, where I was holding a red wad of paper towels over a freely bleeding wound, and then back to my face, where one eye was swollen shut under a ragged eyelid caked with dried blood. He had a hand resting on the butt of his gun, alert in that way that cops are.

He began with, "Who else is in the house, sir?"

"It's fine. I mean, nobody. I live here alone. I mean, my girlfriend lives here with me, but she's away at school right now. So it's just me. Everything's fine. I just had a problem with, uh, something that, uh, came into the house. Some kind of . . . animal."

"You mind if I come in, sir?"

There was no right answer to that, since he clearly thought I had a butchered prostitute in here somewhere. I stepped aside without a word. That "sir" shit was irritating me. He was my age. I went to parties with this guy in school, watched him play teabag twister with underwear on his head.

Burgess, I thought. *That's his name. Franky Burgess.*

He walked past me and I said, "I'd turn on a light, but the power's out. Must have, you know, blown a fuse or something."

He gave me a look that suggested what I just said gave him a whole new perspective on my mental state. I could read his face perfectly because the living room light was on.

"Oh. Right," I stumbled. "Guess it's back on now."

I blinked. Had it been on this whole time?

The place was a mess. I mean, it had been a mess before (the blood I dripped on the carpet actually blended with a nearby coffee stain) but where we were standing gave us a clear view into the kitchen, where drawers were flung open, a roll of paper towels had fallen onto the floor and a pile of plastic lids had spilled out of a cabinet. A couple of steps after that and he would have a view of the main bedroom, where it looked like a bomb had gone off. Oh, and there was an alien spider monster trapped under an overturned laundry basket with a piece of furniture piled on top of it.

The cop moved into the kitchen and I followed him. I heard a skittering noise from the bedroom and saw the spider trying desperately to escape between the plastic bars of his laundry basket prison. The cop gave no notice. He looked at the bloody box cutter on the counter, then glanced back at me and my several bloody wounds. I stepped casually backward, stopping in front of the bedroom door, leaning against the door frame as if I wasn't somehow trying to block the view of the room with my body.

"Yeah, that," I said, nodding toward the little knife, "I cut myself a few times, no big deal, I was . . . trying to get this thing off me. I think it was a possum or something, I couldn't get a look at it. It was clawing me up pretty bad."

He was looking past me, into the bedroom, and said, "Can you step aside, sir?"

Screw it. Let this thing bite his eyes out, what do I care? *Go right in, Franky.*

I stepped aside and Franky the Cop entered the bedroom. He surveyed the carnage, then finally looked down on the overturned basket. Five little armored legs writhed around between the plastic slats. The cop casually looked away, glancing into my closet with disinterest. Finally he looked back at me.

"So, did you kill it or what?"

The beast was right there in the basket. In full view. Jaws clicking against the plastic, a sound like a dog gnawing on a bone. It had gotten a few legs entirely through the basket and was now pulling its body through. All of this went entirely unnoticed by Officer Burgess.

He doesn't see it.

"Uh, no. I tried to trap it."

The thing had its head out of the basket now. Franky looked down. Nothing to see. He looked back at me.

"Have you had anything to drink tonight, sir?"

"Couple of beers, earlier."

"Have you taken anything else?"

26

"No."

"Can you tell me what day it is?"

The spider had a third of its body out of the basket. There was a thick piece of armor around its abdomen that was wedged in between the plastic strips. It had four legs working on the problem.

"Thursday ni—uh, I mean, I guess it's Friday morning now. November fourth, I think. My name is David Wong, I'm currently standing in my home. I'm not high."

"The neighbors are worried about you. They heard a lot of noise in here . . ."

"You try waking up with some animal biting you in your sleep."

"This isn't the first time we've been out here, is it?"

I sighed. "No."

"You put some weight on top of that basket there."

"I told you, I was trying to trap it—"

"No, the basket was you trying to trap it. I'm thinking the weight is on there because you thought you *had* trapped it."

"What? No. It was dark. I—"

The monster pulled the widest piece of shell through the bars. Halfway out. The difficult half.

"Is it possible you made all those cuts yourself? With that knife in there?"

"What? No. I—"

I don't think so . . .

"Why do you keep looking down there?"

I took a step back out of the room.

"No reason."

"Do you see something down there, Mr. Wong?"

I turned my eyes up to the cop. I was sweating again.

"No, no."

"Have we been seeing things tonight?"

I didn't answer.

"Because this wouldn't be the first time, would it?"

"That was . . . no. I'm fine, I'm fine."

I focused on not looking down at the basket. The chewing sounds had stopped.

I couldn't hold out anymore. I looked down.

It was gone.

I felt my bowels loosen. I glanced around the room, checked the ceiling. Nowhere.

The cop turned and left the room.

"Why don't you come with me, Mr. Wong, and I'll take you to the emergency room."

"What? No, no. I'm fine. The cuts are no big deal."

"Don't look minor to me."

"No, no. It's fine. Put it in your report that I refused treatment. I'm fine."

"You got any family that live here in town?"

"No."

"Nobody? Parents, aunts, uncles?"

"Long story."

"There a friend we can call?"

"John, I guess."

I was glancing everywhere, trying to spot the spider, no idea what I'd do if I did.

"Well, tell you what, give him a call and I'll hang out here until he shows up. Keep you company. In case the animal comes back."

I couldn't think of anything that would make this guy leave, short of punching him and forcing him to haul me to jail. That hardly seemed like a solution, though.

The cop can stay as long as he wants, I thought. *As long as he doesn't go to the toolshed.*

Franky the Cop turned to me at that moment and said, "I'm going to have a look around outside."

I let the cop go out the back door, but didn't offer to follow him. I guess he wanted to do a walk around of the yard to make sure there wasn't a corpse out there. Let him. As soon as he was out of sight, I moved back through the kitchen, into the living room and then through to the bedroom. I flipped on the light, checked the ceiling, checked everywhere. No spider. I heard the muffled sound of steps on crackling leaves and saw the cop outside, passing the window with a flashlight. I headed for the bathroom, soaked a washcloth and cleaned the dried blood off me. I got a Band-Aid on my shoulder and cleaned up the eyelid, flinching with every stinging touch. I went into the bedroom, searching for the monster, even looking in the laundry basket in case the thing had decided to return for some reason. I put on a shirt and tried to push down my hair, thinking I could present a picture of a stable citizen for the cop and make him feel better about leaving.

Before he asks to see the toolshed.

I grabbed my phone from the bed and dialed John one last time. Three rings and then—

"Hello?"

"John? It's me."

"What? Who?"

"We got a situation."

"Can it wait until after work tomorrow?"

"No. There's something in my house. A—"

I glanced around for the cop.

"A creature. It took a chunk out of my leg and then it went for my eye."

"Really? You kill it?"

"No, it's hiding somewhere. It's small."

"How small?"

"Size of a squirrel. Built like an insect. A lot of legs, maybe twelve. It had a mouth like—"

I turned and saw the cop standing in the bedroom doorway.

I nodded sideways toward the phone and said, "This is John. He's on his way."

"Good." He nodded toward the back door. "Do you have a key to that toolshed outside?"

I pocketed the phone without saying good-bye to John.

"Oh, no. I've lost the key. I mean, I haven't been out there in months."

"I've got a pair of bolt cutters out in my trunk. Tell you what, let me open that up for you."

"No, no, that won't be necessary."

"I insist. You don't want to be stuck without your lawn implements. You can finally rake all these leaves out here."

We stared each other down. Man, this just kept getting better and better. I found myself wishing the spider would jump down and eat this guy.

"Actually, I think I have a key."

"Good. Get it."

I went into the kitchen and plucked the toolshed key off the nail next to the back door, where it had been in plain view the entire time. Franky the Cop let me lead the way outside to the shed, staying a few steps back so that he could have time to shoot me in case I decided to wheel on him with fists of fury. I held out the key and took a deep breath. I slipped it into the padlock and snapped it open. I pulled the toolshed door slightly ajar and turned to Franky.

"What's in here . . . I, uh, collect things. It's a hobby, that's all. And as far as I know, there's nothing illegal here."

Though you could say some of it is, uh, imported.

"Could you go ahead and step back, sir?"

He opened the little shed and stabbed the darkness with a flashlight beam. I held my breath. He went right to the floor with the light, where a body would be, I guess. There wasn't one there, not right now, and instead he illuminated the crust of grass on the wheel of my lawn-mower. Then he flicked the flashlight beam to the set of metal shelves along the back and side walls. The beam hit a glass jar the size of a can of paint and illuminated the murky liquid inside. Officer Franky Bur-gess stared at it, waiting for his eyes to register what he was seeing. Eventually he would figure out it was a late-term fetus, a head the size of a fist, its eyes closed. It had no arms or legs. Its torso had been re-placed by a jointed mechanical apparatus that hooked around to a point like the tail of a sea horse.

I manufactured a chuckle and said, "Heh, uh, I got that off eBay. It's a, uh, prop from a movie."

The cop glanced at me. I glanced away.

He shined his light back onto the shelf. Next to the jar was an ant farm. The tunnels between the panes of glass had been dug neatly to spell out the word HELP.

Next to that was my old Xbox, the cables wrapped around it.

He moved the light down a foot, to the shelf below. He passed over a stack of old magazines, not noticing that the top one was an old, faded issue of *Time* depicting a swarm of Secret Service agents around a dead Bill Clinton, the words WHO DID IT? blasting across the picture in red. Next to the magazines was a stuffed red Tickle Me Elmo doll, the fur faded with dust. At the moment the light hit it, its sound box crackled to life and in a cartoony voice it said, "Ha ha ha! Five and three quarter inches erect!"

I said, "It's, uh, broken."

Franky the Cop inched the beam to the next object, a mason jar containing a twisted, purple tongue suspended in clear liquid. Next to it was a duplicate jar, only with two human eyes floating side by side, trailing a tangled tail of nerves and blood vessels. The cop didn't notice that when the beam swept past the jar, the eyes turned to follow it. Next to the jars was an old battery from my truck, matted with smears of black grime. The light made it to the bottom, where it found a red plastic gasoline can sitting on the floor next to an old CRT computer monitor with a screen that had been shattered by a gunshot. Next to it was the one thing I didn't want the cop to see. The Box.

We heard crunching leaves behind us.

"Yo, what's up?" The cop and I turned to see a dark figure with one hand swinging the orange coal of a burning cigarette. John. "Hi, Franky. Dave, sorry I sent you all those pictures of my dick. I hope that's not what caused you to injure your eye."

The cop put the flashlight on John, maybe to make sure he wasn't armed. John wore a flannel shirt and a black baseball cap with the word HAT on it in all caps.

Franky the Cop thanked John for coming over. I was hoping he would back out of the toolshed because each minute he stood there made me more and more nervous. My eye and shoulder were throbbing. The wind shifted and I picked up the scent of alcohol from John.

The cop swung the flashlight beam around and spotlighted the floor of the toolshed again. Light fell on the box, and I mean *the* box, the olive green box we'd found in the back of that unmarked black truck. It looked like a serious box. It looked like something you'd want to look inside of, if your job was to keep people safe. Franky nodded toward it.

"What's in the green box there?"

"Don't know."

That was sort of true, I guess.

John said, "We found it. You can't get it open."

That was also true. *Franky* couldn't get it open.

I said, "You can take it back with you, if you want. Put it in the lost and found at the police station."

The cop clicked off the flashlight, then asked John if they could go inside and talk. He then gestured toward the toolshed with the flashlight and said to me, "You want to close that up while I have a word here with John?"

I said that seemed like a fine idea and their shoes crunched through the leaves until they reached the light of my back door. I closed the toolshed and clicked the padlock shut, then let out a sigh of relief. The relief lasted approximately four seconds, the time it took me to realize John and Franky the Cop were now back inside the house with the murderous alien spider. I hurried back inside and saw John and the cop in my living room having a low conversation out of my hearing, the cop I guess was asking John to babysit me and to call if I showed more signs of craziness. I moved closer and barely heard John say, ". . . Been real depressed lately . . ." and wondered what kind of portrait he was painting in there.

I scanned the kitchen for the spider, being sure to check the high ground. No sign of it. I closed some of the open drawers and cabinets, tried to straighten the place up. I made it all the way out of the room before I turned and realized that cabinets would be an ideal hiding place for the little bastard. I'd be getting out my cereal tomorrow morning and the fucker would launch itself at me. Could I search through them without drawing Franky's attention? Better wait. Instead I checked the bedroom, again under the guise of straightening up. I looked under my blankets and then under the bed. I pushed around the clothes in my closet, I checked behind the door. No spider.

When I came out, I saw John and the cop were on the front porch. Progress. John was thanking the man for coming out, saying he hoped Franky would remember me in his prayers because I could really use it right now because my life was really a mess and I was just a complete pathetic loser struggling with my weight and financial problems and alcohol and erectile dysfunction. I decided to join them before John could defame me further.

The cop was already walking back toward his patrol car as John said, ". . . And his girlfriend is away and she's only got one hand. She lost it in an accident. You can imagine the problems that causes."

Franky was desperately trying to escape the conversation, talking into the little radio mounted on the shoulder of his uniform, letting headquarters know that everything was under control here. John and I watched him go. Then we heard a skittering by our feet and saw the goddamned spider run past our shoes. It vanished into the darkness, heading right toward the cop.

I jumped off the porch, waving my hands. "Wait! Franky! Officer Burgess! Wait!"

The cop stopped just short of the squad car and turned to me. I opened my mouth, but the words retreated back into my throat. A bundle of thin black legs appeared over Franky's left shoulder, touching his bare neck. And he couldn't feel a thing.

From behind me John said, "Franky! Franky! Don't move, man! You got something on you!"

Franky put his hand on the butt of his gun again, looking alertly between me and John as if his crazy person troubles had just multiplied. The monster crawled over Franky's shoulder and put legs on his cheek.

John screamed, "Franky! Do this!" John made a brushing motion on his own cheek, as if waving away a fly. "Seriously! You got something on your face!"

Franky, oblivious to his situation, did not follow these instructions. He started to say something about us not moving any closer. I lunged, throwing my hands toward the little monster. I never made it. Franky did something to me that dropped me to my knees, gasping for air. It was some kind of chop to the throat and man, it worked.

I looked up and for the second time tried to warn Franky and for the second time I was unable to. The spider crawled around to Franky's chest and then, in a blur, burrowed into his mouth.

Franky flailed backward and flung himself to the ground, his head thunking against the squad car's door on the way down. Franky clawed at his mouth with his hands, gasping, choking, spasming. I backed away, crawling backward on my ass through the leaves. As I retreated, John advanced, saying, "Franky! Franky! Hey!"

Franky wasn't responsive. His arms were locked in front of him, fingers curled, like he was being electrocuted.

John spun on me and said, "We gotta get him to the hospital!"

I sat there in the grass, frozen, wishing I could just go back inside and crawl under the covers again. John threw open both back doors of the cop car. He dug his hands under Franky's shoulders.

"Dave! Help me!"

I got to my feet and took Franky's ankles. We wrestled him into the backseat of the squad car, John backing out through the opposite door. We closed it up and John took the wheel. I slid beside John as he hunted around the console for a switch. He found it, flipped it. A siren pierced the night. He shifted into gear and tore down the street, red and blue flashing off every window in the neighborhood as we raced past. We blew through an intersection. I pulled on my seat belt and braced my hands against the dash.

"That thing came into *my house*, John! It came into *my house!*"

"I know, I know."

"I woke up and that thing was biting me. In my bed, John!"

We turned the corner, rounding a closed restaurant with FOR SALE painted on the windows in white shoe polish. We passed the blackened shell of a hardware store that had burned down last year, we passed a trailer park and a used-car dealership and a 24-hour adult bookstore and a skanky motel that never had any vacancies because lots of poor people lived there full-time.

"It was in my house, John! Do you get what I'm saying here? Franky couldn't even see it. It was on his face and he couldn't see it. It was *in my house.*"

I felt my body push against the armrest on the door. Tires squealed. John was taking a corner car chase–style. Two blocks up was the concrete parking garage for the hospital, the lit windows of the hospital itself looming up behind it. I peered back through the wire screen separating us from Franky, who was laying motionless across the backseat, eyes open. His chest was heaving, so at least he wasn't dead.

"Almost there, man! Hold on, okay?"

I turned to John.

"It crawled in his mouth! Did you see it?"

"I saw it."

"Are they gonna be able to help him? You really think the doctors can do somethin'?"

We squealed into the parking lot and followed a sign that said EMERGENCY. We skidded to a stop in a covered drive-up to the emergency room. We threw open the back door and dragged out Franky, then clumsily lugged him toward a set of glass doors that slid open for us automatically. Before we got five feet inside, a couple of orderlies came and started barking questions at us that we had no answers to. Somebody rolled up a gurney.

John started talking, telling the guys that the cop had had some kind of a seizure, that he had something in his throat, definitely to check his throat.

There was a flicker of red and blue lights out of the corner of my eye—a second cop car turning in fast across the parking lot. They probably saw John and me tearing ass through town and followed us here. The orderlies were rolling away Franky and a third guy showed up, a doctor I guess, taking his vitals. I turned to John to tell him about the second cop car but he had already spotted it. I followed him back out to the sidewalk.

"Think we should hang around?" he asked.

"I don't think so. I'm already on probation."

"Dave, they're gonna come get us. They'll wanna know what happened."

"Nah, I don't think this thing's gonna be a big deal. Probably send us a nice card for getting Franky to the hospital. Come on."

We took off walking, since it didn't seem wise to go back home in the stolen cop car. We went around the edge of the lot as the approaching police car whooshed past us. It skidded to a stop next to Franky's vehicle and two cops spilled out and went inside. We silently cut across the lawn and crossed a street with a traffic light blinking yellow. We cut through the darkened parking lot of a Chinese restaurant called Panda Buffet, which did not in fact serve panda meat as far as we knew. Behind it was one of the city's many abandoned properties, the depressing twin buildings of an old tuberculosis asylum that had been closed since the sixties, the gray bricks tinged moss-green.

John lit a cigarette and asked, "So what do you think that thing was?"

I didn't answer. I found myself scanning the dark plane of each parking lot we passed, studying the shadows, looking for movement. I noticed my steps were hurrying me unconsciously toward the pool of light under the next streetlamp. We passed into the parking lot of a tire place with a ten-foot-tall tire mascot standing by the street. The mascot was made of real tires, with mufflers for arms and a chrome wheel for a head. Some joker had used white spray paint to draw a penis on the front of it in the anatomically appropriate spot.

John said, "So that thing crawled into his mouth, what do you think it was doing?"

"How should I know?"

A blur of red and blue zipped by. Another cop car, lights flashing. Thirty seconds later, another one. John said, "Man, these guys really gather around one of their own, don't they?"

We walked on, hesitant, a sick feeling in my gut. Two more cop cars flew by. One had different markings, state cop I guess.

"They're just going there to check up on him, right? John?"

"I don't know, man."

"Let's get home, we'll see if they got anything about it on TV."

But he had stopped, saying, "No point, all you'll get is the news after it gets filtered for the reporters. We'll get better information if we go back down there."

"We'd just be in the—"

I stopped at the sound of a distant scream.

John said, "You hear that?"

"No."

Another cop car zipped past. How many of those did we have in this town?

"Come on, Dave."

John took off walking back the way we came. I stood my ground. I didn't want to go back there, but—and I'm not ashamed to admit this—I also didn't want to walk back to my place alone, in the dark. I raised a hand to touch the spot on my eye where I had been bitten, raw flesh under a Band-Aid. I winced as the pain in my shoulder stopped me before I could get my hand up there. The chunk taken out of my skin there was getting sorer by the minute. I was about to tell John to have fun without me when—

POP! POP-POP!

The sound of distant gunshots, like firecrackers. John started jogging back across the tire store parking lot, toward the hospital. I let out a breath, then followed.

27 Hours Prior to Outbreak

We arrived on the hospital grounds to see that all hell had broken loose. Six cop cars were parked haphazardly around the emergency room entrance, lighting up the parking lot like a dance floor. There was an ambulance, its rear doors open. People were spilling out of the hospital entrance, their heads down like they were running the trenches in a war zone. One lady came out in aqua blue scrubs, one side of her blond hair matted down with blood. There was a clump of onlookers on the far side of the lawn that included three or four wheelchairs, maybe fifty yards from the hospital. It looked like they were gathering patients there, getting them away from the building. One cop was talking to them and gesturing with his hand, karate chopping the air with each barked command. His other hand held a pistol pointed at the sky.

POP! POP! POP!POP!POP!

More shots from inside. John, possessing a genetic defect that makes him walk toward danger, strode down toward where it looked like some cops were trying to set up a perimeter around the chaos. Somewhere, Charles Darwin nodded and smiled a knowing smile.

We came upon two cops blocking the sidewalk, a fat black one with glasses and an older guy whose face was all mustache. John stepped off the sidewalk as if to walk right past them on the grass. Black Cop put out a hand and told us to stop, in a tone that suggested if we didn't he would Taser us until our blood boiled. We backed off, stepping aside as paramedics hustled the bleeding-head lady past us. She was crying, holding her head, saying over and over again, "HE WOULDN'T DIE! HE JUST WOULDN'T DIE! THEY SHOT HIM OVER AND OVER AGAIN AND HE—"

John tapped my shoulder and pointed. A boxy truck was pulling up, blue with white letters on the side. I thought it was some kind of paddy wagon but when the doors opened, a SWAT team spilled out.

Holy shit.

John moved off the sidewalk and up onto the lawn in front of the building. There were some benches there, and a ten-foot-tall bronze statue of a lady in old-timey nurse's garb holding a lantern.

Florence Nightingale? I followed John and we joined a small crowd of onlookers.

Gunshots. Rapid shots, dozens of them. Gasps from the audience. I could barely see down there but I could make out people running out of the building, frantic. One lady fell down and got accidentally kicked hard in the face. Then, a man came out supported on the shoulders of two hospital staff, his right leg missing from the knee down. Or at least that's what it looked like, keep in mind we were still far enough away that the door looked about the size of a postage stamp, and I was trying to look through a growing crowd in front of me. That's why I can't be totally sure about what happened next.

First, a man in a black SWAT outfit came running out of the building, screaming something. I couldn't hear him from where we were standing but to this day John insists the man was screaming, "Run away!"

Then, shots. Loud, sharp, close. Next came the screams. Screams from every single human being close enough to the lobby to see what was going on. Three cops near the entrance ducked behind the parked patrol cars and trained guns on the sliding doors.

A man lumbered out.

Every gun barrel followed him.

It was Officer Franky Burgess.

He was wearing his cop uniform pants and a red shirt . . . no, that's not right. It was a white undershirt, stained with blood over 80 percent of its area.

People crowded around, blocking my view. John craned his neck and said, "It's Franky. Everybody's got their guns on him, like he's dangerous. Did he shoot all those people? Hey, move, buddy. I can't see."

Frustrated, John went to the nurse statue and, to my horror, climbed it. He got up to where both hands were on her shoulders, his shoes planted on her forearms. Florence's face was planted in John's crotch.

I waved at him. "John! Get down from there!"

"I can see him. It looks like they're talking to him. I don't see a gun. Oh, shit. Look at his arm. Dave, his right arm is broken. And I mean it's almost broken at a right angle, and Franky doesn't even act like he cares—oh, wait. Something's going on . . ."

A cop voice from nearby said, "Get down from there! You! Get down!" John ignored him.

A burst of gunfire. Everybody ducked.

"They're shooting him!" shouted John. "They're shooting a lot! You can see bits of him flying off! He's still up! Holy shit he's—HOLY SHIT! He just grabbed one of the SWAT guys. He grabbed him by the ankles and is swinging him around like a baseball bat! He's knocking the other guys down!"

"Bullshit! John, get down from there!"

"He's biting a guy now! He's eating him! A cop! He's got him by the neck!"

"WHAT?!?"

More shots. Screams. Suddenly I was awash in a panicked current of swinging elbows and shoulders. John jumped down from the statue, and ran with the crowd, as fast as he could. Over his shoulder he yelled, "DAVE! HE'S COMING!"

I took two steps, and somebody slammed into me. My face bounced off wet grass. I climbed to my knees in the stampede. A woman nearby screamed at the top of her lungs. I spun and between running figures saw a shirt stained red with blood.

Franky.

Standing right there, left arm jutting grotesquely just under the elbow, blood dripping to the grass from a protruding shard of bone.

Police were shouting in the distance, commanding us to get down.

How did he beat them here? He cleared half a football field in five seconds.

Franky's torso was riddled with puckered bullet wounds, leaking red. His chest heaved with excited breaths, his punctured lungs whistling with each inhale. The broken arm was moving, twitching, the bones tearing free of skin and curling like tentacles.

What the shit?

Cops ran into position. I saw one SWAT guy fumbling to cram a new magazine into the little submachine gun he had. They shouted orders at each other, and at the crowd. Franky opened his mouth, opening wide like a yawn. And just for a second, I thought I saw the face of the spider, nesting there behind his teeth, filling the cavity with its black body.

Then, the Franky monster let out a noise like I had never heard before. It was a shriek, like microphone feedback. But more organic and pained, like the sound a whale would make if it were on fire.

The ground shook from it. My bowels quivered. I think I shat a little. I saw people hitting the ground all around me, saw guns fall from the hands of cops. I clapped my palms over my ears as the pained shriek of Franky the Monster filled my bones. Franky's back arched, his mouth opened to the sky, howling. Blood was spurting from a dozen bullet holes. It was the last thing I saw before the world swam away and went black.

I came to and sat up. People were standing around, nobody running. No sign of Franky. Some time had passed. The horizon was shitting a sun, casting a glow on a layer of fog that was settling in the low areas like puddles of ghost piss.

I saw John about ten feet away, on his feet but bent over at the waist, gripping his pants at the knees. He was blinking, as if trying to focus his eyes.

"John? You all right?"

He nodded, still looking at the ground.

"Yeah. I'm thinkin' that sound he made melted our brains. Did they get him?"

"Don't know. I just came to."

A white truck pulled up with a dish apparatus on the back. It had a TV station logo on the side. We were about to be on live TV. I tried to fix my hair with my hands.

Hospital staff in aqua scrubs were walking people back into the building. It looked like every policeman in the state was here, taking statements from people. I realized John and I should probably get going, before we got asked a bunch of questions that, once again, we didn't have any non-crazy answers for. Not just about tonight, but everything. I turned toward John but John wasn't there anymore. I went looking for him, giving one pair of cops a wide berth along the way. I thought about just going home without him, but then I saw him standing out by the street and talking to a goddamned reporter.

I stomped over there, walked right in front of the camera and was about to grab him by the collar and drag him away when John said, "Oh, shit!"

I followed John's gaze and said, "Oh, *shit*."

The reporter lowered her microphone and said, "Ooooh, shit."

Army guys, a lot of them. National Guard, I guessed. They were wearing that grayish urban camo they wear these days. They had parked a green truck across the intersection where the hospital driveway met the road. Cars were lined up trying to get out, and soldiers were going down the line and issuing instructions to angry drivers.

Up by the truck a soldier raised a bullhorn and said:

"ATTENTION. DO NOT LEAVE THE AREA. THERE IS A SIGNIFICANT CHANCE YOU HAVE BEEN EXPOSED TO A CONTAGIOUS PATHOGEN. LEAVING THE AREA COULD LEAD TO SPREADING THE INFECTION TO YOUR FAMILY AND FRIENDS. BY ORDER OF THE CENTERS FOR DISEASE CONTROL YOU ARE NOT TO LEAVE THE AREA. PLEASE GO BACK TO THE LOBBY OF THE HOSPITAL WHERE YOU WILL BE GIVEN FURTHER INSTRUCTIONS. THIS IS FOR YOUR OWN SAFETY. WE APOLOGIZE FOR THE INCONVENIENCE AND YOU WILL BE RELEASED AS SOON AS IT IS DETERMINED THAT YOU DO NOT POSE AN INFECTION RISK TO THOSE AROUND YOU. THANK YOU FOR YOUR COOPERATION. IF YOU ATTEMPT TO LEAVE THE AREA YOU *WILL* BE PROSECUTED. *DO NOT ATTEMPT TO LEAVE THE AREA.*"

John tossed down his cigarette, stamped it out and said, "Let's leave the area."

"Yeah."

We left the reporter behind and circled around, looking for a way out. We found the AMBULANCE ONLY entrance around the block had a Humvee across it. The soldiers were forming a perimeter, camouflage dots looping around the grounds. We looked around behind the building, where there was a little strip of woods separating the hospital grounds from town. Same scene, with the addition of some guys unloading spools of razor wire from the back of a truck.

John spat and said, "This might sound like an odd thing to say right at this moment, but I wish those guys were wearing hazmat suits."

"Yeah or at least something covering their mouths."

"There wouldn't happen to be a door around here, would there?"

"A door . . . ?"

"You know. One of the—"

"Oh. There's not one in the hospital as far as I know. That would have been awfully convenient though."

John thought for a moment, then said, "What about BB's? It's right on the other side of the trees there." BB's was a convenience store about two blocks away, but on the other side of that little wooded area. Among those trees was a deep drainage ditch we'd also have to cross.

"Man, I don't know . . ."

He edged around to get a look at the Guardsmen standing between us and the woods. He said, "Come on, we wait 'til that guy goes to help unload some more of that wire, then run right through the gap there. But if we're gonna do it, we have to do it now, before the sun comes all the way up."

"And what makes you think those other guys won't shoot us in the head?"

"They're not gonna do that. All these guys know is they got up in the wee hours of the morning to fence off a hospital because a guy went on a shooting rampage and they're afraid some diseases may have escaped. They don't know there's a, you know, monster situation going on."

"And you know all of that how?"

"TJ Frye is over on the other side. You remember TJ? Came to that party a few years ago and stuck his dick in the jelly? He's like a sergeant now. Said they haven't been told shit."

"Well, they're gonna chase us."

"Yeah but we just gotta make it to BB's."

John stripped off his shirt and started wrapping it around his face, like he was ready to join some riot in the Middle East. "Cover your face, unless you want them to identify you and show up at your house in an hour."

Peering through a quarter-inch slit of wrapped T-shirt, we crouched low and stayed in the shadows until we reached the narrow stretch of lawn between us and the woods. We stayed like that for about fifteen minutes until one guard left his post to accept a cup of coffee from another. We sprinted. I immediately slipped in the wet grass and fell on my face. My shirt mask slipped over my eyes. I scrambled to my feet and just ran, as hard and fast as I could, nearly blind. I heard shouted commands but no gunshots.

A branch slapped me in the face and I knew I had reached the woods. I stumbled and clawed the shirt away from my eyes just in time to feel the ground give way under me. I was sliding down an embankment of wet grass and dead leaves, then splashed into freezing ankle-deep water. It was dark. There had been an early morning gloom out on the lawn but it was still midnight under the trees—no sign of John, or anyone else. I sloshed through the water and scrambled up the other side, pulling myself up with handfuls of weeds, knocking aside discarded grocery bags and flattened plastic Coke bottles.

A hand latched around my ankle. A different hand latched around my wrist. John up top, one of the soldiers on bottom. For a ridiculous moment I was pulled in opposite directions like a cartoon character, both men shouting frantic instructions at me. I tried to kick free and accidentally kicked the guy in the head in the process. It worked.

In three seconds, John and I were out of the woods and sprinting diagonally across a parking lot, through the bay of a car wash, down an alley and toward the gray bricks and rusting Dumpster that was the ass end of BB's convenience store. I risked a look over my shoulder—

"SHIT!"

There were no fewer than ten soldiers following us now, the two in the lead carrying black plastic pistols with neon-green tips. They looked like toys, but I knew they were Tasers. I was eager to avoid my fifth lifetime Tasering if at all possible.

The restroom door was on the exterior of the store, around the corner to our left. I rushed up to it, grabbed a rickety knob and—

"Locked!" I said, trying to catch my breath. "The key! Inside! You have to get the key from the counter inside!"

John shoved me aside, reared back, and kicked the door. The whole knob and latch mechanism exploded. We crammed ourselves inside, pushing the broken door closed.

One . . . two . . . three . . .

"Hey! You two! Get the fuck out of there and lay the fuck down on the pavement before we have to—"

The soldier was cut off in midword.

I pulled open the door to find we were surrounded by panties.

We stepped out of the ladies' dressing room at the Walmart on the opposite side of town. John and I had traveled about 2.5 miles in approximately zero seconds. Right now, at BB's, several very confused National Guardsmen were staring at an extremely filthy, and completely empty, public bathroom.

We stepped into the aisle of the nearly empty store, two muddy men with T-shirts wrapped around their heads. John unwrapped his and said, "What is this? Walmart?"

So, I wasn't completely honest with the psychiatrist about the whole thing with the mysterious door in the burrito stand and the Asian dude who disappeared into it. John and I have identified half a dozen of those doors around town, and we know where they lead: to each other. The only thing is you never knew to which of the other doors they were going to take you, it was basically doorway roulette. I mean, you're not going step out in Beijing or anything, it's always another door around town. All the ones we've found, anyway. But they never seem to go to the same place twice. Why? Because this whole town is fucked up, that's why. I keep trying to tell you that. You don't want to come here. It's exhausting.

John and I didn't draw much attention as we moved through the store since, at this particular store in this particular town, we weren't even the filthiest people there. We just walked right out the front door and headed back toward town along the shoulder of the highway. It was a wet, chilled morning under a lethargic November sky that had rolled out of bed and thrown on an old, gray, grease-stained T-shirt.

John said, "Did you hear? They never found Franky."

"Wonderful."

"What do you think happened? You think that bug thing took over his brain?"

"Hey, why not?"

"You think he's gonna turn up again?"

If you're asking yourself why the men with guns chasing us couldn't just use the magic door and follow us right to Walmart, it's because for most people, the doors are just doors. Same as for most people, the spider monster in my house would have been invisible, just as it was for Franky. Same as how if you'd been in the bathroom with me all those months ago when I saw that shadowy shape outside my shower, you'd have seen nothing. You might have sensed something, just as in your everyday life you might sit in a dark house and feel like you're not alone, or have a nagging suspicion that something slipped around a corner just a moment before you looked. The feeling can usually be expressed by the phrase, "Of course there's nothing there. *Now*."

To be clear, if you've actually seen a ghost, that doesn't make you like us. A ghost sighting is usually nothing more than your brain trying to put a familiar face on something that does not have a face at all.

John and I, on the other hand, can see what most of you can only sense. We're not special, it's just the result of some drugs we took. Just for future reference, if you're ever at a party and a Rastafarian offers you a syringe full of a slimy black substance that crawls around on its own like The Blob, don't take it. And don't call us, either. We get enough bullshit from strangers as it is.

25 Hours Prior to Outbreak

English should have a word for that feeling you get when you first wake up in a strange room and have no freaking idea where you are.

Hotezzlement?

I was cold, and every inch of my body was in pain. I heard a crunching, like the jaws of a predator grinding through bone. I pulled open my eyes. I saw a dragon standing proudly atop a hill before me.

The dragon was on a TV screen, beneath it was a video game console with a tangle of cords snaking across green carpet. I blinked, squinted at the sun burning in through a cracked window. I turned, hearing my neck creak as I did, and saw John sitting at a computer desk in the corner, staring into the monitor and holding a bottle full of a clear liquid that I'm sure you wouldn't want to try to put out a fire with. I sat up, realizing I had been covered up with something in my sleep. I thought for a moment John had thrown a blanket over me but closer inspection revealed it to be a beach towel.

John glanced back at me from his computer chair and said, "Sorry, I used my spare blanket when I got that leak in my car."

I looked around for the source of that animal crunching noise. I found Molly laying behind the couch, with her head crammed inside an open box of Cap'n Crunch cereal. She was eating as fast as she could, trying to use her paws to keep the box in place.

"You're letting her do that?"

"Oh, yeah. Cereal is stale anyway. I don't have any dog food here."

The dragon sat frozen on the television, the intro screen for a video game John had apparently been playing while I slept on his couch.

"What time is it?"

"Around eight."

I stood and felt my head swim. I rubbed my eyes and almost screamed in pain from the wound there. My shoulder felt like it had taken a bullet and it seemed like a pair of elves were trying to escape my skull through my temples using tiny pickaxes. It wasn't the first time I had woken up at John's place feeling like this.

My phone screamed. The display read, AMY. I closed my eyes, sighed and answered.

"Hey, baby."

"Hi! David! I'm watching the news! What happened?"

"Shouldn't you be in class?" Amy had failed a pretty basic English class last semester because it was a morning class and she kept sleeping through it.

She said, "They cancelled it. Oh, it's on again. Turn to CNN."

I talked around the phone to John, told him to switch over the TV. He did, and watched as an early morning shot of the chaos at the hospital filled the screen. The name of the city was displayed along the bottom. National news.

John turned up the sound and we heard a female reporter say, ". . . No history of drug use or mental illness. Frank Burgess had been with the department for three years. Authorities are combing the area for Burgess but police say the number of wounds he sustained in the standoff make his turning up alive, quote, 'highly unlikely.' Meanwhile, the hospital remains under quarantine due to unspecified infection risks that have only added to the anxiety in this shell-shocked community."

They cut to a shot of our enormously fat chief of police, giving a sound bite in front of a bank of microphones.

To Amy I said, "Man, our chief of police is getting huge."

Amy said, "They said thirteen people were hurt and I think three people died but there could be more. Did you guys hear about this last night? When it was all going on?"

A pause on my end. Too long. Finally I said, "We heard about it, yeah."

"Uh-oh."

"What?"

"David, were you there? Were you guys in on this?"

"What? No, no. Of course not. Why would you think that?"

"David . . ."

"No, no. It was nothing. Guy just went crazy, that's all."

"Are you lying?"

"No, no. No."

She said nothing. She and the therapist knew the same trick. Filling the silence, I said, "I mean, we were *there* but we weren't really involved . . ."

"I knew it! I'm coming down."

"No, Amy. It's nothing, really. It's over. We just happened to be in the area."

I heard John say, "Hey! It's me!" I turned to the television.

Sure enough, John's face filled the screen. The reporter's voice-over covered the audio, saying, ". . . But for every hour Burgess remains at large, fear and paranoia are bound to keep growing in this small city."

On TV, John's voice faded in: ". . . And then we saw a small creature crawl into his mouth. I wasn't two feet away, I saw it clearly. The thing wasn't from this world. I don't mean alien, I mean probably interdimensional in nature. I think it's obvious from what happened tonight that this being possessed some powers of mind control."

I closed my eyes again and groaned.

Amy said, "I'm coming down. I'll take the bus."

"Forget it, your classes are more important. If you fail English again I think they can kick you out of the country. I think it's in the Patriot Act."

"Gotta go, honey. I'm late for class."

"You said you didn't—"

"We'll talk about it later. Bye-bye."

I killed the phone and looked for my shoes.

"You goin' back home?"

"I can't stay here, John."

"Yeah. But, you know. You had that thing in your house."

"You think there's another one?"

"I don't know, but—"

"What do you want me to do, have the place sprayed?"

"No, I'm just sayin'. That thing, it crawled inside Franky and seemed to take him over. Well, that thing turned up in *your* bed. Are you assuming that's an accident? Because maybe we should consider that it was there for you."

I can always trust John to think of things like this.

"It don't matter. Okay? Your couch isn't long enough. It kills my neck on the armrest. So, it's moot."

"Well, you're not gettin' the bed."

I took away Molly's cereal box, which was now just empty cardboard bent in the shape of a dog head. I said, "You sounded crazy on the news, by the way. I hope you know that."

"What? I was tellin' the truth."

"To what purpose, exactly? The only people who'll be convinced by that are people who're already nuts. I can see you've got your blog up right now. For what? So you can tell the whole nonsense story and be one more nutjob ranting on the Internet? It doesn't do anybody any good. It just makes you look crazy. It makes both of us look crazy."

"Hey, aren't you going to be late for your court-mandated therapist appointment?"

"Fuck you."

I glanced at my watch. He was right.

The drive through town was surreal. I had to go past the hospital (okay, I didn't *have* to but curiosity got the better of me) and it had the air of a natural disaster. News vans were parked outside of barriers that were blocking the street. Cops were at a checkpoint, directing traffic away from the parking garage entrance. Three blocks later I had to wait at an intersection for five minutes while a row of green trucks rumbled past. Military. I suddenly wanted to get far away from there.

I had half hoped I would find the psychiatrist's office closed today, as if the aftermath of a shooting rampage would be treated like a national holiday. No such luck. People got to make a paycheck I guess.

I barged in before I realized there was somebody else in the waiting room. Should have looked in through the window or something, I would have waited outside if I'd known, since the potential for really awkward conversation seems pretty high in the waiting room of a psychiatrist's office. I tried to think of a plausible excuse for turning around and leaving. The best I came up with was to grab the potted plant in the corner and just walk out, as if it was a rental I was repossessing. I decided not to.

The lady in the waiting room didn't even turn to me when I came in, she was transfixed by a television in the corner tuned to Fox News, covering the shooting. Jesus, slow news day. People get shot all the time, right? I found a chair as far away from her as possible. I grabbed a magazine and held it in front of my face. Seemed to be a lot of articles about wedding dresses.

"It's happening all over, you know," said the woman from the other side of the room. She was probably forty-five or so, hair a desperate shade of blonde.

I said, "What's that?"

"Demon possession. All over the world. You see news from the Middle East and such and you can see it spreading like wildfire."

"Uh huh."

"It's easier now, now that all the souls are gone."

"Hmm." I flipped the page in my bridal magazine, acting engrossed in the ads. The only thing worse than always being the craziest person in the room is when suddenly you're alone with someone crazier. She was still talking.

"Did you know the Rapture happened already? In 1961. The Lord called all the souls up to Heaven. But the bodies were left behind. That's why the people walking around today don't seem to have souls. It's because they don't. You see that story last week, the man who was being chased by the police in a stolen car? There was a newborn baby in the backseat? He just threw it out the window. A baby! People these days are just common animals. Because their human souls are gone, see."

I lowered the magazine and said, "That's . . . not a bad theory actually."

"They called it the mark of the beast. But they don't need a mark. They reveal themselves as beasts, with time."

The door to the office creaked open and out walked a gorgeous teenage girl. For a baffled second I thought this was somehow my therapist, like maybe she was filling in today. But of course she was just a patient and Dr. Tennet was behind her. The crazy woman in the waiting room stood and thanked the doctor and walked out with the girl. The lady hadn't been there for treatment. She was just giving her daughter a ride.

Right off, Dr. Tennet asked, "What happened to your eye?"

"Got in a fight with John. He said counseling was a waste of time and I told him I'd be damned if I'd hear him insult you and your profession."

"You look like you haven't slept."

"How can I, with what's going on? Have you been watching the news today? Do you know if they found Franky?"

"He wasn't expected to live, was he? Did you know him?"

"What? No. Why would I have known him?"

"You called him Franky."

"Well I went to high school with him. But that was years ago. I didn't have anything to do with what happened if that's what you mean."

"Not at all."

"Because I didn't."

"I'm sorry if I made you feel accused."

I glanced out the window at the exact moment a green truck rumbled by on the street outside.

"Why are there so many army trucks? This all seems like an overreaction, don't you think?"

Not letting me change the subject, Tennet said, "I would like to come back to what you talked about last time, about having to hide your true self from the world, and feeling like you are powerless to become the type of person who would not have to hide. Just now, you seemed to feel I was accusing you. I'd like to talk about that if we can."

I stared out the window and chewed a fingernail. Man, I did not want to be here. In this office, in this town, in this life. I wanted to just walk out. I knew at some point the cops were going to scoop up John—he'd appeared on goddamned television right in the area they were trying to quarantine—and that meant eventually they'd come get me, too. What the hell was I doing here?

Because you have nowhere else to go.

I said, "I don't know. Twenty-four hours ago I'm sitting here trying to justify believing crazy things, and one day later the whole town has gone crazy. So, in my mind the rest of the world has now caught up to my craziness which means I should be set free." I rubbed my itchy eyes and said, "There are real monsters, doc. I'm too tired today to say anything else."

He said, "I read some of the things you and your friend posted on the Internet. Sometimes you speak of yourself as if you are a freak, or a monster."

"Well, metaphorically. I mean, aren't we all? The woman in the waiting room just now basically told me the same thing."

"An incident like last night always brings out those kind of feelings, I suppose."

I considered for a moment, then said, "Can I ask you a question, doc?"

"Of course."

"What would you say if I asked to use your computer there, on your desk? Right now, without you having a chance to delete anything."

"Of course, there is confidential patient information that I couldn't—"

"Let's say I could promise I wouldn't look at any of that. In fact, let's say I just want to look at your Internet browser history. How would you feel about that?"

"It would be an invasion of privacy, of course. And I have credit cards and logins—"

"I'm talking about the porn, doc. Would I find nasty schoolgirl porn on there? Maybe interracial stuff? Incest fantasies?"

"I feel like you're trying to get a reaction from me. If you're not feeling like going through with the session we can continue on Monday—"

"No, listen. When I'm with Amy and I ask to borrow her computer, she passes it right over. No questions asked, no hesitation. She could sit there and look over my shoulder and watch me sift through every single file, and she wouldn't flinch. She has nothing to hide. It'd be the same if I had a machine that could peer into her mind—she'd be fine with it. She's comfortable with what she is. But, on the other hand, if she's visiting and she asks to use *my* laptop? Man, there is so much depraved shit on there that if she saw it all, she'd call the cops. If she could see what goes through my mind when I see another girl walk by, she'd burst into tears."

He nodded. "So you feel like you have to hide a part of yourself, and she doesn't."

"I'm saying it's like that with everybody. There are two kinds of people on planet Earth, Batman and Iron Man. Batman has a secret identity, right? So Bruce Wayne has to walk around every second of every day knowing that if somebody finds out his secret, his family is dead, his friends are dead, everyone he loves gets tortured to death by costumed supervillains. And he has to live with the weight of that secret every day, that tension gnawing in his guts. But not Tony Stark, he's open about who he is. He tells the world he's Iron Man, he doesn't give a shit. He doesn't have that shadow hanging over him, he doesn't have to spend energy building up those walls of lies around himself. You're one or the other—either you're one of those people who has to hide your real self because it would ruin you if it came out, because of your secret fetishes or addictions or crimes, or you're not one of those people. And the two groups aren't even living in the same universe."

"You believe you're Batman."

I closed my eyes. "What did you say the hourly rate for these sessions was again?"

"I mean you're in that category, you feel like the people around you would react badly if they knew what you really thought and believed."

"Not because they'll think I'm crazy. They already think that. But because of how they would react once they knew the truth. You know how people are. That's what you write books about, right? Group panics and all that?"

"You think the truth would cause mass hysteria."

I shrugged, and nodded toward the window. "Look out there. You'll see."

He said, "That's actually more true than you know. Don't repeat this, but it appears I'm going to be called in to work on this case. The hospital shooting, I mean."

"What, like as a profiler or something?"

"Oh, no, no. I'd be offering my assistance in dealing with the public. It's the panic that is the primary concern, you see. Making sure no one gets a hair trigger, some poor soul waiting by their back door with a hunting rifle, shooting at a shadowy shape in the backyard that turns out to be their neighbor. Fear can be fatal and, as I suppose you see on my bookshelf, I'm . . . something of an expert."

I thought, *That has to be nice, to have a job where fear is something that happens to other people.*

I stared out the window and said, "Do you ever get scared, Dr. Tennet?"

"Of course, but you know these sessions aren't about me—"

"And besides, in your world, everything has some harmless explanation, right? It's always bees. Even this thing with Franky. Your job will be, what, to go up to a bank of microphones and assure everybody that it's all bees?"

"You feel like I was being dismissive of your fears. I apologize if so."

"So does anything scare you, doctor? Anything irrational?"

"Of course. Here, I'll volunteer my most embarrassing example. I feel like I owe it to you, to make up for the bee story. Are you a fan of science fiction?"

"I don't know. My girlfriend is."

"All right, but you know *Star Trek,* and 'Beam me up, Scotty'? How they can teleport people around?"

"Yeah. The transporters."

"Do you know how they work?"

"Just . . . special effects. CGI or whatever they used."

"No, I mean within the universe of the show. They work by breaking down your molecules, zapping you over a beam, and putting you back together on the other end."

"Sure."

"That is what scares me. I can't watch it. I find it too disturbing."

I shrugged. "I don't get it."

"Well, think about it. Your body is just made of a few different types of atoms. Carbon, hydrogen, oxygen, and so on. So this transporter machine, there is no reason in the world to break down all of those atoms and then send those specific atoms thousands of miles away. One oxygen atom is the same as another, so what it does is send the *blueprint* for your body across the beam. Then it reassembles you at the destination, out of whatever atoms it has nearby. So if there is carbon and hydrogen at the planet you're beaming down to, it'll just put you together out of what it has on hand, because you get the exact same result."

"Sure.

"So it's more like sending a fax than mailing a letter. Only the transporter is a fax machine *that shreds the original*. Your original body, along with your brain, gets vaporized. Which means what comes out the other end isn't you. It's an exact copy that the machine made, of a man who is now dead, his atoms floating freely around the interior of the ship. Only within the universe of the show, *nobody knows this.*

"Meanwhile, you are dead. Dead for eternity. All of your memories and emotions and personality end, right there, on that platform, for-ever. Your wife and children and friends will never see you again. What they will see is this unnatural photocopy of you that emerged from the other end. And in fact, since transporter technology is used routinely, all of the people you see on that ship are copies of copies of copies of long-dead, vaporized crew members. And no one ever figures it out. They all continue to blithely step into this machine that kills one hundred percent of the people who use it, but nobody realizes it because each time, it spits out a perfect replacement for the victim at the other end."

I stared at him.

"Why did you tell me that?"

He shrugged. "You asked."

His face showed nothing. I thought of the Asian guy, casually dis-appearing into the magic burrito door, walking out somewhere else. And in that moment I *almost* asked Tennet what he knew, and who he was.

I don't know. Maybe it wouldn't have changed anything.

18 Hours Prior to Outbreak

Hours went by, and the cops continued to not show up at either my house or John's apartment. All morning I was worried sick about what I would say when they brought me in, but then afternoon came and I was even more worried about the fact that they *weren't* coming after us. That meant things had gotten so out of control that we were no longer on their list of priorities.

Come midafternoon, I found myself at work, standing behind a counter, trying to peel the magnetic antitheft tag off a DVD with my fingernail (a DVD is a disc that plays movies, if they don't have those by the time you read this). I know I've complained about the pain in my eye and shoulder more than once but I want to point out that the bite on my leg was also starting to hurt like a son of a bitch.

I would have called in sick, but I had used up all of my sick days for the year and couldn't take off again until January. I take a lot of sick days, most of them self-declared Mental Health days, meaning I wake up in a mood that I know will lead me to assault the very first person who asks me if the two-day rentals have to be back on Wednesday or Thursday.

I had worked at Wally's Videe-Oh! for five years, been a manager for two. I started right after I dropped out of college. At the time I had heard that Quentin Tarantino got discovered while working at a video store, and I think I had it in my head to try to work there and write a screenplay. It was going to be about a cop in the future with a sentient flamethrower for an arm. At age nineteen, that seemed like a pretty sound plan. The thing about not having parents is you don't have anyone to tell you you're heading down a path paved with grossly inaccurate expectations of what the world owes you.

The people who raised me—and I'll leave their names out of this—they did what they could. Nice people, real religious. Kind of treated me like I was a little African refugee kid they had rescued. They knew my story, knew that I had never known my dad. Years later when I got in trouble at school and got kicked out because of that kid that died, they were real supportive. Took my side all the way through, then shortly after they moved to Florida and hinted that maybe things would be better if I stayed behind.

My birth mom is living in Arizona, I think, staying with a dozen other people in an arrangement that could be called a "compound." She sent me a letter two years ago, thirty pages scribbled on lined notebook paper. I couldn't make it past the first paragraph. I skipped down to the last sentence, which was, "I hope you are stockpiling ammunition like I told you, the forces of the Antichrist will first seek to disarm us."

I scraped the plastic theft sticker off the DVD, put it back in its case, then picked another case off the stack. Pulled out the disc, started scraping off the tag. I looked around, saw there was only one customer in the store. A guy wearing a cowboy hat. His jeans looked like they were painted on.

The TV we had mounted in the far corner of the store was supposed to be playing a promotional DVD but I had switched it over to Headline News, with the sound down and the closed-captioning turned on. They had been going back to the "hospital shooting" every twenty minutes or so. The cowboy with the tight pants came up to the counter with a copy of *Basic Instinct 2* and *2001: A Space Odyssey*. How could he walk in those jeans? Did they inflate when he farted?

I glanced up at the TV and saw a reporter standing in front of a street barricade. Closed-captioning mentioned something about cops having to break up an angry crowd trying to get in to see loved ones at the hospital. The cowboy gave me his membership card and I punched in the number. His account came up as:

NAME: James DuPree

OVERDUE: ø

ACCT STATUS: A

COMMENTS: THIS MAN HAS WORN THE SAME TROUSERS SINCE HE WAS A TODDLER.

Many memos had circulated at Wally's about abusing the customer comment box on the computer. We have John to thank for that. He worked here a few years ago, after I begged the manager to let him on. John was fired a few months later, but not before he managed to add something to the "Comment" field for pretty much every single customer he served:

NAME: Carl Gass

COMMENTS: If he doesn't have late charges, and you tell him that he does, he LOSES HIS FUCKING MIND.

_____

NAME: Lisa Franks

COMMENTS: Had sex with her on 11/15.

_____

NAME: Kara Bullock

COMMENTS: Thinks I have an English accent. Don't forget.

_____

NAME: Chet Beirach

COMMENTS: Always smells like fish. I think he fishes for a living. He's sensitive about it so don't bring it up.

_____

NAME: Rob Arnold

COMMENTS: It's the white Patrick Ewing!

_____

David Wong

NAME: Cheryl Mackey

COMMENTS: Had sex with her on 7/16.

I gave the cowboy his change, glancing over his shoulder at the TV every chance I could get. They were back to old footage from the hospital, the camera showing close-ups of bullet holes in walls and shell casings on the floor. The cowboy turned to follow my gaze, saw the TV. "That's some scary shit, ain't it?"

I said, "Yeah."

"Whole world's comin' to an end, that's what I think."

"Yeah, probably."

"Nigger in the White House."

"Yeah."

The cowboy left. He stuffed his wallet into his back pocket and I imagined it shooting back out again, squeezed by the sheer pressure of the fabric. I grabbed a DVD and went back to peeling off stickers.

I had gotten written up six weeks ago because more DVDs were stolen on my watch than either of the other two managers. Not sure what I was supposed to be doing to stop it, other than running out and tackling the kids who tried to walk out with the goods. The problem, I decided, was the magnetic antitheft tags that would activate the door alarm were in the DVD cases, not on the discs, so it only took the thieves minutes to figure out they just had to pop the disc out of the case and stuff it in their pocket, leaving the case and the theft tag behind. Yes, this town has people who are actually too poor to afford a computer and Internet connection to just pirate the movies that way.

So I wrote up this angry e-mail to the head office, saying the antitheft system was idiotic and that if they were serious about people not stealing discs, then they should put the antitheft tags on the discs themselves. They agreed, and I and two other employees spent about twelve hours sticking these stiff little stickers to all of the new releases in the store. The plan worked beautifully. That is, until last Thursday, when a customer brought in a disc that had been scratched to hell be-

58

cause the theft sticker came unstuck inside his DVD player. It jammed the little tray when it tried to eject the disc and he had to pry it out. Two days later, a customer brought in a broken DVD player. When his disc got stuck thanks to the sticker, he wound up breaking the disc tray on the machine trying to free it.

I wasn't at the store that day, I was on one of my many "sick" days. But when I came back I was greeted by twenty-seven e-mails from managers and regional managers and other people I had never heard from before, telling me that every antitheft sticker had to be removed from every DVD by November 5th.

I bring this up in case you were wondering why in the holy hell I felt the need to come in to work in the middle of what appeared to be some kind of monster infestation. The answer is that if I took one more sick day I would be fired, and if I didn't get these stickers off by the deadline I would be fired, and even if I could talk my way out of one firing I sure as hell couldn't talk my way out of both. And if I was fired, soon after society would decide I wasn't earning my electricity and water and my house and my food. And they'd be right. If you think that's a bad reason to come to work in the middle of all this, then I'm guessing you're still living with Mom and Dad.

I glanced up at the TV and saw something new. Security camera footage, from inside the hospital. In color, but in a frame rate that made the people appear to blink down the hallway, teleporting five feet at a time. There was a shot of a woman running in terror. They cut back to the studio and some older guy in a suit, an expert of some kind they had brought in. Then they cut back to the security video and I froze.

I heard the DVD I was holding fall to the counter.

Did I just see that?

They played it again. The first frame was Franky, in the hall of the hospital, holding a nurse around the throat. The frames rolled forward. A security guard came into frame, hand out, trying to talk Franky down. Next frame, same players, limbs in different positions. Looked to be about one frame per second. The next frame was what got me.

At the top of the screen appeared a man in black. And I mean all black, head to toe. A solid black shape. Next frame—one second later—he was gone.

I stared. They cut back to the anchor. The closed-captioning lagged behind but I didn't think I saw any mention of the mysterious figure in the hall.

My cell phone screamed. I picked up.

"Yeah."

John said, "Dave? Can you get to a television?"

"We got one on here. I saw it."

"The thing in the hall?"

"Yeah. Man in black."

"Shadow man."

"Whatever."

"Man, this isn't a joke anymore."

"It wasn't a joke before, John. A bunch of people died."

"You know what I mean. You better sleep with your crossbow tonight."

"I don't have the crossbow. The cops confiscated it, remember?"

"Okay, then I should come over. I'll bring my lighter. We'll sleep in shifts."

"No. Wait, bring your what?"

"Come on man, how do you know Franky won't show up there?"

"He's surely dead by now."

"I didn't say he wasn't."

"I'm busy, John."

"Sure. I'll try to come up with a plan."

"Whatever."

"Watch the shadows."

"Hey, John, don't do anything stupid—"

I was talking to a dead phone.

17 Hours Prior to the Outbreak

DISCLAIMER: *The following sequence of events was relayed by John to the author after the fact, and no attempt was made to corroborate this version of events through witness interviews. While there is no evidence directly contradicting any of this account, much of it seems highly unlikely.*

John wound up needing five hours to find Franky Burgess.

That may sound impressive to you, considering there were rows of trained, uniformed men fanning out across several square miles around the hospital all day Friday without success, but it actually took longer than John was hoping. It wasn't until 8 P.M. that he found himself face-to-face with Franky across a pane of dirty glass, and he had been hoping to have the whole situation wrapped up while it was still daylight. Night is when bad things happen in Undisclosed. Well, bad things also happen in the daytime but at least you can see where you're going when you're running away.

Anyway, in early November, night falls at around six. So after getting off the phone with Dave at the video store at three, John had spent an hour driving around in his Caddie and getting a sense of the situation around town. The manhunt, which seemed to involve several hundred police, volunteers and National Guardsmen, appeared to be focused on the wooded area east of the hospital, and the empty houses and trailers around it. It made sense from their point of view, he supposed. They were looking for a spot where a deranged and wounded man would crawl off to die. But they weren't going to find Franky. It wasn't going to be that easy.

There were local cops who had to know better, who had to know that the situation at the hospital had been that other thing, the kind of business that pops up in Undisclosed every few years when the town decides to start coloring outside the lines. John was picturing the chief trying to nudge the National Guard in that direction, maybe suggesting that they expand the search, and that maybe additional precautions should be taken with the quarantine. Special hearing protection, perhaps. Or hazmat suits. And instead of just the hospital, maybe rope off the whole town. Or state. But then that would lead to a lot of awkward questions and the chief would quickly back down and just pray that the whole thing would come to nothing. If only it ever worked out that way.

John, on the other hand, was thinking "monster" from the start since, you know, the situation was caused by a monster. It was just a matter of figuring out what kind of monster it was. There are really only two kinds of monsters in the world, which you already know if you've been watching horror movies: Breeders and Non-breeders. So for instance, Frankenstein's monster would fall into the second category if he was real. He's a freak, a singular being and once you kill him, he's gone. Problem solved.

The Breeders are an exponentially bigger problem. Within that group you've got slow breeders like vampires (if they were real, which they're not) which breed in a small-scale controlled way, but mainly to avoid extinction rather than spread. But then you've got the fast breeders, like zombies (if they existed, which they don't) where breeding is all they do. They are basically walking epidemics, and are the worst of the worst-case scenarios, because such a creature could, hypothetically, wipe out civilization. This is humanity's greatest fear, which is why at the moment half of the world's horror novels, movie posters and video games have zombies on the cover. So in any situation like this, step one is to find out what category of creature you're dealing with. Step two is to anticipate what the creature is going to do next, based on what you determined in step one. Then step three is you find out if the thing can be killed with a chainsaw.

This particular case was a fairly straightforward situation of a small creature taking over a man's head and controlling his body. That is a really specific thing for a creature to do, John thought, requiring countless specialized biological adaptations. So it was unlikely that it was just some kind of Frankenstein-style genetic mistake with no goal beyond stumbling around biting people until somebody shot it enough times. So, logically that would mean it was a Breeder, and that the taking over of a human body was done to facilitate breeding. What had John worried was that the little shit looked like an insect, and in the normal course of things, insects are notoriously fast breeders. So it could be a worst-case scenario. John suspected that *somebody* up the ladder had already arrived at that conclusion, which is why on this fine autumn afternoon you couldn't pull up to a stoplight in Undisclosed without finding yourself in a Humvee sandwich. It's also presumably why the hospital had been roped off.

So, how do we find Franky?

In John's estimation, that would come down to how much of Franky's brain was still intact. His body still functioned despite the damage it had taken, so the basic nervous and muscular systems must still have been operated by his own human brain. So there surely had to be some remnant of Franky's instincts and impulses in there. And Franky was a cop.

John could think of five shops in town that sold donuts, none of which said they had seen Franky when John called. Where else did cops eat? John drove past a half dozen fast-food franchises, and didn't see Franky inside when he passed. It was getting frustrating. Only two hours of light left now. Then, John swung by a Waffle House and found what he was looking for:

Waffles.

He was good and hungry by that point and let's face it, it had been a "eat breakfast for dinner" kind of day. Blueberry waffles, hash browns, washed down with a beer he found in his jacket.

Around five, John dropped by Munch's trailer. Mitch "Munch" Lombard was one of the three bass players in John's band Three Arm Sally, and had been since high school. He was also a volunteer firefighter which meant he had a police band scanner at his place. John figured he could stay on top of the manhunt and come up with a new plan.

There were a bunch of dudes there already and everybody was playing Guitar Hero and drinking that purple mix of 7Up and cough syrup that sent John to the hospital last year. Steve Gamin came by with a huge bag of frozen McNuggets he had stolen from the McDonald's where he worked. They fired up the Fry Daddy and ate McNuggets for an hour. There was a Japanese chick there who was either drunk or just really goofy. Either way she could barely stand up and laughed at everything that happened. John took a hit of something that he realized gave him the ability to speak Japanese. Or at least he thought it did. He made words that sounded like Japanese to the girl and every time he did, she laughed so hard she almost pissed herself.

He hadn't forgotten his mission. Occasionally John would hear excited voices over the police scanner and would make everybody be quiet. But eventually everybody got so fucked up they wouldn't do it. Head Feingold and his girlfriend Jenny McCormick stopped by with a case of wine she won in a contest and it was a party all of a sudden. A while later, Head went outside to puke and fell asleep on the deck. John found himself making out with the Japanese girl but she started calling him by a different name and he suddenly realized she had been confusing him with another guy all night. Do all white people look the same to the Japanese? John got off the sofa and told her he had to use the bathroom, then quietly threw on his jacket and headed for the door.

Dark outside. *Damn it.*

John saw Head passed out on the deck, under the grill. He turned around, went back into the trailer, grabbed a comforter and a pillow. He went back out to the deck where Head lay and put the blanket over him and wedged the pillow under his head. Just as he was about to leave again, John heard the scanner crackle to life behind him. The dispatcher was reporting that staff out at the turkey farm west of town were complaining that some vagrant was stealing turkeys. The responding cop said in that coded way cops do, that they had bigger fish to fry.

John, on the other hand, jumped off the deck and threw himself into his old Cadillac. He buckled his seat belt, which he always did because he never knew when he would need to ramp something. He made the engine growl and told the headlights to fuck the night.

John had inherited the old Cadillac from a great-uncle who passed away the previous summer. There had been quite a heated debate among the family about who would get stuck with the terrible car, as no one wanted to have to deal with the process of scrapping it. John volunteered and had been driving it ever since.

Creedence Clearwater Revival blasted from an old cassette as John bumped down the highway. He hated Creedence, but Uncle Pat loved them, apparently. Or maybe that was just the last tape he had been listening to when all of the buttons on the ancient sound system stopped working. Either way, the tape was now in permanent play mode, playing through side A, reaching the end, automatically reversing and playing side B. Forever. As loud as it would go. You couldn't stop it, you couldn't eject it. Where there should have been a volume knob, there was only an empty hole, not even a little shaft that you could maybe grab with a pair of needle-nose pliers. On each end of the Caddie's dash were large lumps where John had wadded up towels and held them over the speakers with electrician's tape, hoping to muffle the sound. It did not. Creedence was determined to be heard.

John headed south down the highway, left onto a curve that transitioned to a rural paved road with no painted lines, and across the overpass. Then around the lake, heading toward a row of enormous, low, blue buildings. Turkey factory. There was a gravel lane to the right, and John took it so hard he thought he was going up on two wheels. The Caddie bumped and growled on the dirt road, rear end fishtailing like it was on ice, bits of gravel smacking the floorboards with a sound like popcorn.

John scanned the grounds for any sign of Franky. He wasn't feeling so good, the waffles and hash browns and beer and McNuggets and wine and the Japanese girl's ChapStick sitting hard in his gut—

WHUMP

"OH, SHIT! SHIT!"

He had hit somebody. They were writhing on the hood as John's feet stomped around trying to find the brake pedal. A face was pressed against the windshield and it was—

"FRANKY! SHIT!"

John slammed on the brakes and the Caddie spun out on the gravel. Franky held on.

John reached into his backseat for the chainsaw, then realized there was no chainsaw in the backseat because he had forgotten to drop by Dave's place to get it from his toolshed.

Franky reached around through the driver's side window and snatched at John's shirt. John shrugged away from the hand and dove for the opposite door, pushing his way out and rolling onto the ground. He ran. John's fists pumped toward the light of the turkey building, pulling frozen breaths around the cigarette butts piled up in his lungs. He heard footsteps behind him.

John reached the building. There was the door. John yanked it open.

The fucking smell. Holy shit. It was one of those stinks that seemed to generate its own warmth. Mold and poop and rotten meat. It hit him like a wall. It looked for a moment like there was a foot of snow

David Wong

inside the building, just white as far as the eye could see in that impossibly huge space. Turkeys. Turkeys so thick you couldn't see the ground, white feathers and thin little twitchy heads and, here and there, a rustle of flapping wings, birds jumping and thrashing and squawking and flailing through the air, demonstrating turkey flight as one of God's failures.

John was running again, kicking through turkeys, sucking in air, accidentally eating a feather. Looking for a weapon. Where does a turkey farm keep the chainsaws? Thinking fast, John clutched at the nearest turkey, spun and hurled it at his pursuer. Franky caught the bird like a flapping medicine ball, studied it, then turned and ran out of the building.

"Goddamnit," yelled someone from behind John. "You gave him another turkey! You're payin' for it."

It was a couple of guys in gray coveralls. To the one who looked like he spoke English, John said, "Weapons! We need weapons! That's the guy! Franky! He'll be back after he eats that turkey! Get a chain—OW—"

A turkey bit him on the ankle.

Wait, not a turkey.

One of those fucking spider monsters.

"Shit!" John kicked the spider off his shoe, hard enough that he expected it to go flying like a punted football, but it was kind of clinging to his shoe and it only landed about ten feet away. One of the dudes in coveralls behind him started shouting something in Spanish.

John turned to them and said, "Kill it! Help me kill that thing! I think Franky shit it!"

The dudes seemed to be running away. Hopefully they'd come back with a chainsaw. John backed up, realizing he'd kicked the spider to a spot where it'd be between him and the door.

More flapping and gobbling. The turkeys were going crazy where the spider had landed. John could see the spider appeared to be attached to a turkey somehow. Then, one of the spider's legs shot out, becoming rigid and ten times as long. It impaled four turkeys as if on a skewer, punching through them with little sprays of blood and feather. The spider extended another tentacle and did it again. Four more turkeys skew-

66

ered. Again. Now there were four rows of turkeys joined at the central point where the spider's body was.

The X-shaped cluster of turkeys rose as one body, as tall as a man. Two rows of turkeys forming legs, two forming arms. The turkey Voltron took tentative, lumbering steps toward John. He couldn't help noticing that after a few steps, the two turkeys it was using as feet had been pulverized into a pink, feathery mess. John stood frozen for several seconds while he tried to decide if any of this was in fact happening. He decided that running was the best option either way.

He ran across the building, spotting another door on the opposite wall, kicking turkeys as he went. He shoved through the door and, as if in answer to a prayer he had been too drunk and stoned to pray, there sat a filthy white pickup truck with a faded cartoon turkey on the door, the engine running. John threw himself into the driver's seat, grabbed the gearshift on the steering column and realized it was the turn signal. He looked down to find the stick on the floor when a bundle of wings, feathers and stench punched him in the face. He'd been hit in the jaw with a turkey fist.

John slapped at the turkey, trying to shove it back out of the window, unsuccessfully. He found the crank to roll up the window and the turkey gobbled frantically as it was squeezed by the glass. Behind it was the row of turkeys and the rest of the turkey man's body. John threw the truck in gear and stepped on the gas, hauling the thrashing body of possessed turkeys alongside.

Steering with his right hand and punching a confused fist turkey with his left, John smashed through a chain-link fence and plowed through a stack of bags of turkey feed. He cranked the wheel, nearly crashed right into the building he had just left, and found himself heading back toward the overpass, wind gushing through the gap in the window and filling the interior of the truck with feathers.

The road curved but John didn't, and suddenly he was bouncing over rough terrain, the turkey collective exploding in angry gobbles with each bump. And then the terrain was gone. He was tilting in the air.

Impact. The steering wheel punched him in the face. John heard a splash. He had time to think, *Franky is alive and Dave doesn't know it.*

Before everything went black.

12 Hours Prior to Outbreak

At around 9 P.M. I locked up Wally's. I hadn't heard from John since he'd called in the afternoon, which I considered to be a good thing since it meant he had probably forgotten about the whole thing and fell asleep on his sofa watching UFC fights.

Watch the shadows.

That had been the advice from John. Please. This is freaking Undisclosed. That's like reminding a passenger on a Brooklyn subway not to fondle the hobos in their bathing suit area. I went home and did a room-by-room search of the house. Nothing out of the ordinary. Also nothing in any of the closets, or in the attic, at least as far as I could tell from sweeping the space with a flashlight from the hatch in the hallway. I decided I should check the crawl space under the house, and then I decided fuck that.

Still, I left every light on. I remembered the power outage that accompanied the little bastard showing up last time and I was ready for that, too. I had an LED flashlight in my pocket—compact, but powerful enough to light up half the backyard—and a bundle of six red road flares next to the bed that I had grabbed from my stash in the toolshed. I sat on the bed so that my back was nestled in the corner, the whole room visible from there. I got out my laptop.

From the webcam window Amy said, "What happened to your eye?"

"I told my psychiatrist about you. She got jealous and came at me with a knife."

"It was the hospital thing, wasn't it?"

"No."

"I got a bus ticket, I'm coming down tomorrow."

"Amy. No. Get a refund. It's nothing, the whole thing was overblown. A guy just went crazy and shot some dudes."

"That's not what John said on TV."

"That's between me and John. You know how he just says shit sometimes."

"The news says the army is there."

"It's just the National Guard or something. They're just trying to reassure people, after nine-eleven the strategy has always been to over-react to every little thing rather than risk being wrong once."

"So what happened?"

"I just . . . it's nothing. A guy went crazy and it was scary and now it's over. Really."

"Okay. I'm still coming down, by the way. You need me. You're upset and I can tell. I've seen you like this. You're scared and you're trying to act like you're not."

I sighed. "If I tell you what's going on, will you back off?"

"Maybe."

After a long, dramatic, silence I said, "I saw something last night. It kind of disturbed me."

Her eyes lit up. "Really? What?"

"John, he . . . he accidentally sent me a picture of his dick."

She wrinkled her nose. "Ew. You sure it was an accident?"

"Ah, I knew you'd find a way to make it worse, dear."

She said, "You look terrible."

"I just need to sleep. I needed to hear your voice first, that's all."

"Ah, that's sweet. What do you want to talk about?"

I glanced out of the window again. No stars tonight. I said, "Just hypothetically, you'd be okay without me, right? Seriously, if something were to happen to me, you'd move on? Find somebody better?"

"I hate when you get in these moods, David."

"Just tell me you'd be okay. I'll sleep better."

"I love you."

"I love you, too."

"I'll be down tomorrow."

11 Hours, 45 Minutes Prior to Outbreak

John's feet were wet. It was dark. He tried to remember where he was. Had he passed out in the kiddie pool again? Water was running over his shoulder.

Hey, there's a steering wheel.

Okay, so he was in a vehicle of some kind. He couldn't see shit out the windshield. Feet freezing. Something racing past the glass . . .

Bubbles?

John's knees were getting cold now. He reached down and dunked his hand in water and thought OH SHIT I AM UNDER WATER HERE JESUS OH JESUS

His head was all muddled and he started slapping stupidly around the unfamiliar console. He turned the windshield wipers on. No effect. More bursts of bubbles flew past the windshield as his precious air escaped through a hundred cracks in a craft not made to be submerged.

MY AIR, thought John, crazily. *THAT IS MY AIR LEAVING.*

Belatedly he realized the water soaking his left arm was pouring in from the partly open window next to him. He turned toward the door and took a face full of wet turkey.

John shoved it aside and clutched at the door handle. He kicked at the door. It felt like somebody had stacked two tons of sand on the other side. He pushed with both feet and was shocked when more freezing water came raining in. Truck filling fast. Submerged to his chest now, the cold water like needles in every muscle. John was hyperventilating, crazily trying to pull the door closed again to keep the water out.

Five seconds later he was sucking air out of a tiny gap at the roof of the truck, slurping metallic-tasting, stagnant water with each breath. And then, silence.

Blinking. Under water. Frozen from head to toe. For the first time since he emerged from the womb, John wanted to take a breath and *was not allowed.*

MY LAST AIR HOLY SHIT I HAVE TASTED THE LAST AIR OF MY LIFE THE AIR THAT IS IN MY LUNGS IS THE LAST AIR I WILL EVER GET THIS IS BULLSHIT MAN

Suddenly there was open water to his left, the door that had been impossible to push open moments ago having gently drifted open on its own. A huge bundle of connected, drowned turkeys floated there. John lunged toward the door, found to his horror that he was glued in place and decided once and for all that this had to be a nightmare.

SEATBELT YOU STILL HAVE YOUR SEATBELT ON YOU STUPID BASTARD

His fingers were numb in the chilled water, making the task of freeing himself almost impossible. So dark. John realized he was seeing only by the dashboard lights, which were still on somehow. He mashed the seat belt clasp and after an eternity felt the belt loosen. He was so thrilled by this that he celebrated by releasing all of the air he had been holding in his mouth. John watched his life run away from him in a swarm of silver bubbles.

NO COME BACK MY LAST AIR COME BACK AIR

John frantically swam after his bubbles, shoving dead turkeys aside. Water in his nostrils, burning. The bubbles didn't float up, but rather flew off to his left. The assholes. He chased them. Had to get the air back.

Seeing lights. Brain shutting down? John swam after the bubbles and toward the lights. Then he broke through the surface of the water.

He blinked water out of his eyes, and saw streetlights above him. He looked back and saw a pair of red taillights, only a couple of feet under the water, like the eyes of a lurking sea monster. The water was only about eight feet deep and he had only been about five seconds away from drowning in it. Jesus.

John sloshed through the water, climbing the embankment and clawing at weeds to pull himself up, as red and blue lights twirled their way toward him from the highway.

Now they show up.

An hour later, John found himself in handcuffs in the back of a squad car. He'd been totally unsuccessful in his attempts to impress upon the police that they needed to rope off everything in a ten-mile radius and set it on fire. He was equally unsuccessful in getting any of the cops to loan him a cell phone. His wouldn't turn on and in fact there was still quite a bit of water dripping out of it. He needed to get in touch with Dave.

Another car pulled up. Not a cop car—a flashy silver sports car. A dude in plainclothes got out, flashed a badge and talked to the cops. Ah, finally they got the fancy police on the case. Now they'd get something done. The fancy policeman eventually came over to John's squad car and pulled open the door.

"You're John, right?"

John said, "Listen to me. You guys need to get to David Wong's house." John told him the address. "Franky is still alive, he's mobile, and he's got shit crawling out of him. He's full of turkey now and I think he's going to Dave's place next."

"Now why don't you just calm down for a moment. I take it you've been drinking tonight?"

"No more than usual. We're wasting time—"

"Who brought you out here?"

"I drove myself. I thought I'd find Franky here and I did—"

"What did you drive?"

"My Cadillac."

"Well, it's not here. You sure you didn't come with your friend David? You two are the monster guys, right? With the Web site and all that."

"Listen to me. I think David is at his house and if Franky is heading there, you want to get there first."

"Uh huh. Because you think Franky will hurt Dave. Because he has 'shit crawling out of him.'"

"I thought you said you had heard of us. Dude, if you don't get over there, and fast, *Franky is the one that's in danger.*"

6 Hours Prior to Outbreak

I woke up in my bathroom, startled. I had nodded off while pooping. Long goddamned day.

Three in the morning now. I tried to call John, got his voice mail, which was typical. John had set up his life perfectly so that he could get in touch with me anytime he needed something, but all of my calls to him were carefully screened. Everything always on his terms. I stumbled through the house, knowing that going to bed while it was still dark was out of the question, but at a loss as to what to do otherwise. The laptop was still on the bed, so I went to CNN's Web site and found the video clip of the report with the security camera footage. The walking shadow, floating down the hall. Three other people visible in the frame, none looking at the shadow or reacting in any way. Just as Franky didn't react when the alien bug thing was right in front of him. Invisible.

I moved the slider on the Web site's video player back and forth. Rewind, play. Rewind, play. A black ghost floating down a hospital hallway. And nobody notices.

Forget it. This is ridiculous.

I closed the laptop. I threw on a jacket and stuffed the flashlight and one flare in an inside pocket. By the time I got to the front door, Molly was at my knee. Wagging her tail, sensing adventure. Together we strode into the night.

We walked six blocks to the late-night burrito stand. I leaned against a wall and ate from a wad of aluminum foil, occasionally grabbing chunks of chorizo and tossing them to Molly, who hurriedly swallowed each so she could immediately beg for another. There was a bottle of red Mountain Dew at my feet. I glanced at my watch.

Still more than three hours to kill until sunrise. I wrapped up the remaining half burrito and tossed it into the trash can. Molly watched this act of wastefulness with an expression like she had just seen her entire family die in a fire. I mopped orange grease off my hands with a half-dozen napkins.

At this hour, there were five other people eating at the tables in front of the burrito window—this establishment's entire business model was catching the drunks who were pushed out of the bars when they closed at two. There was a pair of couples that looked college age—all four of them drunk off their asses, celebrating the fact that they would be young and pretty forever and ever. Then there was a short, fat guy off by himself in a biker jacket. I found his Harley behind him, in the parking lot. I wondered what his story was. Maybe he's riding across the country, and will be in Ohio by this time tomorrow.

I wondered which of the five were Batmen, and what their secrets were. You couldn't tell by looking. That was the point.

Molly and I were shuffling back toward my house when I noticed there was a silver Porsche parked on my street. To say that was unusual is a ridiculous understatement. This was White Trash lane, one house without a front door, another sealed shut with yellow police tape. My little bungalow had my 1998 Ford Bronco parked in the front. Sitting in the driveways of the next three houses was a 1985 Pontiac Fiero, a '95

David Wong

Geo Tracker and a 2004 PT Cruiser Woody. At least my property taxes were low.

The Porsche was crouched low along the gravel shoulder in front of the doorless house I thought was abandoned, three doors down from mine. The gleaming machine looked like it had been warped here right off a showroom floor. Even the tires looked scrubbed down to a pure layer of factory rubber.

I made it to the house and scanned around the yard. Nothing unusual. I was going to have to clean those gutters soon. The gigantic tree back there was dying and dropped every leaf by the first week of October. The leaves were ankle-deep but I knew they'd eventually blow into my neighbor's yard. The old guy who lived there seemed to like doing yard work so I think that worked out for everybody. I let the dog poop in the yard and let myself in the back door. I passed into the living room and there was some freaking guy sitting there.

He sat in my tattered recliner, making himself right at home. Probably forty or so years old, dark hair with a little gray at the temples, about three days' growth of beard stubble that followed an angular jawline. He had a chin butt. He wore a leather jacket that had been manufactured specifically to look worn and faded right off the rack, over a black button-up shirt that sat open at the collar with the top three buttons undone. He wore jeans and cowboy boots, legs crossed casually. He looked like he had been clipped out of a catalog and I immediately knew this was the owner of the Porsche.

I said, "I think you wandered into the wrong house, buddy."

He did exactly what I knew he was going to do, which is reach into an inside pocket and pull out a little leather ID wallet. He flipped it open.

"Good morning, Mr. Wong. I'm Detective Lance Falconer. You and I are going to have a talk."

5 Hours Prior to Outbreak

Molly went right to the stranger in my living room. He scratched her behind the ears, then she curled up at his feet.

"Pretty dog. How long have you had her?"

I hesitated, thinking at first this question was some kind of a trap. He was a cop, after all. Then I decided that was silly and that he was just trying to be polite. Then I realized his being polite was itself a method of getting me relaxed and accustomed to answering his questions, and that in fact it was part of a trap.

"She's my girlfriend's dog. She likes to bite people in the crotch, out of nowhere. You know it's almost four in the morning?"

Lance Falconer glanced over at a framed picture on top of my television. It was a picture of me, looking chubby and pale and my hair looking like it was being blown around in a hurricane, standing behind Amy with my arms wrapped around her, looking over her, her mop of red hair under my chin. She wore sunglasses and a huge smile, I wore the expression of a man worried that a stranger was about to steal my camera.

"That your girl?"

"Yeah. We're engaged."

"She live here?"

"She's away at school. Learning to be a programmer. What's this about?"

"Can I ask what happened to her hand?"

The guy was good. Amy's normal right hand was visible in the picture, holding a $5 stuffed elephant she had won at a carnival game using only $36 worth of tickets. Her left arm hung down almost out of frame. But if you were observant, down at the very edge of the photo you could see a little sliver of blue sky where the arm ended at the wrist.

"She lost it in a car accident years ago."

"Did you go to see her? Is that where you've been tonight?"

"No."

"Where'd you go?"

"Burrito stand. What did you do, break in?"

"Door was unlocked. I had reason to think you had been the victim of a violent crime so I let myself in."

"I'm pretty sure you can't do that, detective."

"I'll give you a phone number where you can call to complain. I have my own entry on the voice mail tree. Your friend had some concern that maybe Franky Burgess had come after you. You know, the guy who attacked twenty people at the hospital yesterday. Then I asked the local cops if anybody had talked to you yet, and was surprised to find that nobody had. In fact, around the police station any mention of your name just yields awkward silence."

"Well, as you can see, I'm fine. That door you came in works as an exit, too."

"A moment of your time, please. You understand we're in the middle of the biggest manhunt this state has ever seen. I don't see a whole lot of chance Franky is still drawing breath but you can imagine why we'd like to find him and put everybody's fears to rest."

"Why aren't you out helping then?"

"I had to make sure he wasn't here, didn't I?"

"Well, you're free to have a look around."

"Thank you, I did. He *was* here, wasn't he? Yesterday?"

"Yeah."

"Right before he started shooting and biting people at the hospital. Just minutes before, in fact."

"Yeah."

"And was he acting strange at all?"

I could feel my face getting hot, the heat radiating up from my jaw-bone. Starting to feel cornered.

Maybe you should have said Franky was never here . . .

"No, he wasn't ranting or anything. He didn't say much."

"He was responding to a call from a neighbor saying you were making lots of noise and screaming."

"Yeah. I mean, it wasn't all that. There was a thing in my house, it woke me up. Bit me."

"A 'thing'?"

"I think it was a squirrel or a raccoon or something."

"When officer Burgess left here, he seemed normal?"

"Yeah, yeah, like I said. Just told me to be careful. He was more worried about me than anything."

"And you and your friend John didn't drive Franky to the hospital? Because eight witnesses saw you. And they got you on a security camera. And your friend talked to a member of the staff, saying Franky had some kind of seizure. And he talked to a news crew, on camera, and said that Franky was infected with a tiny alien parasite."

"Oh, right. John is . . . weird. You know. Drug problem."

"But you say Franky seemed normal when he left."

"I mean . . . he was normal when he walked out. It was out by his car, he started having problems. We loaded him in his car and drove him to the hospital."

"Nothing led up to the seizure? No strange behavior? No tics or spasms or words not making sense?"

"No, no. He seemed fine. You know, he didn't seem like he was on drugs or anything."

"What was in his throat?"

I was taken aback. I had been looking around the room, avoiding the detective's eyes. But when he said that, my attention snapped right to him. He noticed.

"What do you mean?"

"Your friend, John, he told the staff to check Frank's throat."

"Oh, yeah. Yeah. I don't know, when he started having his seizure or whatever it was, he started grabbing at his throat. Like he was choking."

"Had he been eating something?"

"No."

"Smoking a big cigar, maybe? Got surprised and swallowed it? Maybe he had a wad of chewing tobacco?"

"I don't know, I don't know. We were just trying to help."

"What are you hiding?"

"NOTHING."

I almost screamed it.

I gathered myself and said, "I'm just—I'm just freaked out about this thing, like everybody. And now you're here accusing me and I had nothing to do with it—"

"Have you heard of the Leonard Farmhand case?"

"No. Wait . . . was that the guy that was kidnapping women and performing surgery on them in his basement? Up in Chicago?"

"That's right. Well, I caught Farmhand. He had an IQ of 175 but I caught him. And do you know why? Because I got in the same room with him. That's all it took. See, I have an internal bullshit sensor that has yet to be beaten. And every time you open your mouth, Wong, all the lights start blinking red and smoke starts whistling out."

Falconer rose from the chair. He was a good four inches taller than me, though part of that was cowboy boot. He continued, "Here's my theory, as it stands right now. I think you knew Franky somehow, before all this. You and your friend. And I think you had something to do with his going apeshit."

"Well, that's your opinion," I said, lamely. "Seriously, Franky and I didn't know each other. I hadn't seen him in six or seven years, probably since high school. And how exactly do you think I went about driving Franky crazy? Mind control?"

That's right, have fun connecting these dots, asshole. Stick your hand in this hole and you'll draw back a bloody stump.

"Maybe he wasn't a friend. Maybe he was a fan."

"I don't have fans, detective. I work at a video store. John does, he has a band. Ask him."

"I did. I've been asking him things for a couple of hours now. So, you guys believe this town is haunted?"

I sighed.

"No."

"Really? You and John don't talk about this? Because he's full of crazy stories."

"We're not crazy. I'm not, anyway."

"What's Zyprexa?"

"What?"

"You have it in your medicine cabinet."

"Oh. Yeah. That was . . . that was nothing. Just . . . stress. I'm seeing somebody about it."

"And that guy you shot with a bow and arrow because you thought he was a monster?"

"A crossbow. It was a misunderstanding."

"The guys down at the station, hearing them talk about you and your friend, they think you're in some kind of a cult. They say three neighbors moved away in the last year alone, because they were scared of you. You were the last guy to see Franky before his episode and everybody had some bullshit excuse for why you hadn't been interviewed yet. Like *they're* scared of you."

"People are . . . stupid."

"You know, at the hospital Franky tore out an old woman's throat with his teeth."

I felt myself take an unconscious step back toward the door. This guy was breathing all my air.

"Is that right? That's terrible."

"He was also heard speaking another language."

I didn't answer.

"So here's my theory, Wong. My theory is that last night wasn't Franky's first visit out here. I think he's a part of your little cult following. I think you and your friend scrambled his brain, probably slipped him a drug and told him it'd give him magic powers or whatever it is you're into. And I think he hurt a whole bunch of people because of it."

"You claim to have a top-notch bullshit detector and you let *that* theory come out of your mouth? That a couple of local dumbasses have mind control powers? I kind of want you to charge me with that. The trial would be hilarious."

He showed me the most unsettling smile I've ever seen and said, "I've enjoyed this conversation. I mean that. You've given me what I love most. A puzzle. See, I get bored, real easy. Most cases put me to sleep. Everybody knows who it is, the rest is just a grind, trying to fill a file cabinet with evidence for the prosecutor to take to trial. But now? I'm like a kid a week before Christmas, rattling gifts under the tree to find out what's inside. I just rattled yours and, boy, there's something *cool* in here."

He opened the front door. A business card appeared in his hand.

"Call me if you decide you want to talk more about this and save us both some time. Otherwise, I'll be seeing you around."

When I heard the Porsche growl past the house ten minutes later, I was still standing in my living room, staring at the door the detective had passed through. I was sweating like a bottle of beer at the beach.

I dug out my phone. Dialed John.

Voice mail.

2 Hours Prior to Outbreak

It wasn't the longest night of my life, but it was way up there. I've had my share of terrified, sleepless nights and I've developed a pretty good survival system involving nothing more than mental alertness exercises, positive thinking and amphetamines. Don't worry, I have a prescription. Or at least the guy who sold them to me did.

I was in for a brutal crash later, but that was Day David's problem. Night David was trying to stay alive. And, it worked. I was out on my porch when shafts of light started burning through the trees in my front yard, and I almost cried at the sight of it. It was the first time I could remember that I had seen two consecutive sunrises.

Ironically, at that point I was too jacked up to sleep. And not just from the orange capsules that were dissolving in my system. I had come up with a plan of action during my long wait. First, get the shit out of my toolshed and dump it somewhere. Maybe in the river. Then, get out of town for a while. Let all this blow over. Where would I go? Didn't matter. I could do anything. Hitchhike to San Francisco and live on the beach. Join the circus. The *where* wasn't important. I had been in a rut, that's what I realized. I needed to shake things up. Lose this weight. Learn karate. Wait, did I accidentally take four of those pills instead of two? Wow.

It seemed like a good time for a shower. My laundry basket was still overturned. I lifted it up a few inches and stuffed all the clothes I was wearing under there. I made my way into the bathroom—

Molly barked. She was staring at the door and I heard a car pull up. I heard Creedence, and a look through the curtains revealed John's old Cadillac. *Thank Christ.*

Footsteps on the porch. I yelled, "Don't open the door yet, I'm naked. Give me one minute."

The door opened behind me.

I turned and was face-to-face with Franky Burgess.

Franky opened his mouth. A thin stream of liquid squirted out as a greeting. I had the thought to throw up an arm to shield my face from whatever it was, but before the muscles could twitch into action there was a *bang* and a blueish flash. I felt the floor hit me in the back. I stared at the ceiling, ears ringing, vaguely realizing that the stuff Franky spat had combusted in midair with enough force to knock me on my ass.

I blinked, dazed. Franky stepped over me. He was carrying what looked like several red-and-white grocery bags in each arm. He went into the bedroom. From the floor I saw the Cadillac outside my open front door and had time to make the conscious decision to race out there and drive naked across America, before I felt the forearm close around my neck.

Franky, now with the strength of several Frankys, yanked me to my feet and marched me toward the bedroom.

Molly barked. She bounded toward us, past us, out the door, into the yard, into the distance, barking the whole way. She was not going to get help.

I could see into the bedroom now but couldn't make sense of what was there. There were four huge, white, bleeding dead birds on my bed. *Chickens? Turkeys?*

I was trying to puzzle through the situation. Were these birds for me? Like a gift, or an offering? They were laid out and dripping blood on my sheets, like some Aztec sacrifice on an altar.

I said, "Uh, thank you for the turkeys, Franky. Is your name still Franky?"

"Shut up."

Franky's voice was muffled, like he was talking around a mouthful of food. He held me in place, both of us watching the bed intently for . . . what? Franky's arm—the broken one—felt weird. Something long and dry snaking around my torso. I didn't look down.

Movement on my bed. The sheet was rippling, like somebody had poked their fingers up from under the mattress and was wiggling them. Several somebodies. Dozens of fingers.

I heard fabric rip. A slit formed in the sheet and a tiny version of one of those spiders, no more than two inches long, crawled out. It went right for the nearest turkey. It was quickly joined by another. And another. Within seconds my bed was writhing with dozens of the spider larvae, like maggots on a slab of meat.

With every ounce of strength and adrenaline and terror I could muster, I twisted out of Franky's grasp and spun toward the door. I made it into the living room before Franky tackled me. I twisted around and from a position flat on my back, punched him in the face as hard as I could. It felt like I broke my hand. He shrugged it off and pinned my arms, his legs straddling my chest. I looked right into his eyes, and saw the gaping stare of a terrified young man. He was hissing something at me, a whisper from deep in the throat. He leaned his face down close to mine. I couldn't make out his words, they were just choking sounds like an old man on a respirator. He leaned closer. I could smell his breath.

"They are everywhere," he hissed. "Do you understand me? They are *everywhere*."

"Franky! Can you hear me? Get off me!"

Then, I saw it. When Franky opened his mouth, I was looking at *the spider*. Its tongue, where Franky's tongue used to be, behind his teeth. It had simply taken over the lower half of his skull. I pictured the way its leg was able to glue itself to my shoulder and shuddered. The spider was a part of Franky now. Maybe the spider *was* Franky at this point.

Running footsteps, on the porch. Franky and I both looked and saw John hurl himself through the front door.

I screamed, "JOHN! IT'S A BREEDER!"

John didn't stop. He hurdled the coffee table while screaming, "YOUR KEY! I NEED YOUR SHED KEY!"

Shed key? What was he doing? Borrowing my lawnmower?

"Listen," Franky hissed, focusing back on me. I realized he was trying to talk through his parasite, and struggling to do it. "They're everywhere. It could be anyone. Do you get it? *Anyone*."

Franky screamed. A long, segmented *thing* came out from his mouth, out from the parasite hiding within. It looked like a black earthworm, but longer, with a little spike on the end like on a scorpion's tail. I was expecting the thing to come down and sting me or something. Instead it curled up toward Franky's own eye. Franky screamed again. The worm thing plunged into his eyeball.

I heard a small engine rev to life, from outside the house. I had the crazy thought that I'd see John racing around the house with my lawnmower, screaming, "Thanks for letting me borrow this!" before throwing it in his car and driving off.

Blood dripped down on me from Franky's punctured eye. His hands found their way to my face and throat, clawing at me mindlessly. Fingers trying to pry open my mouth.

The engine sound was in the house now. Deafening. A shadow fell over us.

John.

Something in his hands, something loud.

The engine sound revved to a mechanical scream, then bogged

down as if with effort. There was a sound like carrots in a blender. Wetness rained down on me.

The blurred metal teeth of a chainsaw ripped through Franky's neck. John worked the machine down, rocking it back and forth as it tore through spine and muscle and tendons, his hands streaked with red. Franky's head fell free from his shoulders, his wet hair bonking me in the face.

The rest of his body held itself above me for a few seconds, then pounded down on me with dead weight that knocked the air from my lungs.

The saw shut off and I could hear John yelling questions at me. His hand appeared on Franky's shoulder and together we rolled the corpse off me. I sprang to my feet, looked down at my body in disgust. I looked like an infant somebody had inexplicably taken to all-you-can-eat rib night.

John said, "You, uh, all right?"

I sprinted to the bedroom door and slammed it shut. I struggled to catch my breath and said, "My bedroom! It's infested with baby versions of those spider things, they're all over my bed, eating turkey. My bed, John! They were in my bed! Larvae! This whole time! We've got to do something!"

"Did they . . . eat your clothes?"

"Listen. The army has quarantined the hospital but it's not doing any good because *the spiders are out.* They're *here.* Here, John! What are we going to do? If we let just *one* of those things out into the world . . ."

"Okay first of all we—wait, where's the head?"

We both looked down at Franky's headless corpse, now laying in the living room on a spreading pool of blood. There was no head. *What the—*

"LOOK! SHIT!"

Franky's head was making a run for it.

The spider's legs were protruding from the severed neck, and they were scurrying the head through the open front door. I ran, following the crawling head out onto the porch. I stomped on the head with my bare foot, pinning it to the welcome mat. I started to yell to John to get the chainsaw when the asshole head bit my foot.

I yanked the foot free of Franky's teeth, then reared back with my other foot and kicked the head so hard I felt like I broke four toes. The head sailed ten feet through the air until it bounced off the windshield of Detective Lance Falconer's Porsche, which had chosen that moment to pull into the driveway.

The head left a pink smear on his windshield, then rolled off his hood and back at my feet. I grabbed it in both hands, teeth facing away from me so it couldn't bite my dick off. A hugely confused Falconer emerged from the car to the sight of me standing naked in my driveway, covered in blood and covering my crotch with a severed head.

I'm David Wong and I'm here with a special message about AMPHETAMINES.

"PUT IT DOWN!"

Falconer's gun was out.

I said, "One minute."

I ran back inside, made it to the bedroom, opened the door, threw the head inside and slammed the door shut again. My brief glimpse of the room revealed the hatchlings had made it halfway across the floor. I ran into the bathroom, grabbed two towels and stuffed them under the door. That wouldn't hold long . . .

"ASSHOLE! PUT. YOUR. HANDS. UP. NOW."

Falconer had come inside, gun still trained on me.

I said, "Okay. Calm down. There's good news and bad news. The good news is we found Franky. The bad news is we got bigger problems."

"Wait," interjected John, from behind the detective. "You're Lance Falconer!"

"Shut up or I will shoot you in the face."

"That was driving me nuts all night. You're the detective who caught the Father's Day killer, right? Didn't you throw him out of a helicopter?"

Falconer didn't answer. John said to me, "He's famous. I saw this whole thing about him on A&E—"

"Shut the fuck up. Did you kill Franky?"

John said, "It was self-defense. And he stole my car, he drove it here and I had to walk all the way from the police station. Got here just in time, he was raping Dave when I walked in."

"He wasn't—"

"SHUT UP. Both of you. You're coming with me." To me he said, "Put some pants on."

"Fuck you. This is my house. I make the rules. You take your clothes *off*. John, get the Twister mat."

Falconer asked, "Are you high?"

"A little."

"What's in the room? Why are you sealing it up?"

John, thinking quickly, said, "Infection. Franky had it. It's the reason they quarantined the hospital. It's—it's like a virus that—"

"Stop. You're lying."

To me, he said, "What's in the room?"

"Look. I respect your bullshit detector. Everything that I'm about to say is true. Read it in my eyes. There are factors at work here that you would not understand, and that we do not have time to explain. There is nothing more you can do here, detective, other than to get out of our way. You came here to find a man. You found him. He's lying at your feet. Now go home."

Falconer gave me a hard look. He lowered his gun, strode past me, and threw open the bedroom door.

His eyes went right to the bed. What he saw were four bloody turkeys—no, that wasn't right. What he saw were four bloody turkey *skeletons*, laying on my bed among piles of feathers. The larvae had all but stripped them clean, within minutes. What I saw, but Falconer did not, was that the spiders were now in the carpet, on the walls and crawling around the glass of the bedroom window. They were growing at an impossible rate, some already the size of a fist.

I felt a single drop of sweat fall down the back of my neck, trickling down my spine. I took a reflexive step back. One of the spiders crawled across Falconer's shoe. He wouldn't have noticed if he'd been looking directly at it.

"What is that in there, some kind of ritual? Voodoo bullshit? Trying to summon a ghost or demon or whatever you guys do?"

"No. I told you. Detective . . . you're not going to solve this one."

"Sure. I understand." He holstered his gun.

Then, in a blur he grabbed my arm, spun me around, and slammed me against the door frame of the bedroom. He got my right arm up behind my back and pain exploded down my shoulder joint, the ligaments twisting around bone. I screamed.

To John, Falconer shouted, "BACK."

Cold steel on my right wrist—handcuffs. Falconer pushed me into the bedroom. He shoved me to my knees, among the newborn spiders. I heard John shout, "NO! NO!" but Falconer spun and put his gun on him. With his free hand he looped the handcuff chain around the metal frame of the bed and snapped the remaining cuff around my other wrist.

I was on my bare knees, hands chained around the bed, and I could feel itchy spider legs crawling up one of my thighs, over my feet.

Falconer stood, held his gun on John and said, "Now. I'm not unlocking that until you've explained *everything*."

100 Minutes Prior to Outbreak

Amy peed a lot when she got tense.

A nervous bladder and a three-hour-long bus ride don't make for a great combination, but worrying wasn't something she could just turn off (her roommate at school had taught her some tai chi but that wasn't the sort of thing you could do on a bus without being asked to leave). She couldn't get David or John on the phone, and that was weird. Really weird. David always picked up unless he was in the shower or his phone was dead, but she had been trying since early in the morning. And John, free spirit that he was, had Amy on his list of "must answer" calls. He knew she didn't call him unless it was a big deal and/ or she couldn't raise David. She never abused this privilege.

David had sounded so ominous the night before, getting in one of his moods where he thinks the whole world depends on him and that he's about to let everyone down. It was Amy's job to take his mind off it when he got like that and it usually wasn't all that hard. He was a guy, after all. A guy with a thing for red underpants. But nothing was helping this time and Amy was once again frustrated by the distance.

David needed her and there were things you just couldn't do over the phone or a webcam. The school was only 130 miles away but she didn't drive and, quite frankly, David couldn't afford to make the trip. Not just because of the $60 in gas he burned every time, but the time missed at work. That's why she had bought a Greyhound ticket within five minutes of getting off the phone with him the day before.

From the window seat on the bus, she dialed him again. With her phone to her ear, she stared out at the trees zipping by, imagining a little running man out there trying to keep up with the bus, jumping over obstacles as they flew past. Four rings, then voice mail. Again.

She tried hard not to be clingy. She had been on the other end of that with her last boyfriend, a guy who had never touched a girl before and therefore thought if she was cut open, a gush of rainbows and unicorns would spill out. Calling five times a day, showing up unannounced, kind of acting like one of those sleazy photographers who follow celebrities everywhere. It was no fun and David, more than most people, demanded distance. He was the type to reflexively push other people away, never figuring out that the gnawing feeling inside him is what the rest of us call "loneliness." You have to ease people out of that. It takes time.

But, with David's history, she had earned the right to assume the worst when she didn't hear from him. It had come to the worst more than once.

She felt her bladder swelling. Where was her body getting the liquid from? She hadn't drank anything since breakfast. She wondered how long it was until the next rest stop. The bus had a bathroom but it was gross. Really gross, like on a medical level. It looked like it hadn't been cleaned since the Bush administration and there were probably things crawling on that toilet seat that she didn't want anywhere near her private parts.

90 Minutes Prior to Outbreak

Alien spiders crawled toward my balls. I felt one on my neck and shook it off with a shrug. I thought I had another one in my hair. One got into my armpit and I crushed it against my ribs with my bicep. I tried to squash them with my knees. Falconer must have thought I was having a seizure.

John tried to construct an argument to dissuade Falconer, saying, "AAAH! SHIT! FUCK! DETECTIVE! NO! THIS IS BAD!"

Trying to control my voice I said, "Listen. Franky had something inside him that took over his brain. It laid eggs. They hatched. They're in here. They—"

I paused to shake off a spider on my ear, like a dog flinging off water after a bath.

"—they're crawling around but you can't see them."

"Because they're invisible, right?"

"Yes! Yes, they AAAAHHH—"

One of them bit my ear. I squished it off with my shoulder.

Something crashed behind me. There was a scuffle, and grunts. I looked back and saw John had gone after Falconer. Falconer threw him off, hitting him hard in the nose with an elbow. He pointed his gun at John's face.

"You're fucking crazy. Both of you. What did you give him? What drug did you give Franky?"

"Goddamnit, we're going in circles. They had him in the hospital long enough to get blood, they said so on the news! Did tests show anything? Anything at all?"

"*So you understand my confusion.*"

A spider crawled up my neck, over my chin. It tried to push its way into my mouth and I spat and tried to wipe it off by rubbing my face on the bedspread. I couldn't dislodge it. Its tiny legs pushed it past my lips.

I bit it. I cut it in half with my front teeth and ground it up with my molars, spitting and gagging on an intense salt taste that made my whole body convulse.

One of the spiders crawled off the bed, across the handcuff chain, and onto the underside of my forearm. I started to scrape it off, then stopped.

I twisted my body around to face Falconer and said, "Look. At my arm. Watch."

"I don't see any—"

"No, I know you don't, yet. Wait. Just wait. One of those things— they're like little spiders or bugs—it's sitting right there. It's . . . going to start eating soon. And I'm pretty sure you'll see—GAH!—"

I hissed in a breath and clenched my teeth. The inch-long larvae bit down with its tiny mandibles and ripped up a chunk of skin. Holding it with its two front legs, it started munching on me. A second later, it repeated the process, tearing with its mandibles, ripping up a tiny patch of tissue, eating. And again.

I pressed my eyes shut, trying to block out the pain, the itching of tiny legs on my feet and calves and thighs and ass and back. Tried to escape, to block out the fact that I was being eaten alive by arachnids. For some reason the only thing I could replace it with was the image of being eaten by tiny clowns.

Man, I'm not even sure those were amphetamines . . .

I opened my eyes and the expression on Falconer's face almost made the whole thing worth it. From his point of view, a strip of skin the width of a pencil was spontaneously vanishing from my arm, leaving a trench of blood and pink fat behind. What did he think? That I had a flesh-eating virus? That John and I were faking the whole thing with horror movie makeup, as part of an elaborate and gruesome prank?

I said, "If you leave me here, by this afternoon I'll look like those turkeys up there. Wet, red bones. They're all over me. And I see at least three of them on your pants. There's one on the sleeve of your jacket. If we don't . . . exterminate these fuckers *somehow*, they'll breed and they'll be everywhere and nobody will be able to stop them because *nobody else can see them.*"

He lowered his gun.

"Detective, only the three of us in this room understand what's happening here—*AAGH!*" I growled as the bug took another bite. Hungry little bastard. "*And . . .* only we can stop it. And if you don't help us then it's just me and John and we're just a couple of dildos. Please, unlock these goddamned handcuffs."

Falconer thought about it for what seemed like a day and a half but was probably just a few seconds. He dug in his jacket pocket for a tiny set of keys, tossed them to John and nodded in my direction.

Instead of unlocking the cuffs, John said, "Hold still," then grabbed a nearby shoe and started slapping my arm with it.

"Ow! Goddamnit—"

The baby spider fell off and John ground it into the carpet with his foot. He went to work on the cuffs with the tiny key and was able to unlock them after only 137 or so tries.

I hurriedly grabbed some khaki pants and a T-shirt I found draped over a nearby chair and flew from the room. We slammed the door and crammed the towels under the gap once more. John squashed half a dozen bugs that had escaped into the hall, and cleaned off the ones we found crawling on Falconer. I yanked on the clothes and kept right on walking, out the front door.

With all of us standing in the yard, John said to me, "All right. Get everything you care about out of this house. I'll get my lighter. Do you know what your insurance policy says about intentional fires?"

Falconer said, "Shut up. Don't do anything. Let me think." He dug a phone from his pocket. "I'm going to let you in on a secret. The whole world is not against you. We've got help in this town, pros who actually get paid to worry about public safety. I've got a fed hotline number they gave us, I dial it and describe what I've seen here and they'll have this place surrounded and locked down in ten minutes. I'll tell them what you told me and we'll all figure it out like professionals. I'm tellin' you, there's a whole non-white trash world out there, fellas."

Studying the ragged gouge in my forearm, I said, "You still don't, uh, fully understand the situation, detective. There's a reason we didn't just do that from the start. There are . . . let's just say some powerful people who not only know what's going on in this town, but kind of get off on it."

"What we're saying," added John, "is that the whole world is in fact against us."

I said, "But either way, I'm gonna go gather up my stuff. I'm obviously not staying in this infested shithole." To John, "You got room in your trunk, right?"

"Yep."

"How about we go up to the burrito stand after this?"

"I was five seconds away from saying the same thing."

Falconer had turned his attention to his phone call. He was still alert, though. I got the feeling the man was alert when he was fast asleep. This would be a delicate operation.

Studying the floor for any signs of wiggling, I hurried through the house and returned to the yard with my laptop, a garbage bag full of clothes I pulled from the dryer and a mostly full bottle of Grey Goose

I found in the freezer. I grabbed a half-full bag of dog food from the kitchen, in case Molly showed up again.

I declared my packing finished and started to leave, then felt like slapping myself when I realized what I had almost forgotten.

On the wall of my living room was the one contribution Amy had made to the decor: a velvet Jesus painting that looked like it had been copied from an airbrush job on the back of a van, in the dark. It had belonged to her parents, who had probably bought it off of some roadside stand in New Mexico. Amy's parents were gone, however, and this terrible painting was one of the only things she'd kept from their old house. I grabbed it off the wall and took one last look around. The rest of my stuff could pretty much go.

Outside, Falconer was putting away his phone and I said to him, "Come around back, I need to show you something. In the toolshed."

"What is it?"

"Well, I don't know what it is. That's the point. I think you need to see it before the feds get here though." To John I said, "Can you put my stuff in your trunk? I want to show him the box."

John dug out his keys and started unlocking his trunk. I led Falconer around the yard, to the still-open shed. I gestured toward the green box on the gravel floor, at those weird hieroglyphic symbols across the front.

"Pretty weird, huh? Found it."

"And?"

"It can't be opened. Not by you and not by me. We've only had it open once and what's in there is weird as shit."

"Okay, well, I'll show it to the feds when they get here—"

From the shelf Elmo said, "Eight inches erect!"

"—But I'm not clear how this is relevant to . . ."

Falconer stopped, probably because, like me, he smelled smoke. He gave me a look that would have made cancer apologize, then ran like hell. Falconer rounded the house in time to see John emerge from the front door with his "lighter," a Vietnam-era flamethrower he had bought off eBay. Completely legal, by the way.

Behind him, flames were turning the rest of my worldly possessions into smoke and ash.

Falconer clinched his jaw and said, "Oh, you stupid white trash fucks. What have you done?"

I said, "We've taken care of the problem, is what we've done. Same as always. There was nothing for the cops to do here. Or the National Guard or anybody else."

Sirens rose up in the background. I've got to say, nobody reacts faster than the fire department.

Falconer grabbed me, spun me around, and for the second time slapped on handcuffs. I could not have cared less. I felt relief for the first time in two days. All-consuming flames roared through the infested house, and the whole ordeal was finally over. Franky and the spider larvae would burn, and there would be no outbreak.

10 Minutes Prior to Outbreak

Falconer's Porsche sat so low to the ground that I had to squat to get into it. The interior smelled like the leather shop at the mall. I saw I had dragged some muddy leaves from outside onto the spotless carpet and I felt like I had desecrated it. How could you drive a car like this without going crazy with worry? How could you eat a burrito in this thing? You'd be in constant fear of squirting refried beans everywhere. I have no idea how he afforded such a car and I thought it would be impolite to ask. Maybe he sold drugs on the side.

I sat awkwardly, the handcuffs digging into my lower back. I could see my bedroom window from where the Porsche was parked, orange flames licking up behind the glass, eating the curtains.

On the sidewalk in front of the Porsche sat John, another set of handcuffs holding his hands behind his back (actually, he got those white plastic zip tie cuffs—I got the metal ones, so clearly Falconer recognized me as the more dangerous suspect). John was watching my house burn to the ground as a dozen firefighters rolled out hoses from the two trucks. It was strangely serene. If this ordeal had been a movie, this would play under the credits.

But Falconer was *pissed*. He was moving from one fireman to the next, flashing his badge and shouting for them to back off. They were doing no such thing. I had gathered from Munch (John's friend, bandmate and part-time fireman) that neither cops nor firefighters take kindly to the other group telling them how to do their jobs. This was a *fire*, they were fire*fighters*, and by God they were going to put that shit out.

Neighbors were gathering. House fires are already good entertainment in a neighborhood like this, where the primary forms of recreation are drinking alcohol and inventing excuses to keep the unemployment benefits coming, but the address made this one a bigger deal. They knew who lived here. Everyone had heard the rumors. I saw two people filming the scene with their phones.

Another fire truck pulled up and one of the crew went up to John. I recognized Munch Lombard in his firefighting garb, his neck tattoos making him look less like a fireman and more like the lead singer in a novelty rap/metal band with a firefighter theme, maybe named something like Fahrenheit 187. The two men were having a surprisingly casual conversation, considering one of them was sitting on the ground in handcuffs and behind the other was a raging inferno slowly transmitting a bungalow into the atmosphere via a thick column of black smoke. Water arced into the air from one of the hoses. My bedroom window exploded and fingers of fire clawed at the siding, leaving blackened marks behind.

Falconer was on his phone again. More rubberneckers showed up. None of it mattered. At the end of the day, all that happened was Franky had a bad encounter with something nasty. Something *Undisclosed*. One of the risks of the job in this town. Some people got hurt, but now Franky was dead and the nasty things inside him were disintegrating in a twelve-hundred-degree house-sized blast furnace. As for Detective Lance Falconer, well, he was good and pissed, probably because his evidence was going up in smoke with it. He'd probably push to get John and me charged with two dozen crimes, everything from obstructing a police investigation to public nudity. Let him. It'd come to nothing. The chief knew what town he worked in. Sure, he'd put somebody on the case, then come back a month later and tell the prosecutor there's not enough to take to court. Then it'd all quietly go away. Again. I'd been through all this before. Nobody wants what goes on in this town to get out. They'll sweep it under the rug. Just like the incident with the pizza delivery guy—I take a few hours of mandated counseling, and in exchange I don't tell people what's really going on and start a panic.

I watched flames dance in every window in front of me. The house burning down wasn't even that big of a deal in my life. I could stay at John's place until I found an apartment or trailer somewhere. Besides, I still owned the hunk of land the house was about to fertilize with its ashes. Could sell that for a couple thousand dollars at least, right? See? Everything would be fine. My eyes slipped closed. So little sleep in those thirty-plus hours since the bedspider showed up.

My phone screamed, from my jacket pocket. That had to be Amy, since the only other person who ever called me was sitting on the sidewalk with his hands cuffed behind his back. As were mine, so the phone would just have to ring.

Something caught my attention outside.

Just around the corner from the bedroom, a firefighter was on the ground. Laying facedown, in the grass. I was about to yell at one of the firemen standing around to go help, but another guy was already heading over there. He got his companion up on his knees, but he was clutching his throat. Probably just swallowed some smoke. Or ate something too fast.

Nobody else was coming to help because out front, things were getting complicated.

A city cop car got there first, making a total of six vehicles parked along the street including my truck and John's Caddie. An RV with a square blue logo on the side trailed right behind it, what I assumed was from the "feds" Falconer mentioned. I guessed the Centers for Disease Control. I suddenly realized how much inconvenience this whole thing had caused a lot of people.

Out from the RV filed guys in those white space suits they use to protect themselves from germs, with the hood and the big clear plastic faceplate. They kind of stood around aimlessly when they saw that the structure they were supposed to quarantine was in fact going up in flames, was being attended to by firefighters *and* was surrounded by a crowd of two dozen gawking Midwesterners. Some of the space suit guys approached the firemen, and were almost certainly explaining why they couldn't remain on the scene unless they got some of those suits of their own, since there was an unknown flesh-eating biological pathogen on site and the place was under quarantine. The firefighters were presumably pointing out that they didn't have any of those suits on hand and they couldn't leave because, you know, the fire still wasn't out. Then Falconer and the two local cops joined the conversation, presumably to explain that, oh by the way, this was also a crime scene, what with the dead headless cop, arson and willful destruction of evidence.

Behind them, a Humvee rolled up and the street in front of my house was now a goddamned stationary parade. Out stepped an officer from the National Guard, who I guessed was the guy put in charge of the manhunt for Franky, who appeared to loudly be asserting that this was his show since roasting behind those walls was the man he had been charged with finding. Behind them, a white channel 5 news van pulled up, shitting a cameraman from the rear doors before the wheels even stopped turning. Meanwhile, the crowd of bystanders was doubling every five minutes, as text messages flew furiously through the air to announce that the coolest freaking thing ever was going on down at the old Wong place right this very minute. The whole situation was devolving into what John would later refer to as "a fucktard circus."

I shifted my gaze back behind the house.

Oh-oh.

The fireman was flat again, his protective hat laying a few feet away. His friend nowhere to be found. Maybe he went for help?

Suddenly, several things hit me at once:

1. That the fireman was missing his head;

2. The fact that the hat that was laying a few feet away still had the head in it;

3. The realization that this was not the body of the guy who was hurt earlier—this was the guy who came to help;

4. A fist, which smashed through the window and knocked me out cold.

When I came to a few seconds later, I was being dragged through glass and people were screaming. I landed with a thud on the grass outside the Porsche. A pair of arms coated in the black sleeves of a firefighter's coat were clenched around my chest, dragging me across my lawn. Something was clasped in one of the hands, red and white and shaped like a horseshoe. My vision came into focus enough for me to realize it was a human jawbone, complete with a full set of teeth. One of the molars had a silver filling in it.

With each passing foot, things got a little warmer and a little smokier, which my bell-rung brain finally realized meant I was being dragged toward the fire. I thrashed to get out of the man's grip, my hands still pinned behind me in handcuffs. The burst of panic-fueled strength got me free, for the moment anyway, and I tried to crawl away from him. A boot came down on my back. I fought and managed to roll over.

The fireman—a huge, strapping guy—was missing the lower half of his face. Where his jawbone should have been, and presumably had been all of his life until a few minutes ago, was the mouth and a dozen black wiggling feet of my spider. It looked a bit charred in places.

Halfface Firefighter threw off his fireman's jacket. He lifted his right arm, and two thin, sharp, white protrusions emerged from his wrist, kind of like Wolverine's claws except when Wolverine pushed his out, his hand didn't immediately fall off, as happened here. From the wrist stump the two protrusions grew and sharpened. Then, a red split appeared at the man's wrist, growing down to his elbow. With a wet tearing sound, his forearm pulled itself into two lengthwise halves, the two bones of the forearm splitting apart like blades opening on a pair of scissors.

Halfface Firefighter Scissorarms brandished his new appendage and leaned down.

His forehead exploded.

Gunshots hammered the air. Screams from all around. Halfface Bloodyhead stumbled back.

It was Falconer, advancing behind his enormous chrome handgun. It fired again, and again, shots punching bloody holes in a firefighter-issue T-shirt. But the man just would not go down.

I was up and on my feet and running, off balance and stumbling with my hands pinned behind me. I heard Falconer let out a frustrated, growling scream. I spun and saw Halfface grab the detective around the base of the skull. He forced Falconer's head down to waist level, then turned his body away from him. Holding Falconer's face directly in front of his buttocks, Halfface farted. Falconer collapsed to the leaves, as if dead.

Another gunshot smacked Halfface in the shoulder. Annoyed, he held up his scissored arm. The two sharpened bones rotated at the elbow joint. Slow at first, and then faster and faster until they were twirling at the elbow like a band leader's baton, whizzing through the air and throwing off flecks of blood and meat.

Halfface Firefighter Bloodyhead Spinbones strode toward the burning house with purpose, directly toward my bedroom window, where a column of fire was rushing upward, causing the gutter above it to melt and sag like saltwater taffy.

Starting from the foundation, he angled his spinning appendage into the wall, tearing a ragged hole in the siding and insulation behind it, making a sound like a jackhammer. He made a vertical gash about chest high, leading up to the bottom left corner of the broken window.

Cops screamed commands around me. One was tending to Falconer, the other was shouting about backup.

Halfface finished his cut, then made another one a few feet to the right of it, again ending at the window. He was turning the window into a door.

"Hey! Dave!"

It was John. His plastic handcuffs were cut but he still wore the loops around his wrists like a pair of cheap bracelets. Munch came running up behind him, looking panic-stricken. He was carrying a huge set of bolt cutters.

"Turn around!"

Halfface bashed out the rest of the glass with his remaining fist. Then he reached through the window and pulled.

A burning section of wall fell at his feet. Behind it was the charred, melting springs and frame that had been my bed. The flames roared, fueled by the new rush of oxygen.

John took the bolt cutters from Munch and went to work on my handcuffs. To Munch he screamed, "RUN! TAKE DAVE'S BRONCO! THE KEYS ARE IN IT. DRIVE UNTIL YOU'RE SOMEPLACE NOBODY SPEAKS ENGLISH!"

My hands were free. Explosions erupted a few feet away—a cop going to work on Halfface with a riot gun. The monster was down on his knees. I saw a shot blow a hole in his neck and his head flopped over, dangling by a tendon.

There was victory, for about three seconds. Then . . .

The cop started screaming.

The cop next to him started screaming.

The nearest firefighter started screaming.

They were clawing and swatting and scraping at themselves, trying to knock away tiny biting monsters that they could not see. Then I looked back at my house, and understood.

I just killed the world.

Black wiggling shapes fanned out from the hole in the wall, spilling in waves over the broken boards and plaster on the lawn, disappearing into the grass.

A firefighter ran up with a bullhorn, raised it and shouted, "WARN-ING! WE HAVE TOXIC FUMES! EVERYONE—AND I MEAN EVERYONE—LEAVE THE AREA IF YOU DO NOT HAVE BREATHING APPARAAAAAAHHHH!!!"

A spider was eating his eyeball.

A bystander, shooting the scene on his phone, had a baby spider on his hand and another in his hair.

I couldn't breathe. This was not happening. This was not possibly happening.

A hand on my elbow, pulling me away. John saying something I couldn't hear. Everything was silent. My brain had frozen up. People were running.

It all seemed very familiar.

John was pulling me along. I caught the eyes of Detective Falconer, who was back up, now trying ineffectually to help a heavy teenage girl get the spider off of her neck. His look spoke clearly:

Take it all in, white trash. You did this.

He was right. Before the fire, we had the parasites imprisoned inside the house. The feds could have roped it off, sealed it up, kept all the bystanders safely away. They could have taken their time figuring out how to neutralize the threat. We could have told them what we knew, told them not to get within a hundred yards without mouth protection and to bury the house under a mountain of concrete. Instead, the fire had drawn a crowd. First the firefighters with no protection, and then the gawkers who crowded around like a goddamned all-you-can-eat parasite buffet. They would all die. Maybe everyone would die. Maybe the parasites would own the planet. And it would all be my fault. It was the DVD sticker situation all over again.

We ran. We bumped into CDC crews with holes chewed through their space suits. We shouldered past confused National Guardsmen. We dodged the Action 5 News camera guy and a lady reporter demanding an interview from someone, anyone.

We piled into the Caddie. It stank of turkeys, possibly because there were two turkeys in the backseat. Live ones, pecking at the seat cushions. John cranked the ignition and Creedence Clearwater Revival blared from the dash. He stepped on the gas and we ripped through a band of yellow police tape somebody was trying to string up.

Probably a little late for that, buddy.

Outbreak

Amy decided she was fighting mankind's most ancient battle: physical impulse versus human dignity. Her bladder felt like it was filled with knives, but the bus toilet was not something a human should be allowed to touch without wearing a wet suit. Would she give in to animal impulse and surrender her human dignity? She would not. Actually, she tried to go back there about fifteen minutes ago but it was occupied and there was a guy in there making weird noises. So, she was back in her seat, counting the miles to the nearest bathroom. Not far, now. They were right outside of town, already past the tractor dealership.

On the seat next to her was a white cardboard box from a bakery not far from the university, containing what was probably the finest food ever produced by the human species. They were red velvet cupcakes with a cheesecake filling and a cream cheese icing. There were only half a dozen in the box but you could barely finish one of them before you had to go sit down somewhere and stare at the ceiling. It'd sit in your belly like a bag of concrete but you'd have no regrets. The fat and sugar hit your system so hard that with every bite you just wanted to give the world a hug—

Oh, no . . .

The bus was stopping.

Amy stood up and saw cars. Cars and cars and cars, stopped dead on the highway leading into town.

Her heart sank.

This was . . . surely just a car accident or something. Not every bad thing that happened revolved around David. Surely.

Surely.

She was already dialing. But this time, no voice mail—a recorded message from the cell phone carrier saying all circuits were busy.

A helicopter swept overhead. Low.

Ohhhhh . . . crap.

Across the aisle of the bus, a couple of college-looking guys in vintage clothes and thick-rimmed glasses were whispering frantically to each other, huddled over the screen of a cell phone.

"Excuse me. Are you guys getting a signal?"

"Internet still works. Look."

The guy held out the phone and Twitter was up. If you're reading this in a future where the Twitter fad has passed, Twitter was a Web site where people posted short little messages, usually from their phones, for the world to see. So, at any moment you could go on their site and see what the world at large was talking about, in real time. The main page of Twitter would always list what subjects were hot or "trending" at the moment. So when news broke, it broke on Twitter first—if a plane crashed near New York, people on the scene would start Tweeting about it within seconds, long before the first news camera showed up. Within minutes you'd see "#NYPlaneCrash" pop up on the trending topics.

The number one topic on Twitter at this moment was:

#ZOMBIEOUTBREAK

Exodus

John's old Caddie had a huge engine that would qualify as a human rights violation if built today. It roared down the road, chugging gas and farting a blue cloud of dinosaur souls.

"They're sealing off the town!" John screamed over John Fogerty. "Munch told me! They've got the highway and Route 44 both blocked."

We weren't heading to the highway, however. We would never have made it even without the roadblock—John's Caddie wasn't exactly hard to spot and we were being pursued. Fortunately, we knew a shortcut.

John tossed his phone into my lap and said, "Call Shiva! Tell her to meet us at the water tower!"

"Who?"

"Shiva! My girlfriend!"

"That's actually her name?"

"I think so!"

"There are absolutely no bars on this phone." I pulled out mine and said, "Shit! Mine, too!"

"Goddamn we get shitty coverage here!"

Burrito stand. The tires screeched us to a stop. We spilled out and I yelled, "TRUNK! TRUNK!"

John stopped in his tracks and said, "Molly!"

I spun and there she was. She was by the trash can, her paws pinning down a scrap of aluminum foil while she hurriedly ate the remaining half of a chorizo burrito.

John fumbled with his keys and got the trunk open just as we heard in the distance, "DON'T FUCKING MOVE!"

Goddamned Lance Falconer, sprinting down the street, gun in hand. Holy shit that man could run.

I abandoned my stuff and sprinted to the back door of the burrito stand. The good news was it would get us out of there. The bad news was that the destination was a crapshoot and only one would work.

Come on water tower, water tower, water tower . . .

We opened the door and squeezed into the utility closet. A blink later the door changed in front of us and we stepped out to—

"PANTIES! SHIT!"

We were at the Walmart dressing room. No good. If the feds had blocked off the highway at city limits, we were still on the wrong side of it. John said, "Back in! Back in!"

Back into the dressing room. A blink. The smell of burritos hit us. We stepped out of the door at the exact moment Falconer skidded to a stop in front of us. He leveled his huge automatic at my face and said, "FREEZE!"

We ducked back inside. I heard Falconer yanking the door back open a split second before we emerged at a destination that stank of liquor and disinfectant.

"Shit!" hissed John, surveying a display of Jägermeister. "We're at the liquor store." Specifically, the restroom at the rear of the store. "What now?"

"Maybe if we wait here, he'll wander away."

"He's not gonna do that, he'll search the burrito stand for a hidden hatch or something. Then he'll search our car and interrogate the burrito guy to see if he's in on it."

I glanced around. "What's going on?"

The liquor store was packed. People were hauling armloads of bottles up to the counter and somebody was arguing with the cashier.

"People stocking up."

"Screw it. He won't be expecting us to pop back out. We'll go out and right back in. Third time's a charm."

We shoved back into the liquor store restroom just as a guy nearby piled Jäger and half a dozen Red Bulls into a shopping basket.

A blink. Burrito smell.

I peeked out of the utility closet. A hand grabbed my collar and threw me to the ground, knocking the air from my lungs. A knee was on my back.

Falconer screamed, "HOW ARE YOU DOING THAT?"

"WE TOLD YOU! Just fucking let us go!"

"*Shitbird*," Falconer growled, "you need to understand that it's going to be *martial law and rioting* within the hour. That means if I put a bullet in both of your heads and leave you here, *nobody will fucking care*."

I said, "Listen! Listen to me! Everything that has happened has happened because they wanted it to."

"Who's 'they'?"

"I DON'T KNOW! Find out! You're goddamned Lance Falconer!"

John said, "Don't you get it? You're wasting your time, we're just a couple of inconsequential dipshits in this whole thing. The people behind this will take out all three of us. We're all pawns. Well, you're a pawn, we're a couple of Gummi bears your retarded little brother stuck on the chessboard."

I felt the knee lift from my back. I looked up at Falconer towering over me, I met his eyes and found it easier to look into the barrel of his gun.

He said, "See, I would let you go so you can try to jump the quarantine, but *I would like to not be responsible for destroying the world today.* I'd sooner let everybody in this town past those barricades before you two fucks. I don't know if you've noticed, but disaster follows you *everywhere you goddamn go.* Now we're going to—AAAHHH!"

An orange blur had attached itself to Falconer's crotch. It was Molly, her teeth buried right in the detective's junk.

John grabbed my jacket and we stumbled into the closet. I pulled the door shut—

Cornfield.

"Yes!" screamed John.

We stepped out of a blue Porta-Potty, the middle one in a row of three at the edge of a construction site. To our right was the legs of a half-finished water tower.

In our various experiments with the doors over the months, we'd only found one—this one—that took you outside city limits. But not by much. No more than a quarter mile to the south of us we could see dots of military vehicles, parked along a road bisecting the field. A little bit of the cordon encircling the city. John pulled out his phone and said, "No reception. Man, you think they're jamming the signal?"

"Dunno. If so we just gotta get far enough away, they're not blocking it for all of America, right?"

"Well. Highway's about a quarter mile that way."

We went stomping across the expanse of broken cornstalks and mud of the harvested cornfield, tracing a similar path from that summer night when we saw the black convoy and found The Box. Fifteen minutes later, we got a good look at the traffic jam on the highway, a line of cars that extended across the horizon as far as we could see in both directions. In the distance to our left was the roadblock, a cluster of flashing police lights, Humvees and the muted echo of somebody shouting into a megaphone. They were trying to get cars to cross the median and go back the way they came, but due to people refusing to comply, or confusion, or just the general dipshit dysfunction of crowds, the whole process had resulted in gridlock. We both flinched as a helicopter swept overhead.

A day and a half ago I was at work playing browser games on the PC and trying to think of what to get Amy for her birthday. Suddenly it's the freaking apocalypse.

John glanced at his phone, then stuffed it back in his pocket. Ten minutes later we made it out of the cornfield and onto the grass along the shoulder of the road. We took a right, putting Undisclosed to our backs. To our left was a wall of cars and semis forming an automotive Great Wall of China that snaked over the next hill.

When we crested that hill, we saw that the shopping center just outside of town—a U-shape strip of stores encircling three sides of a huge parking lot—had become a gathering place for refugees. The parking lot was packed with vehicles, and more were parked in the grass along the entrance leading in. As we got closer we saw people standing around, on their phones, trying to get in touch with loved ones behind the barricades.

That prompted John to pull out his phone.

"I've got bars! Well, a bar."

He dialed and said, "Hey! Shiva. It's me. Huh? No, no. Look, Sheila, Dave and I need a ride. We're right outside that strip mall with the Best Buy. They got the roads all blocked—what? Yeah, I don't know. Did you say zombies? No. Your friends are morons. What? No. Why would we have anything to do with it? Uh huh. That's fine. Can you still pick us up? Hello? Shiva?"

He put the phone away and said, "Call got dropped. Also, I think she broke up with me."

"I wasn't trying to eavesdrop but, uh, did zombies come up in that conversation?"

"Yeah, apparently the Internet is full of zombie rumors. People are stupid."

"I guess that's not any stupider than the truth."

We made it to the shopping center parking lot. On one end was the

Best Buy, on the other was a now-closed movie theater. Between the two was a row of storefronts, half of them unoccupied.

John said, "I didn't know they had a Cinnabon out here."

"We got to get a ride, John. My feet are killing me."

We walked past a parked Greyhound bus and John said, "You think they'd let us on there?"

The bus was empty. I said, "I don't know. Where's it going?"

"Who cares?"

"Good point. Find the driver and see if you can buy a ticket. Or bribe him. I have four dollars."

"I have zero dollars. You might have to blow him."

I peered through the smoked front windows of the Best Buy and saw the store was absolutely packed with people, staring up at a massive bank of televisions along the back wall.

We went in and shouldered our way through the crowd. They were watching live news coverage of the chaos in Undisclosed on three dozen flat-screen TVs of various sizes. The Action 5 News Team was finding as many ways as they could to say the same thing over and over—that there was some kind of unspecified crisis in the town, that they didn't know the nature of it but that it was huge and terrible and that we should all remain calm but glued to our televisions. Then they threw it out to star reporter Kathy Bortz, who was standing about one block from my house:

"Thank you, Michael. Look behind me. Fire trucks. Police cars. Military Humvees. A large RV that appears to be a mobile command center from the Centers for Disease Control. Numerous civilian vehicles. Behind them, a raging house fire. There is mass confusion here, folks. We heard gunshots when we first arrived, we have been told there are at least three bodies but that's all we know. Personnel are—what was that? Did you catch that, Steve? Back on me. Ready? Personnel are swarming the scene. They're trying to push back onlookers, as you can see quite a crowd has gathered around. Information has been hard to come by but what we know is that this is the same address where less than an hour ago neighbors called in reports of a shouting, bloody, naked man carrying what appeared to be—what's that? Steve? No, there's something on my—AH!"

Kathy swatted at her hair, like a woman who has realized a bee has nested there. Only two people in the Best Buy saw that it was not a bee.

She screamed. There was another scream, a man this time. Her camera guy, apparently, because the screen jerked and suddenly we were looking at the reporter's feet. She wore tennis shoes. I always remember that part.

The knees of her pantsuit came into frame next. She was shrieking, convulsing. She fell flat into the grass. While the Action 5 News audience watched, the face of Kathy Bortz fell into frame. A three-inch-long strip of flesh was missing from her forehead, pink skull showing in the gash.

Gasps from the crowd around us. On the screen, Bortz shrieked, and shrieked. The strip of eaten flesh on her face grew, edging down, across her eyebrow. The invisible-to-everyone-else carnivore quickly chewed across her eyelid, then dug into her eyeball, spilling pale fluid down across the bridge of her nose.

The shot cut back to the male and female anchors. Perfect-haired anchor Michael McCreary blinked, looked off camera and said, "What the *FUCK*?" His female coanchor turned to lean behind the desk, and vomited.

The air in the store was charged with panic—that bottled-up, impotent panic of a crowd that doesn't know how to act on it. Should they riot? Loot the place? Burn it down? Should they stampede out of there? To where? Cinnabon?

Instead, everybody just kind of stood shoulder to shoulder, mumbling to each other. A black woman next to me was crying, covering her mouth with one hand.

My cell phone screamed and half a dozen people around me almost shit their pants. On the screen it said:

AMY.

"Amy! Can you hear me?"

"Yes!"

"Did you hear the news?"

"Yes, David—"

"Listen to me! We're okay. John and I both, we got out of town. Now, we may have to come up there and stay with you for a bit, we can't go back to town because—"

"David. Stop talking. Did you not get any of my voice mails? I got on a bus to [Undisclosed] this morning—"

"Shit! Turn around! Amy, it's chaos in there. Get off at the next stop and—"

The background noise had cut off from her end and I knew the call had gotten dropped. No bars on the phone.

"Shit! John, she's on her way down here!"

"No, that's good news, man. She'll be coming in on the highway, right? We figure out how far the bus got and we'll meet her there. Hell, if we head north we'll run into her at some point."

My phone screamed again. Text message this time, from Amy.

The message said simply, WHAT IS HAPPENING.

There was a photo attached. I opened it.

All of the warmth in my body drained out through my feet, all my life and strength forming a puddle on the tile floor.

The photo was of my burning house. Taken from not twenty feet away.

I sat down, an act that was not entirely voluntary. I was in a forest of legs. My head was swimming.

John was talking to me. "Dave? Dave. What's happening?"

"She's at my . . ."

I swallowed.

"She's at my fucking house, John. Amy. She took the bus this morning and she went to my house. To find me."

"She's . . . I'm sure she's fine. She's smarter than both of us put together, she'll—"

"I have to go back for her."

"You're damned right."

He pulled me to my feet. I shoved my way through the crowd, knocking rudely through shoulders and elbows.

In the parking lot John said, "All we got to do is get back to the water tower, take the door, get back to the burrito stand. With any luck the Caddie will still be there—"

"We can't walk. We have to, uh, borrow a vehicle. Something that can drive right the hell across that cornfield."

"Look." He pointed. "Left of the Greyhound."

There was a very muddy pickup, on jacked-up suspension. In the bed was an equally muddy dirt bike.

I was praying that the keys were in the truck. They weren't, and the truck was locked.

Looking around nervously, we rolled the bike out of the truck bed. I had only driven a motorcycle twice in my life, and hadn't crashed either time. John had actually owned one a few years ago, but had crashed it twice. We didn't discuss it, I jumped on and John climbed on behind me. I kicked it to life, and we were off. Across the parking lot, onto the grass, into the stubble and mud of the cornfield.

We bounced along the ruts and John had his arms around my rib cage so tight I thought he was breaking bones. I told him to loosen up because I couldn't breathe. I aimed the bike right at the vertical columns of the tower, brown at the seams where they had been welding the plates together. I saw the blue Porta-Potty at the base, as it grew out of a speck in the distance. November wind froze my ears and cheeks. I felt like I was watching myself do all of it from afar.

They couldn't have Amy. They could have me, they could have John, they could have Undisclosed and the Midwest and America. I'll cede all of that to them, whoever they are. But they don't get Amy. She's off the table.

Amy had already lost her family, in that car accident years ago, the same one that took her hand and left her tethered to a bottle of pain pills she could never allow out of her sight. She lost her brother, she lost her home. The world owed her more than it would ever be able to repay but by God, it was going to have to try.

The reporter's face kept flashing through my mind. A flesh-eating spider, chewing through her eye—

Stop it.

—and Amy was closer than that. Closer to the infested house than the reporter. How in the hell had she gotten so close? Why didn't they stop her? Maybe the National Guard had gotten her by now, or the CDC. Maybe they'd just hold onto her until they got all of this under control.

They will never get this under control.

I was numb all over, a combination of the cold and the vibration and the panic and exhaustion. I couldn't feel the bike jolting over the ruts in the field, I couldn't feel John's arms around me, I couldn't feel the half-dozen wounds that had been complaining all over my body.

I pulled up to the Porta-Potty, found the kickstand and said, "If it looks like the feds have it under control, we find somebody in charge and—"

John was not there.

I jumped off the bike and looked back. There was a tiny figure way off in the distance, frantically waving his arms and running. He had fallen off somewhere around the first third of the trip.

No time to wait for him. I pulled out my phone and wrote out a message to him in an unsent text, telling him to give us thirty minutes to get back before getting as far away as he could. *Somebody* had to stay on the other side of those barricades. I left the message on the screen and laid the phone on the seat of the dirt bike. Couldn't use it in town anyway.

I went to the door of the middle Porta-Potty and whispered, "Burrito stand."

To be clear, the doors absolutely did not work that way. It was just wishful thinking, or a prayer.

I opened it, stepped inside.

The plastic Porta-Potty door clapped shut behind me. I knew I wasn't at the burrito stand. There were no burrito smells. There was noise. Panic, from outside. I opened the door and had a split second to register that I was in the restroom at BB's.

Shouted commands, panicked screams. Gunshots.

I wanted to turn back to the door, to retreat to the field. Instead I found a gun barrel pointed in my face. I threw up my hands.

"No! Don't—"

Leviticus

John heard muffled gunshots as he approached the toilet, and they sounded *close*. Sound waves are a funny thing but he swore the noise was coming from inside the blue plastic shitter.

He reached the door and was about to yank it open when he had second thoughts. Wait, if there were dudes with guns at the other end of the "door" or portal or wormhole, could they shoot through it? Was that what he heard? If he opened it, would a hail of bullets fly out? Would a dude with a machine gun spring out at him? Or had some soldier or cop been taking a shit when Dave burst in, so now the two of them were having a gunfight, pressed chest-to-chest in the tiny booth?

Unarmed and with no other plans for the day, John took a deep breath and pulled open the door.

Filthy, chemical toilet. A crumpled bag of Doritos on the plastic floor. Empty toilet paper roll.

John climbed inside. Closed the door.

Nothing happened.

You could feel when the doors worked, there was a change in the air, and a slight smell like the gas that comes out of aerosol cans of whipped cream before the cream comes out. When he opened the door, he was unsurprised to find it was just the field again.

He tried it ten more times.

Finally he gave up and stepped out of the booth, and noticed something for the first time.

Blood.

Splattered on the inside of the door. Blood, and bits of pink something—

Brains.

—that he couldn't identify.

In that instant the whole sequence suddenly made sense. John sat down in the cornfield and tried to think of a dozen ways to talk himself out of it. The same rationalization—the exact same—that was running through the heads of dozens and dozens of people inside those army barriers up ahead. The families of those firemen, and the friends and coworkers of that reporter, and all of the other people who had died in an instant when everything went to shit: death was something that happened to *other* people. Strangers. Extras in the background. *We* don't die. *They* die.

John lit a cigarette. He finished it. He climbed on board the dirt bike and said, out loud,

"All those fuckers are going to pay."

30 MINUTES
EARLIER . . .

A half hour earlier, while Dave and John were still trudging across a cornfield after having emerged from the water tower Porta-Potty . . .

Amy was finding it hard to breathe. Everybody on the bus was restless and nervous, bottled up in there with each other, cut off from the outside world. The phones were dead. Traffic had stopped—cars in front, cars behind. She was sick with worry and she had to pee so bad she didn't know if she could actually make it through the process of standing, walking to the back and sitting down again on a toilet.

The bus driver got up and announced that he had gotten word over the radio that the highway had been shut down for the rest of the day and maybe the next, due to a chemical spill. The two guys in the seats across the aisle scoffed. They *really* wanted it to be zombies.

The driver said there was a shopping center ahead, that traffic was being diverted there and that once there the passengers would have the option of arranging for other transportation, or reboarding the bus and taking it back through the stops in reverse order. All Amy knew was that there were stores at the shopping center and that those stores had bathrooms.

After that, it would just be a matter of finding another route into town. If she had to walk, she'd walk. She hadn't brought walking shoes but it wasn't that far. She'd show up at David's front door with cupcakes and show him the blisters on her feet and he'd give her a hug and try to peel clothes off of her. Then they'd sit on his porch in the autumn chill and eat cupcakes and drink some of that amazing coffee from that Cuban place and they'd talk about . . . whatever this situation was, and laugh about the Internet dorks giddily whispering about zombies.

The bus veered off onto the shoulder and rode it until the turn lane for the shopping center. As soon as it rolled to a stop, Amy shakily headed for the nearest doorway. She wasn't even paying attention to what store she walked into, she just knew that on her dazed trip to the restroom, she passed a lot of televisions and cell phone kiosks and a gauntlet of muttering, worried people. She sat the cupcakes on a shelf outside the door because it seemed weird to take them in.

It's amazing how your body affects your outlook on the world. Using the bathroom and walking around and splashing some water on her face, it made all the difference in the world. With that physical tension gone, the situation seemed so much less bleak. She probably wouldn't have to even make the hike into town, surely there had to be another route—one of those gravel back roads that looped around the cornfields if nothing else—then find somebody in the parking lot going that way. She wasn't sure why the bus didn't just take one of them, but maybe they had some kind of policy against leaving the main roads.

Amy emerged from the bathroom, grabbed her cupcakes and caught a new, weird vibe in the store. Everybody was standing and gawking in the same direction. She followed their gaze and saw they were watching Best Buy's rows of huge TVs, all of which were tuned to the local news. It cut to the anchor, who said a curse word she had never heard used on the news before, and his co-anchor leaned over and started gagging.

What in the world?

Amy almost asked the lady next to her what was going on, but then she noticed somebody talking on their phone and pulled out hers. Ah, service was back. She dialed and—

"Amy! Can you hear me?"

"Yes!"

"Did you hear the news?"

"Yes, David—"

"Listen to me! We're okay. John and I both, we got out of town. Now, we may have to come up there and stay with you for a bit, we can't go back to town because—"

"David. Stop talking. Did you not get any of my voice mails? I got on a bus to [Undisclosed] this morning—"

"Shit!"

The phone cut out.

"David? Can you hear me? What's going on? The Internet thinks there are zomb—"

Nope, call got dropped. She redialed, and immediately got that stupid "all circuits are busy" message.

The scene on the TV changed, and suddenly she was looking at David's house and . . .

Oh my God.

It was on fire.

Why would that happen? Did David even know? She held up the phone, zoomed in on the TV screen and snapped a shot of the burning house. Juggling the cupcake box so she could text with her one hand, she sent David a simple message:

WHAT IS HAPPENING

It said it was sent. Who knows if it actually got through. Meanwhile, the room around her was freaking out. People were murmuring and crying and arguing and cursing at their phones. Somebody rudely slammed into her from behind on their way to the door. She dropped the cupcake box but it landed right side up so she thought it was okay. She needed to find a chair. She needed to sit, and breathe, and wait to hear from David, and focus on not crying.

They sold office chairs over at the far side of the store and there were people sitting in them but something about the sight of the short redhead fighting back tears made three different guys give up their seats at the same time. She took the one in the middle.

She waited, and waited. She tried to call, circuits busy.

It wasn't as bad as she was making it out to be. Didn't David say they had made it out of town? And that they were fine? That's what mattered. She suddenly realized how hungry she was. Was there anything to eat at this place other than those disgusting cinnamon rolls at Cinnabon?

There wasn't. Ten minutes later she sat at a table by the window, picking tiny bits off of an enormous sticky cinnamon roll and stared at people freaking out in the parking lot. She needed to keep an eye on the bus, it still had her suitcase on board and she needed to make sure it didn't leave with it.

The driver was back at the bus, opening up the luggage compartment to drag out bags for people who were bailing out on the trip. A tall guy with long hair and muddy pants was bothering the driver about something, and the driver was telling him no. The guy reminded her of—

"JOHN!"

Amy ran out the door and across the pavement as fast as her designed-purely-with-cuteness-in-mind shoes would let her. John was startled to see her. Before he could speak, she threw her arms around his torso.

"Oh, thank God. Oh my God, John. I can't believe you're here."

John still looked baffled and said, "Yeah, I fell off but . . . I mean holy shit, Amy, I thought that . . . Anyway. It worked out so, great. Great. Oh my god."

"Yeah."

John said, "We should head north, get as far away as we can, and just kind of regroup. Need a ride though, I'm trying to get a spot on the bus but apparently that's not allowed . . ."

John looked around. Amy looked around. At the exact same time both of them said, "Where's David?"

Revelation

Vultures. Big, noisy, circling, mechanical vultures. That's what Amy thought of as she saw, for the first time in her life, half a dozen helicopters circling around in the same sky. A couple of them were news choppers, the rest looked like army. Buzzing, that soft thwupping fading in and out as their blades chopped up the air. If you ever see more than two helicopters over you, you can be sure that something terrible has happened.

Amy made John take her out to the water tower and the toilets. John went to the one on the far right and opened it, showing her that it was just a toilet, showed her that if he went and stood inside, nothing happened. She made him do this about twenty more times. She suggested he try the other two, he said that he had done that and that they, too, were just toilets.

Amy hated crying. She hated crying more than she hated puking. And she would rather puke on live television than cry in front of John right now. She wasn't a large person under normal circumstances but when she cried she could feel herself shrink two feet. She instantly got demoted to child, everybody making soothing sounds and apologizing for things they didn't even do. Strangers inviting themselves to put an arm around her shoulder like she was a five-year-old lost at the bus station.

And she was a crier. She cried when people yelled at her, she cried when she got frustrated, she cried during particularly sad commercials. But it was just crying. She didn't get hysterical. She didn't fall apart. But everybody treated her like she did, because her eyes were so quick to start leaking when things went wrong. And now, as John opened the toilet door and again she saw nothing but blue plastic walls and a whiff of poop chemicals, she felt that hot sting in her tear ducts and knew they were going to betray her for the ten thousandth time.

The thwupping got louder and one of the helicopters seemed to be swooping really low on its passes. It was a huge thing with two blades. She could feel their pulsing in her gut.

A black semi truck was turning down the lane, heading right toward them. Watching it warily, John said, "We have to get out of here. We'll regroup and come up with a plan. But if they catch us then it's over, we can't help him."

"One more time."

John glanced back, toward the truck, and then toward the tiny army men in the distance and the bright orange fencing they were stretching across the field, sealing off the town behind them. Tiny shouts from a bullhorn were drifting through the air. Yells from angry and scared people. Honking horns. All of it playing under the terrible hollow drumming of the helicopters—the soundtrack of every worst-case scenario.

John obeyed. The toilet was just a toilet.

———

You haven't really experienced the full range of human emotion until you've cried your eyes out while hanging on for dear life on the back of a dirt bike bouncing across a cornfield in the freezing cold. Amy and John made it back to the shopping center, which was clearing out fast. They returned the motorcycle to the pickup, propping it up by the tailgate because they couldn't get it lifted up into the bed. Maybe the owner would think it just fell out.

Cars were filing out and heading up the highway, because rumor was spreading around that they were going to expand the quarantine to include the shopping center and everything for a few miles on the other side of it, but who knew if that was true.

The Greyhound was boarding, ready to just dump everybody off at the stops where they had been picked up. Amy thought she could get the driver to let John on board—the guy wasn't made of stone—but John thought that would make them too easy to find if that detective came after them. It made sense, and she got her bag and watched the bus lumber down the highway without them. It was the right decision, but they were now stranded.

Amy would never be able to eat at a Cinnabon again for the rest of her life. They sat there, at the same table she was sitting at when she spotted John an hour earlier. John was on and off his intermittently working phone, first trying friends in town to see if they happened to be outside of city limits when everything went crazy. Those calls wouldn't even go through. Then he tried some people he knew outside of town, but the ones who answered had their own problems.

Amy suggested getting a ride to the airport about ten miles away and renting a car there, but John said he had some things on his driving record that would ensure he would never be able to rent a car for the rest of his life. Amy didn't have a license, so that shot down that idea. It was just so freaking frustrating, David needed breaking out from a military zombie quarantine and his saviors couldn't get a ride from Cinnabon.

John paused in his phone calls to shove the remaining third of the cinnamon roll into his mouth when his phone rang. He picked it up and mumbled, "Munch! Where are you?"

John's friend Munch Lombard had not in fact fled the country in David's truck as John instructed him, but simply went to his parents' farm outside of town. He promised to come get Amy and John in fifteen minutes or so, but John wasn't comfortable waiting at the shopping center that long so they agreed to meet him at the John Deere dealership a mile up the street. They took off walking. Amy's left foot felt sticky and she was pretty sure it was actively bleeding in her stupid shoes but she said nothing because broken blisters were unimportant when the world was in crisis. She kept telling herself that over and over again, wincing with ever step along the highway.

Fewer and fewer cars passed them going north. More and more green trucks passed them going south. She was fairly sure that by sundown there would be more military personnel encircling Undisclosed than there were people inside it. All of that, between her and David.

Soon, John was driving David's Bronco, Munch in the passenger seat and Amy sitting in the smelly backseat. The truck had stunk of rotten eggs for years for reasons no one could explain. They turned off onto a gravel lane snaking into dense woods, the canopy of trees blocking the sun and fast-forwarding the clock to the mid-evening hours. The lane was barely wide enough for one vehicle and Amy wondered what they did when two vehicles met going opposite directions. Did somebody just have to slowly back all the way out? Did they flip a coin to decide who?

Amy tuned in to the conversation between Munch and John to hear Munch say, "Yeah, I mean, they're playin' that clip of the reporter's face getting eaten every five minutes."

"What are they saying it is?"

"Some kind of virus. Maybe something the terrorists released. Eats your skin. Eats your brain. Makes you crazy."

"Jesus. That's the story they're putting out there to calm people down? That's really worse than just saying zombies."

"My dad and grandad have been huddled around the TV since it happened. They think it's Revelations. Though I can't remember anything that messed up even in the bible. The face-eating part I mean."

They rounded some trees and came to a closed gate, and behind it sat a shiny black pickup truck. Behind the wheel was a big guy with a dark beard and aviator sunglasses, who Amy thought looked like John Goodman's character in *The Big Lebowski*.

Munch muttered a curse and got out of the Bronco. The guy stepped out of the black pickup, then reached inside and pulled out a shotgun. John got out and Amy followed his lead, thinking that it had taken society all of two hours to degenerate to the Shotgun stage.

To the shotgun guy John said, "Hey, Daryl."

"Daryl" nodded curtly but didn't answer. Then Munch said, "Come on, Dad, don't embarrass me. Let us through."

Shotgun guy, who Amy gathered was Munch's dad, and whose name was Daryl unless John had gotten it wrong, said, "They're from in town, right? They were in the city when the outbreak happened?"

"John was, she wasn't. That's his friend, Amy."

Amy waved.

Daryl Shotgun said, "Make you a deal. Drive him back to the National Guard checkpoint they set up outside town, let 'em check him over and if they give him a clean bill of health, we'll talk. But until then he ain't gettin' past this gate. Him and nobody else. We already had refugees wandering around out here, tryin' to see what they could steal."

"Come on, Dad. They're homeless. They can't get back in town, they got nothin', they left everything behind. Don't be a dick."

"Don't push me, Mitchell. We talked about this."

John said, "If it makes you feel better, if I was infected you'd know it. I saw a guy get it right in front of me and it took hold of him within one minute."

"Who are you, again?"

Munch said, "Goddamnit, Dad. That's John. From the band. You've met him half a dozen times."

Daryl nodded and said, "From the band. Of course."

John said, "Look, don't let me in. It's fine. But she needs a place to stay and she was never in town, she was on her way in when they shut down the highway."

Amy was about to speak up. She wasn't staying here with these nut-jobs, the place had post-apocalyptic rape cult written all over it. Daryl rendered it moot.

"Maybe she wasn't in the city, but she's been with you all day. Right?"

Munch laughed, shook his head and said, "Unbelievable. Fuckin' unbelievable."

John said, "No, no, it's fine. I'm not trying to sow discord in your family here. I shouldn't have asked. We'll be on our way."

Daryl said, "That's right, you will. And I'm gonna tell you the same thing I told everybody else who's come up to this gate. 'Til a man in uniform comes and gives the all-clear, and maybe not even then, if you show up here again you ain't gettin' the courtesy of a warning shot."

The look on John's face said he was wondering if he could get the shotgun away from Daryl and smash in his nose with the stock. Amy was pretty sure John could do it, the guy looked fat and slow. But then John snapped out of it and they headed back to the Bronco.

As they did a three-point turn in the lane to head back out into the chaos, Amy sighed and said, "What now?"

"Back to plan A. We head north. Put some distance between us and the bullshit. If we get caught and thrown in jail or quarantine, it's over. So for right now, the goal is to not do that."

She crossed her arms and blew some dangling hairs out of her eyes and said, "I don't like going farther away from him. I mean David could be hurt or running away or who knows what. And we're just . . . leaving him."

John was silent for a moment and Amy detected that there was something he wasn't telling her. But either he'd tell her or he wouldn't, she'd learned that she couldn't press John like she could David. Every conversation took place on his terms.

John said, "Oh, don't worry. We'll be back. But we're coming back strong. We're coming back to veto all this shit. But we got to load up first."

And Amy thought, *he doesn't believe that.*

The Maps and Shit

As they drove, instead of the highway, **John** only saw blood and brains, splattered on a filthy blue plastic door.

BOOK II

For the concept of the zombie, we can thank two parties: ants, and a dog who probably died more than ten thousand years ago. Let us start with the dog.

First, you must imagine humanity as it would have existed at the time. Agriculture is a new concept, a radical practice that must have seemed like magic. Settlements are becoming larger. Humans everywhere are struggling with the transition from living in sparse, nomadic tribes hunting gazelle and gathering berries in the woods, to everyday life in close proximity to dozens of strangers in something that could be called a village.

All of this would have been a startling and hugely stressful change for our ancient ancestors. Yes, on one hand there is suddenly more food and comfort and spare time than the species had ever known. But maddening complexity arises at every turn. Language explodes. Man evolves the ability to think in words, essentially creating an entirely new schematic for his brain with which he will create abstract thought for the first time. And along with it, questions. Man needs to understand his place in the universe, and his relation to his creator. But this is not the beginning of science. It is the birth of superstition. What he does not understand, he fills in with this newfound cognitive power. The universe that this man inhabits will be one born from the astonishing new power called "imagination."

Already at this point, superstitions about the dead would have arisen; decaying flesh is a playground for infectious disease and bacteria—man would have long realized that too much time spent in the presence of the dead means sickness or even death for one's self. They find burying or burning the dead in a special place, away from the rest of the tribe, prevents this.

So one day, some nameless and now long-forgotten man dies. He is buried in a shallow grave by his friends, as is now their custom. But along comes a dog, or a wolf, which smells under the loose soil the irresistible scent of slightly putrid meat. The dog digs and finds a hand. It pulls it up from the soil with its jaws, but then becomes distracted in its task and runs away. Along come the deceased man's friends once more, and what do they find? A pale, dead hand, pushing up through the soil, as if clawing for the sky. Their friend, though still clearly dead, attempts to escape from his grave and walk! And thus the undead enter our cultural memory once and for all. That image, of the pale, decaying hand emerging from the grave, can still be found on endless movie posters and horror novels. From that primal fear would develop the mythology of the zombie and the vampire and countless other incarnations across time and cultures.

But why does this haunt us so profoundly? After all, a shambling, decaying man should present less of a physical danger than a quick, strong, able-bodied man who wishes us the same harm. If anything, such a man would be easier to outrun, outwit, and eventually put down. Why would mankind spend a hundred centuries obsessing over such an easily vanquished opponent?

For the answer, we must look to the ant.

As I alluded to, even before civilization began to emerge, agriculture must have seemed to early humans an inconceivably brazen attempt at playing God. Why, to refuse the nuts, berries and game that were naturally placed before you by providence and to instead *plant and grow your own*? It would be the ancient equivalent of some mad scientist today promising to grow a child in a vat. This bitter divide among early man finds its way into our mythology with the story of Adam and Eve—the decision to abandon the self-sustaining garden in favor of food that only grows reluctantly from the ground by "the sweat of thy face." But this kind of audacious assault on nature—an act not observed in any other of the world's creatures—required man to accept (or believe, if you prefer) that he was unique. Blessed. Divine. The planet is there for the taking and he must believe that he is destined to subdue it. Thus mankind embraces his identity as an eternal creation, a being above and beyond the physical. A being capable of choice, where all of the other beasts and fishes function according only to the simple arithmetic of crude instinct. A bear's actions can be boiled down to hunger, or fear. But a man is capable of *decision*, because he has this indefinable but all-powerful spark. This is what makes him man.

But then man observes the ant.

Clearly no individual ant possesses this same spark. No ant ever created a work of art, or felt love, or loyalty. No ant ever thought through a decision—ants mindlessly follow pheromone trails, to the point that if the leader forms a circle, the colony will follow it around and around, endlessly, until all have died from exhaustion.

Yet, they create vast colonies, with separate chambers for the hatching of eggs and waste and storage. They grow and harvest fungi for food. The tunnels are designed with ventilation to the surface to carefully regulate temperature and air quality. A human would need years of formal study to learn all of the various principles and skills required to build a structure as complex as those created by the "mindless" ants.

So what, then, makes humans so special? Of what good is this explosive wonder we call imagination, or the internal monologue we call our "mind" or "personality"? Of what value is the divine "spark" that we believe grants us dominion over all, including those ants? All of our greatest achievements can apparently be duplicated without it.

That is why we fear the zombie. The zombie looks like a man, walks like a man, eats and otherwise functions fully, yet is devoid of the spark. It represents the nagging doubt that lays deep in the heart of even the most zealous believer: *behind all of your pretty songs and stained glass, this is what you really are. Shambling meat.* Our true fear of the zombie was never that its bite would turn us into one of them. Our fear is that we are already zombies.

8 Days, 12 Hours Until the Massacre at Ffirth Asylum

John noted that somebody could actually chart in miles per hour the speed at which the panic and bullshit rippled outward from Undisclosed.

They left the highway to get gas about an hour north of the town, and at that point everything still seemed just a couple of ticks off from normal. The convenience store was busy but not crazy. John bought cigarettes and two Red Bulls and even chatted with the girl at the counter about what was going on. She talked him into getting a couple of hot dogs that had been slowly rotating in their warmer for a week or so. Amy grabbed a huge bag of strawberry Twizzlers and the biggest Diet Mountain Dew they had. Amy paid and John promised to pay her back. Then he had a moment of panic when he wondered if the guy who wrote his paycheck every two weeks was even still alive. Or if the bank where he had his checking account was still standing. If not, then what? He had *nothing*. Just the clothes on his back.

Then, when he and Amy stopped at another convenience store just twenty-five miles up the road, both of them urgently having to use the bathroom for different reasons, the place was a madhouse. The lines to the gas pumps led all the way to the street, blocking traffic as people waited to turn in. All of the bottled water, milk and bread had been stripped from the shelves. An Indian guy behind the counter was arguing with someone about a per-customer limit he had just imposed on everything in the store at that moment. Everyone was on their phones, yelling about packing up, getting the kids from basketball practice, heading to Mom's house. *Yes, now,* they'd say. A curfew was coming. Martial law was going to be declared for the whole tri-county area. Or the whole state. Or the whole country.

"Terrorist attack" was the key word in all the conversations. A biological weapon, released by a cop who went crazy and became a jihadist. The stuff made the skin rot off your bones, ate through your brain, made you kill your family. Highly contagious. Countless infected may have gotten out of the town before the government sealed it off. We could all be infected for all we knew. Some thought this was what the government wanted. Some thought the government itself released the pathogen.

John and Amy got out of there as fast as they could, not even stopping to buy a courtesy item which Amy said was her normal policy when using the bathroom at a business. John said that was the kind of rule that got suspended during the apocalypse.

John was trying to stay calm because Amy was getting worked up and panic has a way of multiplying when you have two people's fear flowing back and forth, creating a feedback loop. She kept asking questions that he didn't have answers to. Wouldn't somebody from the government come looking for them for breaking quarantine? Wouldn't they know to look for the Bronco? He didn't know.

They were heading back to her dorm at the university because they had literally nowhere else to go. But Amy kept asking questions about that, too. Wouldn't they come looking for them there? If the infected were dangerous, shouldn't they get some guns or something? John thought all of those were great questions but he wasn't entirely clear what he was supposed to do about any of them. Say they dumped the Bronco. Then what? Walk? Steal a car?

Yes, somebody would eventually come knocking at the dorm if they stayed there too long (though he thought the government had bigger fires to put out at the moment) but goddamnit, they needed to stop somewhere and sit down and reorganize. He had just slept for a couple of hours the night before, in a chair at the police station. He just needed to . . . reset himself. Get something to drink.

Yes, it would be nice to have the flamethrower plus a shotgun and ten or twenty boxes of shells. They didn't. He also didn't have the cash to buy a gun, but even if he did, he was pretty sure if they stopped at a Walmart they would find the line to sporting goods wrapped around the store. All of the guns would be gone, along with all of the ammo and cleaning kits and knives. Also gone would be the camping supplies, the water purification tablets, the tanks of propane, the batteries, the hand-cranked emergency radios and so on. This is a part of the country that created a nationwide ammunition shortage the day after they saw a non-white president won an election. They've been waiting for this shit.

Not that John could criticize, because he knew better than any of them what was coming—what was *really* coming—and here he was, driving in the night in Dave's beat-up Bronco, without so much as a flashlight in the way of emergency supplies. Not that he would put it like that to Amy. *Goddamn* he needed a drink. Just to get things back on an even keel.

John cursed himself. Or rather, he cursed the past version of himself for so thoughtlessly screwing over the current version of himself. Everything that would come in useful right now was in the trunk of his Caddie. The Caddie that was parked outside of the burrito stand the last time he saw it, but that by now was either impounded by the government, or stolen, or on fire, or flipped over in a riot.

They were on the exit ramp headed to Amy's campus when her phone chimed to announce a text message (by playing "One Night in Bangkok," a private joke between her and Dave). Amy opened it, then scrunched up her face like she'd just watched a waiter at a restaurant slap a squealing live pig on the table in front of her.

John said, "What?"

"It's . . . a text. From David."

She said nothing else. John's brain seized up.

"And?"

She read it off her screen: " 'I want you to know that I am fine. They have asked us to stay here as a precaution. Ignore the rumors, everything is fine and they are treating me well.' "

John and Amy both were silent for several seconds. Finally, both burst out laughing.

Amy said, "If David wrote that, I will eat this phone."

John said, " *'They're treating me well'*? I want you to seriously imagine those words coming out of Dave's mouth. He wouldn't say that even if they were treating him well."

"They might as well have had him speaking Japanese."

"I have his phone in my pocket, by the way."

The laughter died as quickly as it had come and Amy said, "Why would they send me a fake text?"

"I bet they sent them to everybody on the network. Probably the same one. Trying to pacify the people on the outside, to keep them from beating down the barriers to get into town. Think about it, you got husbands separated from wives, kids separated from parents. Imagine you go out of town to go see a concert or something, you leave the kid with a babysitter, then head back home to find the road blocked by a wall of National Guard trucks, telling you you can't see your child, who by the way is trapped inside ground zero of a bio-weapon outbreak."

"Do you have any idea how mad David will be when he sees this? Sending this out in his name like that?"

John didn't say anything. Just let that conversation fade. For now, the goal was to get her away, and safe, and to sit down somewhere quiet and figure out what to do next. Over a beer.

The bullshit reached Amy's dorm ahead of them, so John's final estimate was that it traveled at about 80 miles an hour. Of course, bullshit picked up speed exponentially in the information age—the situation in Undisclosed would make a newscast in Japan within the next two hours, and Internet rumors would assure everyone everywhere that they were all equally in danger of a terrorist/zombie attack.

The common room on Amy's floor was packed with students, gathered around a TV mounted to the wall. It was tuned to CNN, which John guessed meant this was the most CNN anyone in this building had watched in years. It was clear from the coverage that nobody had gotten a camera crew inside the town after the Action 5 News team got eaten. They did have three short video clips that they showed on a loop, all of them shot with shaky cell phones and presumably uploaded to the Web before all of the communication lines went dark. The first was the least exciting, showing a crew of National Guard putting up temporary fencing around the hospital. They were working fast, using a huge drill thing attached to a backhoe to punch holes in the dirt while a crane filled said holes with poles three times as tall as a man. The view cut to a roll of absolutely sinister looking razor wire on the ground, then to a group of guys standing guard, holding assault rifles that John recognized as M4s, as he had gone shopping for one that last summer.

Still no hazmat gear on those guys. Jesus.

Finally one of the soldiers shouted something at whoever was holding the camera and the clip abruptly ended.

Then the next two clips were prefaced by the anchor warning that the following scenes were very disturbing, and that you should leave the room if you were a giant pussy. They then cut to the second clip, shot from inside a car that was creeping along downtown, the driver presumably trying to steer while holding their phone out of the window to record what looked like some bodies laying in front of a smashed-up storefront (John recognized it as Black Circle Records, on Main Street—it hadn't been smashed up quite as much the last time he saw it). The shot zoomed in on a mutilated body laying facedown. Well, part of it was facedown, the torso part. The pelvis was a twisted pink mess, and the legs were turned all the way around, so that they were toes-up. Suddenly one of the legs snapped into action, bending at the knee as if the legs were going to get up on their own and walk away without the rest of the body. The shot cut to black before we could see if they did.

Finally, they cut to a grainy scene shot from an upper-story window, looking down at the street below. There were three soldiers in a standoff with a lone guy who was holding a curved object that looked like a scythe—it was hard to make out from that distance. The soldiers were shouting commands at the guy, gesturing for him to get facedown on the ground. He advanced on them and they opened fire, all three of them. The clip had no audio but you could see repeated puffs of gunsmoke drifting into the air and bits of flesh flying off the guy. He never went down. He didn't even stumble. Instead he reared back and threw the scythe thing at the nearest soldier. The soldier grabbed his neck and went down.

The other two soldiers ran.

The camera view started shaking, which John interpreted as the cameraman going nuts and probably yelling to the other people in the room about what had just happened. This got the attention of the monster below, who turned and looked up, directly into the camera, and thus into the eyes of everyone in the dorm common room.

The man reached into his coat and pulled out another scythe. John had a split second to realize he had actually pulled out one of his own ribs, before he hurled it at the window, shattering it.

Everyone in the common room flinched.

The scene cut to black.

A kid at the front of the room with black hair, a beard, and horn-rimmed glasses said, "Now tell me that wasn't a zombie."

John's college career had been brief and he had never lived in a dorm room. This one reminded him of a prison cell. Amy and her roommate slept in bunk beds. They had no TV. There was a bathroom and shower that they shared with the people in the next room. There was a little mini-fridge next to the window, a hot plate sitting on top of it. Not even enough floor space to do a push-up. Not that he hadn't lived in worse.

In one corner John found a familiar sight, what he thought of as Amy's "nest." At the center was an old beanbag chair that looked like it had come from a garage sale or a vintage store. Surrounding it was her Apple laptop, a rolled-up, half-empty bag of Cheetos, an open box of Cocoa Pebbles cereal that she would eat dry, and four empty bottles—orange juice, orange juice, Diet Mountain Dew, water. If she were at home you would also find two prescription bottles there, one pain pill and one muscle relaxer that John knew she took for her back. She probably kept those in her purse, shit like that would get stolen in a college dorm. You could sell OxyContin for ten or twenty bucks a pill here. Price would probably go to ten times that now that the apocalypse was here.

You stop that apocalypse shit. Keep your head, John.

Amy had the lower bunk, which John knew because on the wall next to it she had taped up a little world map with a dozen cities in Europe and Australia bearing red stars she had drawn on with a Sharpie. Cities she wanted to visit someday. John noticed she had added a star to Japan since the last time he had seen it. He tried to imagine Dave walking around the streets of Tokyo. It was like picturing RoboCop in Middle Earth—

"John, you've met Nisha, right?" John had. Amy's gorgeous Indian roommate. She was on the top bunk in pajama pants and a tank top, glued to her phone and tapping in Facebook updates. A bottle of absinthe leaned against the wall next to her, a textbook nearby served as a tray for an ornate glass, sugar cubes and a disposable lighter. Saturday night!

Nisha said, "Okay, I am freaking out over this. Did you see that zombie video?"

Amy said, "Yeah, it's crazy. David is still there. In the town."

"Who?"

"My boyfriend."

"Oh, wow. I'm so sorry. Is he okay?"

"We don't know. Nobody knows anything. John was there when everything happened, he just barely made it out."

She looked at John. "Oh. Wow. And he's not . . . infected or anything, is he? He didn't get bit?"

"No, no. He was way away from everything when it happened. They actually let him out at the checkpoint, they checked him over and said he was fine."

"Oh, that's good."

"But don't tell anybody, okay? People will freak out. You know how people are."

"Oh, totally."

"Do you mind if he crashes on the floor tonight? Tomorrow we'll make some calls and go back and pick up David."

Pick up David, John thought. *Like he just needs a ride.*

John thought the absinthe looked like it had barely been touched.

"Absolutely," said the roommate, even more oblivious. "Hey Pizza Factory is doing their two-for-one thing tonight."

John thought,

Brains, splattered on blue plastic.

As Amy said, "Okay. Yeah. Yeah, we need to eat. Uh, John, what do you take on your pizza?"

A part of John realized this was crazy, but another part of him wondered if there would be such a thing as pizza a week, or a month, from now.

"John?"

"Meat. I want meat on it. All of the meat that they have."

Amy sank into her beanbag chair and John noticed she called the pizza from speed dial. Nisha nodded to her absinthe bottle and said to John, "Wanna drink with me?"

Well . . . it would be rude not to at this point.

8 Days, 1 Hour Until the Massacre at Ffirth Asylum

Amy couldn't help but notice that after John had gone on and on about how tired he was and how he'd had no sleep because he was busy rescuing David the night before, he was still going strong at midnight. He and Nisha finished off the absinthe but then Nisha went down the hall and came back with another bottle of some kind of liquor or other. It had a pirate on the bottle. John was getting talkative and was suddenly in action hero mode. "We need weapons, that's the first step," he said. "We may have to improvise something. All those assholes gotta pay."

Pay for what?

He was getting loud and that made Amy nervous because, apocalypse or not, it was against building policy to have overnight visitors from off campus and if the RA caught John in the room she'd make him leave. And then what would he do? Sleep in the truck? But now, he and Amy's roommate were getting drunk and downing pizza and making a party out of it.

Uh, everybody deals with crisis differently . . . I guess?

They asked Amy if they could use her laptop and they both huddled over it, refreshing the news Web sites and all of the social networking hubs over and over and over again, even though nothing new was coming out of Undisclosed and Amy was pretty sure nothing new would come out until daytime. If nobody had reporters on the inside and the phone lines were down, then all that was coming out were the stupid rumors. Sitting there and sucking up the rumors wasn't doing anyone any good, it was just following the crisis as a form of entertainment. The crisis that David was stuck right in the middle of. Amy didn't think either of them even noticed when she got up, put on her jacket and walked out.

There were still a lot of people in the common room. The channel got switched to Fox News and a panel of experts was desperately trying to fill airtime by finding ways to rephrase the nothing that they knew, over and over again. She thought it was fascinating how the coverage on the Internet and the coverage on TV were from alternate universes. TV was all "terror . . . terrorist . . . Al Qaeda . . ." and the Internet was "zombies . . . zombies . . . zombies . . ."

Amy just kept walking toward the elevator and headed down, out of the building. She needed air.

The campus was buzzing. The hot dog truck was pulled up in front of the building and there was a line three wide and ten deep in front of it.

Amy walked past because she wanted to wish Spiro the hot dog guy a happy birthday—his was one of the over two hundred birthdays programmed into the calendar app on her phone. He smiled and told her the hot dogs were free tonight, one per customer. Not because of his birthday, but because of the other thing.

She passed a flyer posted to a utility pole with a huge letter Z on it, which she ignored, but then she passed another one, and another. Then she arrived at the visitor's parking lot and found one under the windshield of David's truck (and all of the other cars) and read it:

* Meeting *

Z

POWDER KEG

2nd Street
Every Day at Noon

- SURVIVAL
- BASIC WEAPONS TRAINING
- GENERAL PREPAREDNESS

IT'S HERE. BE READY.

Zombie nerds. They probably had the flyers already made up for this. There was nobody creepier than the zombie nerds, college guys who not only watched zombie movies and read zombie novels and played zombie video games, but actually formed clubs and collected zombie-killing weapons. Gun shops around there actually stocked zombie targets, and special zombie bullets with glow-in-the-dark tips. Not toy bullets, mind you. These guys would go out in the woods and train and shoot and defend to the death their right to stay in childhood until age thirty-five.

She climbed inside the truck. She wasn't going anywhere. She had never learned to drive, her car accident happened not long before she would have been due to take her Driver's Ed courses in high school. She never got back around to it after she went back to school and now the thought of it terrified her. She didn't know how *anybody* did it. Hurtling down the highway at 65 miles an hour while a barrage of other cars come flying toward you like huge cannon shells, whipping past in the next lane, just five feet from your own squishy body. If at that moment one of you nudges your steering wheel at the wrong time, two seconds later your body is a bunch of spaghetti wrapped around bundles of twisted steel. She'd yell at David for eating while he drove, a Coke between his legs and a hamburger in one hand, steering with two fingers, at night. It's like nobody in the world gets how fragile life is. How fragile our bodies are.

Amy got the crying to stop about ten minutes later. Her tear ducts were getting sore. She turned the flyer over and found a pen in her purse. She held the flyer to her thigh with the stump of her left wrist, and began writing with her right. She was making a list.

1. Call the Centers for Disease Control.

John said that's who was on the scene of the house fire, which made sense because this was sort of a disease. If so, at some point they had to establish a hotline for people to get in contact with their loved ones inside quarantine. There'd be riots otherwise. They were still Americans, there was still such a thing as the Constitution. All she needed them to do was confirm that David was okay, even if she wasn't allowed to see him or talk to him.

2. Exhaust all means of contacting David.

One way or the other, it didn't seem plausible that the government could really shut down *all* forms of communication. Not in the twenty-first century. She could have John post a message to him on his blog, she would post on Facebook, she would e-mail him, she would try the cell again. Write a paper letter addressed to the Undisclosed quarantine operation sent ATTN: David Wong.

It was driving her crazy, not knowing. Where was he right now? At this moment? Wandering free around town? In a temporary CDC plague tent or something? Crashing at John's old place? She thought for a moment then jotted down:

3. If David is in CDC custody, get him a care package.

His house had burned down. That meant he needed . . . everything. Clothes. Heartburn pills. Replacement contact lenses in case he lost one. Dandruff shampoo. Some Oreos. A book.

One more idea occurred to her. It should have come to her sooner. She wrote:

4. Contact Marconi?

"Marconi," if you haven't heard of him, was Dr. Albert Marconi. He wrote books and hosted a show on the History Channel about monsters and ghosts and stuff. David and John knew him because their paths had crossed a few times. If anybody knew what to do, he would. Heck, he was probably on his way here. Probably started calling his producer and packing his bags the moment that "zombie" video hit the news. Then, with resolve, Amy filled in the last item:

5. If none of the above can be done, get into the quarantine.

Getting *out* of a quarantine was hard, but getting in would be the easiest thing in the world, right? All you had to do was show up and say you were infected. She wouldn't even need to lie—she had spent twelve straight hours with somebody who was at Outbreak Ground Zero. Just tell them that. Instant ticket in. The problem would be figuring out how to find David once she was in there—if the government had him somewhere, they may not allow them to stay together since they're not married. If they didn't have him, finding where he was in town could be a chore. Still, just being inside the city would put her 90 percent closer.

She folded up the paper and put it in her purse. There. Now she had a plan. She felt better. She would get some sleep and get a fresh start with John tomorrow.

7 Days, 13 Hours Until the Massacre at Ffirth Asylum

Amy started trying to wake up John at nine in the morning. He didn't get up until two in the afternoon. He was cranky and despondent. When she suggested calling Dr. Marconi and asked him if he had a phone number for him, John mumbled that he would "take care of it." After she reminded him six more times over the next two hours, finally he got on her laptop and started doing something or other, which she took as progress until she leaned over him and realized he was on the freaking Web site for Marconi's TV show, trying to find a phone number. *She* could have done that. *Eight hours ago.* John wound up calling a number that she was pretty sure was for ordering DVD box sets of Marconi's show, and leaving a rambling voice mail that no sane human being would respond to.

Then the rest of that evening was spent trying to find John a place to stay. But all of the hotels in town were booked with people unable to get back home to Undisclosed and all the news media converging on the area. They wound up having to put him up in a motel an hour away, so now John would have to make a two-hour round trip every time they needed to do anything. So here are all the other people running around in a panic trying to stock up to survive the end of the world, and Amy and John were farting trying to find a hotel and . . . *ugh.*

She wasn't going to cry.

Oh, and Amy paid. For everything. John said he was expecting a paycheck from the temp job he had working for a DJ doing parties and weddings and stuff, but of course said DJ lived in Undisclosed so who knows if he got out or if he was dead or if he was a monster.

So anyway, that was Sunday gone.

6 Days, 18 Hours Until the Massacre at Ffirth Asylum

Amy had taken to avoiding the common room because there was almost a party atmosphere there. Sure, people would talk about it like it was this big national tragedy, but you could tell they were into it, like it was something they could seize on to break up the routine. Just one more bit of drama that played out on the big common room TV.

The big news Monday morning was that the government had scheduled a press conference, the first one since all of this happened. It was also streamed on the Internet, so Amy could follow it from her phone in her dorm room, away from the spectators. The stream on her phone was delayed by seven or eight seconds for whatever technical Internet reason, so it created a weird effect where she could faintly hear the guy leading the news conference say a line down the hall before he'd say it again on her phone a few seconds later. She was alone, John was at the hotel and her roommate was down the hall with the crowd.

First, the guy—a middle-aged guy with a young George Clooney haircut—announced a phone hotline they had set up, but said to please not call with inquiries about loved ones. The number was purely to report that you or someone you knew were showing symptoms of infection, so they needed to keep those lines free since containing infection had to be first priority. He read off the number and Amy hurriedly dug the zombie flyer out of her purse and jotted it down.

The guy also said that they had set up a patient treatment facility at the Undisclosed hospital, and that all infected and suspected infected were being transported there and given the best care possible. In the meantime, they were imposing a strict sundown curfew in the city, and they would be going house to house to check for infected individuals. The guy was good at his job, Amy found herself actually feeling better. As horrible as John had described the situation and what they had seen, this guy here seemed on top of it.

Then, something weird happened.

The guy was winding down the press conference with some generic lines about how they were busily researching the outbreak, and urged people to neither believe nor spread irresponsible Internet rumors. Then CNN abruptly cut back to the anchor and everyone in the common room *screamed their heads off.* This completely baffled Amy, as the anchor was just a lady in a pantsuit. But then she remembered the delay. She had five solid seconds to tense up her whole body while she waited to see what they had seen.

The anchor quickly said that they had exclusive new video that had just leaked from Outbreak Ground Zero, and in the middle of her sentence they cut to a grainy video, shot from inside a car at night. The chaos had already started before they got the camera up—there were screams and confused shouts from within the car, inhuman growls from outside. Glass shattered. A fist punched through, a grotesque face biting at the cameraman. A flash of light and a pop filled the interior of the car—a gunshot. The monster recoiled from the window. There were plenty more behind it, four or five hands now pushing in through the glass. More gunshots.

A female voice in the car screamed, "DRIVE! DRIVE!"

Squealing tires. Another relieved voice rasped, "Oh, my God, oh, my God, that was so close . . ."

The view swung across the street. Amy thought she saw a reddish dog trot past. She thought, *Molly?*

The woman holding the camera phone had rested her arm so that the camera was now pointing at her lap, but continued recording—that's why the viewers knew she was doomed before she did. While the woman held a nervous conversation with the driver, a crimson stain started forming across her abdomen. Then a puckered hole formed in her belly, like she was being shot from behind by the world's slowest bullet.

Guts spilled out onto her lap, a tangle of wet sausages.

The woman screamed.

The clip cut to black.

Amy shut off her phone. She breathed. She called John and got his voice mail. She paced around her dorm room for a few minutes, trying to think of what to do next. Then she went into the bathroom and threw up.

6 Days, 6 Hours Until the Massacre at Ffirth Asylum

John saw Amy's messages piling up on his phone and by Monday night he wanted to throw the thing through a fucking window. He knew how serious the fucking situation was, he could turn on a TV or look out his window—his motel was down the block from a Pentecostal church and he could see people piling through the door. On a *Monday*.

And oh, by the way, he wanted to say, he had been friends with David for ten years before Amy even knew his fucking name. John felt the loss in ways she couldn't even conceive. He didn't need her calling him every five seconds to tell him to do, what, exactly?

John had promised himself he wouldn't drink today, he had overdone it Saturday night. But by Monday evening he started to have that swimmy, flu-feeling in his head and gut and realized it was stupid to try to put himself through rehab on a week when he needed to be 110 percent. He'd stick to beer, though, that much he decided. He got a twelve-pack and settled in for the night in the motel room, watching the news carefully for updates.

He'd call Amy tomorrow.

From the Journal of Amy Sullivan

Tuesday 11/8:

Lines everywhere. Lines at the stores, lines at the gas station. Everyone is freaking out. People are leaving town and heading north, new people are showing up from the south like refugees. The National Guard has extended the quarantine zone out five more miles from around [Undisclosed]. Class cancelled. I haven't slept.

No answer from John all day. Tried to call Dr. Marconi myself. Left a message.

Wednesday 11/9:

Left John nine messages. Campus and the rest of town is now under a curfew. I think they are going to come looking for us. We SHOULD NOT STILL BE HERE.

Decided I'm not going back to the dorms. Staying with some guys who live off campus. Didn't tell anyone in the dorm where I was going.

Rumors from inside quarantine are crazy. News has a rumor that the CDC had to pull all of their staff out of the hospital treatment facility. Government denies it. Hopefully David isn't there either way.

Thursday 11/10:

FINALLY talked to John in the P.M. Suddenly he's all bluster, says if we don't hear anything by SATURDAY NIGHT—one week after all this started—then he and I will go down to [Undisclosed] ourselves and break David out on Sunday. Told him I didn't need to break him out, I just needed to know that he was okay.

Meanwhile, getting calls on my cell from unlisted numbers. I don't answer them.

Friday 11/11:

Got a call from Nisha, said somebody from the government showed up at the dorm looking for me.

I called John. Voice mail. All day. Voice mail.
I cried again. Broke my streak.

Saturday 11/12:

Absolute information blackout from [Undisclosed]. No more video clips, no new information. I am going crazy. I can't keep food down. A week. Where has David been sleeping that whole time? Is he in pain? Is he hungry?

The government FINALLY put up their Web site for families and friends of outbreak victims to search for names. Three categories— Quarantined, Status Unknown, and Deceased. The Quarantined list was HUGE, hundreds of names. David wasn't on it. It was in alphabetical order but I read the list four times to make sure they didn't just put his name in the wrong spot. Then I moved on to Status Unknown, and he wasn't on there, either, and then I decided it was a stupid list because whose status do we actually know at any given time? They could have the whole world on there. I just closed the browser.

No return call from Marconi. When I tried to call John, got voice mail only. Again.

Left a message reminding him that tomorrow was the day. I gave him a location & told him to pick me up there at eleven A.M. No reason he can't be up and around at that hour.

Scared. Excited. Going to see David tomorrow one way or the other.

18 Hours Until the Massacre
at Ffirth Asylum

Amy wasn't sure if she had been more freaked out about the crazy bustle of the campus earlier in the week, or the ghost town that it was now. Campus had emptied, everybody had left to go back home to Mom and Dad, scared the university would get swallowed up in the expanding quarantine zone. Well, those who had parents, anyway.

That morning, Amy wound up spending a solid hour just trying to get dressed, standing in the "guest room" at the house where she was now holed up (a huge old house occupied by three gay guys she had met in a pottery class). The "guest room" was just a converted attic covered in Bollywood movie posters and full of discarded exercise machines that had each once starred in their own informercial. The hour was spent almost entirely standing over her suitcase in her underpants, trying to figure out what would be practical to wear in this situation. After imagining a hundred different scenarios for what they'd see once they got down there, she finally realized that the quarantine staff would probably seize everybody's clothes and give them hospital pajamas or something. So the best bet was to wear something she didn't care about losing to an incinerator.

So then she was running late, and still had to go to the drugstore. She'd been avoiding it all week because she thought it'd be a madhouse like everything else. But it, like everything else, was eerily empty now.

Also empty? The shelves. There were handmade signs everywhere about per-customer limits. She wanted to get both of her prescriptions filled, but they were out of Oxy and could only do a partial refill of the muscle relaxer. She tried not to let the guy at the counter see how much this freaked her out, doing the math in her head to see how long the painkillers would last her until she was basically flat on her back and unable to stand up (answer: nine days). Then again the quarantine would be full of doctors so they probably had all kinds of stuff there.

She bought nasal strips—couldn't sleep without them. She wanted some over-the-counter allergy pills. All gone. She looked for antacid tablets for David, all those were gone but they had some tropical-flavored Tums that even in an emergency nobody would buy.

Tampon aisle was bare. She also noticed the condom case was empty, though she figured that was a little too, uh, optimistic anyway. She did successfully get some sensitive-teeth toothpaste and the one brand of deodorant that didn't give her a rash. Finally, the candy aisle. Twizzlers were gone, but she did get some Red Vines, which were basically like stale Twizzlers.

She could have kept going around and around the store for the rest of the day thinking up things she and David might need, but she was already running late and if John arrived at the meeting site to find she wasn't there, he might freak out.

In her message, Amy had told John to pick her up at a bus stop in front of a huge Mexican restaurant that was impossible to miss. She took only one change of clothes, her bag full of pharmacy stuff, and her pillow. With her back the way it was, the pillow was a necessity. She could not sleep on any other pillow. They could have everything else, they could send her into quarantine wearing a potato sack. But they weren't getting the pillow away from her.

She got to the bus stop at three minutes until eleven, and saw the white Bronco round the corner right at eleven on the dot. She took a deep breath and said a prayer.

14 Hours Until the Massacre at Ffirth Asylum

Two hours later, Amy was still sitting at the bus stop.

It hadn't been John coming around the corner and it hadn't been a Bronco, it was a different make. Some hillbilly behind the wheel.

She called John for the fifth time. Voice mail.

As she hung up, two guys walked past her on the sidewalk carrying shotguns. Right there in broad daylight.

She was freezing, her butt numb on the bus stop bench, sitting there with her pillow on her lap. She called the front desk of John's motel to ask if they could check on him (they wouldn't). She called Nisha, to see if she'd heard from him (she hadn't).

No crying. She imposed a no-crying rule until further notice. She had eaten half a dozen of the Red Vines.

An SUV pulled over about a block down. Four guys got out of it, all of them carrying hard plastic cases that were shaped like they held rifles. Some had little briefcase-shaped ones that she guessed held pistols or some other kind of littler gun. They all headed off in the same direction.

She stared at her phone, willing it to ring.

At around 1:30, she finally got John to answer his phone.

"Hello?"

"John! Oh my god. Where are you?"

"I'm, uh, at the motel. What's happened?"

"What do you mean what's happened? I'm here at the bus stop."

"Okay are you taking the bus here or . . ."

"What? John? It's Sunday."

Pause.

"The buses don't run on Sunday?"

"John . . ."

"Yeah? What's wrong? Are you crying?"

She took a moment to compose herself, failed.

"Hello? Amy?"

"John, we were supposed to go down to the city today. To see David."

"Oh, yeah, okay. I didn't hear your voice mail until just now. My phone has been messing up, I think the network is dropping a lot of calls because of the—"

"Are you coming?"

"Oh, I don't think so. Today isn't good, I'm really sick. Think it's food poisoning. Probably something going around at the motel, everybody has it. But it's probably for the best anyway, I think we should hold off. But I've been doing a ton of research. It turns out the government has put up a list of names on their Web site. I haven't been there yet but let me give you the address—"

Amy hung up on him, and turned off her phone.

It was, she would have to say, the angriest she had ever been in her entire life. She took a dozen deep breaths, trying to remember the techniques from the meditation class she had taken (somebody claimed it could do as much to control pain as any prescription painkiller, *ha-ha*).

She only had one other option. She dug the zombie flyer from her purse, unfolded it, and dialed the hotline number the guy had given out during the press conference.

She punched her way through a series of voice options, then when she reached an operator said, "Uh, hi. My name is Amy Sullivan. My boyfriend's name is David Wong. His house is where the infection started. Both of us were there. I'm showing symptoms. I think I should be quarantined but I'm two hours away and I don't have transportation."

Long pause on the other end.

"Please hold."

After a minute, a friendly sounding male voice came on the line and said, "Ms. Sullivan?"

"Yes, sir."

"We'll come get you. Stay exactly where you are. Don't panic."

"Okay. Do you know where the bus stop is in front of—"

"We know where you are. We'll be there within thirty minutes. Please stay where you are. If someone else approaches you, ask them to stay at least fifty feet away. Remain calm."

Thirty minutes? So they did have people in town.

She hung up and bit into a Red Vine. She felt stupid. This is what she should have done all along. She'd be in Undisclosed before dark.

13 Hours, 30 Minutes Until the Massacre at Ffirth Asylum

Dark. Thirsty.

I had been hospitalized only once before, for a concussion and some cuts and a fractured eye socket I suffered in a car accident, and for a minor gunshot wound unrelated to the accident. I don't remember any of it clearly, it happened during a period of my life that is mostly lost to my memory. But one thing I do remember is the long, slow, touch-and-go bob to consciousness that came with the artificially induced coma of anesthesia. Sights and smells drifting in under the haze of nonsense dream logic, and a sense that the world had skipped ahead in time without me. And under it all, the thirst. This was like that.

My last solid memory was stepping through the Porta-Potty, stepping out of the BB's restroom door and into a shouting, shoving crowd that had gathered behind the store. The people were being herded into that spot by National Guard—confused, scared kids with assault rifles and no protective gear. Somebody started shooting and a head burst like a balloon next to me, the dead guy flailing back through the door I had just exited.

Days had passed since then. I knew that. I could feel it in my sore joints, and I had a vague sense of cycles, of consciousness and unconsciousness—sleeping through a night, drifting in and out of a day that was just as dark. I had been moved, and moved again, rolled down a hallway on a gurney. I remember having an IV in my arm for a while, and then they took it out, and then put it back. I had been outside at some point, behind a fence, talking to other people. I remembered screams, and panic. All of it just flashing through my brain, like headlights passing a bedroom window at night. There and gone. Meaningless.

Sleep.

Awake.

Dark.

I had eyes. I felt the twitch of my eyelids opening and closing, though the view remained the same either way. Was I blind?

I moved my right arm. I couldn't feel the dragging weight of plastic tubes attached, so I had been unhooked at some point. With some effort I lifted my hand to my face, to see if my eyes were covered. They were not. I blinked. I tried to lift my head, and groaned—a bolt of pain fired up my neck. I looked around for the glow of a digital clock, or a slit of light under a door, or blinking green lights on a console measuring my vitals.

Nothing.

I tried to sit up. I peeled my back off of the sheets, but my other arm wouldn't come with me. I tugged on it and heard the clank of metal and felt cold steel around my wrist. I was handcuffed to the bed.

That is never a good sign.

I peeled apart dry lips and croaked, "Hello?"

Nobody would have heard it unless they were sitting on the bed with me. I tried to swallow and give it another shot.

"Hello? Is anybody out there?"

Something about the echo of my voice told me I was in a small room.

"HELLO?"

I waited, for the sound of a shuffling nurse's footsteps outside, or even the jingling of keys and a burly prison guard to tell me to shut the hell up or he was going to put me in solitary.

Nothing. I thought I detected the sound of water dripping, somewhere.

Suddenly I was certain—absolutely certain—that I had been abandoned here. No question, they had stuck me in a building, chained to a bed, and left me here to die of thirst. They didn't even leave a light on. I'd lie here, for days, pissing and shitting myself, like a neglected dog in a trailer park whose owner was off doing meth somewhere.

"HEY! ANYBODY?"

I yanked at the cuffs. It didn't do anything but make an irritating noise. I couldn't even see a door.

There isn't a door, they just built up a brick wall over the opening, or locked me in a shipping container and bulldozed a thousand tons of dirt on top of it or sank it to the bottom of the ocean.

"HEY! HEY!"

I got one leg up—neither was restrained as far as I could tell—and kicked at the railing the cuffs were attached to. I had no strength in the leg. The railing didn't give.

"HEY! GODDAMNIT!"

"Sir?"

A tiny voice. I froze.

Did I actually hear that?

I blinked into the darkness, stupidly, looking for movement. Somebody could have been sitting on my lap and I wouldn't have seen them.

"Hello? Is someone there?"

"It's just me." Sounded like a little girl. "Can you be quieter? You're scaring us."

"Who are you?"

"I'm Anna. Is your name Walt?"

"No. My name is David. Who's Walt?"

"I thought they called you Walt earlier. When they brought you in."

"No. Oh, okay. Wong. They probably said Wong, that's my last name. David Wong."

"Are you from Japan?"

"No. Who else is in here?"

"Just us. You me and Mr. Bear."

"Okay, Anna, this is going to seem like a weird question but is Mr. Bear an actual bear or a stuffed bear?"

"He's stuffed when grown-ups are around. Sorry if I scared you."

"What are you doing here, Anna?"

"Same as you. We might be sick and they want to make sure other people don't catch it."

"Where are we?"

"Why didn't you ask that question first?"

"What?"

"It didn't make sense to ask me what I was doing here if you didn't know where here was."

"Are we in the hospital?"

No answer.

"Anna? You there?"

"Yes, sorry, I nodded my head but I forgot that you couldn't see me. We're in the old hospital. In the basement."

"Then where is everybody? And what happened to the lights?"

"You can ask the spaceman when he comes by again. There were lots of them here before but everybody has been gone for a while."

I didn't need to ask who the spacemen were. Guys in contamination suits.

"How long has it been since they've come by?"

"I don't know, I don't have my phone. It was two sleeps ago. I'm sure they'll be back soon. Maybe they close on the weekend."

"Do you remember when they brought you here?"

"Sort of. They came and got my dad and they told us we couldn't go home and moved everybody downstairs to the special hospital. And, that's where we are now." In a whisper she said, "I think we should be quiet now."

"How old are you, Anna?"

She whispered, "Eight."

"Listen to me. I don't want you to be scared, but they left us here with no power, and no food, and no water. Now hopefully they'll come back and take care of us but we have to make plans assuming they won't."

"If you drank all of your water you can have some of mine."

"I . . . do I have water? Where?"

"On the table next to you."

I reached over with my right hand and hit a row of shrink-wrapped bottles. I dug a bottle out and drank half of it and went into a coughing fit.

"Sssshhhhh. We really should be quiet. There's a box of granola bars and stuff over there, too, but they're not very good."

"Why are we being quiet?"

"I think I hear the shadow man."

I choked on my water.

"Shhhhh."

"Anna, we—"

"Please."

We laid there in silence, floating in still darkness like a pair of eyeless cave fish.

Finally Anna said, "I think he's gone."

"The shadow man?"

"Yes."

"Describe him to me."

"He's a shadow with eyes."

"Where did you see him?"

"Over there."

"I can't see where you're pointing."

"Over in the corner."

"When? When did you see him before, I mean?"

She sighed. *"I don't have a clock."*

"What . . . uh, what did it do?"

"It just stood there. I was scared. Mr. Bear growled at him and he eventually went away."

I had read somewhere that you could get out of handcuffs if you broke the bone at the base of your thumb. Or maybe just dislocated it? Either way I'd have to find out if my legs were strong enough to do that.

The issue would then be trying to get the presumably locked door open one-handed. Maybe Anna could help.

I said, "Okay. We have to get out of this place."

"They told us we couldn't leave."

"Anna, you're going to find out soon that grown-ups aren't always right. We . . . let's just say that it's better if we're not here when that thing comes back. But if it does, I don't want you to panic. I don't think it's here for you, I think it's here for me."

"Yes, that's what he said."

"He talked to you?"

She hesitated. "Sort of. I could hear him. I don't think he had a mouth. Like Hello Kitty."

"And . . . what did he say?"

"I don't want to repeat it but I don't think he likes you."

I said nothing.

Anna asked, "Do you want Mr. Bear?"

"No, thank you."

I pulled my hand as far out of the handcuff as I could, which wasn't far. I could feel the little knob of bone stopping it, two inches down from the thumb. If I yanked it hard enough, surely it would scrape off that bone, and the blood would lubricate it. Be a matter of not passing out from the pain. And me not being too much of a pussy.

Metal scraping. I was about to ask Anna what she was doing when it registered that—

HOLY SHIT THAT'S THE DOOR THE DOOR IS OPEN

I sat up and threw aside the blanket. The room was bathed in light, a pair of powerful flashlights in the doorway, side by side like the eyes of a giant robot that had poked his head up through the floor. I was momentarily blinded by the light, but I squinted and looked to the corner, yelling, "Anna! Get—"

The words died in my mouth. The room I was in, now fully illuminated by the flashlights, contained a small bedside table, a toilet, a filthy sink, and one bed. Mine.

I was absolutely alone in the room.

On the floor was a tattered, filthy old teddy bear.

Gloved hands grabbed me, holding me to the bed. It was two dudes wearing decontamination space suits, but the suits weren't white—they were black, and they had pads on the arms, torso and thighs like body armor. Their faceplates were tinted, so you couldn't see the face of the wearer.

The cuff was removed from the bed rail and locked around my other wrist. Leg irons were placed around my ankles. I was dragged from the bed and marched down a long hallway lined with rusting steel doors just like the one I had been yanked through.

There were other people here, roused to life by the sound of us passing their cells. I heard an old man screaming for his wife, or daughter ("KATIE!!!! KAAAATIE! CAN YOU HEAR ME??!?") with no response. I heard a scraping from behind one door, like somebody was clawing to get out. I heard someone beg for food, I heard someone beg for pain pills.

At the moment I passed a particular door, a male voice on the other side said, "Hey! Buddy! Hey! Open this door for me. Please. It's my wife, my wife is in here and she's bleeding. I'm begging you."

I stopped.

"I'm here. What's—"

The gloved hands clamped on me again to pull me along.

"Hey! Are you gonna help that guy? Hey!"

No answer from the guards. From behind me, the desperate voice begged and howled and wept.

The hallway came to a bend and continued to the right, but I was stopped in front of a TV screen that had been mounted on the wall. There was a speaker mounted below it, with a "push to talk" button. The screen blinked to life and there was a man in another decontamination suit, this one the normal, friendly white like you'd expect from a government agency. The face behind the clear Plexiglas mask was familiar to me, the neatly cropped silver hair and weathered wrinkles.

"Good morning, Mr. Wong. How are we feeling today?"

"Dr. Tennet? What the hell are you doing here?"

Am I dreaming this?

"If we just keep answering each other's questions with questions this conversation won't go anywhere, will it?"

"I'm feeling like shit. Why are you here?"

"You don't remember?"

"Obviously not."

"What *do* you remember?"

"A bunch of guys in space suits were shooting people in BB's parking lot. Guts sprayed all over me. Next thing I know I'm chained to a bed in this prison. And now my therapist is here for some reason."

"Prison? Is that where you think you are?"

"There are tiny rooms with locks and handcuffs and I can't leave. Call it whatever you want. How long have I been here?"

"You honestly don't remember? Anything at all?"

"No."

"You've lost all memories from your arrival until now? Think hard for me."

"I don't remember anything, goddamnit."

"I completely understand your agitation. But I'm going to have to beg for a little bit more of your patience. I'm part of the team sent to observe you and the others. We're trying to get you well."

He looked down and was doing something with his hands. Tapping on a laptop. Making notes. Immune to the sound of muffled suffering echoing down the hall behind me.

"Doctor, is somebody going to help those people back there?"

"That would be . . . ill-advised. I assure you that the patients who actually need help are receiving it. Again, this is not a prison."

"So am I free to leave?"

"If I'm satisfied that you've stabilized, you'll be free to rejoin the others in quarantine."

"Where's that?"

"Over at the hospital grounds. The primary quarantine area."

"But I can't leave there?"

"I'm afraid not. The government would have some very strong words for me if I were to let any of you wander out."

"Where am I now?"

"In the old Ffirth Asylum, the abandoned TB hospital just down the street. Temporary REPER command center and patient processing."

I thought he said "raper" and decided then and there that I had lost my mind.

"The *who* command center?"

"R-E-P-E-R. Rapid Exotic Pathogen Eradication slash Research. A not widely publicized task force for situations like this."

"*What situations* are 'like this'?"

"You and I have had this conversation before, by the way. I know what you're about to ask next."

"Are John and Amy here?"

"And once again, I can tell you we have three Johns—Washington, Rawls and Perzynski. But no Amys."

I had a dozen follow-up questions: Were they okay? Did they get out of town? Where were they now? But I knew this asshole wouldn't answer them.

"Wait, did you say 'rejoin'? So I've been in quarantine before?"

"We brought you over for testing, but we're ready to transport you back."

"Testing."

"Yes, we're still trying to perfect our method of detecting the infection."

"And this test wiped out my memory."

"That's merely a side effect, one I do believe is temporary."

"How long have I been here?"

"Here, or in quarantine in general?"

"Let's go for the second one."

"Ever since the outbreak."

"*And how long ago was that?*"

"Longer than most of us would have preferred to stay, let us just put it that way."

Oh, fuck you.

"And you get to keep us here, forever, until you figure out how to cure the infection?"

"If you have a better idea, you be sure to let us know. Trust me, no one is enjoying this. The best thing you and everyone else can do is cooperate."

He finished his laptop work with a flourish of key taps and looked me in the eye.

"So. In that spirit, tell me how you are feeling."

"Why is it dark in here?"

"Electricity is out to much of the town. We have diesel generators but they are insufficient for the whole facility, so we are forced to pick and choose. Other than your missing memory, are you having any other symptoms? Dreams, hallucinations?"

"Well if I was, I wouldn't remember them, would I? You know, because I'm missing my goddamned memory."

"Of course. How are you feeling, physically?"

"I have a headache and my joints hurt."

"Those are expected side effects of the tranquilizers and being bedridden, and also should pass quickly. Do you remember why you were put under tranquilizers in the first place?"

"Any question you ask me that begins with the words 'do you remember' is going to be answered with 'no.'"

"Ha. Understood! Do you feel like you are up to rejoining the others?"

"The others? How many others are there? Can you tell me that?"

"In the primary quarantine area? Nearly five hundred. At one time."

Jesus Christ.

"And how many of them are people like me, who you know goddamned well aren't infected?"

"Now David, can't you see that I do not know that?"

"Do I fucking look infected?"

"Ah, I see. Due to being muddled by the medication, you are missing some key information about our circumstances. It turns out that appearances are not a perfect indication of infection. Not, unfortunately, until it's too late. So hopefully you understand that we must take precautions."

"Dr. Tennet, can you hear the fucking people behind me, screaming for help? Can you hear them over this intercom thing?"

"Which people? The gentleman asking for help with his wife? We lost two staff members trying to help that man's poor 'wife.' If you open that door, you'll indeed find what looks like a very frail, wounded woman. If you get within striking distance, you'll find that woman is the transfigured tongue of a grindworm."

"A *what?*"

"I'm sorry, we have to come up with names for the organisms the parasite transforms its victims into. Without getting into detail, let me just say that we spent sixteen hours trying to recover our two staff members from the creature, their screams echoing down this hall the entire night, and next day, as they were slowly twisted to pieces. The creature has been spitting splinters of their bones under its door ever since. So hopefully you'll understand why we're leaving that door locked. 'Fool me once,' as they say."

"So . . . you just lock everybody up and wait for us to turn monster?"

"As I said, we're making progress. But, regardless, this conversation is only wasting time and taxpayer money at this point, when all I need to know is if you feel up to joining the others out in the fresh air and sunshine of the hospital lawn. We need your room, to be perfectly frank."

"Yeah. Whatever."

"Great, great. If you turn to your right and continue down that hall, you'll find an elevator."

"And then what will—"

The monitor blinked off.

One of the two guys behind me told me to hold still, and unlocked my cuffs and leg irons. He pointed, and through a speaker in his helmet said, "End of the hall."

I said, "What about the girl?"

"Sir, move to the end of the hall."

"There was a little girl in my room, named Anna. I don't know if she snuck in and back out or what but she was in there right before you guys arrived."

The guy gave a glance to his partner. Uncertainty? The partner said, "Move to the elevator, or you're going back to the room."

I obeyed, my unsteady footsteps echoing in a dim hallway where the only illumination was dribbling out of a set of emergency lights to my left. Way down at the end was a barely lit elevator standing open.

Halfway down I turned and looked back for the two guards. Not there. Just lonely blackness beyond the pool of emergency light.

Goddamn did this seem like a long walk. My legs were weak and shaky—how long had I been strapped to that bed? What kind of drugs did they have me on? I felt my face and had no bandage there, just a little bump where the spider had bitten me. Where were John and Amy? What happened to the town? Had the world ended? Why did this hallway smell like shit?

"*Walt.*"

A whisper, behind me. I stopped, and held my breath. Had I actually heard it?

I continued, the elevator waiting right up ahead in the darkness, barely enough light inside to fill the tiny space.

I stopped again. I thought I could hear smaller, lighter footsteps trailing mine. Or maybe an echo.

I whispered, "Anna?"

Not sure any sound actually came out.

I turned and walked as fast as I could toward the open elevator, without breaking into what could be called a run. I made it inside, spun around and punched the button that said "1." All the other buttons from there up had been covered with electrician's tape.

Nothing happened. I was standing under what seemed like a 25-watt bulb that was slightly brighter than a candle. Dead silence.

No, wait. There was a faint sound. Not footsteps. A light scraping, then a brief pause, then the scrape again. The irregular rhythm of some-body trying to drag or carry an awkward load, or maybe just trying to walk with a severely wounded leg.

Getting louder. Closer. I could now make out a smacking, sticky sound, like a person loudly eating pasta right next to your ear.

I punched the "1" button again. I punched the "Close Door" button. I punched the "1" button again. Then I mashed the buttons under the electrical tape. All of them.

"*Walt.*"

That wet sound, scraping toward me. I could hear it clearly now, not ten feet away. Moving faster.

"*Walt. Walt. Walt.*"

The door closed.

If they didn't want the patients at the Undisclosed Ffirth Asylum com-mand center slash patient processing facility to feel like prisoners, they were doing the world's shittiest job. In the light I saw I was wearing a green prisoner jumpsuit. When the elevator arrived at the top, two more black-suited space men roughly dragged me out, put a black hood over my head, and threw me into the back of a military truck.

The hospital was just a couple of blocks away, but the trip took twenty minutes. We drove, stopped, waited, drove, waited again, then an alarm went off and I heard an electric sound like a garage door opening. We rolled forward for five seconds, then the sound again, and the clicks of latches. Then there was another gate opening, followed by the opening of the doors of the truck. I felt sunlight and a blast of cold air hit my hood. I was dragged out and told to lay flat on the grass. I was told that if I raised any part of my body before commanded to, I would be shot.

Holy shit.

They yanked off my hood. The truck left and I risked craning my neck enough to see a chain-link fence roll shut behind it. I turned the other way and saw that there was . . . another fence. I was in a gap the width of a city street, between two tall fences that were each topped with coils of Fuck-You razor wire. The inner fence, the one opposite the one the truck had just slipped out of, was opaque—they had attached tarps or some plastic sheets to it. The goal was clearly to make sure the separation between the hospital quarantine and the outside world was absolute. The plastic sheets were colorful and had printing all along them. The one nearest to me said 91.9 K-ROCK ROCKTOBER ROCKOCALYPSE.

I wondered how long they'd leave me laying like this, but soon a gate in the inner fence slid open and a voice from a PA system told me to go through. I obeyed, and entered quarantine, apparently for the second time.

I don't know what I was expecting to find inside the gate, but it was just the hospital lawn. The building itself was immediately to my right, the front lawn of the hospital stretching off to my left. The sun hatefully spat daylight into my eyes—how long had it been since I'd seen the sun?—and I gathered it was probably midafternoon or so.

My first thought was, "Ribs." Meat smoke hit my nostrils, like being downwind from a barbecue joint. I heard voices. Somebody laughed.

Hell, it's a party.

What was stranger than that was what wasn't there: men in space suits carrying guns. I assumed I would be roughly dragged in and told to go report to this tent or to submit to some tests or shit. But I was on my own. No soldiers. Nobody who looked official. No staff.

Instead, a smattering of tired-looking people in jumpsuits, some with hospital blankets wrapped around their shoulders, were staring at me like they were expecting someone else. When they saw it was me, they all shambled away without a word.

Well, screw you, too.

I spotted a pillar of smoke a hundred yards or so away, off near the fence that wrapped its way around the perimeter of the hospital grounds. A fence that did not exist the last time I was here, and that was covered entirely in garish ads that were each . . . *wrong* somehow, like they didn't have a big enough tarp and covered it in rejected billboards somebody had laying around in a warehouse (SUBWAY: COME TASTE OUR NEW BEARD!). I wandered toward the fire, having absolutely no idea what else to do. It was the same strategy I employ at parties: find the food first. My lungs quivered at the contact with the chilled air. Not an unpleasant feeling. Kind of felt like freedom.

"Hey! Spider-Man! Spider-Man's back!"

The voice came from above me and I admit my first reaction was to glance around for the actual Spider-Man. Why not?

He wasn't here. I found the source of the voice, a black dude poking his head out of a fifth-floor window of the hospital. I had no idea if he was talking to me or somebody else, so I kept walking. I couldn't help but notice the window he was yelling from was not open—the glass was busted out. That seemed weird to me.

I passed a fat lady in a dark green janitor's jumpsuit like mine, sleeping under a blanket on what looked like a waiting room sofa that had been dragged out into the yard. The upholstery was discolored, like it had been rained on. I kicked an empty water bottle. It skidded and bounced off another one. Trash was everywhere. I noticed somebody had knocked over the Florence Nightingale statue, laying on its side like they had just toppled a dictator.

I shuffled toward the bonfire, a lot of people were congregating over there. Everybody wearing jumpsuits, either green like mine, or blood red.

Tennet, tell me this is not a goddamned prison yard.

I passed the main entrance to the hospital. The sliding glass doors were propped open with two overflowing garbage cans. From the dim reception area inside it appeared the whole building was without power. Postapocalypse. How long has it been? A year? I wondered if the White House was trashed like this, the Lincoln Bedroom full of refugees. Or zombies.

I caught a whiff of that meat smell from the fire and my stomach growled. How long since I'd eaten? I felt slightly thinner, though that could have been due to the huge jumpsuit I was wearing. A clump of red jumpsuit guys were up ahead, talking and eating from bowls. I was going to ask them where the food table was but at the sight of me they all stopped talking, giving me a look like I was a cop and they were all hiding joints. Everybody had patchy beards. Greasy hair. Nobody shaving, nobody showering. On the ground were discarded plastic forks and paper plates tattooed with old grease stains and muddy shoe prints where they'd been stepped on a dozen times.

The huddle of red suits on the opposite side of the bonfire also fell silent. The bonfire, by the way, was a crackling pile of smashed furniture, wooden pallets, at least one mattress and bundles of what looked like blackened sticks.

Everybody looking at me now. I scanned around for some fellow green jumpsuits but there was just one guy who looked about eighty years old and another middle-aged woman who looked like a schoolteacher. Her eyes showed no signs of even vague interest in this situation. The biggest of the reds, a guy with shoulder-length blond hair and more neck than head said, "We about to have a problem here?" He had the voice of a man with four testicles. His jumpsuit was zipped down to reveal an Iron Cross tattoo on his sternum.

"Not that I know of. Can somebody point me toward the food?"

Nervous glances. Was the food a sensitive subject around here? Nobody seemed to have barbecue ribs.

Four-balls said, "You playin' a fuckin' game here, bro?"

"*Have we met?*"

"Man, just fuck off."

"If I agree to fuck off will you tell me where the food is?"

The man scowled and said, "Ask Sal where the food is. Go ahead. He's right there."

He nodded toward the bonfire. A skinny guy with a bandage covering one eye said, "Let it go, man. Walk away." He said it to *me*.

"Why am I the one who has to walk away? Maybe I wanna enjoy the fire?"

Four-balls stepped toward me and said, "Dude, you got five seconds to walk away or else you're goin' in there with Sal. I don't give a shit what anybody says."

"Wait, do you have me confused with someone else?"

"Whoa, whoa!" from behind me. It was the black guy from the window. Green suit. "Easy, man. Easy. Dude just got outta the hole."

Four-balls said, "I don't give a shit."

Black guy grabbed my sleeve and pulled me away, saying, "Let's go inside, it's cold out here."

I went with him, and realized he hadn't come alone. Four more green suits were with him. What, were we on teams? What the hell was this? Had I stepped into some weird alternate dimension? Again?

"Man, we didn't think you were comin' back," he said. "This is just in time, too. We got the warning buzz about forty-five minutes ago so truck gonna be here any time."

I said, "I didn't understand one word of that."

Just short of the front door he stopped, leaned into my ear and screamed, "WE GOT THE WARNING BUZZ FORTY-FIVE MINUTES AGO SO THE—"

"My hearing is *fine*. I don't know who you are. I've lost time, I have no memory of all this. Last thing I remember everything was going to shit out there, out in the town. Then I woke up in the basement of the old creepy-ass TB asylum down the street. In the 'hole,' is that what you called it?"

The black guy rubbed his head and said, "Shit. You get knocked over the head or somethin'?"

"No, they said it was a side effect of whatever they did to me over there."

He let out a breath, glanced around nervously and pulled me inside the hospital. The place was absolutely trashed. Once upon a time, there had been a huge oval-shaped desk right inside the doors where you could check in with a row of secretaries who'd log you into their computers and put a band on your wrist, filtering out the people who didn't have insurance. Now there were just ragged splinters and deep gouges in the tile where the desk had been roughly ripped from the floor.

The black guy said, "Firewood. See, their plan is to take the easy stuff first—stuff close to the door—and burn it. That way, when we're all more tired and sick a month from now, the only wood left will be the shit that's hard to get to on the tenth floor. Makes good sense if you're a fuckin' idiot."

"How long? Tell me. How long since the outbreak happened?"

"'Bout nine days. You don't remember nothin'?"

"Holy shit, we trashed the hospital this bad in nine days?"

"Oh, no, man, the CDC had staff here keepin' things in order for the first few. Then they bailed out. We done all this since Wednesday. This is Sunday."

"And no, to answer your question, I don't remember anything after showing up here. I don't even know your name."

"Name's TJ. I knew John before all this. You and I met once at a party but you probably don't remember that for a different reason."

"Wait, is John here? The guy said—"

"No, man. We got a lot to talk about. Let's get up to my room, come on."

He led me to a stairwell that was pitch dark and, despite everything that had transpired, still smelled like hospital—old food, chemicals, death. I'm going to get rich one of these days selling a hospital disinfectant that doesn't stink of despair.

We emerged into a fifth-floor hallway and there wasn't anybody there who wasn't in a green jumpsuit. TJ announced, "Look who's back!" A chubby black guy who looked like he'd been dozing in a wheelchair said, "Spider-Man! You escape or they let you out?"

Before I could answer, TJ said, "Let him out, dumped him off in the truck just now. He's still groggy from when they sedated him." To me, TJ said, "You hungry? They feed you?"

"If you got food, I'll eat it."

"Then follow me." He continued down the hall. I got the feeling he was trying to pull me away from a conversation with Wheelchair Guy. From behind us he said, "Gonna need him out in the yard in about ten minutes. Buzzer sounded a while ago."

TJ said, "We heard it. We'll be there."

We reached the last door at the end of the hall. Two hospital beds, some cardboard boxes on the floor that looked to be full of Ramen noodles, energy bars and bottles of water. In the opposite corner there were a dozen plain white plastic jugs, looked like old Clorox bleach bottles with the labels ripped off. Something was written on them in Sharpie but I couldn't read it.

"David! Yay!"

That came from one of the beds where a white girl with dreadlocks, thick-rimmed glasses and a pierced nose was turning a sheet of paper into origami. She was wearing a necklace that it took me a moment to realize she had made by stringing line through a half dozen of those red plastic caps from syringes. She gave me a smile that I thought would make cartoon songbirds come land on all of our shoulders.

TJ hurriedly closed the door behind me and said, "Got a complication here, babe."

Dreadlocks Girl got a crestfallen look and said, "Oh, no. Please tell me—"

"No, no, it's not that. He can't remember anything."

TJ looked at me and said, "Right?"

"Yeah."

"You recognize her?"

"I'm sorry, no."

Dreadlocks said, "Like amnesia? He doesn't remember his own name or anything?"

"No, I remember everything until, uh, this. All this started. National Guard coming in and all that. I remember getting grabbed by some dudes and then I woke up in the dungeon. A little while ago."

"You don't know what they did to you? Over there?"

"Nope. Sorry."

She said, "I'm Hope, by the way." To TJ she said, "Maybe it'll all come back to him?"

TJ shrugged and went to the window. The same busted-out window he had yelled from when I first showed up on the yard.

I said, "If you don't mind replaying conversations I'm sure we've had already, can I ask what the hell is going on in general?"

TJ said, "Well, we're in quarantine, and beyond that we don't know shit. This hospital was full of CDC in biohazard suits for the first few days, they had all of us confined to rooms with guards in the halls. But then some of the guards got infected and that turned ugly. Screams from the halls. You look out there, those aren't coffee stains on the tile. Then that was it, they bailed out. All the staff. Some of them got evacuated—you could hear helicopters on the roof—some they just left here, now they inmates like us. Some got taken across the way, where you just were. They just left the hospital to us."

I joined TJ at the window and scanned the fences at the edge of the yard, trying to see what was behind them. I saw the tops of some white tents, but not much else. We weren't high enough to see much into the distance.

I said, "So, what, the CDC just retreated over to the other building?"

"CDC gone, man. They left, these other people swept in. REPER. National Guard gone, too, they pulled out to the perimeter around the city. Left my ass behind."

I said, "Wait, you're the TJ John mentioned? You were on the scene the day it all started."

"Yes, sir. National Guard. Deemed an infection risk. Some REPER motherfucker thanked me for my service, took my rifle and sidearm and left me on the wrong side of the fence. There's more than a dozen of us in here. Least there was anyway. The first bunch of us on the scene didn't have Level C suits or nothin'. Clusterfuck."

From behind me Hope said, "Here" and handed me a crunchy granola bar, a little bag of peanuts and a "fun size" Snickers bar.

"There's no hot water left from lunch or else I'd have made you some Ramen. Coffee's gone, too. Didn't last long. There's bottled water on the floor there."

TJ looked appalled and said, "Damn, girl. He gets the last Snickers? Almost had to wrestle a dude for that." To me he said, "Don't talk to nobody too much, all right? As you can probably tell from Owen down there—that was the dudebro with the big-ass hair and neck—things are kinda tense. Tell people you're tired or you got that stomach flu or that you got a migraine. But I wouldn't let it slip about the memory thing. No need for a complication. They all still need you out there, red and green both, so let's not upset that balance until we got to. You're our Spider-Man, and we don't got a backup."

"Okay why does everybody call me—"

A buzzer sounded, an angry noise like the expiring shot clock in a basketball game.

TJ said, "Showtime. You can eat that on the way down. Just follow my lead. Don't say more than you have to."

He picked up two of the bleach bottles from the corner and hurried out the door.

———

There were half a dozen of us clomping down the stairs by the time we reached the bottom. I had been shocked when Wheelchair Guy got up from his chair to follow us, for some reason it never having occurred to me that he was just using the chair as a chair and in fact had no disability. In the stairwell, Wheelchair said, "Owen been tellin' people that he was gonna cure the whole next batch. Sayin' it ain't worth the risk."

TJ said, "Well we gonna have to talk to Owen. But it don't matter now, we got Spider-Man back. He hasn't failed yet. You're not goin' to, right, Spidey?"

I started to answer but he cut me off with, "You do this, we'll get you some rest. You probably just dehydrated is all."

Out through the lobby and back into the yard. Everybody out there was standing and staring. Not at me, but at the fence, at the gate I had just come through.

Man, there's no guard tower or anything. What would they do if we just tried to run? Just charge that gate when they open it . . .

Nobody spoke. I could hear the bonfire crackling. Somebody had thrown some more fuel on it since last time, piling the scraps into a pyramid shape to create that jet engine afterburner effect, for when you wanted your bonfire really, really hot. If there were soldiers on the other side of that fence, they weren't chatting or shouting instructions or doing anything else. I couldn't even hear idling engines. It really did feel like we were alone and I couldn't shake the idea that we could just walk out. Maybe everybody with guns fell back and figured they would stop the outbreak at city limits. So why not break out of here?

And what makes you think the "infection" stopped at city limits, hmmm? Last time you saw these guys in action they didn't exactly have shit under control.

There was a faded white line painted into the lawn, forming an arc around the gate like an NBA three-point line. No one crossed it. No one got within twenty feet of it. I opened my Snickers and shoved the whole thing into my mouth. I dragged my peanuts from my pocket—they had an American Airlines logo on the bag—and sat down on the grass.

TJ roughly grabbed my elbow and yanked me to my feet.

"Do not fuckin' do that," he hissed. "Shit, man, you forgot everything."

I started to ask him if those two flimsy fences were really the only thing between us and freedom, but he shushed me. He leaned into my ear and whispered, "Listen, man. Buzzer sounds an hour before new arrivals. Buzzer means nobody gets within 'run for it' distance of the gate. It goes off again right before it opens, as a final warning. In a few seconds, truck gonna come through there. It's gonna be full of new inmates, people they rounded up off the streets because they might be infected. They get processed over at the asylum and run over here. Then you gonna look at 'em and make sure they're clean. Right?"

"And how exactly am I gonna—"

But I didn't need to finish that sentence.

Check them for spiders.

Because I can see the spiders.

I'm the Spider-Man.

I glanced down at the two white jugs TJ had set at his feet. I found Hope standing behind me. She was chewing on her thumbnail. Nervous. Everybody was nervous. The air hummed with it. The fence closest to me displayed a picture of a woman's lower body wearing only underwear, a pink slogan saying VICTORIA'S SECRET CHRISTMAS PANTY BLOWOUT.

There were some faint clicks and clanks in the distance—having heard it before, I knew it was the outer gate sliding open. Beyond the plastic sheeting of the inner fence, a military cargo truck rumbled in. We heard truck doors open and shut. Engine. Exterior gate again. Silence.

The shot-clock buzzer sounded once more, and the inner gate finally rattled open on its own. Laying on the grass, in the exact spot where I had been minutes ago, were four people. All of them young, looking to be college age. Three guys, one girl. The three guys were in green suits, the girl in red. Their hands were bound behind them.

"Goddamnit," muttered Wheelchair Guy from somewhere behind me. "Wish they wouldn't lay them on the ground like that. Those dudes are gonna get a shock one of these days when Carlos comes up for a snack."

I swear that every other sentence somebody uttered in this place sounded like a foreign language. It was starting to piss me off.

The four new citizens of the Undisclosed Spider Quarantine stumbled awkwardly to their feet and shuffled into the yard. The split second the last one was through, the gate slid shut on its own. The mechanism was fast—I'd say two full seconds from fully open to locked.

The huge blond-haired guy—Owen, TJ had said his name was—shouted to them, "Welcome to quarantine. Please listen carefully to what I am about to say, and don't talk until I'm finished. This will save you a lot of questions later."

His voice echoed through the yard, huge lungs making the words split the air like a rifle shot in the woods.

"As you can see, there ain't no guards here. There ain't no feds, there ain't no soldiers. They ran out on us several days ago. And that's just fine with us. We have food and water and medical supplies, you are welcome to whatever you need. That's the good news. Bad news is there ain't no mail. There ain't no phones, there ain't no Internet, there ain't no televisions or radio. What we've got, don't get a signal. We are *cut off*."

Owen paused, to let that sink in.

"Also, there's no power. Maybe it'll come back and maybe it won't. We've been getting by without it and we will continue to get by, until somebody gets their shit together and comes and lets us out of this prison. Okay, so now that you're caught up on all that, let me get to the important part. There's a little more than three hundred of us in here. And not a one of us you see here is infected."

Pause again. He made eye contact with each of the four, individually.

I thought Tennet said five hundred . . .

"Yeah. That's right. Only reason we're still stuck here is because even after nine days, the feds ain't come up with a test that works. So they're guessin'. And I'm gonna bet that none of you are infected, neither. So here's how we do it. We got an expert here, who can spot infection on sight. He's gonna look you over, and once you've got a clean bill of health, we'll cut off those handcuffs, take you indoors and get you set up with a room and some blankets and whatever else you need. Sound good?"

Nobody answered.

Owen looked at me. The new kids looked at me. Everyone else looked at me. I was not breathing.

TJ said, "Do it, and then it'll be done."

He walked me up to the first guy, a geeky-looking kid with acne cheeks. He was squinting because he had apparently lost a pair of glasses at some point. TJ said, in a voice that suddenly reminded me he had spent some years in the military, "I'm going to need you to open your mouth for me, sir."

The kid's eyes darted around, looking for someone to rescue him from all this.

Man, chill out. I just need to check to see if a mind-controlling spider monster has possessed your head.

He opened his mouth. Looked like a regular human mouth. Lots of cavities in his back teeth.

I said, "He's fine."

The kid closed his mouth and his eyes at the same time. Relief rolling off him like a boulder. All at once it hit me that I was the most powerful man in the quarantine.

TJ said, "What's your name, sir?".

"Tim," said the geeky kid.

"Welcome to quarantine, Tim. We're glad to have you." TJ spun him around and pulled out a pair of wire cutters. He snipped the plastic bands that served as handcuffs and the kid immediately rubbed the deep red marks on his wrists.

I moved to the next kid. Tall, square jaw. Probably played high school or college basketball. Without me asking, he opened his mouth and moved his tongue around, making sure I could see everything. Confident. Here was a guy who'd never failed a test in his life, mental or physical. Probably be a senator someday. Perfect teeth.

I said, "Yeah, he's fine."

This one said, "Kevin" as TJ snipped off his cuffs. "Kevin Ross. And I can climb that fence in about ten seconds if we can get something draped up over that razor wire. Rip up some carpet from in there, something like that."

TJ said, "Yeah, that thought was thought before. Didn't work out so well."

Two people left now, the girl and a kid with curly hair who reminded me of Jonah Hill's character in *Superbad*.

The girl was next. She was a hippie. I could tell, even dressed in a red prisoner jumpsuit. She had some haphazard braids in her hair, and that dopey trusting look in her eyes, like she was seeing the goodness of your soul at a glance.

She gave me what I can only describe as a tragic smile and in a shaky voice said, "Hi. What's your name?"

"David. Just open your mouth for me, okay?"

"I feel like I'm going to be sick, David."

"I'll stand off to the side, then. This'll only take a second."

She smiled again. A tear ran down her cheek.

I said, "Come on, open up."

She did. She was a smoker, apparently, the front teeth had some yellow. Not a single cavity, though. Good for her.

She was fully crying now.

I said, "It's fine, it looks fine. You can calm down, okay? We'll all get through this." I put a hand on her arm. Look at me, acting all in charge and professional.

Don't worry! I'm the expert!

She whispered something between sobs that I couldn't make out.

"What was that?"

"Check again."

"I can if you want but—"

"Because a week ago I had a pierced tongue, with a stud in it." She squeezed her eyes and sobbed, trying to suck in breaths to get the words out. "And now I don't."

"What? I don't under—"

But I did understand.

She woke up one morning, and realized her mouth was not her own.

Oh Jesus no no no.

She held her mouth open, extra wide this time. I didn't want to look. But I couldn't help it. And, of course, I saw it. Between her lower front teeth and her lower lip, two black mandibles rested there.

I recoiled in horror, and everybody nearby reacted with me.

Owen was already on the move, striding toward the girl from behind, with purpose. She went down to her knees, weeping.

TJ got in front of me, pushing me back away from her. I said, "Okay, okay. You, uh, you said you got a cure, right? We've got a procedure here?"

TJ said, "Cover your ears, man." He was cramming something into his ears, it looked like cotton balls. The people around me were covering their ears with their hands.

"But why are—"

Owen stepped up behind the girl, pulled an automatic pistol from his waistband, and splattered her brains all over the grass in front of her.

Her body flopped to the ground. The other three new arrivals flew into a panic.

I had thought everyone was covering their ears for the gunshot, but then the piercing shriek started, the cry of the spider creature. I wedged my fingers into my eardrums as hard as I could. I could still feel it vibrating my bones.

They worked fast. Owen—who I noticed had cigarette butts wedged into his ears—flipped the girl over. I could see the spider trying to detach and crawl out of her skull now, growing out of the girl's mouth like a huge, grotesque black tongue. TJ uncapped both jugs, then carefully poured the contents of one jug into the other. Mixing something. After a moment, steam or smoke emerged from the opening of this new concoction. Owen stepped back and TJ poured the entire contents of the jug into the girl's mouth.

The shriek was cranked up to a level that sent a tremor through my guts. The spider thrashed. The girl's cheeks and lips dissolved under the acid, the liquid running out of ragged holes in her skin. The spider was dissolving, too, legs falling off as it thrashed.

Eventually, its horrific cries died down, and it was still.

Owen stuffed the pistol into his pants and grabbed the girl's feet. He said, "Come on, before Carlos comes calling."

The one I'd been calling Wheelchair Guy shouldered past me and grabbed the girl's wrists. They dragged her toward the now-roaring bonfire. On the count of three they tossed her corpse right into the blaze, sending an explosion of sparks heavenward. The flames tore into her flesh and I smelled what I had mistaken for smoked barbecue ribs just minutes ago.

Then, finally, I saw.

Bones.

In the bonfire. Bones and bones and bones. It was full of them. Blackened skulls and ribs and pelvic bones and straight leg and arm bones jutting out like sticks. Hundreds and hundreds of bones.

The girl's hair was burning. Her jumpsuit was peeling off of her in black strips, like the skin on a hot dog roasted over a campfire. I was *just* talking to her.

I will remember that smell for the rest of my life. I will never eat meat again.

Owen said to me, "Get over it, bro. You got one more."

"No. *No.* That . . . *cannot* be the only way to do this."

Owen growled, "Bull *shit*. You didn't have no problem when it was Sal you were callin' out. Now you lose your fuckin' nerve?"

"Man, I don't remember—okay, look, that was then. That . . . that's the past and it doesn't matter now. I can't do *that* anymore. I'm sorry."

There was a commotion behind me and TJ shouted, "Hey! Stop! Don't!"

He was shouting at Kevin, the basketball player kid. He was sprinting toward the fence. The kid leaped, landing halfway up the fence with his fingers hooked in the links. He scrambled up toward the razor wire—

He fell. He hit the ground like a crash-test dummy. Limp, dead weight. A pool of blood spread below his face. A chunk of his skull was missing.

I never heard the shot that took him out. I whipped my head around, looking for the gunman. I saw no one. In the sky were just some birds, gliding along with wings outstretched, riding the thermals, circling lazily overhead. Maybe they were buzzards, hearing the sounds of death like a goddamned dinner bell.

TJ said, "Stupid motherfucker. What, he thinks we're all here because none of us know how to climb fences? Shit, I could have gave him an extension ladder, got one in the maintenance room."

The Jonah Hill–looking kid was paralyzed with fear. His hands were still bound behind him. His eyes were wide, his lips were white, his mouth clamped so tight it was pressing the blood out of them. Owen walked up behind him and put the pistol to the back of his skull.

"You check him, or else we cure him right now. Him and everybody else who comes through that gate. Fuckin' Carlos runnin' around here, that's bad enough. Now multiply him by three, or six, or a dozen. The feds will come into this place a month from now and find nothin' but chunks of meat and bones and crawlin' nightmares. Well I got a wife I'm gonna get home to. I got a kid I'm gonna get home to. The feds left us in here. Left us to get torn to pieces. We're all we got. But when that gate finally opens and they give the all-clear, I'm walkin' outta here. As a man. Help me, or don't. It's up to you."

To the kid I said, "Open your goddamned mouth or he's gonna shoot you in the head."

The kid obeyed. I pulled at his lower lip, then his upper. The kid had braces. I saw nothing else.

"He's fine."

Owen said, "You sure about that, now?"

"Yeah."

Owen stashed the pistol and used a pocketknife to cut the kid's hands free.

"What's your name, kid?"

"Corey. I think I'm gonna pass out."

Owen grabbed a toppled wheelchair and sat it upright. "Sit down before you fall down."

Corey did, putting his head in his hands, trying to wake up from what he surely thought was a terrible dream. Owen, TJ and Bruce the Wheelchair Guy went to go get the basketball player's body away from the fence and presumably onto the fire. More bones for the pile.

From behind me I heard a warbly voice say, "This isn't right. How can they allow this? Where's the government? Where's the army? Where's the police?"

That was that first kid I'd checked, Tim, the geeky one. Without turning to face him I said, "I think we're on our own, man."

The men were dragging the basketball kid's body toward the fire. I couldn't watch this again. I turned to face Tim, who was sitting on the ground, cross-legged.

"Hey, I don't think you're supposed to sit on the grass. They get mad."

"Why?"

"It . . . upsets Carlos apparently."

"Who's Carlos?"

"I dunno. The groundskeeper? I kind of just got here myself."

I could feel something, a rumble at my feet. Faint, like somebody using a jackhammer nearby, or thumping bass-heavy music. But there was no sound, just the tremor in the earth. Then, people were running and shouting. TJ was sprinting toward us and waving his arms.

"Get up! Get off the ground!"

That finally convinced Tim, who unfolded his legs so he could get up—

His face froze, in an expression of confused shock. His jaw flexed, his mouth working to form silent words. His eyes met mine and I had the thought that this is what people look like when they're suddenly stabbed from behind in an alley.

"Hey are you—"

He howled in pain. He pushed himself off the ground but he looked like his butt had been glued there. He screamed again, a garbled and halting sound, as if it was coming through a microphone that kept cutting out.

Summoning the thrashing, animal strength of a fox ripping off its own leg to get out of a trap, Tim got his feet underneath him and pushed his body up off of the ground with everything he had. He rose a foot off the grass, and in a brief moment I could see that something was still tethering him there. It looked like he was shitting spaghetti. A bundle of thin, writhing tentacles, turning and curling and spinning. Working their way up into his bowels from below, like a puppeteer.

Tim sat hard back on the ground. He screamed one last time, then spasmed into a seizure that mangled the scream into a spastic *UCK-UCK-UCK* chant. His eyes rolled back into his head. Sprays of blood erupted from his mouth. I thought I saw one of the thin, yellow spaghetti tentacles flick up between his teeth. Tim's body thrashed once, twice, three times. There was a huge, wet slurping sound, and then he slumped over sideways.

When he did, he left behind a wad of guts the size of a potato sack. The yellow tentacles reached up and dragged the pink pile under the dirt, leaving behind nothing but a gopher hole in the ground, soaked in blood.

An out-of-breath Wheelchair Guy stopped behind TJ and said, "Fuckin' Carlos, man. Told ya we shoulda killed him when we had the chance."

TJ, seeming amazingly calm—

—*because he's seen this several times before oh goddamn oh holy shit*—

—sighed and said, "Well. We didn't know then what we know now, did we? What's important is that we do know it now. And that we follow procedure."

He stared at me. "Right, Spider-Man?"

I didn't answer.

Owen stomped up behind them and jabbed his finger at me.

"He didn't spot the girl. You notice that? Far as I'm concerned, that's the last I want to hear about his so-called one hundred percent hit rate, bro."

"Told you, he's still groggy from bein' in the hole."

"Yeah, and about that. What went on over there? We don't know, do we? That may not even be the same fuckin' guy. He looks like he don't even know who he is."

TJ rebutted, "Yeah, and that girl was wearin' red. Or did you not notice that, Owen? That's three reds in a row. That's easily three out of every four infected that was in a red jumpsuit when they burned. What does that tell you?"

"You want to have a talk about that, TJ? We'll convene a panel. You, me and my Beretta nine millimeter. How about that?"

"*Fuck* you, man."

I love the way black guys say "*Fuck* you." Emphasizing the first syllable hard, like a verbal punch. I wondered if they practiced it in front of a mirror. TJ and Owen stared each other down for a minute, then TJ turned his attention to the curly haired kid. Corey.

"Come on, let's go inside. It's gonna stink real bad once all three bodies get to burnin'. Oh, and welcome to quarantine."

Everybody headed upstairs. TJ said, "You should get off at the second floor and see the doc. He's been askin' about you, let him see about your memory and all that."

Fuck that. I wasn't heading for the second floor, or the fifth. I was heading to the roof.

I had to get out of this goddamned madhouse. I wanted to get up there, to look out, to see what exactly was holding us in. TJ followed me, trying to tell me that we had done all this before, and that I myself had declared that there was nothing to see. He did not seem surprised when, after hearing this, I still insisted on going up.

Five minutes later we were ten stories up, standing among the silent air-conditioning units and the bird shit, looking out over the red and green figures loitering in the yard below. The wind picked up, garbage blowing around with it, fluttering paper plates and food wrappers. The trash was starting to pile up against the western fence like a snowdrift. And among all this, the inmates, clumps of red and clumps of green, huddled in conversation. It looked like the world's shittiest Christmas pageant. It had been a mild (uh, mid-November?) day but up here, on the cusp of evening, it was goddamned freezing. I didn't care. I paced from one ledge to the other, scanning the landscape. The pulsing grip of a panic attack was slowly squeezing around my brain.

Past Dave was right—there was nothing to see. A fence, another fence, and then the town. There were a few white tents set up outside the gate, but there were no guards walking along the fence with rifles, nothing.

That's not enough. That's not enough to fucking keep me in here. Why am I still here? Jesus the smell of that girl's burning hair . . .

I asked TJ, "Where are the shooters?"

"The what?"

"The guns, man. The snipers or whatever who shot that kid. They didn't shoot from the asylum, it's too far away."

I stared off toward the asylum, the big, depressing mossy gray brick box sitting nestled among some trees next to a smaller identical box, as if they had a bunch of those bricks left over from the main building but not enough to build another whole one. No sign of men with rifles on the roof over there. Or anyone, really.

TJ pointed to the sky.

I followed his finger, to where the birds circled lazily overhead. I shrugged. "What am I supposed to be seeing?"

"Man, talkin' to you . . ." He smiled and shook his head. "Like you a time traveler. No, wait, it's more like you're a caveman they just un-froze. 'What is this strange devilry, future man?'"

He pointed up again.

"Sniper drone. Three-three-eight-caliber rifle mounted under an Unmanned Aerial Vehicle. Computer-assist targeting, can put an anti-personnel round into your brain from a thousand yards out. Did assassinations in Afghanistan, a lot neater than the Hellfire missiles that'd take out the Tango and the entire kid's birthday party the Tango was attendin' at the time."

I looked up at a pair of tiny black crosses drifting below the clouds. I liked it better when I thought they were vultures. He continued, "Not that it don't have the missiles, too. Them drones, they look tiny up in the sky but on the ground they're pretty big, almost as big as a real plane, and those Hellfires it's got under the wings, if we stood one up here it'd be almost as tall as you. If things got outta control down here, drone could launch one down into the yard and take out thirty of us in one shot."

" 'Unmanned'? So this place is being patrolled by robots?"

"No, no. Remote control. Somewhere there's a dude sittin' at a console, cup of coffee on his right, jelly donut to his left, and on his screen is a black-and-white shot of this hospital turnin' around and around real slow. He can go to infrared at night. Switch to thermal in case there's too much fog or if we get clever and try to create a smoke screen for cover. Maybe he's lookin' at us right now. Wave to him. But don't make any threatening moves, man can zoom in so that your head will fill his screen. Gun barrel is stabilized by computer, automatically compensates for vibration, wind speed, everything."

"Okay, okay." I ran my hands through my hair, thinking. "Okay, so, the operator is down there in one of those tents? Like, uh, if we could get somebody over there and beat the shit out of him . . ."

"No, no, we been over all this before. Drone operations is several states away, in Nevada, believe it or not. The 17th Reconnaissance Squadron. Creech Air Force Base, just outside of Vegas. And even though it's eighteen hundred miles or so from here, he hits his little red 'fire' button, the command reaches the drone point-seven-five seconds later."

"*Fuck.*" I bent over at the waist.

Breathe. Just breathe.

"I know, right? Weird to think that all the taxes you and me ever paid wouldn't even replace a broken wing on that shit. Just try to calm down, alright?"

"Okay, so there's two of 'em up there?"

He nodded. "I'd say one's a spotter, probably set to scan the whole grounds at once, the other's got the guns—"

"Okay, so how about we—"

"And before you ask, no, we can't all rush the walls at different spots at once to give 'em too many targets to hit. They got ground-based hardware outside the fence, unmanned units called Gladiators. Just look like little Jeeps only with no place for a driver to sit, guns mounted on the back. Between them they got sensors in the ground that detect vibration, they got motion detectors, body heat sensors, lasers, all that shit. Anything bigger than a bunny rabbit tries to sneak through, somethin' bad will happen to it. And no, we don't have any way of tunneling out. Even if we had equipment—which we don't—and the means to do the work without the UAVs noticin'—which we also don't—where do we tunnel to? We got no intel about the situation out there, other than the fact that the damned REPER command center is right over there. I mean I know the geography and you probably do, too, but even if we could find an exit spot with nice, soft dirt, one that's secluded, and not too far away, how do you know you don't pop up right into a patrol? Six weeks of diggin', wasted."

"There's that word again. REPER. You ever hear of that in your life before this week?"

He shook his head. "Nope. But when shit went bad last week and the CDC pulled out their people, this REPER took their place. You see the gear on those guys? Hazmat suits tricked out with Kevlar, modified M4s with targeting HUDs in their damned faceplates. You think they came up with that gear overnight? Shit, each of those suits probably cost half a million bucks. That's specialized equipment, and all these dudes know exactly what they're doin'. They sweep in and suddenly they're in charge. They're ordering around us National Guard like we answer to them, and nobody says shit otherwise. They tell me to stay behind and I'm like, bullshit, I'm gettin' on that chopper. But guess what? Here I am. Never seen anything like this."

I walked back across the roof, to look out at the rear of the building and the little strip of woods that from up here looked like the end product of a Brazillian bikini wax. Smoke rose in the distance, maybe somebody else's house on fire. I heard no sirens.

TJ followed me and said, "You know, this conversation is a lot more discouraging the second time 'round."

I said, "But there's nobody *here*. That's what I can't get over. The whole operation on this side looks like it's staffed by like two people. So what, it's all just the drones and sensors and shit?"

"Well, yeah, they tryin' to keep down the infection risk. They don't need people like me swellin' the ranks of the infected. And if you ask me, the automated shit seems like it's workin' just fine. You saw that kid try to climb the fence."

From behind us a female voice said, "You should write down everything he said up to now, so he doesn't have to do it all again if your brains get scrambled next week."

Hope had joined us on the roof.

I said, "I just don't accept that there's no way out of this place. I mean it wasn't built as a prison, right? It was built as a hospital. No way they've covered everything."

Hope laughed, and to TJ she said, "It's so funny to see him go through the five stages again."

I said, "The what?"

TJ explained, "It's the same for everybody they dump in here. First it's the confusion, right? 'What's happening, where am I?' That's stage one. But then you go to stage two: pissed off. 'How can they do this to us, man? I got rights.' Okay, then there's stage three. Defiance. 'I gotta get outta here, there's gotta be a way out.' Stage four is the depression. 'Why me, man? Boohoo. I wanna go home, I wanna see my girl.' Then hopefully you land at stage five, which is, 'we got to make the best of this situation, and be smart.'"

"I really made it all the way to stage five before?"

Hope said, "Oh, no. You stopped somewhere between stage two and three."

12 Hours Until the Massacre at Ffirth Asylum

John's head was pounding.

He tried to call Amy back, but she was ignoring him. He had a sick feeling that began around his navel and extended all the way up to his scalp. No doubt that was partly due to the huge egg breakfast he had eaten at sunrise to help absorb some of the vodka and Crown Royal he had flushed through his system, but the feeling was mostly due to the fact that he had clearly hit one of his patented Rough Stretches. Those bits of his life where every string of shitty luck converged into one horrible knot that everybody blamed him for. As if he had chosen things to work out this way. *No, Amy, I did not just decide to bring about the apocalypse this month.*

Times like this, you just gotta disconnect from the world and ride it out. It was a process he and Dave had, the two of them rarely hitting low points at the same time, one always there to cheer the other up and to pull them off the sofa to go hit the "town" (Dave always made air quotes around "town" when referring to Undisclosed, since the party train only ran through two bars and Munch's trailer.)

John glanced around, half expecting to see a disheveled Dave pulling himself up from some spot on the floor. He'd be squinting, his hair matted down, looking like he'd just been shit out of a dinosaur. He wasn't there, of course, and wouldn't ever be there again. John immediately wanted to go back to sleep on the floor.

Wait. Whose floor? Where the hell was he? John had told Amy on the phone that he was back at the motel, but that was because he didn't want to admit that he didn't actually know. He was in somebody's basement. There was a full bar down here. Maybe a frat house? He was close to campus, he knew that. The last thing he remembered was coming down here and watching round-the-clock apocalypse coverage on their sixty-inch TV, then someone introduced him to the modern wonder that was the Irish Car Bomb (Guinness, Baileys, and Jameson) and the next thing he knew, his cell phone was shooting noise bullets into his temple and the clock said afternoon. John surveyed the floor around him and saw a lot of tall black guys. He had gotten drunk with the basketball team, apparently.

John stumbled to his feet and spent a few minutes looking for his shoes. He never found them, so he figured he would just trade with one of the guys there. He put on a pair of Nikes he found by the door that were downright huge—seemed to be size 18 or so. They looked newer than his own but he figured he could catch up with the guy later to see if he wanted to trade back. Some people like shoes that are a little more broken in . . .

John realized he was staring at the wall and that some time had passed without him realizing it. Brain was still trying to boot up, loading all of the extra shit into the task bar. Finally he made himself get up and head out. Amy was going to do something rash if he wasn't there to calm her down. He hit the cold air and found the Bronco parked haphazardly across the lawn. John cursed when he saw some jackass had spray painted ZOMBIE ASSAULT VEHICLE on the door, but then recognized it as his own handwriting.

He pulled out and saw the dorm tower looming ahead. He actually wasn't more than five or six blocks away from Amy's bus stop at the Mexican place. Awesome. He let the Bronco idle for a bit so the heater would have time to warm up.

John found the bus stop easily enough, but instead of a bus, pulled up to it were four windowless, black vans. Yellow tape roped off the whole sidewalk and the parking lot beyond. Guys in black space suits were prowling everywhere.

Amy was nowhere in sight.

John stopped right in the middle of the street, threw open the door off the Bronco and ran to the first van. He yanked open the back door.

"AMY! HEY!"

Nobody there. He ran to the second one. Before he could get it open, two of the space suit guys grabbed him.

"Sir! Sir! You are risking contamination by—"

"AAAMYYY!"

The men dragged John away from the vans and wrestled him to the sidewalk. John got a good look at what they were wearing and it was fuck-ing *terrifying*. The glass on their helmets was tinted so that when light hit it, it glinted blood red. They had armor and machine guns and wires and shit running around like they were on the way to fight a war on Mars.

A third space suit guy came up to them and said, "What, is he family?"

John said, "Yes! I'm Amy Sullivan's . . . dad."

"Sir, do you know—"

"Listen! I'm infected! Take me and let her go! The infection, I got it all over. Look at my enormous inhuman feet!"

The guy said to his coworkers, "Okay, see if you can get ID and let him ride with Otto."

For the second time in nine days, John's hands were bound with the heavy-duty zip tie handcuffs. He was stuffed into the third van, but Amy wasn't in there, either. Twenty minutes later it jolted to a start, and he knew that he and Amy would be in Undisclosed in a little over two hours. He had that much time to think up a plan.

45 MINUTES EARLIER . . .

Forty-five minutes before John would get hauled away in a van . . .

Amy sat and waited at the bus stop bench for the government to get there, watching as four more people with gun cases and army satchels strolled by. Were they like a militia or something? The sight of these regular people wandering around with all that hardware scared her more than the zombie thing. If everything fell apart and civilization came down to this, to guns and people fighting over food and medicine, what would she do? She wasn't strong. She didn't have strong friends. She didn't have a family. The closest she had was David, and what if he was hurt or—

"Excuse me, what's your name?"

Amy looked up, expecting to see a guy in a jumpsuit and gas mask or something. Instead it was a hipster-looking guy with a beard and glasses and wearing a black peacoat.

"Amy."

"Hi. My name's Josh, and we keep running into each other. We sat across from each other on the bus on Z Day. Remember? Then I come back and it turns out you live on the floor below me."

Amy remembered him now, but wouldn't if he hadn't brought it up. He was a nice-looking guy but he also looked exactly like seven hundred other guys on campus. Same build, same beard, same glasses.

Z Day?

"Oh, yeah. I remember."

"Did you lose someone in [Undisclosed]?"

"My boyfriend is there."

"Me, too. Not my boyfriend. I'm not gay. My brother, my nephew and one of my best friends. That's three different people obviously. Are you here for the meeting?"

"Oh, no. I'm just waiting for a ride." She realized in that moment the strap Josh had draped over his shoulder was not a backpack, but a rifle case. "Wait, is this the gun meeting everybody's going to? Because I left all my guns at home."

"You should come anyway." From an inside pocket he pulled out a sheet of paper, and she didn't need to read the details. She recognized the huge letter Z the moment he unfolded it. "When your ride gets here, bring them, too."

"Oh, I don't think they'll want to come. The CDC or whoever is coming to pick me up to take me to quarantine."

Alarmed, Josh said, "Excuse me?"

"Yep, I've wasted a week here and finally I said, screw it. If that's where David is, that's where I want to be. I told them to come get me."

Josh looked nervously down the street in both directions, then said, "Amy, listen. You need to come with me. Give me ten minutes to explain what's going on. If after that you don't think I'm right about this, I'll bring you back here. Hell, we'll drive you down to the checkpoint ourselves. But you don't have all of the information and I'm telling you right now, if you go with whoever shows up here, you will never see your boyfriend again."

Another nervous scan of the street.

"Come on. I'll explain everything once we're off the sidewalk."

Amy sighed and pushed the hair out of her eyes. "So, so many kidnappings begin this way."

"We're going right down there, to the Powder Keg. It'll be packed with people. It's full of rednecks with assault rifles and shotguns, if anyone tries to put a hand on you, they'll be perforated. Come on. There's no time."

He put a hand under her armpit.

"Up."

She went with him. They hurried along the sidewalk, Josh with his hand flat on her back pushing her along and ducking down like they were dodging machine gun fire.

———

The Powder Keg was a gun store/shooting range and not, as Amy had thought, a gay nightclub (this wasn't a snide private joke, it would be days later before she would remember that the nightclub she was thinking of was called the Bomb Shelter). The place was absolutely packed, and the crowd was armed to the teeth. In any other country on earth, this kind of gathering would be cause for an all-out military response.

Josh pushed her through the door and into a crowd. He stopped to tell two burly shotgun-bearing men, "REPER is looking for her. If they show up at the door, tell them we've never seen her."

Amy thought, *Did he say Reavers? Like on* Firefly?

Josh pushed inside, pulling Amy through the crowd behind him to the front of the room, Amy still carrying her bag of pharmacy stuff and her stupid pillow.

He reached a spot where a white bedsheet was hanging in front of a display of earmuffs and safety glasses. Josh put his back to the wall and stepped up on a huge cardboard box of clay pigeons, so he'd be a couple of feet above the crowd. He quieted everybody and said, "Okay everybody, we don't have much time. Now, I need to get something out of the way first thing, I begin every meeting with this. Some of you were dragged here by friends or family, rolling your eyes over the whole 'zombie' thing. If you don't like that word, feel free to pick one that suits you. The Zombie Response Squad was a club promoting physical fitness, weapons training and safety, and wilderness survival. These are skills I believe that every human should possess regardless—they can save your life in the event of anything from natural disaster to civil unrest. The zombie angle was just our way of having fun with it and, obviously, we had no way of knowing that, you know, something like this was coming."

He paused here. That seemed like a really important point to him.

"So if you don't like the word zombie, feel free to mentally substitute any word you wish when you hear it. But for the purposes of this discussion, I am going to use the word zombie. The infected are contagious, they exhibit animalistic and predatory behavior toward other humans, they can survive massive organ and tissue trauma. So regardless of what science eventually figures out about this outbreak, right now, the danger these creatures pose to your personal safety, and the method of dealing with them, fully fits the profile of 'zombie.' So just deal with it."

Josh gestured to a guy in the crowd and said, "Fredo?" That was presumably Fredo's cue to turn on a projector hooked to his laptop. An image appeared on the sheet next to Josh.

Oh my dear god, Amy thought. *They have a PowerPoint presentation.*

Josh said, "Okay, very quickly. Here's what we know. For some of you this will be repeat information, just bear with me here."

A blue slide appeared, with white writing in Comic Sans font. It said, ORIGINS?

"We don't know where the infection originated from. We may never know. Since it behaves in a way that's different from anything known to science, I prefer to think it's man-made. In fact, I also happen to think that the pathogen was specifically engineered to 'zombify' the victims, for the psychological impact. Humans have been scared of walking dead since hunter-gatherer days. Zombies are burned into our genetic memory. I was just reading about that in a book. Fredo . . ."

Next slide. This one had a line graph, starting at zero and spiking rapidly upward. The left-to-right axis was ticking off the days since the outbreak.

"OGZA estimates are that the infection rate within the borders of [Undisclosed] was at twenty percent as of last Wednesday. It exceeded fifty percent yesterday, and will be at ninety to one hundred percent within forty-eight hours."

Gasps from the crowd. Amy thought, *that couldn't be true, could it? And who was OGZA?*

Fredo hit the next slide. It said, WHO IS OGZA?

"For those of you who haven't been to previous meetings and who have been following this story in the mainstream press, let me quickly fill you in. A group of resistance fighters have formed inside town, gathering supplies and scouting secure locations where they can hole up as the situation deteriorates. They call themselves Outbeak Ground Zero Alpha."

He brought up his final slide, which said, SO WHAT ABOUT THE GOVERNMENT?

"One final point I want to make, and I leave this for last because it's what you need to keep with you when you watch TV tonight. An anonymous source within the government has leaked a series of e-mails between the Centers for Disease Control and the task force for Rapid Exotic Pathogen Eradication slash Research, outlining what they call Operation Leppard. From these e-mails we know that REPER determined within forty-eight hours of the outbreak—based on autopsies of infected dead—that the physiological changes caused by the infection are radical . . . and irreversible."

Another "let that sink in" pause from Josh.

"Even if they could kill off the agent of the change—the bacteria, virus, parasite or whatever it is—the subject's entire nervous system is no longer recognizable as human. There is nothing to be done for the infected. From there they have made the logical conclusion that quarantine is not separating the infected so that they may be isolated and cured. They are being separated—and concentrated in one location—so that they can be wiped out in one step. Just like amputating an infected limb."

He let that sink, too.

"And our goal, as of now, is to do whatever we can to help them accomplish this."

The room erupted in cheers.

8 Hours Until the Massacre at Ffirth Asylum

John found himself packed into the most depressing room he'd ever been in—and in Undisclosed, that was really saying something. It was a gymnasium in the depressing old Ffirth TB asylum, a building that had been old, abandoned and almost certainly haunted since his father was a kid. Inside, the place was even more of a rotting, mildewing shithole than out. The long boards in the old gym floor had warped and curled up over time, creating a rippling floor that, if painted blue, would look like the surface of the ocean on a windy day.

He didn't see Amy there but he wouldn't have even if she were—there were partitions with curtains set up to divide the gym into dozens of little rooms containing cots. Teams of guys in those spooky Darth Vader space suits were rolling a cart from one "room" to the next, taking blood samples from everyone. John wondered what exactly they were checking for. He wondered what his blood-alcohol level was.

John's hands were still bound behind him. Everybody else was getting a standard checklist read off a clipboard ("Are you having hallucinations? Any unexplained urges or mood swings? Are you experiencing any unusual sores or lesions in the mouth area?") but they came back to his cot twice after his interview, asking him his name, asking how he knew Dave and Amy, and so on. Finally they asked him if he knew Amy's whereabouts, and John felt a Gatorade bucket of relief get dumped over his head.

They don't have her.

On the fourth visit, they brought a white space suit that contained a smiling, gray-haired guy who John instantly disliked.

"Hello there, John. I'm Dr. Bob Tennet. How are we today?"

"I know you somehow . . ."

"I don't believe we've had the pleasure of meeting, but I know your friend David."

"Right, right, you're his crossbow therapist."

Tennet grabbed a rolling office chair and dragged it over. He sat on it backward, straddling it so that he could cross his arms over the back in a casual, folksy way, which looked absurd in his huge, bulky hazardous-materials suit. He pulled out a device with a series of clips dangling at the end of thin wires.

"Your left hand, please."

Tennet clipped the five clips to John's fingers. At the other end of the wires was a box with a small screen. Tennet punched in some settings. Was this thing going to give him a manicure?

"Now please answer the following questions honestly. They might seem odd to you, but reading your reaction will give us vital insight into your condition."

John said, "Whatever. Wait, you said 'know' David, present tense. Is Dave still . . . around?"

"We'll explore that in a moment. As you can imagine, John, we're working just as hard as we can to give a clean bill of health to the people who don't need our help so we can devote as much time and attention as we can to the ones who do."

"And by help, you mean throwing them behind that goddamned prison camp you've built next door?"

"You feel what we're doing here is unethical."

"Is that . . . some kind of a joke? You can't tell me the government knows what's really happening here. We have . . . rights and shit."

"Why do you say that?"

"Why do I say there is such a thing as human rights? Wait, what is all this? Who *are* you?"

"You understand the irony of you asking that question, when my entire role here is figuring out who—or what—you are. You and the rest of the patients in this facility."

"We have rights either way."

"Human rights."

"*Yes.*"

"But you may no longer be human."

"Jesus Christ. Look at me. You know damned well there's nothing wrong with me. I'm sitting here having a rational conversation with you. In English."

"There is a species of carnivorous turtle whose tongue has evolved to look exactly like the worms local fish are known to eat. The fish swim right into its mouth, going after the 'worm', only to have their heads severed by powerful jaws. If, say, a hypothetical predator of humans had learned to mimic human speech and mannerisms in order to make it a more efficient predator, that would hardly make it human, or guarantee it rights under our Constitution or any common system of morality."

"Holy shit. The whole world has gone insane out there, hasn't it? So you just throw everybody in a concentration camp and figure you'll sort it out later? That's where things are at?"

"Ah, your friend called the quarantine a prison, but you have elevated it to concentration camp! Your generation does have a flair for the hyperbolic when it comes to describing your own adversity."

"Wait, so you did talk to David? So he's alive?"

Tennet looked up from his readout and said, "Let's explore that.

David Wong

That'll be a good jumping off point for us. If David were here, but was infected, would he still be David?"

"*What?*"

"Say his personality remained exactly the same, but the parasite caused his head to transform so that his face was replaced with the face of a leech, complete with circles of tiny teeth for sucking human blood. Would you still consider him to be your old friend?"

"Are you saying he's infected, or are you just fucking with me?"

Instead of answering, Tennet studied the screen on the device hooked to John's fingers and made some notes on his clipboard. "Good. Now let's say the opposite happened. Say he still looked, spoke and acted like David, but was, in reality, an inhuman predator. How would that make you feel? Please answer."

"Are you serious?"

"Please, we have a lot of patients to get to."

"It would make me feel *bad*."

Tennet nodded and checked something off of his clipboard.

"Now let's say that he was not infected, but was sent to quarantine with hundreds of people who are, and that their infection has dissolved the part of their brain capable of making moral decisions. And let's say that they overpowered David, restrained him, defecated into his mouth and taped his mouth shut with duct tape, and left him there to writhe and slowly swallow feces all week, how would that make you feel?"

"Who *are* you?"

A check of the screen. A mark on the clipboard. "Almost done. Now, if you had to choose, either to have Amy Sullivan gang-raped by twenty-seven infected males in town over the course of ten days, or to have David's digestive tract surgically restructured so that his large intestine fed directly into his mouth, which would it be? And please provide support for your answer."

"You're fucking crazy."

Tennet glanced at his clipboard and said, "If you had to choose, and if you were not allowed to see either ahead of time and had no other information to go on, would you rather fight Mindcrow or Gonadulus?"

"This isn't a government operation, is it?"

"If it wasn't, tell me how that would make you feel."

194

"You're behind this. All of this. You people released that thing in Dave's house. You set all this in motion. What's your real name?"

Tennet casually glanced at another page on his clipboard and said, "All right, John, I think we're in good shape here. What we're going to do is observe you overnight—standard procedure, don't read anything into it—and tomorrow morning we'll do this all again, so we can cross-check the results. Between now and then I want you to really mull this over: if you were carrying the parasite right now, *how would you know?*"

John didn't answer. Tennet stood, pulled the clips from John's fingers and as a good-bye, said, "You are now aware that your lower jaw has weight, and that it requires effort for you to hold it up. Good evening."

7 Hours Until the Massacre at Ffirth Asylum

Amy was in the Zombie Response Squad's headquarters, aka an old RV Josh inherited from his parents. Parents who Amy suspected were fairly rich. One wall featured a rack of five guns that Amy had never seen outside of an action movie or video game. Josh insisted on showing them all to her, and the footlocker of bullets and shotgun shells they had stockpiled. She nodded and tried to act impressed but she had no idea what she was looking at. The guns all looked like they would knock her over if she tried to shoot one. Josh insisted this wasn't the case and that he would show her how to shoot if she wanted. He asked her if she wanted anything to drink or to eat or, you know, anything else because he was there for her. Massages, boob inspections, whatever.

Amy couldn't get John on the phone but at this point she expected that and, to be honest, hated his guts for it. Josh was on his laptop now, showing her a map of Undisclosed that somebody was updating with zombie sightings. There was a big red blob in one corner and Amy asked if that meant there were a lot of zombies there or if there was just one flamboyant zombie who was really easy to see.

"Uh, that's the hospital there, they've fenced it off and used it as a quarantine. They've got the place built up like a supermax prison now, but it got so bad that not even the CDC staff could stay inside it. Now, it's a dumping ground. When somebody in town turns up infected they move them there, behind the fences. So that area is pretty much one hundred percent infected, because if you're not but they stick you in there anyway, well, how long are you going to last?"

"But they don't know for sure who's infected and who's not?"

"Right."

"So if your neighbor or whatever calls them and says they suspect you are infected, you get dumped into that camp or whatever. Which is full of hundreds of people who *are* infected and have turned into monsters and stuff."

"That's what we're hearing, yes."

"Oh, wow, that's like the worst thing I've ever heard."

"That's what I was saying at the meeting. If you're the government, and your job is to make sure this thing doesn't spread, and once you've finished sweeping the town and have everybody who might be infected all in this big red blotch here, and you know for *a fact* that they can't be cured, what do you do with the red blotch? I'm thinking one MOAB would do it. Fuel-air bomb that will cook everything within a square mile to four thousand degrees."

"I bet the guy who invented that had a really weird relationship with his mother."

"What?"

"Do we know when they plan to do it?"

"Unfortunately, no."

"I checked the list on their Web site, David wasn't on there at all. What do you think that means?"

"I think it means that keeping people informed isn't their top priority. Look at this."

Amy leaned over Josh's shoulder and watched a black-and-white video clip play out. It didn't look like anything. Some dark squares and tiny dots. At the center were white crosshairs, and some numbers were ticking off in the corners.

"It's aerial video. A military pilot leaked it, I think it's a gun camera. This big dark bunch of rectangles here, that's the hospital. If they zoomed out, you'd see the REPER HQ buildings to the upper left, but it's offscreen on this view. See this? You can sort of see the fencing and stuff around the edge of the quarantine. He'll zoom in in a second, to get a view of the yard . . ."

The shot blinked in as the pilot upped the magnification. Much clearer now—Amy could make out the dots as people, and make out the shapes outside the fence as tents and trucks.

It zoomed in again. Now she could see the people in some detail, enough to tell the difference between someone sitting and standing, and when someone raised their hand to their mouth to smoke or eat something.

She said, "Wait, that's inside the fence? Those are the infected monster zombies? They're just standing around. They look like people."

"No. See this blotch here? That white part in the middle, that's heat. Fire. See all this stuff jutting out on all sides? Look close. Those are bodies. Skeletons, of uninfected victims they've killed. They seem to be burning them in some kind of primitive ritual—"

"DAVID! Look!"

"What?"

"That's David! I see him!"

"Are . . . are you sure? At this resolution I couldn't even tell you which ones are women and which are—"

"Oh my god, he's right there. Oh my god. I have to tell John."

Josh was still protesting, but Amy could have read David's body language from outer space. He was staring at the fence, with his arms folded, and he was *really really mad*.

She said, "We have to get him out of there. Tonight. Or tomorrow morning. How soon can we get down there?"

"Amy . . . even if we wanted to risk a breach of the quarantine, do you want me to point out all of the military vehicles surrounding that place? Plus whatever aircraft this video came from? You heard me say it's a gun camera, right?"

"Then I'll go myself. That's what I was trying to do, get them to take me to that place. That's what I was doing and you stopped me and now I'm here and David is there and they're going to heat it to four thousand degrees."

"Amy . . . if that's really him, and he's in there with those . . . *things*, then it *might not really be him anymore*. In fact, it almost certainly isn't."

"Uh huh. So how soon can we be down there?"

6 Hours Until the Massacre
at Ffirth Asylum

TJ claimed it was around 9 P.M., which he said he could tell by looking at the moon. That sounded like bullshit but it didn't feel like he was off by much. He and Hope were in my room, the latter heating a coffeepot full of water over a Sterno can. She said, "The last bunch of supplies had boxes of macaroni and cheese but we don't have enough heat to boil the water that long. You know it never occurred to me until now how much energy it takes to heat water. I mean, I've had science classes and I understand that's why they use water to put out fires. But like when you're at home you don't think about it. You run a hot shower or let hot water run in the sink while you brush your teeth and you don't realize that somewhere down the line it took like several pounds of coal to make enough electricity to heat it. We are soooo wasteful."

TJ said, "Goddamnit, Hope, why did you have to mention hot showers? You wagin' a psychological torture campaign against me tonight. Don't know what I did to offend you."

She dipped her finger in the water. "Okay, we got two flavors of Ramen and they both taste exactly the same."

There was a moment soon after that, as we sat around the room eating noodles out of coffee cups, hearing muffled conversation from the hall, when everything seemed normal again. We could have been camping. I felt a strange sense of calm and realized what I was feeling was the release of responsibility. Nobody expected me to be at work the next day. Nobody was trying to call me. I had no e-mail to check. Ghost enthusiasts weren't stalking me on Facebook. Our responsibilities were stripped down to the bare biological basics: thirst, hunger, cold. All at once I could see why lifelong convicts got to where they couldn't function outside of prison walls. You're almost functioning more at a level for which the human brain was intended.

I asked TJ, "What's the deal with the colors? The red and green? How'd we wind up on teams?"

"Well, that's the thing. Nobody knows. Everybody went through decontamination and when you stepped out of the chemical shower you were handed coveralls. Half got red, half got green. They didn't tell us nothin' or put us in different sections. Just, 'here, put this shit on.' But it don't take Dr. House to figure out that the reds are way more likely to spider out. Carlos was a red, Sal was a red. Danny, Marcus, that fat Muslim dude. It's not a hundred percent but it's not within margin of error, either. Red means 'high risk', seems pretty common sense. Everybody figured it out before anybody said it out loud. The colors started separatin' to themselves. As colors tend to do."

"Owen has the only gun?"

"Yep. Until somebody finds another. Owen has appointed himself the de facto President of the Quarantine based on the fact that he happened to find a sidearm that got left behind in the melee. Lot of human history works like that."

We had boarded up the broken window, but could still hear the bonfire crackling down in the yard. TJ continued, "The lobby and the bit of yard outside the lobby, that whole patio area, that's shared territory. The second floor, that's where the hospital still functions as a hospital. The doc and two nurses got left behind, they're treatin' the sick. The regular sick, you know. People keep cuttin' themselves on broken glass, about a dozen people got them nasty shits that's goin' around. You ever talk to the doc, by the way? Since you been back?"

"No. Tomorrow." I had a thing about doctors, for a very good reason.

TJ continued, "So, then the third and fourth floors are all red territory. We're here on the fifth and up, those are the green floors. The two sides, we don't shoot each other on sight but it gets tense, as you saw. And you can tell which side has the gun, by who got the lower floors."

"Why?"

Hope interjected, "No elevators. Nobody wants to tromp up and down a million stairs to get to their room. Everybody would prefer to just pile down at the bottom. Owen declared his people got the good floors."

I said, "Why did I wind up back at the asylum?"

TJ shrugged. "Like they'd tell us. Loudspeaker came on and said you needed to go to the gate. Truck hauled you away. That was Friday morning. Now you're back."

"How long can we keep this up? Before the food and everything runs out?"

TJ said, "They dropped in supplies. Truck dumped out boxes of stuff. I assume they'll do it again."

"Yeah, but I'm saying . . . let's say that hypothetically they can't figure out a cure or even a reliable test for the infection. They keep dumping the suspects here in the quarantine and . . . what? We're still here ten years from now? Somethin' has to give, right?"

Looking into his cup, TJ said, "What would you do?"

"Drop a nuke on it. Write a letter of apology to the surviving family members. Send 'em some coupons to Outback Steakhouse as compensation. Rest of the country breathes a sigh of relief."

He shrugged. "That rumor started about two minutes after outbreak. I was hearing that shit everywhere. Man, people got a low opinion of the armed forces, don't they? Watch too many zombie movies. No way they get away with that in the real world."

Hope said, "What if they cover it up? Make it look like something else?"

I said, "What, like fake a gas line explosion?"

"No, all they have to do is poison our food. Then say the infection did it."

That brought silence to the room.

TJ said, "Both of you think you bein' cynical, but you're not. Reality is, if they wanted us dead, they don't have to do anything. Situation we got here is what cops call a self-cleaning oven. Some gang neighborhoods, they'd just let be. Come back in five years and it's all quiet, all on its own. You know, because everybody shot each other. It'd be just like that here, because instead of organizing and figuring out how to work together, we all got paranoid, like Owen."

He stood up.

"It's early, but I'm goin' to bed. No TV and it too dark to read. What else am I gonna do?"

Hope said, "Ugh. The nights are the worst. I'm to where I can tolerate the days as long as nobody dies. But the nights go on *forever*."

TJ said, "I agree. And yet, the night comes just the same. Like the rotation of the Earth don't give a shit what we think."

Hope was making a huge freaking understatement when she said the nights were the worst. I realized when TJ left that I was also exhausted, but it was only after I went to bed that it became screamingly apparent that we had no lights and no heat and were basically living in a third world gulag. I tried to remember what day TJ said it was. Sunday? So the rest of the country was probably watching Sunday Night Football. Or were they? Maybe it was like this everywhere. Everyone in America huddled in the dark, waiting.

TJ and Hope left the room to me at bedtime, so I guessed it was my room. I wrapped myself up in as many blankets as I could find. I knew exactly where to find them, just as I knew where to find the hunk of particle board we used to cover the broken window. My specific memories never came back but a lot of the automatic stuff was still programmed in. I suddenly remembered that I had broken the window by throwing a little television out of it. I couldn't remember why.

I shivered and wrapped up the covers a little tighter.

We had a bunch of emergency kerosene space heaters that had been left behind in a storage building, but not much kerosene to fuel them. Here on the fifth floor we had two of them in the hall and they'd keep them lit for a few hours at night to take the chill out of the air, but that was it. People set pots of water on top to heat, killing two birds with one stone. Some people slept in the hall to be closer to the heaters, but the kerosene fumes stank so bad the stench radiated into my brain and gave me a headache. TJ pointed out that the stuff was jet fuel, after all.

I shivered. Couldn't get warm. Or maybe the shivering was something else. So damned quiet. No TV. No ticking clock. No soft whoosh of heat blowing through vents. Not even the reassuring hum of countless electronic devices that you don't even register until it's gone.

Somebody coughed out in the hall. A dog barked way off in the distance.

I shivered.

I remembered getting into a drunken argument with a guy about American prisons, him talking about the injustice of the system, me talking about how it's ridiculous that we spend forty grand a year per inmate to maintain what are basically super-clean hotels for rapists and crack dealers, complete with a computer lab and TV room and pool tables. But now I understood what he was saying. That knowledge that you can't leave, it's a twisting knife in your gut. All I could think about was that razor wire at the top of the fence, meant to slice your hands down to the tendons if you tried to climb over. My own government put that there, with my hands in mind. Those hundreds of vicious blades hanging fifteen feet over the bloodstains and brains in the grass of the last guy who tried to climb up. But even prisoners knew when their sentence was up, they could tick off days on a calendar, feel themselves progressing toward freedom. But this place? They could keep us here forever. Or poison our food, like Hope said. Or starve us out. Or let the drone operator use us for target practice. Or fill the yard with nerve gas.

I shivered.

I couldn't stop. I laid on my side and brought my knees up, trying to control it. Where was Amy right now? Could she have gotten out of town? How the hell could she, the way they were locking the place down at the end there?

I thought I'd lay there, shivering, staring at the wall until the sun came up. I could sense no sleep on the horizon. But when I heard footsteps in my room later, I realized I had drifted off.

I didn't move. I pulled open my eyes and stared at the wall. I heard nothing, decided I dreamed it. My eyes slipped shut—

My bed shifted. Weight. Gentle, settling in.

I thought, *Hope?*

She was friendly earlier, but were we . . . friendly? Holy shit was that possible? I wouldn't think I'd do that to Amy but . . . here, alone, in this cold place? Would I turn down a warm girl and soft skin and the chance to do the one thing that would let me forget all this? I admitted, I didn't hate the idea. I stayed frozen, on my side, not sure what to do. I thought about reaching back, looking for a thigh or a hip. Casually, you know. Just to see who was there. I wondered if I would find her naked. An entire separate part of my nervous system roared to life at the thought. I moved my hand, slowly. My heart was pumping.

Now watch, you'll roll over and it'll be TJ, wearing a tiny leopard-skin thong.

I reached out and rolled over at the same time.

I grabbed a handful of red fur.

Molly

Note: Do not ask the author how the details of the following sequence of events were obtained. The explanation would only leave you more confused and dissatisfied than would any theory you could come up with from your own imagination.

Experienced pet owners know that if your pet ever goes missing, the first step is not to panic. The vast majority of the time, the pet will simply find its way back home on its own.

Molly knew this, so she hadn't been all that concerned when her male human first went missing nine days ago. In the beginning, things had been in a general state of agitation everywhere Molly went, so she figured it had something to do with that.

That was the day all of the people had been shouting at each other, and running, and falling down. It was hard to find a place to sleep quietly but eventually she found a shady spot between two buildings, and she curled up in the shadow of one of those huge green boxes humans use to store their extra food. This one had some great-smelling poultry in it, maybe four or five days old, but those boxes were hard to get out of once you got into them and she wasn't hungry. She had just eaten the rest of the discarded meal that her human had forgotten to give her the night before.

What passes for language among dogs—made up mostly of a lavishly detailed sense of smell and a well-tuned but cautious sense of empathy for all living things—cannot be translated neatly into English. But if it could, the closest translation of Molly's name for her human, the one other humans called David, was "Meatsmell." His breath always smelled like meat—always, as if he had just eaten some recently, no matter when you encountered him. To a dog that spoke of an awe-inspiring accomplishment. She was proud of Meatsmell's ability to always have access to such riches. She knew she had taught him well.

But she also knew that Meatsmell was always getting confused. Molly knew that he couldn't look after himself, and that he depended on her. She guarded his house every night, keeping all of the predators and bad guys at bay. She sometimes let him pet her, feeling his stress and agitation melt way as he did so. She also kept dropped food picked up off the floor, and fished out the edible items when he would accidentally drop them into those big flimsy bags and take them out to the yard (where anyone could get them!). Molly was certain that Meatsmell would not last more than a day or two on his own.

On the evening of that day, the day when everything went wrong, Molly had woken up after dark, the hard ground having grown cold under her. It had started to rain a little. She made her way back toward home, but that took a long time. She kept having to stop and investigate smells. There was smoke that stung her nose everywhere she went, things were burning here and there and she knew that could not be good news because the humans were already riled up. When things started catching on fire that rarely calmed them down. She had stopped and sniffed a patch of fresh blood, and the freshly dead human laying next to it in the rain. A little way down the road, she stopped and smelled another one, sniffing around where some of its insides had spilled out onto the ground.

She got closer to her home and there were several such people laying around, with parts separated and some burned up. One of them was very small. None of them were Meatsmell, she would have known that from far away. The smoke smell was here, too. There was no fire now, but there had been recently. Now, everything was just smoky and cold and wet. She went into the house, because the door was open, and went right to her food and water dishes.

It was all wrong. Everything was all black and twisted. Her water dish had water in it, but it was rainwater that tasted like smoke. There was no food in her dish at all. That is when she knew Meatsmell was in trouble—he would not forget food time. If he had forgotten to feed Molly, who knew how long it had been since he had fed himself.

It was then that Molly had noticed that it was still raining on her as she stood over her bowls. This wasn't right. The wind was still coming in, too. Where was the warmth and light and the endless food smells? She went looking for her bed but even it was cold and wet and strangely flat. She couldn't get comfortable—she hated sleeping in the rain—and trotted around outside the house until she found the small entrance to the space under the floor where she sometimes went when she didn't want to be bothered. It was nice and dry and shielded from the wind. She curled up on the dirt and drifted off, deciding that if Meatsmell came back soon she would let him sleep down here, too.

Light poured into the entrance to her sleeping spot and Molly instinctively moved to go somewhere darker. But then she realized Meatsmell still was not home and that he was probably somewhere scared and hungry and waiting for Molly to come get him.

Molly went on the hunt. Tracking Meatsmell would clearly begin with the last spot where she had seen him—at the little building down the road where he always bought his rolls of spicy meat. She set off down the street under the morning sun. She was disappointed to see that the humans had not settled down one bit after a night's sleep—a lot of men who were all wearing the same clothes, with big coverings over their heads, were shouting at the other people who were all wearing different clothes, maybe telling them that they should all be wearing the same clothes, too. There was a terrible bang and Molly flinched. Noises that loud didn't happen in the normal world, only people could make sounds like that. One of the different-clothed people fell over and they weren't alive anymore.

Molly ran to get some distance from the shouting people, then turned one last time to get a look. She had noticed something curious and had to double-check. One of the people in the different-clothes crowd was not in fact people. He looked just like a person, but he was something else, just pretending to be one. It was the same for one of the same-clothes people, and she got the feeling the other same-clothes people did not realize this. This phenomenon was not new to Molly, but she always took note of it because it seemed to be the source of a lot of anxiety for Meatsmell and his friends.

Molly hurried down the street and arrived at the tiny spicy meat building. No one was there at this time in the morning, but the place was bursting with smells. Not just all of the exotic meat the place cooked in big heaping piles, but of people. Molly sniffed the ground, making a full circle of the hard, cold surface around the building. She picked up the scent of Meatsmell, and the angry man who was trying to hurt Meatsmell, and John.

She followed the scents right to the narrow door, now standing open. She sniffed her way into a little room full of items that were not food. She sniffed and sniffed, in an instant learning the long and dramatic story of a possum who had died nearby a few days ago, then someone stepped in the juices that leaked from his body, then they tracked it into this room. Then a cat slept in here not even one day ago.

Molly was so distracted by the drama of the tiny room's floor that she failed to notice that the sun had gone away. She turned around and went back outside, only to realize she was no longer at the little building. She was now looking at a flat expanse of pavement exploding with fresh smells. Blood. Sweat. Smoke. Terror.

Molly had sniffed and sniffed, taking it all in, replaying through her nose the story of scared men killing other scared men.

There.

Meatsmell had been here. The scent led off toward where lots of the same-clothes men were gathered. Meatsmell was not among them. There was a fence that went both ways as far as Molly could see, and she sensed that Meatsmell was on the other side. So she just needed to find a way in. Shouldn't be a problem. Molly went and found a sunny spot, and curled up and went to sleep.

It took a full week to find her way in. In that time she was chased by some of the same-clothes people, and other dogs, and was almost hit by cars more times than she could remember. But she made it, inside the big building full of terrible smells—layers upon layers of ancient sickness and slow death. Now she was curled up next to Meatsmell and it wasn't raining on them and everything was back the way it was supposed to be. She fell into a deep sleep, inside this huge building full of anxious and tired people, many of whom she noticed were not really people.

4 Hours Until the Massacre at Ffirth Asylum

John had lost track of how many consecutive days he had woken up not knowing where he was. This place was full of people and echoes and creaky boards and mold. Someone was shouting at him to wake up. He sat up on the cot and the first thing he saw was one of the terrifying Darth Vader guys holding a machine gun. John thought, *oh, right. It's this bullshit still.*

Two spacemen surged forward and lifted John off his cot and took him roughly out of the gym and into an old shower room covered in ancient chipped tiles held together by mildew. John half expected to see a dozen naked men in black space helmets snapping towels at each other. Instead he found himself alone, the long-dry shower room now piled high with boxes of rubber gloves and syringes and trash bags and every other thing. He was alone for ten minutes, until he was joined by—

"Detective Falconer! Shouldn't you be wearing a space suit?"

Falconer was wearing his street clothes—jeans, a black turtleneck and an empty shoulder holster under his armpit. Cowboy boots. Little bit of beard stubble. John wondered if the guy would walk from one end of the street to the other without winding up covered in bitches.

Falconer said, "A suit wouldn't help, would it?"

"Might buy you a few seconds. Where's Amy?"

"Who?"

"Dave's girlfriend? Redhead. Only one hand? They snatched her up. Both of us. But I think she got away, they don't seem to know where she is. I don't know if she's in town, or . . ."

"Didn't see her."

"What about Dave?"

"I can ask but they won't tell me either way."

"Because you don't work for the CDC."

"Does this shit look like the CDC to you? You see what those guys were wearing? What they were packing? No, they're not CDC and I'm not one of them. I'm being processed for infected, just like you. I turned myself in. I got them to let me talk to you because I said you might have information, but when we're done, both of us will get tossed over the fence down at the hospital. And it sounds like nobody comes back out of there."

"You turned yourself in? Great plan you had there, detective."

"I am really trying to restrain myself here. Do you understand? This all happened because of you two shitbirds."

"Man, fuck you. I don't think Dave made it out. Did you know that? I'm pretty sure he got his brains blown out when everything went bad. Or if not, they got him after shit went to hell. Either way . . ."

"Well, I'm sorry if that's true. But I can say that I don't know that to be true, either. Some people were killed in that first round of riots but I never heard that he was among them."

John shrugged.

"But, none of this is my main point." Falconer moved to a spot where he could see the gym from where he was standing. Making sure nobody was close enough to listen.

"My point is, I've seen everything I need to see in here. So I figure that instead of rotting in their quarantine, I might as well get to the bottom of this and save the world."

John stood up. *"Now you're talking."*

"Don't get excited. If I think you can help me, I'll get you out of here, too. But you have to prove you can help me first."

John sat. "Okay, fine. Want me to show you some karate or . . ."

"I watched both of you go into a door at a taco stand and not come back out. Where did you go?"

"To a construction site outside of town."

"How?"

"Magic door. No, seriously. Don't get mad. The door is magic. It's not my fault."

"But it didn't work for me. And if the illegal aliens they got manning the grill at that place go through the back door, they're not gonna wind up outside town."

"Correct. Neither will most other people. Me and Dave can do it, so can some other people around town. They're the ones who built the doors. We just stumbled across them."

" 'Doors.' There's more than one?"

"Yeah, they're all over."

"And who are these people who put them there?"

"We'd love to find out. They're very well funded, and very powerful and they dabble in weird shit. They're also almost certainly the people responsible for this outbreak. Which as Dave tried to explain to you, is the work of invisible monsters. I think that Tennet guy is with them. He has that vibe."

"A few days into this situation, CDC, military, everybody pulls out and this new agency—REPER—sweeps in. They got all the right equipment and all the right training for this exact thing. And nobody has heard of them before."

John shrugged as if to say, "Sounds about right."

"These guys, the ones you say are behind this, do they do anything else, other than build magical doors and monsters? I'm having a little bit of trouble figuring out how they make money off that."

"Dave thinks the monster stuff is a side effect, an accident. He thinks they're experimenting under the table with the door stuff, quantum teleportation or wormholes or however they do it, and that when they started dicking around with the fabric of space-time and dimensions and so on, weird shit started leaking through. From, you know. Other dimensions or wherever they come from. But the stuff that came through, don't think of it as just animals that run around biting people. Some of it is intelligent. Superintelligent, maybe. Dark shapes, like ghosts."

John could tell from Falconer's face that he was losing him.

"Detective, all that stuff I just said, we didn't just fill this in with our imagination. We've had encounters here and there, stuff has leaked out from inside the operation. We look like a couple of assholes but Dave has actually worked really hard to put this together. And you've seen enough weird shit in your time here to give us just a little bit of the benefit of the doubt."

"These people, you think they're part of the government?"

"I think that when the government comes to investigate something that goes down here, these guys can make some calls and that shit just disappears. Cases get closed. Also, they've been around a while. Stories about this town go back as far as the history books go. Maybe forever."

"What's so special about this town?"

"Don't know. Maybe there's some kind of electromagnetic conditions that make it ideal for whatever it is they do. Maybe they just got a good deal on the land. Who knows."

"And what's so special about you and David? Why can you use the doors? Why can you see the monsters?"

"Short answer, we're magic. Longer answer, he and I took a magic potion that gave us the ability. The longer still answer is that a drug hit the streets, looks kind of like molasses, or motor oil that hasn't been changed in a decade. The dealer was calling it Soy Sauce. You take it and you change instantly. The veil comes up off your perceptions. When you're on it, the first few hours, you're like a fuckin' demigod. You can slip through time, space, unlock the mysteries of the universe and shit. Then you come down and you feel normal again. But some of the effects are permanent. You become a member of the club."

"That drug, it came from these people, right? All the weird shit comes from them?"

"Yeah."

"You have any of it left? The drug?"

"You don't want to take it. It kills ninety-nine percent of the people who come in contact with it. Mostly in gruesome ways. The dealer who sold it to me, they found him splattered on the walls of his trailer. But in answer to your question, yes, we do have some of the Soy Sauce left."

"Where?"

"I'll take you to it. No bullshit. But we got to get outta here first."

"I agree."

"And I'm gonna take a wild guess and say that they're not gonna agree to release us, even if you wave your badge at the dude guarding the door."

Falconer said, "You're right, for once. But I don't know if you realized it, but these assholes picked the *single most fucked up building in a hundred mile radius* in which to set up their ad hoc HQ. They have generators in the parking lot and power cables draped through windows and boxes stacked everywhere. I'm thinking they have not had time to work out exactly what they would do in the event of something unexpected. Like a fire."

"We're totally on the same page here. Let's burn this shit down."

Falconer closed his eyes, let out a steadying breath and said, "*No,* we just need some smoke. Enough to make them go through the process of carefully moving aaalll of these patients and staff and shit out of the building. All those guys in their bulky-ass space suits tripping over cables, patients tryin' to escape. And in the confusion, we slip away. Now, if I go out there now and occupy as many staff as I can with some ruse, do you possess the resourcefulness to sneak away and create a nice, smoky but *controlled* fire in a trash can somewhere? Without fucking it up?"

John looked him dead in the eye and said, "Throw some rubber gloves in there, it'll smell just like an electrical fire."

3 Hours, 45 Minutes Until the Massacre at Ffirth Asylum

I marched Molly into the hallway, intending to ask if anybody had seen her around before. Hell, maybe she'd been here from the start and we'd just missed each other. I got my answer without asking—as soon as we stepped into the hall a dozen people gathered around and said, "How'd you get a dog in here?"

Molly wasn't talking. She just panted and wagged her tail and let everyone pet her. She was filthy, mud caked on her legs and chest. Was there a spot to dig under the fence unnoticed? *Both* fences?

It only took ten minutes for word to filter down to the yard, and for Owen to call a meeting because apparently he could do that in his role as Only Guy With a Gun, according to Robert's Rules of Order. Shortly thereafter, at least a hundred people were huddled in the yard around the fire pit. The night air was cold as shit, so we all huddled around the smoldering coals and blackened, smoking rib cages, rubbing our hands together and hoping nobody was secretly taking our picture. Kind of hard to run for office later with a photo circulating of you warming your hands over a pile of glowing skulls.

Owen had the automatic in his hand, but wasn't threatening with it. In this setting it seemed more ceremonial, like a gavel. He said, "I don't like it. It don't make sense. That's a big dog, it ain't like a squirrel gettin' past the sensors and shit out there. Dog probably weighs a hundred pounds, if it can make it through, a dude can make it through."

I said, "Well, awesome. If there's a way in, there's a way out, right? Maybe there's a place you can dig under the fence after all, out of sight of the—"

"*Dipshit*," interjected Owen, "we have been around and around that fence. It's *all we got to do, all day,* bro. No, there ain't no good place to cross the fence. There ain't any storm drains, there ain't any big sewer pipes like in the damned *Shawshank Redemption*."

I shrugged. "Well I personally observed this dog, in town, eating a burrito, *after* the hospital was locked down. She was on the other side of that fence and she didn't come in on the last truck. So . . ."

"Speaking of which," Owen said, "What are we supposed to do with it?"

I said, "Why do we have to do anything? To be clear, there's no indication that dogs can get infected, right? So we're not worried about that end of it?"

TJ said, "No, dogs don't get it. Animals and kids, they don't get it."

Owen said, "You'll bet your life on that? All of our lives?"

I said, "So, I'll check her mouth."

"That ain't a hundred percent, neither."

"So, what, you want to put her down? She's our ticket out of here."

"Our ticket outta here is keeping this place safe and secure until we hear the all-clear. There ain't no reason in the world to make a jailbreak even if your dog leads us to a magical train platform that hauls us all to Hogwarts."

Everyone stared at Owen until he said, "I told you, I got a kid. Fuck off."

I said, "Your 'let's remain calm and stay put' speech would be a lot more convincing if you weren't giving it in front of a pile of burning skeletons. So, we kill the dog because maybe she's not a dog and maybe she's some new kind of undetectable monster. We gonna use that same standard on the next human who walks through those gates? Where does that shit end, Owen? Government shows up to give the all-clear and it's just you and a mountain of bones?"

Owen had no rebuttal for this and I have to be honest, I detected relief in his face. He didn't want to have to shoot a dog.

"She monsters out, and it's your ass." Owen stuffed the gun into his pocket and apparently that signaled that the meeting was adjourned. The reds huddled among each other and the greens headed back inside.

I walked with TJ and said, "There's somethin' else to this, but I don't want to jump to any conclusions or anything. Molly really belongs to my girlfriend, Amy. I think Molly showing up here, it's not coincidence. I think she was sent here, as a signal to me. John and Amy—hopefully just John, I guess, with Amy in some safe place—I think one or both of them are out there, and are trying to bust me out or trying to show me how to sneak out."

"So what does that mean?"

"Means I have to figure out what the plan is. But I feel like they definitely have a plan."

Somewhere beyond the fence, an explosion lit up the sky.

3 Hours, 30 Minutes Until the Massacre at Ffirth Asylum

John sprinted across the asylum parking lot screaming, "SHHIIIIIIIT!"

Black smoke poured through the house-sized hole that had been blown in the gymnasium wall. Screams and gunshots chased him. Nearby, a car windshield shattered. There was another explosion, and the shock wave threw John to the ground, scraping his palms on the pavement. Falconer grabbed the back of his shirt and yanked him to his feet.

They made it to the Porsche parked a block away and ten seconds later were tearing through the streets of Undisclosed, drawing the attention of every gun-toting spaceman they passed. And there were a lot of them, clusters of them seemed to populate every corner.

Falconer growled, "That was *liquid oxygen*, dumbass! That's why those tanks had those huge orange warning stickers all over them. They use it in rockets."

"I didn't know! Jesus."

"You didn't know oxygen burns? Where did you go to school?"

"Here! Look around! It's a shithole!"

The Porsche smashed through wooden barricades set up in the street, and on the other side was a ghost town.

Broken glass in the streets. Garbage piled on the sidewalk. The Porsche turned down an alley and John realized that what was crunching under the tires like gravel were brass shell casings from machine guns.

John said, "Holy shit. Is everybody dead?"

"There's a twenty-four hour curfew outside the Green Zone. Inside those barricades we drove through, they've still got military doing foot patrols. But out here, it's lockdown. Nobody on foot, just armored Humvees making sweeps every now and then. Anyone seen roaming the streets out here is presumed infected and either shot or hauled off to quarantine, depending on how far gone they are."

"Christ. How is that legal?"

Falconer shook his head. "I have never seen anything like this in all my days. Everybody you see inside town, all hazmat suits, all the vehicles—that's all REPER. Everybody else has withdrawn outside of town. If we turned right here, we'd eventually run into a REPER cordon at city limits. Get past it, and you're in the Dead Zone—it's a five-mile-wide ring around the city where nobody is allowed. All the houses in that ring have been evacuated, all the businesses shut down. REPER patrols it in armored vehicles. It acts as a vacuum seal between the city and the outside world. At the end of the Dead Zone, you find the National Guard. I'm talking tanks here. Rows of them, guns aimed at the city like they expect *Day of the Dead* to come pouring out at them at any moment."

Falconer pulled off into the yard of an abandoned house, and parked in a spot behind the garage where the car wouldn't be visible from the street.

He continued, "But you see what they've done. What the outside world knows about what's going on in town, is only what REPER tells them. There is no one else. All the phones are jammed. No news crews, no Internet access. The military, they're on the other side of five miles of no-man's-land. Whatever the people are hearing, whatever the government is hearing, comes from REPER. It's their show."

John said, "And I'm pretty sure at least one of the guys in charge is crazy."

"I'll agree with that assessment. Let's just say that I've heard some shit. About what goes on in that asylum."

John said, "Well, what now?"

"We wait to make sure they're not still after us. I'm hoping the shit-storm you left behind back there makes us a low priority. They got to get containment back in place first."

John said, "Can we get to Dave's place? Are they . . . guarding it or anything?"

"Why would they?"

"They would if they knew what was there."

Falconer said, "The drug, you mean. The Soy Sauce."

"Let me apologize ahead of time, detective. Because shit is about to get weird."

3 Hours, 15 Minutes Until the Massacre at Ffirth Asylum

Amy was about to explode. She didn't get mad often, and it took a lot. But once the pin on that grenade had been pulled, there was no containing it. This was something she had in common with David, though he didn't realize it.

Amy's mom, back when she was alive, had said God had made sure to give her brother Jim all of the size and Amy all of the temper. He had been as big as a bear, but was always the voice of reason in an argument—the only time she had seen him fight, it was to defend her. Amy was literally less than half of his size but had that grenade inside her. Her mom called it her "Irish" as in, "now calm down, your Irish is coming out" which, ironically, made Amy furious. Wasn't that racist or something? But the look on Josh's face right now, it was about to get *all* Irish up in here.

"We have to go *now*. We should have left two hours ago. Fine, you don't care about David, you don't care if he gets eaten by a zombie or burned up to ashes, but who knows how many more are in there? Women, kids, who knows? We *have to get them out.* As many as we can."

Josh, not making eye contact, said, "I totally understand you're up-set, but we have to be smart about this. Mike and Ricky aren't here, they're helping their families move before the quarantine swallows this

215

place. And I told you about Zach, he's got food poisoning. He's already in bed. That's three guns we're short. But tomorrow—"

"Oh, for the love of— You know what you are? All of you? Children. Little kids playing pretend, with toys. You've spent *years* obsessing about this and now it's here, much to *everyone's* surprise, it's actually here, and it's 'tomorrow, tomorrow, tomorrow.' Tomorrow, when the sun comes up. Tomorrow, when the weather's warmer. Tomorrow, when we have more help, when things aren't so bad, when everything is aligned just right so that there's no risk of anything bad possibly happening."

"Calm down."

"Screw you!" Amy shrieked it, a sound that tore a hole in the air.

Grenade, Amy, watch it.

"You want to sit here in your little fantasy, your little suburban *womb*. With your laptop, in your little clubhouse, rubbing oil on your guns and congratulating yourself on how brave and strong you turned out to be in the stupid zombie war fantasies that play in your head. You're not a man. You're a boy. All of you. You're little boys because you choose to stay little boys. You don't become a man until you wake up one day and realize that *today the world needs you to be a man.* Josh, so help me, if you don't step up, and become a man *right now,* people will die. Tonight. Not tomorrow."

He didn't answer. He had his MacBook open and was fiddling around with the touchpad, and he had that look on his face that had pulled Amy's pin. A mask of feigned nonchalance. It took practice to come up with that look. Somebody who had been shamed so many times that he'd adapted to simply never showing it, rather than changing to not do things he was ashamed of. She wanted to slap him and slap him and slap him.

"Amy, all I'm saying is—"

"AAAAARRRGGGHHHH!" Amy bent over and screamed at the floor. She didn't know what else to do. Mom was right, if the Lord had given her Jim's body, she would have thrown this kid through the windshield of the RV.

"Fine," she said. "All I want you to do is *give me a ride down there.* Drop me off at the barricades. I'll figure out a way to get across. I'll figure out a way to find David and anyone else who needs help in there and I'll figure out a way to get them out and if I don't, then *I will die.* And that's okay because while I'm dying trying to save the people I love, you'll be back here in your cocoon, playing your zombie video games and jerking off and *dying would be better than watching you do that*."

The side door of the RV ripped open. A short dusky kid who Amy remembered was called Fredo leaned in and said to Josh, "Did you hear?"

"I couldn't hear anything over her."

"Outbreak *inside* the REPER command center. All hell broke loose, there was an explosion, the building's on fire, all their containment breached. Infected pouring out of their holding area."

"Holy *shit*."

"OGZA says fire trucks headed one way, then ten minutes later REPER were going the other. Pulling out. Leaving the Green Zone. Leaving everything."

"They're pulling out of [Undisclosed]?"

"Looks like it."

Amy said, "So what does that mean?"

Josh said, "It means all the manpower is now devoted to keeping anyone from leaving the city, and anybody left behind is now on their own."

Fredo said, "OGZA put out a call for assistance, anybody and everybody with a gun. They said this is about to go from a class two to a class three zombie outbreak."

Amy said, "Is a class three the one where you guys *actually do something*?"

Fredo said, "They said they can get us inside the city. They got friends on the cordon but that's only until the feds change the guard rotations."

Josh hesitated, studying the ridiculous collection of guns on the wall. Finally, he said, "Tell everyone it's a go. The feds shit the bed, and now it's up to us. We roll in thirty minutes."

3 Hours Until the Massacre at Ffirth Asylum

John couldn't help but notice that, while all of Undisclosed appeared to be the aftermath of a post–Super Bowl riot in Detroit, if you had woken up in Dave's neighborhood you wouldn't have noticed any difference. Same old busted windows and same months-old trash bags sitting on porches. John found this comforting.

The big change, of course, was where Dave's little eleven-hundred-foot bungalow had previously stood, there now wasn't much of anything. Just a floor supporting the black frames of two burned-out walls and piles of wet, charred debris. Blackened drywall and two-by-fours and roofing and gnarled wiring.

John really didn't feel anything about this, one way or the other. And not just because he had been the one to burn it down. John didn't get sentimental about houses. Maybe it was because he bounced around so much as a kid, thanks to three different divorces. But he liked to think it just made more sense to not get attached to things. The memories didn't get burned up with a house, or transferred to the new owners if it got sold. A house was just wood and nails. Falling in love with a house or a car or a pair of shoes, it was a dead end. You save your love for the things that can love you back.

Falconer wanted the Porsche out of view, in case REPER came by or somebody tried to steal the stereo or something. One of the abandoned houses down the street had left its garage door open, and Falconer pulled in. John personally thought it was wiser to have the car within lunging distance in case they needed to make a desperate getaway, but apparently desperate getaways were what *other* people did in Falconer's world, while Falconer chased them and told them they had the right to remain silent.

Once parked, John found the prospect of opening the car door and stepping out into the night erased any illusions he had that this was the same old neighborhood. In the rearview mirror, John saw curtains rustle in the dark house across the street. An infected? Or somebody hunkered down, scared that John and Falconer were infected? Who knows. If it was some terrified refugee crouched with a shotgun, John was hoping that the Porsche would put them at ease. No zombie's gonna drive a Porsche.

There you go, with that zombie bullshit.

They eased the heavy garage door down, closing it behind the Porsche. They headed down the sidewalk, at which point John thought he saw somebody slip around a corner, but then realized he didn't. He thought he heard footsteps, but it was a windy night and the sound was a strand of Christmas lights—from last year—tapping against a window at the neighbor's place.

Falconer asked, "The Soy Sauce, was it in the house when it burned?"

"No. I'll show you."

John was afraid Falconer would say, "Great, I'll wait here!" but instead Falconer led the way, striding into Dave's yard like a man with a huge gun. Falconer glanced this way and that, alert but not scared. John followed and made his way around the yard to find the toolshed hadn't burned. It was also still unlocked from when he'd grabbed the chainsaw the day everything went to shit. He reached inside and grabbed a shovel. He tossed it to Falconer.

"The sauce is in a little silver container, about the size of a spool of thread. Inside is a really thick, black liquid. When we find it, don't open it. Not only will the shit kill you if it gets on your skin, but it will *come after you.* Have you seen *The Blob?* It's like that. Only tiny."

"And when you say it will kill 'you,' you mean 'me.' Because you can handle it for some reason."

"Yes. You'll see."

"Uh huh. And judging from the shovel, I assume you buried it?"

"Yeah, around here somewhere. Don't look at me that way, I need you to do the digging, you'll see why. It's not deep. Now, the container is somewhere here in the backyard. I know where. But I'm not going to tell you. I want you to walk to a random spot—what you think is a random spot, anyway—and dig down about a foot."

Falconer didn't move from where he was standing. He plunged the shovel into the dirt right in front of his feet. Three scoops and then—

"Look. Right there."

Falconer looked down, and in the moonlight saw the glint of brushed steel, poking out from the mud. "All right, how did you do that?"

"I didn't. *It* did. The Sauce. When we buried it, Dave just threw the shovel like a javelin and said wherever it landed, that's where we'd bury it. That's where it landed. Where you're standing. Because the Soy Sauce wanted it to land there. Because it knew you would be standing there a year later."

" 'It' knew. So the Sauce is alive."

"Yes, sir."

"And now you're going to swallow some of it."

"That's the least painful way, yeah."

"And you have no idea how it does what it does."

"Let's just say it's magic."

"Let's just say that I need a little more explanation than that if I'm going to go along with this."

John sighed. "Okay, have you heard of nanotechnology?"

"Yeah. Microscopic robots, right?"

"Right, and imagine they can make millions of these robots and embed them in a liquid, so that you now have a liquid infused with the power of all these machines. Got it?"

"All right."

"Now imagine if, instead of tiny robots, it's magic."

John dug the bottle from the mud with his fingers.

"Stand back."

"If you take that shit and you go into a seizure or cardiac arrest, I'm leavin' you here."

"Detective, if I take this shit and it looks like the trip is going bad, fucking *run*."

John squeezed the bottle in his hand. He thought he heard the footsteps again, but decided he needed to stop falling for that at some point. He took a deep breath, and said, "All right. Here goes."

2 Hours, 45 Minutes Until the Massacre at Ffirth Asylum

Amy was rumbling through the night in a crowded RV, heading south, scared out of her mind. Her head was between her knees, staring at the filthy floor and praying silently, as had been her habit since she'd been a toddler. She had realized she was doing it out of reflex. If God was the type who needed to be asked verbally before he would support your side over man-eating monsters, then she wasn't sure what good he would be once he joined. She hadn't been to Mass since her brother Jim was alive. Her faith could be summed up in two sentences, from one of the *Narnia* books. Speaking about Aslan, the lion that symbolized Jesus, a character says:

"I'm on Aslan's side even if there isn't any Aslan to lead it. I'm going to live as like a Narnian as I can even if there isn't any Narnia."

Amy hated—*hated*—the way the grown-ups her parents had surrounded themselves with were so quick to offer prayers and so slow to actually *do* anything. Old women who barely left the house for anything but bingo and congratulated themselves on never drinking alcohol or saying dirty words, thinking God created humans to stay home and watch televangelists and just run out the clock until the day they die. Well, Amy figured you don't need more than five minutes on this planet to figure out that one thing we know about God—maybe the only thing—is that he favors those who *act*. David also believed that, though he didn't realize it.

Guns were clicking all around her. The zombie nerds were pushing all variety of bullets into all varieties of gun parts. Long, gleaming brass bullets, bright red shotgun shells. Guns designed with the elegant lines of sports cars, slick oiled metal and curved textured plastic meant to fit right into your hand. Josh rammed a lever forward on his and it clicked satisfyingly into place. Don't get her wrong, she saw the appeal. She also saw how you could start thinking of them as toys.

Josh held up a blood red shotgun shell and said, "Dragon's Breath. Zirconium-based incendiary pellets, looks like a flamethrower every time you pull the trigger. This is an automatic shotgun with a twenty-round drum. Three more drums in my backpack. We get in a jam, this thing will unleash a wall of hellfire, as fast as I can pull the trigger." He clicked shells into a plastic drum the size of a large saucepan and said, "These shells are fifteen dollars apiece, by the way."

And there it was. She suddenly realized that she'd rather have David or John, either one, armed with a baseball bat, than any of these guys and their video game hardware. David and John had a look in their eye when things went bad—a sad but resigned familiarity. They weren't trained for violence and maybe weren't particularly competent at it, but they weren't going to go pee in the corner, either. Both of them had come from bad homes, both had gotten hit quite a bit as kids and maybe that's all it was. Maybe they just understood something about the world and were more ready for it when things took a turn. She didn't see that look in any of these suburban kids.

A couple of months ago, Amy had come to stay with David over the long Labor Day weekend. At around midnight on Friday night, a crazy guy started showing up. He knocked on the door and said he had a pizza—they hadn't ordered one—and he handed them this filthy pizza box, like something he'd dug out of the trash. David opened it and it had dog poop in it. They called the police, but the guy was gone when they got there. The guy came back, Saturday night. This time the old pizza box had a dead squirrel in it. David threatened the guy, slammed the door in his face. The guy comes back at two in the morning, another pizza box. David doesn't even answer the door, just calls the police again. Again, no sign of the guy when they get there.

At around 7 P.M. on Sunday, the crazy guy starts showing up once an hour. If they didn't answer, he'd stand there and ring the doorbell, over and over and over. The third time, David goes to the door and this time the guy says something to David, through the closed door. Whatever he said, it made David open the door. They exchanged low, heated words, and the guy leaves a pizza box on the porch and walks away. David looked inside, closed it, and threw it in the trash barrel outside. He wouldn't tell Amy what was inside. As the man drove away David yelled, "You ever come within a hundred feet of her again, and I'm gonna tear your throat out with my teeth." Only there were a lot more curse words.

But the guy did come back. At three in the morning. To their bedroom window. They were both fast asleep and Amy slowly woke up and heard whispering, a foot from her head. And it's the crazy guy, whispering *her* name, over and over.

She screamed. David sprang out of bed, grabbed that ridiculous crossbow that John bought him at a gun show, and charged out of the house.

David shoots the pizza guy in the chest and the guy goes down, screaming. But then comes the twist—the guy is carrying a fresh pizza, from a local twenty-four-hour pizza place in town. He works for them. The guy is wearing a clean, new uniform, he looks totally sane and acts completely shocked that he got attacked by a customer. The pizza was for a house down the street. He said he just went to the wrong door.

After all of the legal craziness, with charges filed by the guy and talk of a civil suit for his medical bills, Amy asked David what they'd do if the guy came back some night, in crazy mode. David's answer? "I hit him someplace where I know it'll be fatal."

And he would. Even if it meant jail. He would do it for her.

A kid in the back was trying on a pair of night-vision goggles. There were eight people packed into the RV. Fredo was driving. About 150 people counted themselves among the Zombie Response Squad when the wave of zombie panic hit the university. Seven answered the call when it came time to actually meet the threat—all of them piled in the RV with Amy, clacking the mechanisms on their guns.

Amy was scared out of her mind. But she would push through the fear and finish this. And she would have to hope the men sitting around her would do the same. Amy had read the *Lord of the Rings* trilogy four times, and was starting on her fifth. There was a bit she had memorized when the Ents were marching off to war against seemingly impossible odds (all odds probably seemed against you when you were a big ridiculous walking tree). It was running through her head now and would keep looping from now until they arrived at Undisclosed:

> "Of course, it is likely enough, my friends, that we are going to our doom: the last march of the Ents. But if we stayed at home and did nothing, doom would find us anyway, sooner or later."

Yes, Amy had long ago made peace with the fact that she was a huge, flaming nerd.

Soy Sauce

John twisted the silver bottle. It separated in the middle, along a seam that was invisible when it was closed. He didn't open it all the way— he'd learned that wasn't always wise if the Soy Sauce was "awake."

A thin, black stream leaked out from the crack, it looked like a length of heavy black string had come unspooled. John laid his index finger under the stream to catch it.

Then, several things happened at once.

First, the shuffling footsteps John thought he had been hearing got louder, and faster. They had a hollow tone, like someone stomping around on the floor above your apartment. John and Falconer both spun, looking for the source. Then something leaped off the neighbor's roof, sailing through the air like a huge, weaponized flying squirrel, coming right down on Falconer.

John's brain had a tenth of a second to try to register what he was really seeing when the Soy Sauce made its move. At the exact same moment John's mouth was forming the words—

"FALCONER LOOK—"

—the thin, black string of Sauce coiled around on its own like a snake, in a blink whipping around his finger, over his fingernail, and digging into his skin right at the sensitive spot where a hangnail would form. Pain flashed up John's hand, all the way to his elbow.

Then the Soy Sauce took hold, and the world disappeared.

Dave once described taking a hit of Soy Sauce as like digging up one of those thick fiber-optic lines that feeds an entire city's Internet connection and plugging it into your brain. All those streams of data crashing into your neurons at once, so hard and fast that you simultaneously know everything and nothing at all. John always thought his own description was clearer: it's like an Insane Clown Posse concert where all fifty thousand members of the audience are given their own microphone and sound system, and they all start simultaneously improvising bad freestyle rap verses.

John was introduced to the stuff at a party, when he was barely old enough to legally drink (and had been drinking for eight years). It was given to him by a black dude from Ohio doing a fake Jamaican accent, the guy who would later be found with his guts splattered on the walls of his trailer—the fucker got off easy. It was the same sensation this time as the first. Soy Sauce was not something you built up a tolerance for.

Everything stopped—John was yanked out of his body, out of the world, mind freed from the confines of his eyes and ears and nose and mouth and a trillion nerve endings. A wash of alien sensations crashed over him, like being naked at the bottom of a frantic orgy involving everyone in that *Star Wars* cantina scene.

John found that he was suddenly somewhere else. He was standing among bombed-out buildings, avalanches of brick and wood and glass flung across streets, weeds growing up through cracks in the asphalt. He had leaped forward in time, he didn't know how much. He looked around—or rather, his view panned around, as he didn't seem to have eyes to "look" with. Devastation and broken structures littering the landscape into the horizon and beyond. He saw that the rubble was crawling with life, small skittering things.

John walked—or rather, his view floated—toward the remains of a shattered church. A rotting human head crawled across a pile of ragged concrete, the legs of a parasite jutting below the jaw, the parasite wearing the moldering skull like a hermit crab's shell. Another head trundled by. Then another. Then, another set of spider legs skittered by, this time trailing a tangled wad of guts.

They were everywhere. John looked around—again without turning a head or a set of eyes—and saw the streets were littered with broken and charred corpses, flies buzzing over spilled guts. The head of an old woman—eyes having long rotted out of their sockets, the skull bearing a blunt trauma wound—came wobbling by. The parasite inside opened its mouth and emitted that bone-rattling shriek. A moment later, a second head and parasite came trundling behind it. They started humping.

Then it was gone, John yanked back across time, and now he was in the sky, trees and homes whipping by underneath him. He saw rows of military trucks forming thick layers on either side of a fence—the cordon circling city limits. He flew away from it, zipping up the highway. Suddenly he was inside of an RV. And there was Amy, sitting with a bunch of dudes carrying guns. She was sticking her hand in a box of Golden Grahams, eating them dry like they were potato chips. John tried to speak to her, but of course he wasn't really there.

Focus. Focus on getting back.

And then the world was twisting and flowing around him, the scenery stretching past until he found himself back at Dave's burned-out house, back in his own body, staring at Falconer and the unholy thing that had jumped down at him from the rooftop above.

The scene was frozen before him. John saw that the leaping monster was transforming grotesquely in midair, Falconer still not having so much as tilted his head up to see it. The leaves at their feet were no longer blowing and the world had gone utterly silent. Time had simply stopped. John looked down at his hands, and realized that he could move his fingers, realized that time had not stopped for *him*, but only the rest of the world. John took a tentative step, found that he could move with no problem. Then he looked around, put his hands on his hips and in the stillness said, "Huh."

This particular thing had never happened to John on Soy Sauce before, but that was par for the course because the same thing never happened twice. Out-of-body experiences, time travel, interdimensional travel, invisibility, yes. Stopping time? No. He'd have to tell Dave. If he remembered, that is—unfortunately, the godlike status you sometimes achieved under Soy Sauce, however briefly, was kind of like the boost in sexual confidence you got from beer: nice while you're in the moment, but the next day you don't remember shit. He tried to get over the initial shock of what was going on and assess the situation. Who knew how long the effect would last, and when time would suddenly burst forward again?

Falconer was frozen in place ten feet in front of John, a statue that looked like it was built to pay tribute to good style and bewildered expressions. Suspended in midair two feet above him, was a monster.

John could kind of see where it had been a man once, before the parasite did its work, but it took a few minutes. (Wait, did it? Did minutes exist?) The creature's arms and legs both were spread straight out, so that the limbs and torso formed a sideways "H." Along the arms and legs both were sharp, pointed protrusions of bone, so that the limbs were serrated, like a knife. It was easy to see its method of attack: in a half second of real time, it would wrap the limbs around Falconer's neck and torso and with one brutal squeeze, leave him in three distinct bloody chunks. There was no time for Falconer to react. He was simply not going to survive the attack without intervention.

John walked toward him and thought the ground felt different. It took him a moment to realize that the grass wasn't bending under his feet—like he was walking on titanium Astroturf. His shoes were sticking with each step, where blades of grass were pricking the soles like needles. John went to grab the shovel from where Falconer had stabbed it into the ground, and realized he could not move it. Not even to wiggle it back and forth.

So it was like that. Time was frozen but it was truly frozen—John couldn't actually impact the world in any way. He couldn't kill the monster, or even push Falconer out of harm's way. Well. Shit. What good was this?

Actually . . .

He could find out if Dave was alive.

No, he couldn't leave here. At any moment the Soy Sauce could wear off, time could resume and Falconer would be on his own to deal with the creature swooping down on his head. Or, rather, *not* deal with it. He likely wouldn't even comprehend what was happening before his severed skull was rolling in the dead leaves of Dave's yard. The man was good, but not that good. And so, the venture with the Soy Sauce had all been a big, stupid waste. Getting out of the asylum building, coming here, all of it. When things returned to normal, Falconer would get splattered, John would be on his own, and he would be no closer to fixing things than he was the moment he woke up hungover in the frat house earlier.

Well. Whatever.

John walked over next to Falconer and positioned himself behind, with his hands on Falconer's back. John leaned forward, all of his weight on the man's back (Falconer did not move, of course, it was like leaning on a bronze statue) so that at the moment time returned to normal, Falconer would be shoved instantly out of harm's way. At the same time John would fall to the ground, and hopefully this would thwart the monster long enough that they could do . . . something.

John waited. And waited. Time remained frozen.

A couple of hours (?) later John was sitting on the prickly petrified grass in front of Falconer, annoyed, wondering precisely how long he should babysit this situation instead of striking out and trying to do something else. Finally, he got bored and made his way to the street, walking toward the hospital quarantine. What else was there to do?

John walked through Dave's neighborhood and out into the life-size Undisclosed diorama. At one point he painfully banged his shin on a discarded newspaper that was in the middle of being blown by a gust of wind when time stopped. There were a few stationary vehicles on the roads—not many, with the curfew. John figured the uninfected were living the life of refugees in a war zone, hunkered down with the kids in the basement, hoping that the sounds of all hell breaking loose on their block wouldn't be followed by the sound of their front door getting smashed in.

Out of curiosity, John approached a beat-up pickup truck frozen in the middle of the street, a cloud of exhaust hanging perfectly still in the air behind it. The bed was full of cardboard boxes, cases of toilet paper and diapers. The driver was an elderly black man with a shotgun laying across his lap. His hand was stuck halfway to the ashtray, two inches of cigarette between thumb and index finger, a curling ribbon of smoke hanging frozen over it. John reached his hand in through the driver's side window and tried to push his finger through the frozen smoke. It was as solid as rock.

Weird.

John strolled across town and made his way to the hospital. His footsteps were utterly silent, the quiet here was less like a library and more like having earplugs. Sound waves unable to move the air, apparently. John thought he could hear his own blood sliding through his veins, and his digestion gurgling away. He wondered how long it would be until that drove him insane.

The hospital was now a POW camp. The grounds were surrounded by the kind of high fence you'd see on a maximum security prison, razor wire at the top and everything. Outside of the fence were concrete barriers they'd dropped in to keep somebody from getting the bright idea to just ram through the fence with a truck. Yet, John found no human guards on the outside. Were they all in bed? Instead, stationed every two hundred feet or so was a driverless vehicle. On the back of each was a turret, two thin barrels on each side of a cylinder outfitted with a bank of lenses. Mechanical eyes, with radar or infrared or thermal imaging like the Predator. This place was totally being guarded by robotic sentry guns. *Badass.*

John had come hoping he could just get a look into the yard—if Dave was alive and outside, and if John could get a glimpse of him, that would be enough. But they had covered the damned fence in tarps that, inexplicably, were all printed with misspelled advertisements (blocking the section of fence in front of him was a huge billboard that said TRY THE BLACK ANUS QUARTER POUNDER). He should have known it wouldn't be that easy. John walked all the way around the fencing, a trip that took him at least an hour. Or zero time, depending on how you looked at it. That raised the question in John's mind as to whether or not time would *ever* resume to normal speed. What would he do if it just stayed this way forever? Take up a hobby?

John didn't find an obvious way into the quarantine—he had been hoping that somebody had been walking through an open gate at the exact moment time stopped—and climbing the fence would be no easier in freeze-frame than it would be at normal speed. In fact, the coils of razor wire would be worse in this state of absolute rigidity. John had a vivid image of himself falling into that wire, the blades slicing through his abdomen and shredding his intestines. And John staying like that, writhing in the razors, unable to free himself. Unable to die. For all of eternity.

John completed his circuit and made it around to the front gate again.

John noticed a frozen pillar of smoke that had been drifting horizontally over the fence in the wind, and figured maybe the inmates were all standing around a campfire, roasting weenies or something. If he could just get up high enough to see over the fence . . .

Boom. There were trees right behind him. They looked fairly climbable. It occurred to John halfway up that this would have been impossible two months earlier—the frozen-in-time leaves would have sliced him open just as effectively as the razor wire. But this was mid-November and he had bare branches to grab onto. He was making good progress right up until he banged his head into an invisible force field. Hanging above him was a gray haze and he finally realized it was the plume of smoke from the campfire, pushed over the fence by a gust of wind that John obviously could not feel. He re-routed himself to get past it and, now at a height where he could easily break his neck if he fell—

and lay writhing and screaming, unheard in the eternity between moments

—he suddenly realized that the plume of campfire smoke formed an imperfect bridge right over the fence and into the quarantine.

Fighting every possible sense of balance and self-preservation, John steadied himself on the gray haze and walked over the fence, trying to keep his eyes forward and not on the impossibly flimsy, transparent bridge he was edging across. The footing wasn't bad, though; the tiny, suspended particles of ash had a rough texture, like walking on a huge bar of Lava soap.

The plume got uncomfortably narrow as he got closer to the fire, and as soon as he passed over the fences he had to get down on his hands and knees and crawl. He jumped to the ground because it seemed like a bad idea to walk into the glowing embers of a dying bonfire, even if it was frozen in time. He had no idea how that worked.

No longer focusing on trying not to fall on his head, he finally had time to register what was going on in the yard. There were dozens of people in red and green jumpsuits. Well, shit, he didn't see why the situation in here was any worse than out in town. Nobody had a monster hovering over them and they were all safely behind a fence, guarded by robots. If Dave was here and alive, then it seemed like a best-case scenario. Then John happened to glimpse what was being burned in the fire pit and thought, *Oh.*

John tore his gaze away from the bones in the ash—he had caught himself trying to count the skulls in there and was up to sixty-two when he stopped—and started moving through the still life of the wax dummy quarantine. None of the people standing in the yard were Dave, so he headed for the hospital itself. Fortunately the door was propped open so he wasn't going to have to figure out some convoluted way in—

Dave!

There, next to the main entrance of the hospital. John almost missed him because he was bent over, paused in the middle of tying his shoe. He had an open can of beans sitting on the ground next to him, a little plastic spoon sticking out. And there was Molly, standing next to him, poised to start eating the beans with Dave's attention diverted.

A dam burst inside John, a river of relief crashing through him so hard he almost collapsed.

Dave was alive. Somehow.

His friend was pale, and had lost some weight. A lot of it. And while Dave could stand to lose some weight, he had lost it because he was in a prison camp against his will, eating cold beans and shit. Packed in here with other dudes he almost certainly hated by now, cut off, standing among garbage and broken windows and burning corpses. Because they had left him here. Because *John* had left him here.

And then another dam burst, this time unleashing a black tide of self-hatred that was poised to come crashing over the sand castle of John's mind. But he held it at bay, knowing this was no time to let things go dark in his head. He wanted a drink. Later. For now, he was going to take a shot.

"Dave?" said John, and the words seemed to die right in front of him, swallowed into the stillness of the paused world. It was like the little pocket of time that let John move around ended two inches in front of his face, and that's all the sound could travel. He leaned in closer and said, "Dave, I don't know if you can hear me. But I'm coming. Be ready. Stay near the fence. If anything I'm saying is capable of sinking in, let it be that. Wait for the sound of shit hitting the fan."

No reaction from Dave, of course. John tried to think of something else that could be accomplished while he was here, but he imagined time suddenly resuming while he was standing here, so that the end result of the whole project would be that he was now trapped inside the quarantine with Amy out there trying to rescue both of them. Falconer would be in several bloody chunks.

John headed to the smoke bridge, followed it back over the fence, and nearly killed himself trying to transition from the solid smoke to the tree branches. But he eventually made it to the ground, landing with a jolt on the immovable grass, and started making his way back to Dave's house. John's route took him past the asylum, the main building now with a huge hole in the side that was leaking smoke. And then he saw something that almost made him shit himself.

Shadows. Walking shadows.

This was no trick of the light. These were bona fide shadow men, just like he'd seen in the hospital security video, just as Dave saw in his bathroom recently, just as random folks around Undisclosed had been reporting off and on for as far back as written records were kept. And they were moving. The former Ffirth TB asylum and now former outbreak command center for REPER, was filthy with the shadow men. Moving, twisting through the air. Not frozen, like everything else—one thing John knew about the shadows is that they were unbound by time, which is what made them unspeakably dangerous. Well, that and the fact that they were assholes.

John ran. He made it two blocks before he took a bullet to the shoulder and spun to the ground.

That's what it felt like, anyway. Something had torn open his shirt and left a red gash underneath. He scrambled to his feet, looking around for a gunman. Finally, he looked back the way he came and saw his assailant: a moth, frozen in midair. Tiny, fragile, yet utterly unmovable. John pressed on, toward Dave's house, slower this time, glancing back over his wounded shoulder for trailing shadows.

Back in Dave's yard now, which was unfortunately exactly how he'd left it: with a deformed motherfucker swooping down on Falconer, ready to saw his body into pieces.

This was incredibly frustrating. He had as long as he wanted to form a plan, but since the only thing he could move was his own body, this advantage amounted to nothing more than the ability to throw himself into the monster's jaws instead of Falconer. Even now, he saw how stupid his idea had been earlier, to try to just shove Falconer out of the way. They'd both wind up on the ground, with the beast on top of them. All he'd be doing is supersizing the monster's lunch. John wondered if he had stuffed a weapon in his pocket before he froze time, if he'd be free to use it? After all, his clothes moved with him—

Ah, there we go. He *did* have something.

From Falconer's point of view, John stood in front of him and started to open his little silver pill bottle. Then John got a momentary look of panic on his face, shouted, "FALCONER LOOK—" and suddenly *blinked out of existence.* At the exact same moment, a growling, shrieking, inhuman mass of thrashing limbs fell onto Falconer's back, flinging him to the grass.

Falconer rolled over and whipped out his sidearm in one motion. What was in front of him was a spastic tableau of absurdity.

A grossly deformed once-human monster was rolling around, howling in frustration. It had four jagged limbs full of huge white teeth that it was trying to whip through the air to slash anything in the vicinity.

It couldn't, though, because it was restrained by lengths of cloth that knotted the limbs behind its back like handcuffs. Standing over this flailing, shrieking beast was John, in tiny black jockey shorts, screaming, "Yeah! Fuck you! Fuck you! Fuck yooooooooouuuuu!!!"

Falconer kicked away from the monster and got to his feet. John looked at him and yelled, "What are you waiting for? Shoot him in the mouth!"

The word "mouth" could not be heard over the gunshots.

A minute later John, heart pounding and breathless, untied his pants from the twitching beast and pulled them on. Falconer was reloading. Falconer had put six bullets in the creature's maw but John had no idea what it took to kill a spider—the only one he'd ever successfully killed was the one he drowned with the turkeys. Glancing nervously at the creature, John suddenly remembered the real reason he had made Falconer bring him here. He said, "The box."

"What?"

"The green box, get it out of the toolshed and let's get the hell out of here."

Falconer ran to the shed and said, "Not here."

"Shit! They took it. No, wait. Dave put it in the trunk of the Caddie while I was burning the house. We have to find it. What would they have done with an abandoned car? We left my Cadillac at the burrito place . . ."

"If it was blocking traffic, they'd have impounded it. Maybe. Who knows. Why do we need the box?"

"Trust me, we need it. Or rather, we need it to not wind up in the hands of somebody else. Oh, wait! Damn it!"

"What?"

"It just occurred to me that I could have written Dave a message on a wall using my own shit!"

Falconer didn't ask for clarification on this, he just jogged down toward the garage that held the Porsche, with John in tow. This time John *knew* he was hearing footsteps. Fast steps. A lot of them. Out of breath, John hissed, "Detective . . ."

"I hear it. Move."

It took both of them to open the garage door—it was old and the springs were busted, which meant it was heavy as hell without the lift system to help. John was left to keep it propped over his head while Falconer ran in to start the car.

Footsteps. A stampede. Something had been roused in the night, probably by the sound of the gunshots. John whipped his head around, squinting in the night, nervous mists of breath puffing into the night air.

A crowd rounded the corner.

Blocking the street.

Dozens and dozens of shambling figures, so many that no light slipped between them.

"DETECTIVE!"

The zombies approached fast, coming up the street like a tide. John turned and saw that they were coming from the opposite direction, too, converging like a hammer and anvil. The Porsche started and John was calculating the time it would take Falconer to back out, stop, let John in, pull into the street, and plow through the crowd—

The tires were flat.

It was so dark in the garage he almost didn't notice. Both of the back tires had been slashed—shredded, in fact—and John was going to guess the same went for the front. He was just about to tell Falconer this but at that moment, John felt something touch his face. A caress, like a finger. Only it was definitely not a fucking finger.

That was all it took—John cursed and ducked inside the garage. The door slammed shut, sealing them off from all light.

"Detective! Your tires! Shit!"

From inside the car, "WHAT? GET IN!"

"NO! WE—"

Falconer flipped on the headlights, lighting up the interior of the garage.

There was a giant daddy longlegs spider covering the entire inner surface of the garage door—easily eight feet across. Where the body of the spider would normally be, was a human face.

The creature jumped.

125 Minutes Until the Massacre
at Ffirth Asylum

I was in the middle of tying my shoe when an idea popped into my brain, out of nowhere. Somehow, I suddenly just knew that *Molly was eating my beans.*

"Hey! Stop that! Bad dog!" I slapped her snout away from the can. She licked bean sauce from her nose, sniffed the air, and took off, presumably to find someone else's food to steal. I considered eating the rest of the beans even though they were contaminated with dog spit now, but decided I hadn't gotten quite that low yet. I decided to go back to bed, and took one step inside the main entrance when a drum solo of rapid footsteps approached from the stairwell. TJ skidded to a stop on the tile and said, "Roof."

I thought he had barked at me, but he headed for the stairs and I followed him all the way up. Two dozen people were up there, lined up along the ledge like pigeons. Hope met us as soon as we stepped out of the roof access door. She grabbed my elbow, pulled me to the edge like she was going to toss me over. She leaned close, pointed and whispered, "Look. That's the boom we heard earlier."

I said, "The asylum."

From behind me TJ said, "Now you see all them headlights, lookin' like it's rush hour in Atlanta? All them vehicles headin' off to the north? That's REPER buggin' out. Headin' for the highway."

"Perfect. Let's break outta here."

"I wouldn't use the word 'perfect.' Means the situation out there has gone so much to shit that a few hundred men with body armor and assault rifles decided it's not safe *for them.* Plus I don't see any reason they'd take the rest of security offline. If anything they need it more, right? I bet tomorrow instead of two of them UAVs up there they'll have six, or ten."

"On the other hand," I said, "if they're just giving up containment of the quarantine, that means somewhere right now there's a table full of guys with medals on their jackets trying to figure out exactly what type of bomb you need to vaporize several city blocks, and what would be a cool name for the operation. Something like Operation Cleansing Dawn."

"Damn, man, that is a good name. I'd feel proud to get burned up in somethin' called that."

"You seriously don't think that option's on the table?"

"I don't know, man. I didn't ten minutes ago."

I said, "Don't take this the wrong way, but we're all gonna have to make our own decision here. Me? If I can get my dog to help me figure out how to get outta here, I'm going. And I mean tonight, if at all possible. Cover of dark, while they're good and confused out there."

"Uh huh. So you wind up on the other side of the fence and then what? You're out on the streets, unarmed. You think you just show up at Wally's tomorrow and clock in like nothing ever happened?"

"Like I said, do what you want. But for me the choice between inside and outside a cage is no choice at all."

Goddamn I would not miss the stairs in this place. A hundred freaking stairs to get to the roof and it somehow seemed like even more to get back down. I had gotten down ninety-two of them when, from below me, Hope screamed.

When TJ and I got to the bottom, we found Hope staring terrified at Molly. The dog had something long and horrible and meaty in her jaws. It took me a moment to register that it was a very fresh-looking human spine.

Damn, she was *hungry.*

120 Minutes Until the Massacre at Ffirth Asylum

John was screaming and trying to run directly through the garage door, hoping to smash through it like the Kool-Aid Man. The daddy longlegs creature landed on top of the Porsche, wrapping its legs around the entire body of the car.

Falconer was paralyzed by fear for a whole .5 seconds before he screamed, "GET DOWN!" and reached over the roof of the car with his automatic. He squeezed the trigger and filled the closed space with lightning and thunder. Chunks flew off the monster, but it held on.

"MOVE!"

John saw the rear lights flare up on the Porsche not six inches from his face. He threw himself out of the way as tires spun and the Porsche smashed backward through the garage door. Huge slabs of rubber flew in every direction as the Porsche flung off the ruined remnants of its tires. The car hobbled backward down the driveway, off into the grass, through a mailbox, and into a shallow ditch full of dead leaves.

Immediately John registered good news and bad news:

The good news was the spider was gone—the garage door had scraped it off.

The bad news was that he and Falconer were dead. The street was full of zombies. Fast zombies. The shadows were thick with crouching shoulders, tensed limbs and crazy eyes. The Porsche spun out helplessly, bare rims trying in vain to dig their way out of the muddy ditch.

For some reason, this was the moment the little flame of hope inside John blew out, everything inside him was oddly cold and dark and calm. The crowd washed in, swarming the Porsche. Detective Lance Falconer was yanked roughly from the car like a toddler and dragged away.

It was all happening in silence for John, the desperate screaming and cursing and everything falling apart.

John had time to think—

I am not the star of a zombie movie. I am the guy in the background who gets eaten in the first montage.

—when he was bear hugged from behind.

Eight thin, horrible arms wrapped him up from neck to ankles, squeezing the breath from his lungs, cracking ribs. The spider's shriek filled the world.

105 Minutes Until the Massacre at Ffirth Asylum

Amy jolted awake, ripped out of an awful nightmare that involved something terrible happening to the people she loved. She didn't remember the details of the dream, but didn't need to. That was the only nightmare she ever had.

She was shocked that she had drifted off. If you ever needed proof that we are prisoners of biology, there it is. These could be her last minutes on earth and her body decided to sleep through a bunch of them. Josh was rubbing his finger on the screen of his phone and Amy was pretty sure he was playing a game.

They were absolutely alone on the highway, not meeting a single car coming the other direction, no taillights as far as they could see. Amy moved up and took the empty passenger seat next to the driver, Fredo. He looked more scared than she was. She kept him company. She found out his last name was Borelli and that he was getting a degree in Public Relations, but was thinking of changing his major because a lot of the classes depressed him. Fredo's brother was in the marines, as his father had been, as *his* father had been. Fredo's dad had fought in Desert Storm, Grandad in Vietnam. Brother saw action in Afghanistan. Fredo took classes in PowerPoint. Fredo was really into Japanese anime, but none of the porn stuff, he assured her. He didn't have any friends or family in Undisclosed, but hoped David was okay. They talked about *Battlestar Galactica* for a while. That made the time go by, as Amy knew it would, and soon Josh was telling Fredo to turn and exit the highway onto a country road that Amy knew would eventually take them around the lake, past the woods and the turkey farm/stench factory.

"Where are we going?"

Josh said, "We have to get off the highway before the army's roadblock, this road circles around the lake and comes in behind the industrial park. The friendly checkpoints are there. Once we get through, then we meet up with OGZA."

"Where are they?"

"They set up inside the building REPER abandoned, I guess they left a ton of equipment and supplies behind. But that means they're right there outside of quarantine and they'll be the first to get overrun if the quarantine fails. So the first order of business is to meet up with them and get a status update. But it's a fortified building, and we're all going to be armed. Everything is going to be fine."

Josh turned out to not be full of crap on the subject of getting inside town—the army guys manning the checkpoint on the country road south of the lake let the RV through after a short conversation with Fredo. But then, a few miles later, they met a second checkpoint, one that was approximately ten times scarier than the first. It was a terrifying wall of black vehicles and men in equally terrifying black suits. They had night-vision goggles or something behind their visors that lit up red in the night, making them look like freaking demons.

"Josh? What is this? Who are—"

Josh shushed her, but Amy thought he looked like he was trying with all his might to keep poop from escaping his body. An army of the black-clad men with their elaborate machine guns swarmed the bus, those red eyes floating in the night. Barrels were raised, like they were ready to paint the inside of the RV red. One of the guards went to the driver's side door and Fredo held a one-way conversation with him. Fredo gave the guy the OGZA pass code or whatever, but there was no answer. The guy backed away and conferred with someone else. After a tightly knotted minute, he waved them through. Amy and the seven members of the Zombie Response Squad entered Outbreak Ground Zero.

The power seemed to be out in most of the town and all the stores were closed, but they would be anyway since it was the middle of the night. Still no signal on her phone. Fredo said, "We're six blocks away. Still nothing from OGZA?"

Josh tapped on his laptop and said, "No. Everything has been cut off for the last hour."

Amy said, "We probably just got close enough to the town where the wireless signals are all blocked or whatever. Like maybe they can still send but we can't receive now."

Josh said, "That's probably it," in a way that did not sound at all convincing. "I actually don't know how they were getting around the blackout before."

Fredo said, "Whoa, is that it? The lights down there?"

Josh answered, "That's the quarantine. That's the city's hospital back there behind all that. They got the perimeter all lit up. Look at that fence."

"Jesus," Fredo breathed. "It's . . . right . . . *there*. They're right there behind that fence. Jesus."

Amy could see Fredo's imagination spinning with images of what creatures must be shambling beyond that fence. Or maybe she was projecting, because that's what she was doing.

And David is in there with them.

Wait, why were there advertisements all over the fence? Under one of the floodlights she could see an ad for McDonald's bratwurst.

A chubby guy hugging a long machine gun—a gun Amy recognized as "the gun all of the bad guys use in Vietnam movies"—said, "What do we do if they've been overrun?"

Josh answered, "We'll have to play it by ear," which Amy understood to mean, "We'll turn around and run away and congratulate ourselves for having tried." The RV continued past the quarantine and headed right for the creepiest buildings in town: the old TB asylum, a depressing old building that looked like a giant cinder block somebody had fished out of a swamp, next to a smaller building just like it, both of them looming over a bunch of dead trees.

Amy said, "Okay, that place does *not* look safe."

The larger building was damaged, with smoke drifting from a huge hole in one end. A lot of equipment was scattered around the yard. She saw boxes of supplies on a pallet and at least two hoods from decontamination suits laying in the weeds. They'd all either been killed, or run away in a panic. And this RV full of college kids was declaring it their new safe house.

Josh said, "I bet it's one of the safest locations in town. The feds already did the job of securing all the windows and doors and OGZA says they found a lot of food and stuff left behind."

The RV was rolling to a stop. Amy stared at the massive, smoking hole in the wall and her imagination lit up with the image of some elephant-sized creature, breathing fire, smashing through it with its fists.

Oh, you have got to be kidding me, Sullivan.

Josh said, "That's the gym down there, with the hole in it, but

OGZA got that sealed off so you can't get into the rest of the building that way. I guess some oxygen tanks exploded."

"Were they trying to kill a shark?"

"What?"

Amy didn't answer. To Fredo, Josh said, "You got the flares?"

Without a word, Fredo reached into the glove compartment and pulled out an orange pistol with a comically oversized barrel. He rolled down his window, pointed the gun toward the sky and fired. The lawn was bathed in light, a tiny white star rocketing up, then drifting lazily back to earth.

Josh said, "They're supposed to signal with a light from one of the windows. They have a lantern or something and they'll flash it off and on."

Everyone stared at the darkened building. Minutes passed. No lights.

"Maybe they didn't see it."

Josh said, "Do another one. Do you have a red one? Maybe they missed the last one."

Another flare fired. Another wait. No response from the building.

Vietnam Gun Guy said, "Man, that's ominous as shit. Maybe we should go back."

Josh said, "Hey, this is what we came for, Donnie. If they need help, so be it. That's why we brought all this hardware. This is the real thing here, we're not just playing zombie video games and jerking off here. Everybody load up, we're goin' in."

Amy finally spoke up and said what she had been wanting to say for more than two hours. It was futile, she knew, but she had to try.

"Josh . . . I want you to leave the guns behind."

Vietnam Gun Guy, Donnie, said, "What are we supposed to use? Harsh language?"

Josh asked, "Why?"

Amy took a breath and said, "I don't know how to say this without bruising your ego or whatever, but you've accidentally pointed that gun at my head four times in the course of loading it. Josh . . . I'm impressed that you did this, you're amazing for just making this trip. But *you don't know what you're doing with that thing.* And I think there's a one percent chance you're going to actually need the guns and a ninety-nine percent chance that a stray cat is going to jump out of the shadows and you're all going to shoot each other. And me."

Josh laughed.

"I'm not joking. You're not pixels on a screen. You're flesh and blood. If you get spooked and shoot your friend, he's dead, and dead forever, or in a wheelchair. You'll live with that the rest of your life. *Leave the guns behind.* If there's something in there, we are way, way, *way* more likely to survive if we just run as hard as we can back here, than if you try to stand and act out some video game fantasy. The guns will just weigh you down, Josh."

"We'll be careful, I promise."

"No, you won't, because you don't have the training to understand what 'careful' is. Josh, I'm begging you."

"I'm sorry, but—"

"If you leave the guns here, when we get back, *I will have sex with you.* I'll put that in writing. I am not kidding at all. Your friends can watch. You can videotape it."

"Stop it. We're not going in there without protection, and that's that. And this isn't a video game fantasy, you're insulting all of us when you say that."

As he spoke, Josh was affixing some small electronic device to his shotgun. Amy thought it was some kind of fancy scope, but Josh tapped away at his laptop, and a video window appeared. He swung the shotgun around and the video image swung around with it. Josh had a wireless gun camera.

He handed the laptop to Amy and said, "If we don't make it back, make sure the video gets uploaded to the YouTube channel. The world needs to know what's happened here."

Amy said, "Oh, so I'm not going now?"

"We've got the guns—no, listen—we're going to go make sure it's all clear first. Then we'll come back for you. Don't look at me like that. We're not being sexist here, Fredo's going to wait behind, too, and he's male as shit. He's going to stay behind the wheel, engine running, in case we have to make a quick getaway. You're going to be watching it live, on my gun cam. If things go bad in there and it looks like we're not going to make it out, don't hesitate to just g—"

"I won't. Fredo, you hear that? If I say go, we go, right?"

"Yeah, I'm hitting the gas at the sound of gunshots and screams."

To Amy, Josh said, "Okay, your new job is now to make sure Fredo doesn't leave *unless it's absolutely necessary.*"

To the men in the RV, Josh said, "Regulators, mount up."

Everyone stood. One guy had a little flashlight attached to his gun, and he clicked it on. The kid in back strapped on his bulky night-vision goggles.

Josh said, "Remember, save your ammo. This isn't a video game, we're not going to pick up more along the way. Short, controlled bursts." He turned to Amy and said, "I'll be back. I promise."

Josh took a deep breath and opened the side door. A blast of cold air shouldered its way in. Outside was the sound of wind whistling through the wounded building and suddenly Amy badly wanted that door closed and locked again, to have the warm, metal cocoon sealed off from whatever was out there.

Stop it.

The boys started filing out into the darkness and Amy heard Josh say, "Get your ears on." Everybody pulled out earmuffs or plugs. Protecting against that debilitating monster shriek John had talked about.

The door clapped shut behind them. Amy looked down at the laptop and saw the asylum grounds on the shaky, grainy image from Josh's gun feed, the barrel protruding into the bottom of the camera's view. It lent a feeling of unreality to the whole thing. She wasn't sitting in the middle of a clearly haunted abandoned TB asylum crawling with monsters. It was all just some stupid video she was watching on a computer.

The view bounced along the grounds, approaching the front doors of the old building. The guy to the left of Josh had the flashlight on his gun, the beam whipping wildly around the front lawn like the guy holding it was riding a mechanical bull. The view steadied as Josh arrived at the big, wooden front doors. Flashlight guy grabbed one of the old, tarnished brass handles and pulled. Locked. Josh knocked and said, "Hello? My name is Josh Cox, I've got a team of six armed uninfected out here. We're offering our assistance to OGZA. Is anyone in there?" Nothing. They all stared at the locked door like a bunch of chimpanzees looking at a car engine. "We've, uh, been following your updates until the feed cut out a little while ago. Are any of you still at this location? Princespawn? Direwolf?"

Amy's view whipped downward, as Josh apparently pointed the gun at the ground. The kid with the flashlight shouted, "I can pick the lock." Another voice yelled, "No, you can't." Everyone screaming to be heard over their ear protection.

Josh yelled, "They probably got it barricaded. There's probably some other door they come and go out of. Let's go around. Everybody stay sharp."

The view swung back up to shoulder level again, and the Hipster Zombie Squad edged along the wall of the building, the flashlight beam flashing back and forth, illuminating boarded-up windows and drifts of dead leaves blown against the foundation. Looking for another entrance.

Watching through the video feed was frustrating. Whenever the flashlight beam would swing out of view, the video window would go completely black—the little wireless camera had no night-vision capability. She peered up over the laptop and out of the windshield of the RV in time to see the gang disappear around the corner of the building. The trailing guy, the one who had the night-vision goggles and looked about thirteen years old, was sweeping his gun behind them. Watching their six, just like he saw somebody do in a movie. Or cartoon. He rounded the corner and Amy and Fredo were now truly alone.

"So," she said. "How fast can this thing go?"

Fredo said, "Depends on how much stuff you want me to run over when I do it. Thing handles like a blimp."

Amy returned to her laptop and in the video feed window saw the group had stopped moving. The mic on the gun camera was weak and she could barely pick up words over the background noise. Every time the wind blew, everything was drowned out by a sound like crashing ocean waves. The noise cleared up enough for her to hear Josh say "Where?"

She faintly heard Flashlight Guy yell, "Right there, man. Behind the wheelbarrow."

She couldn't see what they were looking at, Josh had a frustrating habit of pointing the gun camera at the most irrelevant spot possible, lazily aiming the gun at his feet, or the cloudy sky, or right at the head of one of his friends. By the time the camera angle settled on the spot, Flashlight was on his hands and knees, studying the ground in front of him. Did he lose a contact lens? Josh edged in closer, around a rusty wheelbarrow somebody had pulled out of the way, and Amy saw that they had found a basement window. The glass had been bashed out, probably decades ago. But if it had been boarded up, it wasn't now.

Wind howled into the mic, obliterating bits of their conversation.

"—no way they just left it like this—"

"—don't see anybody—"

"—hello? Can anyone hear me? My name is Josh Cox—"

"—No, let's go in—"

Flashlight aimed his beam through the window while the guy with the Vietnam gun—Donnie—got down on his hands and knees, and writhed into the building, the jagged bits of broken glass making it look like a brick mouth was swallowing him whole.

For a moment, nothing happened. Amy could feel her bladder seizing up as she watched the dark basement window bobbing in the gun-cam feed. Finally, Donnie's hands emerged and gestured that the coast was clear. Josh was next, but the camera stayed behind as he handed his gun to somebody so he'd have his hands free to crawl in. The view swirled around as the gun was handed back and forth, and then a moment later Amy was looking at a dim room that looked like an old cafeteria with a faded black-and-red checkerboard tile floor. The view swung back around to the window, then to the floor nearby where a sheet of ancient plywood bristling with curled nails had been tossed aside.

Josh yelled, "They did have it barricaded. Somebody took it off from inside."

As another guy crawled through the window, someone off camera said, "Told you, man. They evacuated, prob'ly for the same reason the feds did. We prob'ly passed 'em on the road comin' here."

Josh said, "You sound relieved, Mills."

"Man, when we didn't get an answer I thought we were gonna find this place full of dead bodies."

"Me, too."

"Hey, if you're suggesting we abort, you convinced me."

Loudly and clearly, Josh said, "Not until we do a sweep of the building." Amy decided Josh just now remembered that everything was being recorded for possible posthumous YouTubing.

The whole gang of six was inside the cafeteria now. Somebody shouted, "Well, we know they was here. Left a lantern behind."

The camera found a green propane camper's lantern in the corner.

Someone yelled, "Anybody know how to light it?" They didn't. After about ten minutes of them farting around and Amy yelling into the laptop monitor to just leave it, Jesus Christ people, they got it lit.

Lantern in hand, they ventured out of the cafeteria and into a hallway. Flashlight Guy went first, Josh right behind him with the camera gun. The lantern carrier followed, casting a soft glow and distorted shadows around the group. The team investigated two other rooms, each time going through this ridiculous SWAT team procedure that Amy had seen in movies, where guys with guns would lean on opposite sides of the door frame while Josh kicked in the door. Both times the rooms revealed themselves to be empty. Amy knew exactly nothing about SWAT procedure, but knew from where Josh's gun camera was pointing that he never checked the corners to his right and left when he entered the new rooms. It seemed even to her untrained eye that this would make these guys really easy to ambush, and this further solidified her opinion that these guys knew even less about how to walk through a building with guns than she did. They reached a door marked STAIRS, did their room-entering dance again, and took a flight of stairs down to a subbasement. They reached a short hallway with some office type rooms—empty—and one serious-looking metal door. Big lock, a steel grate instead of a window. The kind of door you saw in a prison.

It was standing open.

Through the door, the guys entered a hallway that to Amy looked a lot like a prison block. Rusting metal doors lined up on each side, a few standing open. Inside each one they checked was a bed, a sink and a toilet.

Amy thought, *they were not keeping tuberculosis patients down here.*

On camera somebody said, "What's that?" and Josh's gun cam focused on the floor. What was laying there was, for some reason, far creepier to Amy than anything short of a severed clown head.

A tattered, old teddy bear.

A chill ran up her spine, and for the first time she considered asking Fredo if there was a way to contact the guys, to get them to come back, to think up a different plan.

Somebody off camera shouted, "Man, what's that smell?"

"Maybe the old sewer backed up down here somewhere?"

The flashlight beam bobbed down a creepy hallway. Somebody tried one of the closed doors. Locked. They peeked inside each of the open ones. No people, or zombies.

From a foot away from Amy, a voice said, "Anything?"

She almost jumped through the roof of the RV. It was Fredo, peering over her shoulder at the laptop screen.

"They're inside. They found a window to crawl through. Empty so far. They're on the next floor down."

On the video screen, somebody said, "Guys, guys. What's that? There, on the floor?"

The gun camera swept across the floor, finding nothing until it reached one particular door. Something was oozing out from the bottom.

"Oh my God, what is it? Is it blood?"

"That's not blood, man. Smell it."

"Is there a sewer line back th—"

"Shhhh. Listen."

Amy could hear nothing over the laptop's speakers. Donnie, the only guy in the view of the camera, pulled back one ear from his earmuffs, listening intently like a dog.

"There's something in there."

Everyone fell silent.

"You hear it? Something scratching."

Somebody said, *"Jesus fuck."*

Josh aimed the camera, and thus the shotgun, at the door and said, "It's not locked. Look, it's open just a crack. Donnie, open it up. Open it and get out of the way fast."

Slowly, a hand reached in, presumably belonging to Donnie. It pulled the latch on the door and jerked out of the way. The door swung open and—

"OH JESUS FUCKING CHRIST!"

Panic. The camera swung around.

"WHAT IS IT MAN WHAT IS IT? OH MAN THAT'S SHIT MAN THAT'S SHIT COMING OUT—"

"IT'S ALIVE, JOSH, IT'S ALIVE! HOW IS IT STILL ALIVE?!"

"KILL IT, MAN! KILL IT!"

There was the sound of banging on metal. The doorway swung back into view and somebody was kicking the door closed. The camera was pulling back—Josh was backing away. Somebody was whimpering, "Jesus, man. Jesus. Was that his mouth? What was that? Was that a man? What did they do to him?"

Somebody else said, "Was that OGZA? Was that one of the OGZA guys? *Motherfucker*."

"We can't just leave him like that, man, we can't. Jesus . . ."

The camera view was looking at the floor, at the brown puddles. Then it tracked sideways, following the floor and the other doors down the hall.

All of the doors were oozing.

The camera tracked the ooze all the way to the end of the hall, where there was a single closed door, a partially obscured sign that said MAINTENAN at the top.

The door was riddled with bullet holes.

Josh whispered, "Guys. Guys. Pay attention."

The flashlight swung around and lit up the door. Somebody off camera said, "Oh God, oh God, oh God . . ."

Josh said, "Amy, if you can still see this, make sure it's saving the feed for playback later. If I don't get back, tell my parents and sis that I love them. Safeties off, everybody."

Amy said, "Josh! Come back! Come back to the RV! Now."

Fredo said, "He can't hear you."

The camera view wobbled down the hall, the MAINTENAN door growing in the video window. Josh gestured with his free hand, and two guys, Donnie and another guy Amy hadn't seen on camera yet, did their thing, laying against the wall at each side of the door. Josh stood in front of the door. Gun barrels edged into view on his left and his right.

Josh said, "On three. One. Two . . ."

The view shook. There was the crack of a boot kicking a door. This was *not* coupled with the sound of a doorjamb shattering. Instead, the boot gave it another try, and another. Finally the door swung in.

The view whipped around as everybody piled into the room at once. It was a huge room, full of rusting pipes and machinery and barrels and crates.

"THE FLOOR! THE FLOOR!"

The view panned down. Amy yelped.

Someone or something was writhing on the floor of the room.

Grasping hands appeared in the flashlight beam. A face. The thing on the floor reached out at Josh's leg and he kicked it away. People were screaming. Josh was screaming.

"DONNIE! GET THE—"

"HEY! NO!"

Through the gun cam came the sound of rustling—scraping shoes and gasps and shouts. The flashlight beam was spinning. The camera swung over to it and something had Flashlight Guy, throwing him around. The flashlight swept the back wall of the room—

Zombies. Wall to wall. Shambling, caked with mud, advancing.

"THEY'RE COMING OUT OF THE WALLS! THEY'RE COMING OUT OF THE FUCKING WALLS!"

Flashlight Guy was spun around again and his machine gun roared. Amy heard it through the laptop first, and echoing from the building a half second later. That jolted her into the realization that this was happening *right inside the building across the yard,* behind exactly zero locked doors. The same thing seemed to occur to Fredo, who ran back up behind the wheel and buckled in.

The video window was black. The flashlight has gone out. Screams.

"MIIILLLSSS!"

"JESUS CHRIST GET BACK!"

"RON IS DOWN! THEY GOT RON! GET OUT!"

More rustling and jostling around the gun cam. Finally, light appeared. It was the hallway, the lantern still on the floor in front of the oozing door where they'd left it. The view was bouncing. Josh was running away.

The gun camera spun around to face the MAINTENAN room door again. No one was following. The view just froze there, the sound of Josh breathing hard, muttering, "Oh-Jesus-oh-Jesus-oh-Jesus-oh-Jesus—"

From behind the door came screams. Then gunshots.

The view swung again, and Josh was looking into the camera, looking into the barrel of his own gun. He looked like he'd aged ten years. Sweat matted his hair to his forehead. Tears streamed down his cheeks. Blood was running from his lip.

Into the camera, Josh said, "Mom, Dad, Hailey. I love you. To the rest of the world, my name is Joshua Nathaniel Cox. I have just witnessed the first shots of the Z War. Amy, go. Now. We're going to hold them off as long as we can but if we can't stop them, they're going to be right on your tail—"

Something thudded heavily against the door. Josh closed his eyes and swallowed. The camera view swung back around, the view plunging forward, fast, Josh running into the battle. He stopped to scoop up the lantern, then kicked in the MAINTENAN door. He threw the lantern into the mass of thrashing limbs.

The flying lantern illuminated absolute chaos. Bodies falling on top of bodies. Strobing bursts of flame from gun barrels. Gunsmoke filling the room.

From the melee lumbered a big, bloody female zombie with matted hair that made it look like Medusa. The camera, and the gun barrel with it, drew dead center on the target and unleashed a burst of hellfire that tore into the beast. It let out an inhuman shriek and fell, flames sputtering across its ragged clothes.

The view swung to the left. A dark-skinned zombie was trying to wrestle the gun away from another member of the squad. Josh unleashed the Dragon's Breath once more, clipping the target on the shoulder. It stumbled back, and Josh fired again, and again. Each shot blazed out like a lethal Roman candle. Josh was screaming, a battle cry. Donnie was next to him and he opened fire with his Vietnam gun. Side by side, the two unloaded into the room.

"JOSH! IT'S ME! DON'T SHOOT!"

The view swung over to show Flashlight Guy, stumbling over the tangle of smoking bodies on the floor. He joined the other two, raised his gun and the three turned the room into a shooting gallery.

Josh yelled, "WHERE'S MILLS?"

"THEY GOT HIM. THEY GOT EVERYBODY BUT US!"

"I'M OUT! I'M OUT OF AMMO!"

Josh screamed, "GET BACK!"

The camera leveled at the lantern laying on the floor. The barrel jutting up from the bottom of the frame roared once more. The lantern burst into a ball of flame.

The screen flared white, then to total darkness. The sounds of the battle faded to a trio of hurried footsteps and frantic breathing. They emerged into the hall.

"AMY! FREDO! CAN YOU HEAR ME? PREPARE FOR EVAC!"

TWO HOURS
EARLIER . . .

At the sight of Molly and her bloody hunk of meat, TJ screamed, "Holy shit, stand back! Get back!"

I said, "Okay, I *really* don't think she tore that spine out of a living person."

"And how do you know *that?*"

"Because she doesn't have any blood on her paws or her face. I think she just found it. So, you know, let's figure out whose spine it is."

Hope was already walking down the hall, past the bank of dead elevators. Watching the floor as she went.

Blood. A smeared trail of it, where Molly had been dragging the spine. TJ followed Hope, put his hand on her shoulder, and took the lead. I made Molly drop the spine, and grabbed her collar. I dragged her along while we all followed TJ like we were the Scooby-Doo gang. We went down two flights of stairs, and arrived at a STAFF ONLY door in the basement. Behind it was a dark hallway—no windows and no lights. Without a word, Hope clicked on a flashlight and handed it to TJ.

The blood smear ended partway down the hall, presumably at the point before the spine got too heavy for Molly to keep it aloft in her jaws. But there were only three doors: an employee restroom, a break room, and a door that read BOILER ROOM.

The bathroom was clean. Well, not clean, but there were no corpses in there. People were eating calmly in the break room, by candlelight. We went back into the hall again, and stared at the boiler room door.

TJ said he'd go check it out first, since he had the only flashlight, and I thought that was a good plan. He leaned his shoulder against the door, the flashlight held at the ready like it was a gun, when he turned to me and said, "You comin', Spider-Man?" So apparently I was an extension of TJ somehow, which was not mentioned when he apparently volunteered on behalf of both of us.

With Hope and Molly behind us in the hall, TJ pushed the door open and expertly shone the light in one corner, then the other. Ambush points, I guess. Nobody home. There was a massive, dead machine to our right, a pair of huge, armored barrels laying on their side, sprouting pipes big enough for a raccoon to crawl through. Boiler. TJ edged over, checked behind the cylinders, and swept the flashlight across the concrete floor. Nothing. Then the light found another metal door on the opposite side of the room, paint peeling around the edges and stained with rust, and I realized we weren't finished.

The door was standing partially open, wide enough for a dog to slip through. The floor was streaked with red. TJ edged over toward it, and I wondered why we didn't just go get Owen to lead the way with his pistol. What were we going to do if some spidered-out zombie came leaping out at us? Die, to serve as a cautionary tale to the others? Was that our role here?

TJ pushed the door in. Same procedure with the light—corner clear, clear behind the door. Suddenly we were in a room from an earlier century—exposed bricks on every wall, black with grime and patched with cobwebs. A remnant of the original building, buried by multiple renovations. TJ swept the flashlight across the floor and hit a pair of dead eyes, staring up from a white face wreathed with matted bloody hair. A woman, middle aged. Her torso was still wearing a green jumpsuit, but everything from her rib cage down was white bone draped with shredded crimson ribbons.

"Shit. That's Rhonda."

"Okay. And who's the other one?"

TJ hadn't noticed the other body yet, but I pointed and he found it with the light, facedown next to the far wall. It was a guy who looked like his ass had been blown out with a grenade. His abdomen had a flat, deflated shape, disemboweled from the back end. Spine was missing.

TJ sighed and said, "Carlos got 'em."

He approached the facedown corpse and lifted the head with his foot.

"Don't know this guy." TJ did another sweep with his light to make sure that "Carlos" wasn't in the room with us.

I said, "Who is 'Carlos' by the way, other than the monster who eats people's assholes?"

TJ shrugged. "Don't know him in any other capacity. Suave little Latino dude. We identified him as infected, but he didn't show any signs and he didn't seem to know. So we didn't tell him. Then one day with no warning, he transforms right in front of us, like Optimus Prime if he was made of meat. Turns into this wicked corkscrew worm thing and digs into the dirt. Comes up when he gets hungry. Or when somebody sits down. Look."

I followed the beam to a hole in the back wall large enough for a man to crawl through, a pile of brick bits scattered on the floor below. TJ approached it and I said, "Hey, let me get Owen. This operation needs a gun—"

"You're gonna want to see this. Check it."

I very slowly edged closer, trying to see into the jagged hole. "Is there another room back there or—"

"Look."

A tunnel. Leaking, muddy and twitching with insect life. It was lined with red brick and arched at the top, extending to infinity. It was maybe five feet wide and high, but much of the space was filled with ancient, rusting iron pipes that ran along the walls.

He said, "Old steam tunnel. To service another building."

"What other building?"

"Don't know. Maybe one that's not even there anymore. Crawl in there and find out."

"No, thanks. We know it ends past the perimeter, though. And outside where anybody patrols. Man or robot."

"Because your dog got in through here."

"Yep."

For the benefit of the woman waiting tensely in the hall, TJ said, "ALL CLEAR IN HERE, GIRL! WE'RE COMIN' OUT!"

I headed for the door and said, "Am I allowed to call a quarantine-wide meeting, or is Owen the only one who gets to do that?"

"Well now wait, why does this need a meeting?"

I stopped to face TJ just short of the door to the hallway. I lowered my voice and said, "To . . . see who all wants to try to escape from this freaking prison?"

"You want everybody to know about this?"

"Why wouldn't I?"

"Even the reds?"

"I don't think the color teams means anything outside these fences, TJ."

"I'm not talking about that. I'm talking about taking a hundred and fifty or so high-risk patients out of quarantine."

"Now, come on. The 'red equals high risk' thing, that's just talking about the new people, right? Everybody out there has been spider-checked."

"Owen hasn't. A lot of people haven't. They had you check all the new arrivals but a lot of people got grandfathered in because when we suggested a check of everybody, Owen started waving his gun around."

"But if they haven't, you know, monstered out by now then we know they're not—"

"You sure about that? We got no idea when Carlos got infected. The girl you almost missed, she was walkin' around like you and me, parasite and all, for a week or so. Isn't that what she said? How many more like her could we have in here? Think about that, now. You lead somebody outside these gates, you're responsible for whatever they may do once they're out."

"But if I leave uninfected people behind and they get incinerated if the air force nukes this place, then I'm also responsible."

"That's right."

"Goddamnit, TJ."

"Listen. Let's say you're right. Let's say they intend to turn this whole facility into a crater. What that means is, somebody's got to get them to change their mind about that. Whoever gets out of here, the first thing they got to do is get the word out to the chain of command that there's innocent people in quarantine, uninfected. So that group that gets out, it's got to act as a representative of what's inside. Got to put a good face on the quarantine. So it's got to be people we *know* are clean. They're gonna be our ambassadors to the outside world, right?"

"But we don't know how much time we have—"

"I'm not done. *If,* on the other hand, we help infected leak out into the town and they start wreaking havoc, and multiplyin', then the same dudes looking at a map with a little red circle around this hospital are gonna draw a bigger red circle around this whole *town.* Right? And you think your girl is out there. And John, and whoever else in this town you care about."

"That place that makes those Cuban sandwiches."

"Yeah, Cuba Libre. You had their coffee, man? No way we can let 'em bomb that place."

"You see the waitresses?"

"Mmmm-hmm. Whoever does the hiring there, he definitely an ass man."

"All right, all right. So who gets to go?"

"Well, see, Spider-Man, now there's a tough-ass decision we got to make."

Seven people were waiting for TJ and me out in the hall outside the boiler room. In addition to Hope, Wheelchair was there, along with Corey (the curly haired kid who'd come in on the truck earlier), an old guy whose name I didn't know, Lenny (a short balding white guy who looked like Vizzini from *The Princess Bride*) and the two women who heard the commotion and wandered in from the break room.

We told everyone about the tunnel, and the two bodies. Old Guy said casually to TJ, "Which wall is it on, nigger?"

Without blinking TJ said, "North."

Old Guy nodded thoughtfully and said, "That's what I thought. Same boiler used to service the other buildings, before they tore down the old hospital and built this one up on top of it. Probably, oh, fifty or sixty years ago. Now back in those days, if a black so much as brushed past a white woman on a sidewalk, they'd have had him hung by torch-light come nightfall, but of course a lot has changed since then. Me and my friends, we had a bluegrass band back in the 1960s—"

"I think Racist Ed is right," said TJ. "How far to the other end, Ed?"

"Oh . . . you're talking about half a mile of tunnel there, Porch Monkey. Long way to crawl. I couldn't make it, on these knees. You know the workers back then would have a cart they'd lay on, and there was a pulley system and you'd just lay on your back and then down at the end you'd have a big strong nigger turning a crank—"

"Well there's no pulley system in there now, so we got to make some knee pads, or else all our knees will be hamburger by the time we get out the other end. But if Racist Ed is right, there may be seven- or eight hundred meters of tunnel there; that's a long stretch to crawl over brick and mud. If you're in pretty good shape I bet you could make it in twenty minutes, if you're not, and you got to constantly stop and rest your knees, you could be an hour gettin' through there. So first question is, who's up for it? Show of hands."

Everyone but Racist Ed.

"That's eight of us, and that's a pretty big group already. If I could pick the optimal number to take on this mission I'd stop right here—"

"I'm not leavin' without Terry," said the bald guy. "If it comes to that I'll stay behind."

"I wasn't finished! What I was sayin' was I don't expect any of you to leave loved ones behind, but that's *all* you can take."

Wheelchair said, "We gotta tell Dennis and LeRon."

Hope said, "Katie and Danni . . ."

TJ said, "Okay now see we're getting up to more than a dozen people now, take some time to think about it but you get very much beyond that and it goes from a group sneaking through to get the word out to an all-out prison break that's going to provoke a full armed response. No way we can go with more than fifteen people—"

"What about the sick people? And the doc?" said Hope.

TJ sighed and rubbed his head. "What about 'em?"

"Katie's one of the nurses. She said some of the sick are so bad off that they're not going to last long if they don't get to a real hospital. The diarrhea is so bad they're getting dehydrated."

"Babe, how are they gonna crawl through a half mile of tunnel if they're that sick? What if they get halfway through and can't go no farther? We got no way of getting them out and they're clogging up the tunnel for everybody else. It's narrow, real narrow. There's pipes all around. You'll see."

"And what about the doc? He'll have to know."

"*Why* does he have to know?"

"Well for one he's going to notice Katie gone when she doesn't show

THIS BOOK IS FULL OF SPIDERS

up to the second floor to help, and if we don't tell him where she went, he's going to waste time looking for her. Two, we're going to need to take some stuff with us. Bandages, basic first aid. Doc has all that up there. And we're out of the . . . mouthwash. We used the last of it today. We need to take some with us and that means we need the doc to make it."

I said, "Actually she makes a good point with people being noticed gone. Everything is going to fly into turmoil when Owen and the rest notices a bunch of us missing. People will think we got eaten or something. That could turn ugly if it becomes a witch hunt."

TJ said, "Yeah, we'll leave a note."

"Saying what?"

"*I'll think of something.* Fuck, man. Look. We come back and we meet out in the hall in *one hour.* Hope, go get Katie and tell her that if they have sick people up there who can't last a single more day but *are still somehow capable of crawling for a half mile through the freezing mud,* then we'll take them. Dave, go see the doc and get him to make up a jug of mouthwash. But you got to have him put it in something that's not going to leak when it's banging around in the tunnel."

I said, "Okay do you know where the doctor is right now? Or if not, what he looks like so I'll know when I find him?"

TJ stared at me. "The doc? Marconi?"

"Wait . . . he's *here*?"

"Where else would he—Ah, you're pulling that unfrozen caveman shit. Yes, he's here. And he don't sleep. Didn't you go talk to him after you got back from the hole? Like I told you?"

"No . . ."

"You need to go now, man. He's been asking about you."

"The situation is much worse than I had thought," said Dr. Marconi.

He was leaning over an unconscious woman and shining a flashlight into her eye. I had actually only seen this man in person once—every other time it was on television or on a book jacket. The neat white beard, the glasses down on his nose. And here he was, standing in front of me, not dressed in a red or green jumpsuit, but in the same style of three-piece suit I'd seen him in on TV. Only now, the man wearing it looked like he hadn't slept in a decade.

He glanced up at me expectantly and said, "What did you find out?"

"I'm . . . totally lost here, doctor. My memory of this whole quarantine experience only goes back to earlier today. I remember up to the chaos of the outbreak and then the next thing I remember is waking up over at the asylum with no idea where I was or how I got there. I had no idea you were here and I have no memory of us ever speaking."

Marconi turned his back on his patient to give me his full attention. "They wiped your memory?"

"I . . . I don't know. You think they can do that? Just pick a specific bunch of memories and erase it like files on a hard drive?"

"Oh, I'm sure there's no method to do such a thing *safely*. I also do not believe these men give a tinker's dam about such things."

"You mean REPER?"

He shrugged. "If that's what they're calling themselves now."

"How did you wind up here again?"

"Your friend John called me the day after the outbreak, after he got your lady friend clear of the danger. I flew down and offered my services to the task force here, who happily gave me a job and sent out a press release declaring such. You see, by then, amateur video had emerged that revealed to the public that this in fact was not a conventional disease outbreak *or* bioweapon attack. The word 'zombie' was being bandied about. Someone very high in the operation was very happy to fan those flames by attaching a name like mine. If you take my meaning."

I did not.

"When the decision was made to pull the containment staff from quarantine last week, I volunteered to stay behind because otherwise the detained would be left without medical care."

"Wait, are you that kind of doctor? I thought you just had a doctorate in . . . ghosts or something."

Ignoring me, he said, "My instincts turned out to be right because patients that have reported here with seemingly minor symptoms have turned out to in fact be infected with the parasite."

"Holy shit. Really?"

Marconi nodded to a row of large clear plastic pitchers sitting on a nearby cart, and I recoiled to the point of nearly falling down. Each pitcher contained a spider. Two of them were fully grown, another was no bigger than my thumb, the last was at some stage of growth in between. One of the big ones was badly damaged, half of its body missing.

Calmly he said, "They're quite dead."

"You can see them?"

He shrugged. "Sometimes. With great concentration. I do not have your gift, but I know some techniques. Though I should say, and I hope you will not take offense, that I would not accept your 'gift' if you offered it to me in a basket along with a bottle of Glenfiddich."

"And you know how to kill these fuckers, right?" I held up the now-empty bleach jugs I'd brought with me. "You came up with the, uh, mouthwash? The poison? So you're close."

"Close to what? A cure? It is no great feat to kill a parasite in a way that also brutally kills the host. No, I am not close to a 'cure' for what the parasite does to the human body, in that what it does is rebuild the body from the inside out in a way that violates everything we know about human physiology. At this stage I'm simply trying to perfect a way to detect infection."

"I still don't understand how this works. I mean, I've watched these things crawl right up to people's faces and they couldn't see them, but they can merge with your body in a way that somehow blends in, like it becomes just visible enough to—"

"David, how can you of all people still be surprised when our eyes fail us? The human eye has to be one of the cruelest tricks nature ever pulled. We can see a tiny, cone-shaped area of light right in front of our faces, restricted to a very narrow band of the electromagnetic spectrum. We can't see around walls, we can't see heat or cold, we can't see electricity or radio signals, we can't see at a distance. It is a sense so limited that we might as well not have it, *yet* we have evolved to depend so heavily on it as a species that all other perception has atrophied. We have wound up with the utterly mad and often fatal delusion that if we can't see something, it doesn't exist. Virtually all of civilization's failures can be traced back to that one ominous sentence: *'I'll believe it when I see it.'* We can't even convince the public that global warming is dangerous. Why? Because carbon dioxide happens to be invisible."

"But . . . we just have to figure out how to detect them, right? Like, somebody will build a machine or something? Once we can detect them, we can kill them."

"In answer to that, I need only to offer two words: *Plasmodium falciparum*."

"Do I even want to know what that is?"

"Exactly. It's a monster that has slain *several billion* of your fellow man, and you don't even know its name. It's the microscopic parasite that causes malaria. *Nearly half of all human deaths in recorded history* have been caused by this invisible assassin. One could make the argument that *Plasmodium falciparum* is the dominant life form on the planet, and that human civilization exists purely to give it a breeding ground. Yet, until very, very recently we had no idea what it was. We blamed witchcraft and evil spirits and angry gods, we prayed and performed ceremonies and ritually murdered those we believed were responsible. And meanwhile we died. And died, and died. Yet, to this day, you could have *Plasmodium falciparum* on your hands right now, and you wouldn't know. Because after all, if you can't see it, surely it can't hurt you."

Marconi strode out of the room and said, "Follow me." He walked me down the hall and showed me where six rooms were occupied with a total of nine unconscious patients. "Our 'flu' patients. Started showing up forty-eight hours ago with uncontrollable diarrhea. I have a feeling if we still had power to the MRI, we'd find some nasty changes going on inside. Or maybe not. Maybe you have to wait until transformation for that."

"Jesus Christ, they're infected?"

"This is what I wanted to tell you about. Several of them passed your mouth inspection upon arrival. It turns out, there is more than one way for the parasite to enter the body."

"How do they—"

"Did you hear the part about the diarrhea?"

"Oh. Oh, Jesus . . ."

"Yes."

"And . . . you're just keeping them up here? With the sick people? They could spider out at any time . . ."

"I don't think so. The Propofol seems to shut down the process. You see that we have them strapped to the beds as well. It's the best we can do under the circumstances. When the sedative runs out in a few days, well, we'll have a decision to make."

THIS BOOK IS FULL OF SPIDERS

"What decision? Kill the fuckers, doc. Before they get loose."

He said nothing.

I said, "I can get you out of quarantine. And I mean right now. We found a way out."

"You did?"

"Old steam tunnel in the basement. REPER—or whoever—didn't know about it because it had been bricked up. Leads right past the perimeter. We're keeping it quiet but if you want to go, come with me."

"To what end? Where else am I going to be allowed to work hands-on with infected patients? No, I'm most effective here."

"Suit yourself."

"And what do you hope to accomplish, if I may?"

"Uh, freedom? And I don't want to sound like a pessimist, but word on the street is the military has declared this whole hunk of land a loss and is about to drop a big goddamned bomb on it."

"We had a conversation about this, when I first arrived. A conversation that I suppose you now no longer remember. About my book? Titled *The Babel Threshold*? Ring any bells?"

"No. Sounds like it stars Jason Bourne."

"I know time is short, but . . . I think you missed an important point earlier, about these patients. The symptom that brought them up here was diarrhea, not nightmarish spontaneous deformity or propensity for violence. They showed no other symptoms. None. And I'm starting to believe that there are others that show no symptoms at all. And that we may *never* be able to detect the infection, until it's too late. I think the parasite is adapting, learning to stay under cover longer, and more effectively. Now what do you think will be the world's reaction when that fact comes to light?"

My answer wasn't something I wanted to hear myself say out loud. Finally, I said, "So what you're saying is, if the military is going to wipe this quarantine off the map, do I really want to stop them?"

"Think about it. Think about whose purpose is served if the bombs fall. Think about whose purpose is served if they don't."

"How about you just tell me?"

"That would require me to actually know myself."

On the way down, I stopped at the lobby and peeked out of the main doors, to make sure we hadn't aroused suspicion. What few people were still out in the brisk night were gathered by the south fence, watching the sky like they were expecting a tornado.

I wandered out until I found a green—an older, bearded guy—and asked what was happening.

He shrugged. "Somebody shootin' flares over at the asylum."

"Flares? What does that mean?"

"Probably don't mean shit. Could be a kid with leftover fireworks for all we know. But it took a whole three minutes for the rumor to spread around the yard that it meant a posse was gonna break through the fence and set us all free. Give us all Cadillacs for our trouble. Why not?"

Somebody said, "Look! Look! Another one. Red this time."

I turned in time to see the ball of magnesium die and fade to earth. Murmuring from the crowd.

I said, "Well I'm going to bed. If it's a rescue party, throw a rock up at the window or something. And save me a Caddie."

By the time I made it back down to the basement, twenty-seven god-damned people were packed in the boiler room, spilling out into the hallway. A buzzing, murmuring crowd of people who, even though they had been stripped of all possessions when they entered quarantine, some-how all had luggage. Backpacks and garbage bags and various random shit they thought they would need. The people were knocking around and slamming doors and giggling and asking questions and basically con-ducting the least stealthy prison escape in history. The reds were asleep, most of them anyway, but it would take exactly one of them to discover the massive conga line of people piling into the boiler room to blow the whole operation.

TJ was so pissed he looked like steam was about to start whistling from his asshole. Hope was trying to calm him down, trying to work through the logistics.

"What about knee pads, huh?" he said, wrapping electrician's tape around the caps of the two jugs of the binary chemical "mouthwash." "I suppose we came up with knee pads for two or three dozen people in the last half hour?"

"No, but we have duct tape," said Hope, reassuringly. "All people got to do is take off their shoes and tape them to their knees. You know, like Dorf."

"Like who?"

"It works, all right? Katie and I did it and crawled around the floor, from one end of the hall and back again. It's going to be *fine*."

"Well, then that's one of our nine hundred problems solved." To me he said, "If we was smart, we would send one guy through by himself to make sure the path is even fuckin' open. Or that Carlos isn't waitin' at the other end. They'd crawl through with the flashlight and signal back that the coast was clear, so if there's a problem we don't got to turn this whole ridiculous human centipede around. But we can't fuckin' do that because we'd have this huge noisy crowd of people standin' out here for an hour, waitin' to get caught."

"It's only gonna last until somebody else stumbles across the tunnel anyway."

He shook his head. "Racist Ed is stayin' behind, once the last person is through he's gonna stack up some of them cardboard boxes in front of the hole. I already cleaned up the bricks on the floor, so hopefully that'll throw off Owen's dumb ass."

TJ pulled the flashlight from his pocket and said to me, "I'm gonna let you pick. One of us will take point. The other stays behind and goes in last. The point man is the first to get to freedom, but he's also gonna be the first to meet any bad news that might be waitin' up there. Last guy has the easiest escape should things go wrong, but also has to spend the most time back here waitin' for the stragglers to work through their bullshit. Guess it's a matter of how optimistic you are."

"No, it's not. You're in better shape than me, we don't need the whole train to be waiting for me to catch my breath. You go first."

"And you seen enough horror movies to know the black dude don't ever make it to the end."

"We all appreciate your sacrifice, TJ."

"*Fuck* you."

He laughed. So did I.

TJ tied a bandana around his head, Tupac-style, and wedged the flashlight in it above his ear, so it'd work like a coal miner's headlamp. He clicked it, shook my hand, and climbed into the tunnel.

I said, "See you on the other side, TJ."

Hope followed him in. Then Corey. It was on.

What followed was thirty excruciating minutes as one by one, the escapees slowly, clumsily and noisily clambered into the ragged hole in the brick wall. I went around the boiler room, telling people to quiet down, explaining the knee shoe process, and waiting for a red jumpsuit to throw open the boiler room door and ask us what the hell we were doing.

One by one, they went through. The crowd in the boiler room got more and more sparse. As we drew closer and closer to the "holy shit this is actually going to work" mark, the knot in my stomach pulled itself tighter and tighter.

So, so close.

Then there were only five people left. That worked its way down to two, an older woman who in my opinion had no business attempting the crawl (what would I do if we got halfway through and she told me she needed to go back?) and a suave-looking dude who looked like Marc Anthony, the Latin pop singer. Racist Ed was standing guard in the hall and I was supposed to knock twice on the door once I saw the last person go through. He'd wait a few minutes, then come in and cover up the tunnel.

The last pair of shoes disappeared into the bricks and the boiler room had finally disgorged its contents into the tunnel. Was TJ out the other end by now? Surely the fact that we hadn't heard anything was a good sign.

Surely.

Hurrying, I knocked lightly on the hallway door and quickly jogged back across the room to the tunnel. I put my hands on the edge of the hole—

Whoa.

Dark in here. I couldn't see the last guy who went in, and there was no sign of TJ's bobbing flashlight up ahead. All I could see was maybe the first ten feet of muddy red brick before it was swallowed by the darkness. In the sputtering candlelight of the boiler room, it looked like a throat. I could faintly hear the hard breathing and scraping of the crawling refugees ahead, the sound fading in the distance.

I had a flashback to the dark hallway in the dungeon when I was heading for the elevator. The wet dragging sound.

Walt.

Stop that. I squeezed my eyes shut and shook my head. Thirty people had climbed right into that tunnel ahead of me, men and women from age eighteen to early sixties. I'd be damned if I couldn't do it.

My legs would not move.

Brick and mud. Cockroaches skittering along every surface. Spiderwebs spanned the gaps between rusty pipes. It stank of mold and mildew and rot. It stank of the grave. Water dripped from the cracks in the bricks overhead.

The shuffling of knee shoes was completely gone now, not even the echoes reached me. I had stayed behind too long. It was just me and the utter silence and the utter darkness. I remembered a video I had once watched of a wasp outside of a beehive, patiently beheading each bee that emerged from the hole. It accumulated a pile of hundreds of heads before it was done. I imagined a huge wasplike creature on the other end of this tunnel, silently and efficiently ripping the heads off of each muddy, exhausted person who emerged from the other side, tossing them into a pile.

Stop it.

I put my hands on either side of the tunnel. I said, out loud, "Here we go."

But my legs did not move.

I started to whisper words of encouragement to myself, when a massive hand landed on my shoulder and spun me around.

Owen said, "And where do you think you're going, bro?"

Owen pinned me against the wall. Racist Ed strolled past me and started dutifully stacking boxes in front of the tunnel entrance, which made me think maybe he didn't fully understand the plan from the beginning.

Owen said, "Dude, you are a piece of work, you know that? What is that, a tunnel?"

"Let go of me."

"Where does it go?"

"We don't know. Out. Out there somewhere. We got no idea what's at the end of it but we decided whatever it was, was better than being *stuck in here with you*."

"How many people went in?"

"Fuck you."

He slammed me against the wall. *"How many?"*

"About . . . thirty."

"Thirty. And you had no idea what's at the other end. Nobody scouted it first? Nobody crawled through to make sure it was even open at the other end?"

"We—we didn't have time. I—"

"Right, you didn't have time because you were afraid of being discovered. Because *you had to keep this your little secret*."

Racist Ed said casually, "Well, I know where it goes. It runs right out to the old asylum."

We both turned toward him.

I said, "You mean the—"

I was interrupted by echoes of gunshots, cracking through the tunnel.

Gunshots, and screams. Faintly, from the other end, I heard an unfamiliar voice scream, "THEY'RE COMING OUT OF THE WALLS! THEY'RE COMING OUT OF THE FUCKING WALLS!"

The Massacre at Ffirth Asylum

Amy was bouncing in her seat, muttering, "Come on, come on, come on."

The gun cam was in the old cafeteria, trained on the door to the hallway. The other two guys—Flashlight Guy and Donnie—ran past. The camera swung around to find Donnie helping Flashlight climb up through the basement window.

To Fredo, Amy said, "They're almost out! Get ready!"

It was taking forever. Flashlight guy was stuck in the window for some reason, his legs kicking but not making any forward progress.

Josh kept swinging his gun/camera back to the door to see if they were being pursued.

Shrieking.

Not screaming—this was the kind of noise babies make, when they don't know how to put their pain into words. It was Flashlight Guy. His legs were thrashing in the window. Something had him from the other end. Josh and Donnie grabbed his legs, trying to pull him back into the classroom. They pulled and pulled, and whatever had Flashlight from the other end finally let go. Of his legs, anyway.

Josh and Donnie found themselves on the floor of the classroom, with the lower half of Flashlight Guy twitching in their lap. Everything from the waist up was still laying in the basement window. If Josh and Donnie hadn't had earmuffs on, they could have heard Amy scream from the RV.

Josh scrambled to his feet. He trained the gun cam on the window, and the twitching and now-silent pile of meat that was Flashlight's torso. It appeared that something was ripping away at his guts from below, something coming out of the grass, like it had emerged from the earth itself and torn him in half. Josh shot at it, the Roman candle shells blowing Flashlight's guts apart and sending fire streaking into the night beyond the window.

Amy flinched—she and Fredo saw the glowing projectiles streak across the windshield from the side of the building.

The view on the monitor was chaos. Donnie and Josh were arguing. Then Josh yelled, "THE DOOR! WATCH THE DOOR!" and more shots were fired, sharp reports that echoed through the night air.

Donnie screamed, until his screaming parts were ripped out of his throat.

The gun cam raced toward the basement window—which was still blocked by the ravaged remains of Flashlight Guy. The view flew through the window—Josh tossing the gun through ahead of him—and it spun around in the grass until Amy found her video feed was showing the very RV where she was sitting in the distance, weeds partially obstructing the view.

Through the camera's mic, Amy heard a sound like a sponge being wrung out in a sink full of water. Josh screamed and then made a series of harsh grunts. The gun cam was still sitting motionless in the grass. Amy looked over the laptop at the building, then back down at the camera feed, back and forth, looking for something. Anything.

On the laptop, the camera view suddenly moved, being dragged backward through the weeds. The view swung around. Josh's face came into view, laying on the ground, blood pouring from his mouth. He was grabbing the gun by the barrel, pulling it toward him. He was doing something with his other hand, reaching around. His mouth was wide open, making choking noises. Something came up in his throat. His eyes got wide, and Amy had a split second to see a fist-sized wad of Josh's own intestines push out between his teeth before he pulled the trigger and blew his own head off.

Amy jumped to her feet, the laptop clattering to the floor of the RV. She had her hand over her mouth.

Fredo had heard the shot.

"What? What's happening?"

"We have to go, Fredo, we have to go and we have to go now. We have to go. We have to . . ."

"What? What happened?"

"GO! Fredo! They're dead! They're all dead! Go! Please!"

"YOU DON'T KNOW THAT! We don't leave men behind!"

Fredo threw the RV into gear and floored it. Instead of backing out onto the street, he plowed forward, across the lawn and toward the building. Amy stumbled back up to the passenger seat.

"WHAT ARE YOU DOING?"

"Look! They're still alive! They're moving!"

The RV skidded to a stop outside the basement window. On the ground, in the shadows, *something* was in fact moving.

"NO! Fredo, just go! We have to get out of here!"

Fredo yelled, "Josh! Donnie! Answer if you're alive!"

Someone was out there, between the RV and the wall, a lumpy almost-human figure. Fredo peered out at it. Amy hissed, "Don't, Fredo, don't. Back up. Please. Back up the RV—"

Fredo reached inside his jacket and pulled out a serious-looking black handgun. He said, "Donnie?"

No answer. Fredo aimed the handgun at the figure, the glass of the driver's-side door between him and his target. Amy could see Fredo's face reflected in the glass. His eyes went wide. He had time to say, "Holy shi—" before a series of things happened so quickly that Amy's mind couldn't register them all.

While Fredo had been focused on the figure out of the driver's-side door, something smashed through the windshield to his right. Something—a long, pink blur—whipped in through the glass, grabbed Fredo's right bicep, and neatly severed it. The arm, with the hand at the end still clutching the pistol, was yanked through the windshield and out into the night. Before Fredo could scream or even turn to see what had happened, the arm poked back through the broken windshield, now with the gun end aimed at Fredo. Fredo's own hand, now being operated by whatever was outside the RV, squeezed the trigger. Fredo's skull exploded.

All of this occurred over the course of 2.5 seconds. To Amy, all she registered was the shattering of glass, a wet, meaty rip and a gunshot. Then she was covered in bits of glass and droplets of warm blood.

Fredo slumped over, dead.

A Trial by the Fire

Owen was pointing a gun at my head. An impromptu late-night tribunal had formed around the quarantine bonfire. I shivered. The fire had that campfire effect of making your front too hot and your back too cold.

Owen had waited in the boiler room for somebody to come crawling back through, fleeing whatever violence had erupted on the other end. He waited patiently through hellish echoes of shotgun blasts and screams, waited as the report of machine gun and shotguns ended the screams one by one. He waited while I screamed into the tunnel, for TJ, or Hope, or Corey, or anyone. He watched me throw up in the corner and waited while I put my head in my hands and heard those screams echo through my head over and over and over and over again.

Then I had a gun at my forehead and he was pulling me to my feet.

Five minutes later I was standing in a crowd of red jumpsuits. Everybody was out of bed. The echoing rattle of gunshots from a few blocks down the street—right on the back of the mysterious flares that came from the same direction—had everyone awake and at DEFCON 1.

From behind the nine millimeter, Owen said, "Now that you got everybody's attention, why don't you tell them what that shooting was about."

I was so tired. It was the unique type of exhaustion that comes from failure on top of failure. Futility and fuckups take a lot out of a man—I should know, since that was pretty much my whole life up to this point. I didn't have the energy to defend myself.

Those goddamned screams.

"Do what you want, Owen. But don't make a show out of it."

"A show. That's what you think this is, bro?" He shook his head. "All right. Allow me to summarize for the fuckin' jury. You and TJ found an escape tunnel. Instead of tellin' the camp about it, you tiptoed around, gathered up your green clique, and tried to crawl out while everybody else was asleep. You left behind sick people, you left behind pregnant women, you left behind moms who ain't seen their kids since the outbreak."

"They still got drones buzzing around up there. If suddenly the population of this place goes from three hundred to zero, and a goddamned crowd spontaneously forms outside the fence, they're gonna figure out what happened. And then they're gonna rain holy hell down on that crowd. It was either a few of us go, or nobody."

"And of course *you* get to make that decision, all on your own, don't you? See, because none of us are as smart as you. We couldn't have organized a way to do it without dooming the entire quarantine. No, only you."

I shrugged. "You'd have stopped us, Owen. And you know it. You'd have started sticking that gun in everybody's face. Same as you're doing now."

"And why would I ever do such a thing? Because I'm an asshole, right? Here, why don't you tell everybody what happened to all your friends who crawled into that tunnel."

"We don't . . . necessarily know. We heard gunshots and—"

"What happened to them is *exactly what I have been saying would happen* to anybody who tried to make a break for it. It's what I would have explained to you—*again*—if you'd asked. Because from the first day that gate closed on this quarantine, I said that anybody who crossed that line *was gonna die*. Because as far as anybody outside of that fence knows, every single one of us is tainted. And that fence is the only thing keepin' back a tide that will turn the fuckin' rivers into blood. That means all of us in here got to band together. But you, TJ and the rest of you greens, you never got that."

I shook my head. "No. The difference is that we had a chance at freedom and were willing to take it. Unlike you."

"Uh huh. And just to be clear, you were gonna be among the escapees, right? If I'd showed up five seconds later than I did?"

"Hell, yes."

"You don't even know what I'm saying, do you, you arrogant little prick? You're *the only one who can sort infected from uninfected*. If you'd gone through there, what choice would you have left us the next time a truck full of people rolled through that fence? What choice would we have—would *I* have—but to burn each and every one of them? You crawling into that hole would have doomed every man and woman who got shoved through that gate, *bro*. And you'd have condemned me to have to do the killing, in the name of protecting the other three hundred swinging dicks who are trying to stay alive in this quarantine. I get to live with the final expression of every face I put that gun in, for the rest of my life, to smell their fuckin' skin and hair burning, every night, for the rest of my life. And I bet you never even paused three seconds to consider that."

"I don't know. I . . . Amy . . ."

"And if you'd made it through and the feds started raining death on *this* end of the tunnel, all you'd have felt is relief. You'd never have given us a second thought. It's all about saving your own ass. And that tells me that you're gonna sabotage this operation again the first chance you get, for whatever selfish reason pops into your fat, arrogant head. And that means we can't trust your judgment to be our 'Spider-Man' any longer. And that means that as long as you're alive and walkin' around in here, the three hundred—I'm sorry, *the two hundred and seventy*—men and women in this quarantine are in danger. Is there anybody standing here, including you, Wong, who can make a convincing argument otherwise?"

No one spoke. Not even me. The wind howled. The bonfire whooshed and crackled. I looked into the fire and the burning eyes of two dozen charred skulls stared back at me.

I said, "Nope."

Mop-Up

Amy spun out of her seat and crawled to the rear of the RV, knees and hand crunching over cubes of safety glass. She knocked aside the spilled laptop, her knee crushed a box of Pop-Tarts. She crawled and crawled and eventually ran out of RV.

She turned over and pressed her back against the rear wall. She pulled up her knees and made herself as small as possible. Frigid air blew in from the busted windshield and it felt like the tears and sweat were freezing solid on her face.

She huddled, in the cold and the darkness, staring at the dismembered and lifeless corpse of Fredo the RV driver. His right foot was twitching. She couldn't take her eyes off it.

The driver's-side door yanked open. Amy screamed.

Fredo's corpse was yanked out into the night. She screamed again. She pulled her knees tighter, and twisted her hair in her fingers, and squeezed her eyes shut and tried to make it all go away.

There were tearing and smacking sounds from outside, set to the tune of the open door chime from the RV.

Bing . . .

Bing . . .

Bing . . .

She needed to get out, to run, to hide. Or to get behind the wheel and stomp on the gas. Instead, she balled herself tighter, and clinched her eyelids.

Inhuman feet crunched through the glass in front of her. Warmth spread across her thighs and she wet herself for the first time since she was five years old.

The steps came closer, and closer, crackling through the broken glass until she could feel warm breath on her cheek.

Bing . . .

Bing . . .

Bing . . .

BOOK III

Posted on FreeRepublic.com
by user DarylLombard, Nov. 11, 1:31 P.M.

They laughed. They laughed when I stocked up on canned goods, they laughed when I stocked up on ammunition, they laughed when I said the storm clouds were gathering. Same as they laughed at Noah. And, as with Noah, they come clawing at my door as the flood rolls in. Sorry. This is why I was building an ark while you were doing drugs and watching reality TV.

I appreciate all of the prayers and expressions of concern from you over the last week (for those of who you don't know, I live not three miles outside of Outbreak Ground Zero in [Undisclosed]). But we are safe because we have prepared. We have food to last a year. We have water from our own well. We have fuel to last three years. We have guns, and everyone in our family is trained to use them.

On the day of outbreak, one of my son's (the "musician") druggie friends and his little girlfriend came by. You can picture him even without my description—long hair, covered in tattoos, track marks on his arms, showing early signs of HIV infection. A pro-Atheism bumper sticker on his car.

He wanted to shack up with us, eat our food, drink our water, sleep under our protection while the pestilence and depravity ran rampant outside. I pulled him aside by his scrawny arm and said:

"What can you do?"

He looks at me with that slackjawed look and says, "What do you mean, dude?"

"I mean what can you do? Can you shoot a rifle accurately at fifty yards? Do you know how to gut an animal? Or make a fishing net and clean what you catch? Can you fertilize a garden? Or purify water? Can you repair a small engine? Or even gap and change a sparkplug? Can you wire an electrical outlet? Repair a roof when it leaks? Set a broken bone? Can you make your own clothes? Field strip and clean a rifle? Reload ammunition from spent brass? Disinfect and sew shut a wound?"

Of course he said he didn't know how to do any of these things.

He had spent his life playing video games and doing drugs and had probably fathered five welfare babies, demanding the whole time that I pay for their health care. When a pipe leaks, he calls the landlord (at best) or (more likely) just lets it leak. Let the next tenant find out the floorboards have rotted and that every wall is covered with mold. His little girlfriend would be the type to cry about rights for animals because she thinks meat grows in the grocery store display counter. Smoking pot and spitting on our soldiers when they return home from fighting terrorists because she lives obliviously in a little cocoon built from our sweat and blood and tears.

I said to him, "Imagine there's a meteor coming to destroy the world. But some rich men have pooled their resources and built a big rocket ship to get people off the planet. They don't have room for everybody, but you want a seat on that ship. Now, your having a seat means somebody else doesn't get one. Space is limited. Food is limited. What would you tell the man standing at the door? What case would you make for getting a seat on that rocket ship at the expense of another person? What can you offer that would justify the food you would eat, and the water you would drink, and the medicine you would use?"

He said to me, "I don't know, dude. I don't see no spaceship here."

And I said, "What you didn't realize was that you were always in that situation. Only the spaceship is planet Earth, and your creator built it for you. And you had your whole life to make your case for why you should be allowed to stay. Instead, you did drugs, and played video games, and collected welfare. Well, this ship is taking off without you."

That boy walked away without a word.

Maybe I'll see him and his little girlfriend again, out among the diseased and the starving, running from the riots and the chaos. And I will say,

"You had your chance. All your life those 'crazy' preachers were trying to tell you that the day of reckoning was coming. You chose to ignore it. Now it is too late."

This is the way it should be. There are two kinds of people in the world: producers and parasites. When a society gets too many parasites, we need the disaster, the tsunami, the earthquake, the war, the flood, the disease to wash away the garbage, to rinse the safety nets of the slugs that use them as a hammock. Let them fall into the fire, so that the strong, the faithful and the capable will be left behind to rebuild, and renew humanity.

That day has come.

They laughed at me when I stocked up on food and fuel and ammunition.

Who's laughing now?

12 Hours Until the Aerial Bombing of Undisclosed

John was rocked out of unconsciousness by the blast of a shotgun and the warm splash of brains in his hair.

Hands were grabbing him from all over, tugging at the spindly legs of the unholy daddy longlegs creature. When he was free of the monster, John rolled over and saw a cowboy-looking dude in incredibly tight pants holding a smoking double-barrel shotgun. He was wearing earmuffs.

The crowd of people standing around John were surprisingly human-looking for infected, and were pretty well-dressed for zombies. The cowboy said, "You all right, buddy?"

John couldn't think of how to answer that. His ribs hurt and it was kind of hard to breathe. The back of his neck was wet with monster blood, and he had gotten all worked up anticipating his own mortality only to find out it was on back order. He needed a drink so badly he was wondering if there was a gas station nearby that pumped ethanol, and if there would be a way to crawl into the underground tank.

Three burly guys were wrestling the spider monster. The human head at the center was shattered from the shotgun blast, but the parasite inside was still thrashing for life. A massive pickup truck sporting dual wheels and flared rear fenders backed up in the street. There was some kind of machine in the bed, a big red thing with a motor and chutes and wheels. Somebody started it. It sounded like a lawnmower. Only when they started cramming the giant, squirming daddy longlegs into the chute did John realize it was a wood chipper.

There was that terrible shriek, and red slush went spraying into the neighbor's yard. When the last of the creature's eight legs vanished into the jaws of the machine John thought, *well, that's one way to do it.*

John tried to get up, but Cowboy pointed the shotgun and said, "Now, just stay seated for a minute, if you don't mind."

From behind John, Falconer barked, "I'm a cop, asshole! See that on my belt? That's a badge."

Falconer was marched over and forced to sit next to John. Holy shit, did he look pissed.

Cowboy pulled down his earmuffs and said, "Just to be clear, I got nothin' but respect for law enforcement, officer—"

"Detective."

"*Detective*, but at this point in time I'm pretty sure that what you see here is all the law that exists in this town at this here moment. When the feds huddled up behind their barricades on the other side of town, it came down to us to walk these here streets. And now that they left town altogether, well, we're pretty sure that makes this our town. 'Til we hear different."

Falconer said, "I understand. Now you tell me specifically what needs to occur before you let me continue what I was doing."

"You need to convince us that you're not a zombie."

John said, "Do we look like zombies?"

"Ain't you heard? The zombies *look just like everybody else.*"

Falconer said, "This is all some huge prank, isn't it? Is somebody filming my reaction, to put it up on the Internet?"

"Now," Cowboy said, "the infection takes root in the mouth, that much we know. Then it spreads to the brain and then the rest of the body. So there's a real simple test: we have to take somethin' out of the mouth. If you're infected, you won't feel it, because it's not really part of your body. If you're clean, it'll hurt like hell. So I'll let you pick."

From his back pocket, Cowboy pulled out a pair of vise-grip pliers.

"We can take a tooth . . ."

From his other back pocket, he produced a six-inch-long pair of pruning shears.

". . . or a piece of tongue."

11 Hours, 45 Minutes Until the Aerial Bombing of Undisclosed

I was locked in a supply closet while the reds gathered to discuss execution methods. I didn't care. It'd all gone wrong, the kind of wrong that not even Owen properly understood. Otherwise he'd realize he was about to give me a cleaner end than most people on earth were going to get over the coming weeks and months and years. Including him.

Amy was my only regret. I just wished I knew that she was safe, and if so, that I could get word to her not to come after me. Even if she had made it out of town, Amy wouldn't just leave the situation alone. She and I had that in common. Can't stand to be on the other side of a fence from where we want to be. Not a fence somebody else put there, anyway.

I wished there was a way to tell her all that in person. To hug her, feeling her warmth and smelling the fruity shampoo in her hair. If I had that, and if I could hear her laugh one last time, I could carry that with me into eternity and that would be okay.

I kept trying to think back to everything that had happened since I woke up with that spider thing biting me in bed, trying to figure out what I was supposed to have done differently. It was stupid, I knew. Questioning how my life would have gone if I hadn't made bad choices was like a fish asking how his life would have turned out if he'd only followed through on his dream to play in the NBA. I don't beat myself up over my choices. My shame circuits burned out from overuse years ago.

Wait. This started before the spider showed up in your bed.

See, that was the thing, right there. I'd been so busy running around since that night that I'd never really had a chance to stop and put it all together. There was a common thread through all of these events that stretched back even before that night.

Tennet.

Goddamned Dr. Bob Tennet. He shows up in my life as my supposed court-appointed paranoia therapist. Asking me about monsters and trying to get me to work through all of that shit. Then the spider shows up and starts spreading this infection. And who's there the whole time, showing up at quarantine? Dr. Tennet. Monitoring the situation. Watching it unfold. Tapping away at his laptop and recording his observations.

Anyway. So there's two things I wish I could take care of before my execution. People have died with longer to-do lists.

I leaned my head against the wall and tried to make myself smell shampooed red hair instead of hospital sadness chemicals. I dozed off.

11 Hours, 40 Minutes Until the Aerial Bombing of Undisclosed

John was actually weighing the "tooth or tongue" options when Falconer said to Cowboy, "Let me say this as a red-blooded, not possessed by any kind of inhuman organism, all-American man. If you get near my mouth with either of those tools I'm going to shove your head into the ground so hard a Chinaman will see it fly out of a volcano."

Before Cowboy could react, John said, "Hold on. Do you know who this is next to me? This is Detective Lance Falconer."

Cowboy looked like he sort of recognized the name, but couldn't place it. John said, "You can't tell me you haven't seen him on the news. He caught the Portland Strangler?"

From behind Cowboy, a lady said, "Oh my God, it is him!"

"Show them your ID, detective."

Falconer did. The lady was duly impressed.

John said, "We were kind of in the middle of getting to the bottom of this whole thing when you showed up."

Tightpants Cowboy said, "Is that right?"

John said, "Yeah, that is right. It's looking like the government is behind it all."

Tightpants cursed and said, "Son of a bitch. I been saying that since day one. Day *one*." To the guy next to him: "Haven't I?"

Falconer said, "I'm standing up now."

He did. No one objected. A kid in the crowd said, "What's it like to fight somebody on top of a train?"

"Windy." To Tightpants, "What do you mean the feds left town? When?"

"Breach at their headquarters. Somethin' blew up. You didn't hear it?"

"Oh," said John. "We, uh, were wondering what that was."

"Convoy headin' out of town right now. So now we got to do what they couldn't. Which is the way it always winds up. Which is why I been sayin' it since day one. Me and my brother went door to door, within two hours of the feds roping off the town, gatherin' up everybody with a gun and a set of balls. We're the ones who got shit back under control, not the soldiers tripping around in their space suits. We're the ones who put a stop to the looting, we're the ones who have been patrolling the streets every minute of every day, in shifts, outside of the so-called Green Zone the feds set up. There's almost two hundred of us now, working in three shifts, 'round the clock, pumpin' buckshot into zombies and feedin' 'em to Chip back there. Making sure everybody outside that hospital is clean, everybody who ain't gets put down, and makin' sure that hospital stays sealed off until the president grows the balls to drop a couple dozen cruise missiles on it."

This got John's attention. "Wait, what? They're dropping cruise missiles? When?"

"When they grow the balls, like I said."

"We don't have a more specific timeline on the balls situation?"

"Are you askin' because you want it to happen, or because you don't want it to happen?"

"Well what about the people inside who aren't infected? We got to get them out, right?"

David Wong

"Buddy, anybody that's spent a day inside that place is infected by now, five times over. If there's anybody alive in there, they ain't human no more. That's the only thing we know about the infection. Once you get it, there ain't no cure. You're walkin' dead. If you got people you care about in there, you need to treat 'em just like you saw them go into the ground yourself. Picture the dirt goin' in over the casket. Take time to mourn, do what you got to do. But you got to get past that. Feelin' sorry for them, it's like feelin' sorry for the fire that's burning down your house. These infected, they'll say anything, anything at all, to make you let down your guard. They can look just like you and me, can talk just like you and me. Or your neighbor, or your best friend, or your momma. But you cannot hesitate. Think of 'em just like a parrot imitatin' human speech—the words sound the same, but they ain't got no soul inside. You come face-to-face with 'em? You. Cannot. *Hesitate.*"

Nearby, somebody said, "Fuckin' A."

Falconer said, "See, that just makes me more pissed off at the bastards who are gonna get away with this. They're going to turn all the victims to ashes and sweep it all under the rug. Somebody needs to answer for this shit."

About ten different people muttered, "Damn right" or something to that effect.

Tightpants said, "Tell me what you need, detective."

"As you see, I'm gonna need a ride. Unless you know a tire shop that's open."

"What the hell are we waitin' for? Hop in the truck." To another guy Tightpants said, "Tell Bobby to follow me. Everybody else should finish their sweep. We're behind enough as it is. Don't forget to check in on Eve Bartlett, make sure she got her insulin okay."

The crowd started to disperse. John didn't move from the spot where he was sitting in the yard.

Falconer said, "You comin'?"

"Dave is alive. I saw him, when I was on the Sauce earlier. Gonna go find my car and see what I can do."

The look on Falconer's face told John that he thought he was looking at a dead man, but knew that there was also no point in trying to talk John out of it. Instead, Falconer shook John's hand and said, "Don't fuck everything up, okay?"

286

3 Hours, 10 Minutes Until the Aerial Bombing of Undisclosed

The supply closet door was yanked open and I awoke to see Owen there with his co-chair, Mr. Gun. They led me to the yard and I found that it was morning—I had managed to sleep several hours among the mops and buckets, exhaustion catching up with me. The group of reds had swelled, huddled around the bonfire to hear my sentence.

Owen said to me, "We figure we'll give you the choice, bro. You can either crawl through that steam tunnel and whatever happens, happens. Or I can shoot you right here and let your fat ass fuel the fire. It's all the same to me, aside from the second option settin' me back one bullet."

I shook my head and said, "Nah, that tunnel smelled like a grave-yard for dogshit. Am I allowed a piece of paper and a pen to write a note to my girlfriend, if she's even still alive? No idea how she's ever going to see it but I'd feel bad if I didn't make the effort. You know like when you forget to call home on Mother's Day."

Owen didn't answer, because he was looking past me. Something deep in my nasal passages noted that the scent of the smoke took on a more sophisticated tone. Instead of the meaty smell of barbecue mixed with the acrid smell of particle board and veneer, I suddenly smelled the sweet, rich fragrance of pipe tobacco. I turned and there was Dr. Marconi, puffing on his pipe with one hand dipped into the jacket pocket of a pin-striped suit. He looked so out of place here he seemed like a hologram.

Marconi said, "Can I ask what this gathering is about?"

I said, "I been sentenced to die but Owen here has agreed to let me write a note to Amy before he shoots me."

Marconi nodded and said, "I see. You realize, David, that other men do not find themselves in this kind of predicament with the same frequency that you do? I'm beginning to think it's something *you're* doing."

To Owen, he said, "Can it wait fifteen minutes? I would like to pull Mr. Wong aside and take him up to my floor. I actually believe I'm on the verge of a breakthrough with detection but I'll need his skill this one last time."

No answer from Owen. Marconi said, "It really is for the good of all of us, if it works. You can stand right outside my door, if you think this is a ruse to help him escape, though I personally cannot imagine what such a plan would entail. It would also give him the chance to confess his sins, so it would be a personal favor to me, as a former man of the cloth it would weigh on me greatly if I didn't at least offer him the opportunity."

Owen pointed the gun at the sky and said, "If it was anybody but you, doc . . ."

"You know I do not ask lightly." To me, he said, "Will you take this opportunity to let me show you something? And to reconcile yourself with the creator you're about to meet?"

3 Hours Until the Aerial Bombing of Undisclosed

John jolted awake to find himself staring down a shotgun wielded by his greatest enemy: himself.

He had fallen asleep in the Caddie, his shotgun in his lap. He must have shifted position at some point. If he'd coughed, he'd have vaporized his own skull. The sun stared angrily through his windshield. John blinked and threw open the driver's-side door, needing to get out and take a piss. He almost fell and broke his neck—the Caddie was sitting six feet off the ground. Then he remembered.

The night before, he'd parted company with the Undisclosed zombie militia and made the nervous trek on foot from Dave's house up to the burrito stand, only to find the Caddie was not in fact where they'd left it. At that point his only possible hope of finding it again was if it had gotten towed away, back at a stage of the apocalypse when a car partially blocking the street was still considered a priority on somebody's list. John jogged twelve blocks to the towing company impound yard, expecting to be decapitated by a monster at any moment.

The good news was that he wasn't. The further good news was that the Caddie was in fact there and that the tall fence had been cut open by some other looter or vandal days ago. The bad news was that the Caddie was apparently the last seized vehicle before towing was shut down—it was still on the back of the tow truck. The truck was the flatbed type, where the whole bed tilted down to form a ramp and let the car roll on and off—a technology that probably came about because the old hook style yanked off too many bumpers in the course of dragging cars out of handicapped parking spaces.

John had jumped up onto the truck's bed and opened the Caddie's trunk, expecting to find that everything had been stolen. But apparently even the looters who ransacked the impound yard took one glance at the rusting piece of shit and deduced that there could be nothing in the trunk worth the effort of prying it open. That was probably a good thing for both the citizens and law enforcement of Undisclosed. Inside they'd have found the aforementioned shotgun (a custom-made triple-barrel sawed-off), two hundred shells, Dave's blood-splattered chainsaw, the green mystery box taken from Dave's shed, a bag of Dave's clothes, a bottle of Grey Goose, a bad black velvet painting of Jesus and a fucking flamethrower.

The keys had still been in the tow truck (in fact, the driver's-side door was standing open from when the driver had run screaming from whatever mob or unholy terror was coming his way). John spent twenty minutes trying to figure out the controls for tilting down the ramp and never could. It was either take the tow truck itself, or walk. So, for the third time in ten days, he commandeered a vehicle for use in a mission, promising himself he would return it when it was over. He was one for two so far.

That is how John wound up spending the night tooling around town in the tow truck with the Caddie piggybacking. One thing he had noticed when he was out: people. Lots of people. Since REPER had retreated and stopped enforcing the curfew, every street corner had grown clumps of people bristling with hunting rifles and shotguns and revolvers and machetes. John was comforted by that for about five seconds, then he saw the looks in the eyes of these harried, tired, cold, frustrated people and realized they would butcher his ass if he even so much as let out a yawn that sounded too much like a moan.

Just before dawn, John had passed the quarantine, which looked even more impregnable than it had with time on pause. Floodlights and armed drones were all powered up and standing guard. Driving slow to avoid the armed crowds that were wandering across the streets, John had made his way up to the asylum. A crowd was busy up there. Dozens of members of the militia were surrounding an RV parked in the yard. The pickup with the wood chipper was parked next to a long ditch that had been dug in the yard, and the chipper was running.

John had edged closer, as close as he could without exiting the tow truck (which he was not going to fucking do) and saw bodies. The militia was dragging them out of a basement window and laying them in a row in the grass. Another crew was picking them up, one by one, and feeding them into the chipper. The chipper was, in turn, filling the ditch with red slush.

Oh holy mother of—

John had heard a scream at that point, and saw a gang of militia approach from the street, dragging a cursing man covered in tattoos. He was thrashing around and lobbing insults at his captors, insisting on his innocence, and his humanity. The captors conferred with Tightpants Cowboy, who was in charge of the zombie disposal operation apparently. The tattooed man's trial lasted forty-five seconds, then Cowboy vaporized the man's forehead with two shotgun shells. Into the chipper he went.

John got the fuck out of there.

He had headed as far outside of town as he could get without running into the REPER barricades. So, John had parked the tow truck, with the Caddie piggybacking, in a cornfield a mile or so from the water tower construction site, the REPER barricade now standing between there and where he'd spoken to Dave for the last time. He had gotten drowsy, then climbed up to the Caddie because he figured the higher vantage point would give him an advantage if he was ambushed while he slept.

John sat upright and worked his stiff joints. He threw the shotgun into the passenger seat where it clinked off the empty Grey Goose bottle. The gun was a custom-made job he'd bought at one of the gun shows he frequented. It wasn't pretty, but it worked—firing all three barrels would chop down a small tree. He kept double-aught buck loaded into the two side barrels, and a slug in the middle. Give the target a nice variety of projectiles to think about.

He needed to get into quarantine. And not as a patient, either. He needed to get in there with the implements of destruction in the Caddie's trunk. John pictured himself just plowing toward the fence in the tow truck, but remembered the concrete barricades meant to stop somebody from doing just that.

Well, sitting here was accomplishing nothing. John jumped down, pissed for several minutes, then threw himself into the tow truck.

2 Hours, 45 Minutes Until the Aerial Bombing of Undisclosed

Marconi led me up to the second floor, with Owen in tow. He made Owen stay outside of the makeshift hospital within a hospital, telling him there was a risk of him spreading the nasty stomach flu to the rest of the quarantine.

Once on the other side of a door, Marconi muttered, "We have less time than I thought."

"What? Before Owen shoots me?"

"No. Believe it or not, that's actually not our most pressing problem."

He led me to a window and said, "Look. Beyond the fence."

I did. A freaking crowd was gathering out there. "Holy shit, doctor. Who are those people?"

"Looks like everyone."

Hundreds of people. Cars were parked here and there, scattered like toys out beyond the fence. People were sitting on the hoods, or were off in bunches, talking. Everyone seemed to have a gun. I swear one person actually brought a pitchfork.

Marconi said, "Your neighbors, your coworkers, the people who mow your lawn and deliver your mail."

Nobody mows my lawn.

"I don't understand."

"Critical mass, Mr. Wong. They're going to get what They wanted. And I haven't the faintest idea of how to stop it."

"Who? Who's going to get what they want? The mob, you mean?"

Marconi looked me in the eye and said, "We're speaking in private, I assume that we can drop all pretense. This conversation will take longer if we filter everything through a façade of skepticism of the supernatural, and at least one of us doesn't have the time. If I have seen the shadow men lurking about, then I assume you have, too."

I sighed and said, "Yes, doctor."

"So when I speak of an invisible 'They' working against us, you'll not waste precious seconds asking who 'They' are. The shadows, and the men who knowingly or unknowingly work on their behalf."

They.

I often wondered if "they" had an office building somewhere, where They sat around a long, black granite conference table with a pentagram etched into the top. Or maybe They had a headquarters inside a hollowed-out volcano, like a James Bond villain. Or maybe They had the technology to leap effortlessly across time and space, holding shareholder meetings on the surface of Mars, or on top of a plateau in Pangaea circa 200 million B.C.

John and I knew very little about Them, which made me an expert when compared to the general population, who don't know They exist at all. They are people, or at least They assume the form of people. They are wealthy, or at least have access to wealth, or maybe have means which render wealth as we understand it moot. The little Asian man who disappeared into the burrito stand was surely one of Them, as was whoever was waiting for that convoy of black trucks we saw last summer.

But all I have are rumors, stories John dug up on the Internet probably written by people who know even less than we do. Some say it's a cabal of wealthy men who, centuries ago, poured Their wealth into experimentation with the occult. At some point, the story goes, They tapped into a dark power that They saw as one more resource to be exploited, the way that humans would later learn to split the atom and use it to power our televisions and hair driers. Instead, the legend goes, the dark energies that poured forth infected Them, corrupting these men who learned too late that the power They had bought would cost them the last remnants of Their own souls. That's the story, anyway. Shit, for all I know, They wrote that version of the story and the truth is another three layers down. That's how They work.

These days, if you ask John to summarize who They are, you get only one answer: "Well, they're not fucking vampires, I'll tell you that." Then he'll stare hard at you for a solid minute until you walk away.

Marconi tapped the side of one of the jugs that contained the spider specimens. It didn't react, but still I wished he wouldn't do it. He said, "This was always chess, not checkers. I'm not sure you ever fully understood that."

I said, "Tennet. You know that name? Claims to be a psychiatrist but suddenly turns up consulting for this agency nobody's ever heard of? REPER?"

"Oh, he's a psychiatrist. Search his past and you'll find twenty-five distinguished years in that profession, an expert on the virulent nature of fear. And likewise, if it just so happened that he needed to be a plumber in order to be in an advantageous position to observe and influence the situation, then you would find a quarter century of plumbing in his background. And so on. He would be whatever is required."

"Can't somebody investigate him? If his licenses and all that are fake then—"

"I didn't say he would use false documents. I said he would actually have twenty-five years on the job. Whatever job. Do you understand? Again, chess. With a very advanced player who can see many moves ahead. They put their pieces into position."

Marconi checked the vitals on a sleeping patient as he spoke, puffing on his pipe the whole time. I again wondered to what degree Dr. Marconi actually knew anything about medicine.

He said, "In the case of Dr. Tennet, he not only has specialized in treating violent and paranoid patients since the 1980s, but has written multiple prominent books on the subject, and dozens of journal articles. More pertinent to this situation, he has also written extensively on the subject of group paranoia and crowd dynamics in crisis situations. He didn't have to infiltrate the government. When the 'outbreak' hit, they came to him. Do you understand? The pieces are always positioned where They need them."

"Right, and 'They' are dicks."

"But we can't stop there. We need to ask the big question: *what do They want?*"

"To . . . kill us all?"

"Ha! We should be blessed with an adversary with such uncomplicated ambitions. No, war is never about killing the enemy. War is about remaking the world to suit the whims of some powerful group over the whims of some other powerful group. The dead are just the sparks that fly from the metal as they grind it down."

2 Hours, 40 Minutes Until the Aerial Bombing of Undisclosed

John didn't get within three blocks of the hospital quarantine. There were people everywhere. It was like the afternoon of the Fourth of July, when everybody ambles out to the park in loose groups to find a place to watch fireworks. Only instead of carrying blankets and lawn chairs, everybody was armed to the teeth. From the driver's seat of the tow truck, John recognized a familiar cowboy hat and denim-wrapped ass walking nearby. John pulled up to where Tightpants Cowboy was on the sidewalk, shouting orders to somebody. John rolled down the window and Tightpants said, "Did Hank send you out here? We're still four short."

John said, "Uh, no. Is Falconer around?"

"The detective? He went off on his own. Said he had to follow up on a lead."

"Shit. What is all this?"

"It's the end of the world, where you been all week?"

"What?"

"What's your name again?"

"John. Yours?"

"Jimmy DuPree. Pleased to meet you. We're makin' sure the quarantine holds until the air force can blow the shit out of it in about . . ."

2 Hours, 35 Minutes Until the Aerial Bombing of Undisclosed

Marconi said, "I mentioned my book earlier. *The Babel Threshold.*"

"Yeah. I said I hadn't read it. I usually wait for the movie."

"Try to focus, please. Do you understand the significance of the title? You know the Tower of Babel, right? You went to Sunday School?"

"Yeah, sure. In ancient times everybody on earth spoke the same language, then they decided to build a tower that would reach all the way up to heaven. Then God cursed everybody on the job site to each speak a different language to mess them up."

"Exactly. *'And the LORD came down to see the city and the tower, which the children of men buildeth. And the LORD said, Behold, the people is one, and they have all one language; and this they begin to do, and now nothing will be restrained from them. Let us go down, and there confound their language.'* It's right there in the text, Mr. Wong—God's motivation in that story is that he was *afraid.* He limited our ability to communicate because he was afraid that, operating as one, we would challenge His power."

"Man, I hope you're not about to tell me that all of this shit is a curse from God because we built our buildings too tall. Kind of a flat town to impose that lesson on. You'd think he'd take it to Dubai."

"No. But there is a parallel. Are you familiar with Dunbar's number?"

"No."

"You should, it governs every moment of your waking life. It is our Tower of Babel. The restraint that governs human ambition isn't a lack of a unified language. It's Dunbar's number. Named after a British anthropologist named Robin Dunbar. He studied primate brains, and their behavior in groups. And he found something that will change the way you think about the world. He found that the larger the primate's neocortex, the larger the communities it formed. It takes a lot of brain to process all of the relationships in a complex society, you see. When primates find themselves in groups larger than what their brains can handle, the system breaks down. Factions form. Wars break out. Now, and do pay attention, because this is crucial—you can actually look at a primate brain and, knowing nothing else about what species it came from, you can predict how big their tribes are."

"Does Owen have a watch? Because when you told him fifteen minutes I'm not sure if he's going to take that as a literal fifteen minutes, or . . ."

"We'll deal with him in a moment, but I take your point. The salient issue here is that every primate has a number." Marconi gestured to the crowd gathering outside the fence. "Including those primates out there.

Including you and I. Based on the size of a human's neocortex, that number is about a hundred and fifty. That's how many other humans we can recognize before we max out our connections. With some variability among individuals, of course. That is our maximum capacity for sympathy."

I stared at him. I said, "Wait, really? Like there's an actual part of our brain that dictates how many people we can tolerate before we start acting like assholes?"

"Congratulations, now you know the single reason why the world is the way it is. You see the problem right away—everything we do requires cooperation in groups larger than a hundred and fifty. Governments. Corporations. Society as a whole. And we are physically incapable of handling it. So every moment of the day we urgently try to separate everyone on earth into two groups—those inside the sphere of sympathy and those outside. Black versus white, liberal versus conservative, Muslim versus Christian, Lakers fan versus Celtics fan. With us, or against us. Infected versus clean.

"We simplify tens of millions of individuals down into simplistic stereotypes, so that they hold the space of only one individual in our limited available memory slots. And here is the key—those who lie outside the circle are not human. We lack the capacity to recognize them as such. This is why you feel worse about your girlfriend cutting her finger than you do about an earthquake in Afghanistan that kills a hundred thousand people. This is what makes genocide possible. This is what makes it possible for a CEO to sign off on a policy that will poison a river in Malaysia and create ten thousand deformed infants. Because of this limitation in the mental hardware, those Malaysians may as well be ants."

I stared at the crowd outside and rubbed my forehead. "Or monsters."

"Now you're getting it. It's the same as how that crowd out there doesn't see us as human. The way the rest of the country won't see anyone inside city limits as human. The way the rest of the world soon won't regard anyone in this country as human. The paranoia rippling outward until the whole planet is engulfed. This infection, this parasite that dehumanizes the host but is utterly undetectable, it is perfectly designed to play on this fundamental flaw, this limitation in our hardware. *That* will be the real infection."

Marconi emptied his pipe into a bedpan, and pulled out a bag of tobacco.

"Which brings us back to the Tower of Babel. Humans were always destined to be derailed by this limitation in our ability to cooperate. At some specific point, determined by the overall size of the population on the planet and a host of other factors, we *will* destroy ourselves. That is the Babel Threshold. The point at which the species-wide exhaustion of human sympathy reaches critical mass."

"And you think this whole thing, starting with me finding a giant alien spider in my bed, was Their plan to trigger that event."

He nodded. "The parasite's ability to stay undercover indefinitely, the infected showing absolutely no symptoms . . . it's perfection. Anyone can be infected, at any moment, anywhere in the world. If you want to see what the future of life on planet Earth looks like, simply take a glance out that window."

I found a chair and collapsed into it. There was a harsh knock on the door behind me.

From behind the door, Owen said, "It's been long enough, doc."

"Five more minutes won't change anything, Mr. Barber."

Lowering my voice, I said, "Wait, you wrote a book about this happening before it happened? Damn, why didn't you send me a copy?"

"You shouldn't have needed a book to see this coming. No one should have. This is what They've been building toward since civilization began, accelerating as it got closer, like the last sand running from an hourglass. Look at the games children play now. The average child has killed ten thousand men on a video game screen by the time he enters high school. Reinforcing that lesson one button press at a time—the shapes at the other end of your gun *are not human*. And when news of the infection spread, what did the world immediately call the infected?"

"Zombies."

"Exactly. Our culture's most perfect creation—an enemy you are absolutely, morally correct in killing, because they are already dead. Why, you are doing them a favor by smashing in their skulls. We as a species were so primed for this that to get combustion, They only needed the tiniest spark. It actually happened sooner than I expected, but . . ."

He shrugged as he lit his pipe, as if to say, "Eh, can't be right every time."

I said, "Well, you took a long time to say what I pretty much already knew. We're screwed. I mean, to be clear, we're rooting for the bombs, right? That's the only way to satisfy the paranoia, let them blow all this to shit on live TV while the mob out there cheers."

Marconi puffed on his pipe and stared out the window.

I said, "I mean, we absolutely cannot let that part get out, right? The fact that the zombies are undetectable until they're biting your brain? That fact needs to die with the quarantine, otherwise it's going to be a global lynch mob out there. Which means making sure none of them get out, even if innocents die in the process. I mean, it's shitty, but that's all we can do, err on the side of overkill. Right?"

Marconi said, "The sedative is running out. One of my infected patients woke up."

I said, "Jesus. Really? Did you—"

"I've been talking to him all morning. He's still strapped to his bed. I calmly explained to him the situation, and he asked me to leave the restraints on. He said it was the only responsible thing. What do you make of that?"

"I . . . I don't know. But you can't just leave him like—"

"You're right. I can't."

"I mean it's just a matter of time, right? Until he monsters out and kills who knows how many people?"

Marconi studied me.

Owen banged on the door again. Marconi said, "We're coming."

2 Hours, 30 Minutes Until the Aerial Bombing of Undisclosed

To Tightpants, aka Jimmy Dupree, **John** said, "So we know for sure now? They're going to bomb it?"

Jimmy nodded. "You're the one who was askin' earlier about the innocent people inside quarantine."

"Got a friend in there."

"No, you don't. What this is, with the bombs, is a mercy killing. Nothin' more. You need to get that straight."

Staring through the windshield at the fence down the street, John nodded.

Dupree said, "Don't know if you heard the shots last night, but there was an outbreak, from the quarantine. Bunch of 'em found an old utility tunnel that the government, in its infinite wisdom, failed to spot on the blueprints. Few dozen tried to get out. Looked like some militia tried to stand their ground and got themselves torn to pieces in the process. Don't got any idea how many zombies got out into the wild but I spent my night disposin' of thirty bodies. There'll be more, a lot more, if they don't do somethin' about that quarantine. It's a bag of live snakes in a nursery. Well, word finally filtered in, from the feds at the perimeter. The bomb drops at noon. We just got to keep it secure until then, then this whole flippin' nightmare will be over. And if noon comes and nothin' happens, we're gonna surround this place and pour bullets into that fence until nothin' on the other side draws air."

2 Hours, 25 Minutes Until the Aerial Bombing of Undisclosed

I couldn't help but notice that Owen had the reds build up the fire. Looked like they had found some more wooden pallets somewhere. That shit really burned.

To Owen, I said, "You know what? I never got to sit down and write that note to my girlfriend. Marconi used up all my time. And all he did was give me a chili recipe. Do you want it?"

He didn't answer. It was a beautiful morning, though some clouds were moving in. I could actually hear birds chirping somewhere. Birds don't give a shit about the apocalypse any more than we'd care about some species of bird going extinct in the Amazon. Which had probably happened twice already this morning.

All of the reds were awake and standing around me. I looked back at the hospital entrance and saw a smattering of greens standing there. I glanced up at the roof, and there were the rest of them, lined up along the ledge and looking down.

From behind me, Marconi said, "Mr. Barber, I don't know if you can hear the commotion on the other side of the fencing, but we do appear to have larger problems here."

Owen said, "With all due respect, doc, I'm not a fuckin' idiot. Those people are about to riot out there because they figured out this quarantine isn't secure, thanks to last night's breakout. And guess who we have to thank for that?"

"Killing David here will not assuage their panic. It will, in fact, accomplish nothing except to confirm their worst fears about us."

"ATTENTION."

Everybody turned toward the booming sound of a voice coming from a public address system.

"PLEASE MOVE A THOUSAND FEET AWAY FROM THE QUARANTINE FENCE. FOR YOUR SAFETY, PLEASE WITHDRAW FROM THE QUARANTINE PERIMETER TO A DISTANCE OF AT LEAST ONE THOUSAND FEET."

2 Hours, 20 Minutes Until the Aerial Bombing of Undisclosed

John heard the PA system outside the fence announcing something he couldn't quite make out from inside the truck. Warning the crowd away from the gates probably. He pulled the tow truck up through the quarantine crowd, gently knocking over a DO NOT CROSS BY ORDER OF REPER—HIGHLY INFECTIOUS—TRESSPASSERS WILL BE SHOT ON SIGHT sign. Beyond it were the four-foot-high concrete barricades. Beyond them was an unmanned jeep with a mounted gun that John assumed would shoot anyone who touched the fence. Beyond it, the fence itself. For all he knew, Dave could be no more than fifty feet away, on the other side of that chain link. A cheap pair of bolt cutters would get through it in two minutes. But it might as well be the center of the Earth. He needed a drink. They had a little over two hours until either the army inciner- ated this place, or the entire town went apeshit on it. Two-plus hours in which to accomplish . . . what?

The crowd was actually moving back, to his surprise, and then it dawned on him that the military was trying to get the rubberneckers out of the blast radius of whatever they were going to drop on this place. He wondered if he was close enough to be engulfed by whatever came streaking down from the sky. He threw the truck into park.

The PA system repeated its message. John lit one of his last two ciga- rettes. He twiddled with the levers on the console. He heard a hum- ming from behind him and a shadow inched across the cab. Oh, hey, he'd figured out how to work the stupid ramp mechanism. It'd have been nice to have done that before he was forced to steal some guy's tow truck, but that was how every single possible thing had gone so far in this situation. Just a little bit behind the curve, a little slow to figure out the right thing. Story of his fucking life.

John realized at the very least he needed to get this poor bastard's tow truck out of the blast zone, and that leaving it here would be a ma- jor dick move considering he no longer needed it. John got out and climbed up onto the tilted truck bed, released the cable that secured the Caddie and got behind the wheel. He twisted the ignition and woke up the bear under the hood. He reversed off the truck bed, flattening out on the street below. Creedence loudly assured him that a bad moon was rising.

2 Hours, 15 Minutes Until the Aerial Bombing of Undisclosed

Marconi was trying to voice another objection, but Owen wasn't listening—his eyes never left mine. He cut off Marconi in midsentence and said, "All these people in here. All those greens. And look, you got exactly *one* guy standing up for you. Look up, at all the greens up there, watchin' this from the roof. Notice how none of them came down to advocate on your behalf? None of 'em are throwing themselves in front of you and sayin, 'you take him, you got to take me, too!' You know why? Because every single one of 'em knows *you wouldn't do it for them.*"

2 Hours, 14 Minutes Until the Aerial Bombing of Undisclosed

John backed up in the Caddie, and kept backing up. Farther and farther down the street, the tow truck and its tilted bed shrinking in his windshield. He stopped. He thought.

He flicked his cigarette out of the window.

He buckled his seat belt.

2 Hours, 10 Minutes Until the Aerial Bombing of Undisclosed

Owen said, "Dude, this is going to be lost on you. But I need to say it. Because we are going to die, Wong. Don't think I don't understand that. I know the feds aren't gonna let us outta this place. So let me say my bit. I have kept the order in this quarantine since the day the feds pussied out of here. All in all, I'd say it's the best thing I ever done in my life. Maybe the only positive thing I've ever done. And that's all right. Whether it's bombs in here, or bein' torn apart by the mob out there, I will stand before the good Lord and say that I held things together as long as I could. And my final act is to declare you guilty, for the deaths of thirty men and women, and the probable deaths of two hundred and seventy more. I find you guilty of committing the only real sin Jesus ever asked us not to commit: the sin of not giving a shit about anyone but yourself. Doc, step aside."

From behind Owen, somebody said, "They're having a block party out there. Listen."

"What?"

"They're playin' music. Creedence."

They were turning up the volume, too. "Bad Moon Rising" swelled in the distance, getting louder and louder. And under it was another sound, a terrible noise like a mechanical Chewbacca that fell into a rock-crushing machine.

At that moment, John's Cadillac came soaring through the air.

It cleared the first fence and *almost* cleared the second—the rear tires caught the razor wire and started unspooling it from the top of the fence, trailing behind the falling Caddie like the streamers on a kite.

Everyone scattered. The grille of the Caddie plunged right into the middle of the bonfire, scattering smoke and flames and bones to the wind. The Cadillac finally bounced and jolted to a stop among a rain of burning human skulls.

The voice of John Fogerty garbled and died. The driver's door opened and John flung himself out, clutching a sawed-off shotgun. He screamed, "DID SOMEBODY ORDER SOME FUCKING PRISON BREAK WITH A SIDE OF SHOTGUN?"

Guardian: Be advised, a vehicle has breached the quarantine fence along the western side. I repeat, a vehicle, appears to be a civilian passenger car, has breached the fence.

Yankee Seven-Nine: Guardian, are you we looking at containment failure here?

Guardian: Negative, uh, Yankee, the fence appears to be intact.

Yankee Seven-Nine: Okay I need clarification, Guardian, I thought you said it had been breached by a vehicle—

Guardian: Affirmative, there is a vehicle inside the fence, the driver has exited.

Yankee Seven-Nine: Then how is the fence still intact, Guardian?

Guardian: It, uh, appears he went over.

Yankee Seven-Nine: He what?

Guardian: Yankee, I think he ramped it. There's a . . . some kind of truck with a platform on the back and I think he used it as a ramp.

Yankee Seven-Nine: All right, did you say you had a clear shot at the driver?

2 Hours, 5 Minutes Until the Aerial Bombing of Undisclosed

John grabbed my shoulders and screamed into my face. "DAVE! ARE YOU IN THERE? IT'S ME. JOHN. I AM YOUR FRIEND. CAN YOU UNDERSTAND ME?"

"Why are you talking like that?"

I looked inside the Caddie. John had come alone.

"Where's Amy?"

"I don't know! Outside town I think."

"Oh. Thank God."

"Or not. I actually don't know."

Owen strode up and kicked aside a smoldering skull. He raised the pistol.

John raised his shotgun. Their eyes met.

John said, "Owen? What the hell are you doin' here?"

"You are one crazy son of a bitch, John."

To me, John said, "Is he infected?"

"I don't think so."

Owen said, "Ain't none of us infected."

I said, "We . . . don't know *that*."

John said, "Well, whatever. Everybody needs to get the hell out of here! By lunchtime this is all gonna be a crater. Did you hear the announcement out there, Owen?"

I said, "Wait, do you two know each other?"

"Yeah, remember I said I was doing setup for him? This is DJ O-Funk." To Owen, he said, "Hell, I thought you'd be out there on Daryl's farm, ridin' this thing out."

"I was. Went into town on a beer run and got scooped up by the feds. I punched one of those guys in the space suits and I guess they took that as a sign of infection."

I noticed the rest of the inmates were staring at us, shell-shocked, as we held this conversation next to the crashed Caddie and among the scattered pile of smoking human remains. It finally occurred to me to turn my eyes up to the circling drones, wondering if they were zeroing in on our skulls right now. I had a vague thought that we should run for cover, but the entrance to the hospital was a hundred feet away. It'd be a nice, leisurely couple of shots for some guy sitting at a console out in the desert. We could duck in the car, but the drone was also equipped with the kind of rockets that could turn it into two tons of burning steel confetti.

Actually, why hasn't he shot us already?

Dr. Marconi walked up and John glanced at him. "Doc? You been here the whole time?"

"John. I would ask you what you are doing but I fear you would actually tell me."

"I'm just here to get Dave. Now we're gonna get in my Caddie and I'm gonna drive a Caddie-shaped hole in that fence over there. The rest of you can walk right out behind us. Once out, you will owe me a case of beer. Each of you."

Owen said, "You didn't see the big fuckin' guns lined up outside? They'll turn you into chunks in two seconds."

"I didn't see any *big* fuckin' guns, I saw a bunch of *little* fuckin' guns. I don't think they were anticipating Cadillac-driving zombies. But either way, you need to find a way outta here, before they bomb the place."

John ducked into the Caddie and said, "Oh, Owen, did paychecks go out last week before this all happened?"

Owen glanced at me, then John, and said, "How the fuck did you two ever find each other?"

To me, John asked, "You comin'?"

I took to the passenger seat. The Caddie seemed to be listing somewhat and steam was oozing from under the hood. But the engine was still running, so that was good.

John said, "Marconi! There's room in the backseat."

Marconi leaned in and said, "I assume your plan didn't progress beyond this exact moment."

"I try to take it one step at a time."

Marconi shifted his eyes to me and said, "Remember what I said?"

"Yeah, the Babylon Protocol."

He started to correct me, but instead said, "There is a way to beat it.

But with God as my witness, I do not know how any of us will get the chance."

"Just tell me what we need to do."

"Think it through. Think about the symbols we rally around. Think about what binds people together."

"Just *fucking tell me*—"

"I think you already know. David, there needs to be a sacrifice."

"A sacrifice? Why?"

"Think it through."

"What, like somebody has to die? One of us?"

Marconi backed away and said, "Go, before the drone operators finally make sense of what they're seeing and open fire."

We buckled our seat belts. John threw the Caddie into reverse. He backed up, rolling through the fire pit, knocking aside a wheelchair. He cranked the wheel and got the Caddie pointing behind the building, not far from the strip of woods John and I had escaped through on that first night, before there was a big-ass fence there.

The crowd of inmates in front of us split like the Red Sea.

John floored it. The back tires dug down into the mud. We launched forward, barreling toward a section of fence bearing the words, FLAME GRILLED FRIDAY, AT CUNTRY KITCHEN. I braced my hands against the dashboard and heard myself screaming.

The fence never stood a chance. The hood bashed through the first layer, whipping down the layer of plastic sheeting. The fencing was still raking its way down the rear windshield when we hit the second layer of fence, smashing a wooden pole in two, ripping through the chain link. The boundary between quarantine and the outside world was pierced once and for all. And then—

CRASH

—with a cataclysmic sound of metal and plastic splattering against concrete, we hit the vehicle barrier both of us had forgotten about until that moment.

The King Kong fist of inertia punched me in the back. My last memory before I blacked out was the filthy windshield about one inch from my face, and the seat belt then yanking me roughly back. When I came to, the hood was crumpled up in front of me and John was shaking me, saying, "GET DOWN!"

Since I had temporarily forgotten where we even were, I also had forgotten what exactly I was ducking away from. I groggily turned to look outside of the driver's-side window, and saw a hulking camo-painted vehicle with no driver. I had no problem figuring out what it was. I saw a turret on top of it, light glinting off of a camera lens and on either side of the lens were two massive gun barrels.

The machine whirred and the barrels spun on me. The movement wasn't robotic at all, but quick and smooth and purposeful. I froze, mesmerized, staring into the twin black holes and chose that moment to wonder what Marconi was talking about when he was going on about "sacrifice."

EIGHT HOURS EARLIER . . .

Bing . . .

Bing . . .

Bing . . .

The RV's door-open chime wafted through the frozen night.

It was the soundtrack of **Amy's** last moments. The thing in front of her breathed and its breath smelled of exotic dead meat. It sniffed her. A realization washed over her in that cold, dark space: this was how virtually all living things born on earth have died—with teeth tearing through their muscle and bones. We humans have computers and soap and houses but it doesn't change the fact that everything that walks is nothing but food for something else.

A tongue licked her forehead. Amy instinctively threw up her hand to ward off her attacker, and grabbed a handful of fur.

Amy opened her eyes and in the darkness, found Molly staring back at her.

Molly sniffed her again, turned, inspected the Pop-Tarts on the floor among the broken glass, then trotted over to the side door of the RV, staring at Amy and wagging her tail. Dog language for, *I need you to open this door for me because I do not possess hands.*

Strangely, that got Amy's leg's moving again. Molly needed to go out. Amy had responded to that canine nonverbal cue a thousand times. She moved quickly to the door, steeled herself, and pushed it open. Molly jumped into the night, into the still air that minutes ago had carried dying screams and the visceral crack of gunfire. Into the night, where teeth and mindless appetites waited, digesting the entrails of boys she'd been laughing and joking with an hour before.

Stop freaking yourself out and MOVE.

Molly returned, looking at Amy expectantly. Amy stepped into the night air, crouching low, keeping her eyes focused on Molly to keep the terror at bay. The dog was not afraid. Amy got ready to run, trying to decide which direction to go. She looked at Molly, as if hoping for a suggestion.

Molly made a beeline for the basement window.

No.

Molly jumped over two piles of guts that used to be Josh and Donnie, and disappeared into the cafeteria Amy had seen on the grainy camera.

No.

From below, Molly barked. Amy decided that dying out here, in the yard, in the open air, was somehow better than dying down in that dark basement. Molly barked again, but this time it was followed by the sound of shuffling footsteps behind her, somewhere in the night. A lot of them. Something was out here. Down there in the room, Molly was still alive and unharmed. Still, Amy half decided to just go running off into the night. But to where?

She got down on hand and knees and crawled through grass that was slimy and sticky with blood and other bodily discharges that were never meant to leave the confines of their organs. Her knees squished through spilled entrails until she awkwardly climbed/fell through the window.

Amy was blind in the darkness. The lantern was gone, the flashlight was gone. Molly was immediately at her side. Amy reached down to touch her, then grabbed her collar. Molly pulled her along, Amy using her as a Seeing Eye dog.

Amy kicked a corpse and stumbled, catching herself via the pure desperation to not have to crawl through any more guts. Molly led her out of the room, into the hallway, and Amy tried to pull her away from the direction of the stairwell, and the maintenance room down there that she knew was now a mass grave. Molly would not budge, pulling the other way, heading for the stairs.

No.

Amy didn't care what Molly had in mind. She wasn't going down into that basement. Not now, not ever. Not for a million dollars. Not if her life depended on it. Amy pulled one way. Molly planted her feet and pulled the other.

Fine.

Amy let go, and charged off into the darkness of the hall, toward whatever lay at the opposite end from the stairs and the twitching, writhing tomb she knew lay below. She threw her hand in front of her, walking blind, and eventually found a metal door just like the one she was running from.

A locked door.

She ran her hand along the handle and dead bolt, hoping to find a lever but instead finding a keyhole, one requiring a key she did not have. Clawed feet scratched up the floor tiles behind her, Molly coming back to say, "See?"

Amy didn't move. She shivered. Her pants were wet. Her fingers were sticky with other people's blood. Molly barked. Amy grabbed her collar, and allowed herself to be led down the hallway. They reached the end, and the stairs.

Down they went. They emerged onto the cell block and there was the stench of sewage and gunpowder, and there were the doors, and the scratching noises behind the doors. Amy blocked it all out. Molly pulled her along, and Amy knew where they were going. They reached the MAINTENAN door. In the darkness, Amy ran her hand over it and felt puckered bullet holes. She closed her eyes, let out a breath, and said a silent prayer.

She pushed the door open.

What lay beyond the door was Hell. Smoke filled the room, wafting between the rusting pipes and ducts that made the big room look like it was being attacked by a giant robot octopus. It stank like fireworks and burned cloth and scorched meat. A single, tiny white shaft of light stabbed up from the center of the floor from a dropped flashlight. It illuminated just enough of the nightmare so that Amy would be seeing it for the rest of her life. Dead, open eyes stared up at the ceiling. Open mouths, twitching fingers. All of the bodies wearing the same solid color. She felt her stomach turn.

Molly pulled free and stepped across corpses, trotting past the tiny shaft of light, continuing into the shadows beyond. She stopped at the opposite wall, looked back at Amy, and wagged her tail.

Amy focused on the light—she was determined to block out everything else from this nightmare place. If she could just make it there, then she'd have a flashlight, and everything would be a bit better. She carefully stepped over limbs and squishy things and explored with her toes to find the solid floor in between. One step, two, three . . . eventually she got close enough to grab the flashlight, trying to block out the fact that it was curled in three dead fingers. She plucked out the light and made her way toward Molly. The smoke was getting to her now, toxic, stinging fumes that burned her eyes.

There was a hole in the wall. Cinder blocks had been smashed and knocked aside. This was where the monsters had tunneled into the room. She shined the light inside and found that wasn't quite right—the tunnel had already been there. It was made of brick and looked like the old-fashioned sewers they have under European cities. Old rusty pipes and stuff. Did the zombies live down here? Under the town?

Molly pushed past Amy, jumped and scrambled up into the tunnel.

"Molly! Wait!"

It was barely more than a whisper. The tunnel was crawling with bugs and dripping with muddy water. But that wasn't the worst of what she knew lurked in there. Molly scampered into the darkness, the scratches of her claws disappearing into God knew where.

"Molly!"

Amy shined the flashlight down the tunnel, and saw two eyes reflecting back at her. Molly had stopped and looked back at her, but stayed where she was.

No. No, no, no, no, no—

Amy climbed into the tunnel, realizing it wasn't tall enough for her to crouch. She would have to crawl, on her hand and knees, over the bricks. She started, realizing the flashlight was next to useless in her right hand, the beam whipping around crazily as she edged forward. She briefly thought about sticking the flashlight in her mouth, but pictured the dead hand that had been clutching it and decided no way.

She pressed on.

Amy crawled, and crawled, and crawled. The brick ate up her knees and the stump of her left hand and the knuckles of her right that were trying to simultaneously clutch the flashlight and act as her front paw. Molly had taken off, her claws echoing down the tunnel until not even the echoes could be heard, and Amy wondered how long this tunnel could possibly be.

She crawled. Pain flared up each time a bony kneecap struck brick, grinding away at the paper-thin skin between the bone and the denim of her jeans. It seemed like she had crawled for miles, and hours. Water dripped in her hair, and on her back. She pushed through spiderwebs, she squished bugs under her hand, she thought she saw a rat scurry off at the sight of the flashlight beam.

She had to stop and rest. She couldn't take the agony in her knees and fingers. The crawling was pulling and twisting at muscles she hadn't used since she had learned to walk.

She stopped, pulled up her knees and leaned up against the rusty pipes. She shined the light back the way she came. She could barely see the entrance to the tunnel. She shined it ahead of her. No end in sight. Her knees were wet and dark. Blood. She was turning her kneecaps into hamburger. A cockroach crawled across her lap and she swatted it away. Suddenly the thought struck her, and in that moment, in that place, she believed it fully: she had died back in the RV, and now was in Hell. This is what Hell was, a cramped, dark, cold tunnel that you crawled through forever and ever, grinding away the skin and muscle and bone of your hands and then your arms and then your legs, endless brick that chewed away your body until you were just a helpless lump for the insects and rats to come feed on, forever.

She heard a noise. Behind her, from the direction of the room full of dead. Something was coming. That got her moving again. She crawled, faster than before, shutting out the pain, hoping that whatever was pursuing her was as poorly designed for crawling as she was.

Time stood still. All that existed was the bricks and the darkness and the chilled breaths tearing in and out of her lungs. Scuffling, over bricks, from behind her. No way to tell how far behind. She tried to go faster but she was crawling, and fast crawling was slower than slow walking and as she inched slowly along the tunnel she became sure this was a nightmare, the classic nightmare everyone has about being chased in the dark and you try to run but you can't—

Suddenly, there was Molly, ahead to her left. Molly barked. There was an intersection in the tunnel, where you could continue straight or turn left. Molly wanted to take the turn and Amy was in no position to argue.

A few feet into the turn, the tunnel came to a dead end. It was blocked by wood, ancient and covered in mildew. Molly scratched at it. Amy crawled up and pushed Molly out of the way. She sat back on her butt and kicked the wooden barrier as hard as she could. It didn't break but it bounced and cracked.

She pounded it again, and again.

Her pursuer got closer, slithering and slapping at the bricks. She heard it breathing. It would round the corner at any moment—

She screamed like a karate master, lashing out with her exhausted legs, her muddy tennis shoes cracking against the board. And then there was no board, it flew away in one piece, slapping against a tile floor somewhere beyond.

Amy scrambled out, climbed to her feet and immediately fell over, the muscles in her thighs spasming and seizing from the crawl that seemed to have lasted weeks. She forced her way up and swept the flashlight around the room. Next to the tunnel exit she had crawled through was a vending machine, of all things, full of bags of chips and cookies and candy bars. On the other side of it was about three feet of space between it and the wall. She went around, put her back to the machine and her feet on the wall and pushed. It tipped over and landed on its side with a crash that sounded like a building being demolished. It didn't block the tunnel entirely, but it blocked most of it.

She got back to her feet and picked up the flashlight. There was one door out of the room. She was sure it would be locked, so sure, but it wasn't and when she pulled it open, she was bathed in light.

And just like that, she was suddenly in a spacious, well-lit office. There were a dozen computer workstations around the room. The computers were new, the desks were ancient. The place was empty but looked like it had been vacated just minutes before; there were half-full cups of coffee sitting around, one chair still had a winter coat draped over the back. A manila folder had been dropped on the floor, spilling printed forms where it landed. A box of donuts had been knocked onto the floor nearby.

Everyone had left in a hurry.

Amy turned back to the door she had just entered, and listened intently. Nothing from the other side. She checked to make sure Molly was in the room with her, then locked the dead bolt. She stood there a few minutes more, listening for the sound of someone or something struggling to push over the vending machine. She heard only her own pounding heart.

Had she really even heard anything in the tunnel? Or was she running from her own echoes? Or a raccoon?

Amy turned her attention back to the room. It was warmer in here, but not room-warm. She did a loop around the room and found a pair of kerosene space heaters that somebody had remembered to turn off when they evacuated. She turned them back on, felt the warm air waft up at her and she just stood there and shivered and wished she had a change of clothes. She smelled like sweat and mold and pee.

There were two doors leading out of the room. She inspected one and found it was locked from the inside, and she decided to leave it that way. The other led to a tiny bathroom that she was shocked to find had running water. She ducked inside and spent several minutes going about the completely unnecessary yet, in that moment, incredibly important task of cleaning herself up. There was a pump with antibacterial soap on the sink and she pulled down her pants and scrubbed the raw skin on her knees. She cleaned her hand and her wrist and her glasses and even got her hair down vaguely into hair shape. She got to where she recognized the face in the medicine cabinet mirror again. It helped.

She emerged from the bathroom and, out loud, asked Molly, "So where are we?"

But that wasn't hard to figure out, was it? She drew a map in her head of the building and the tunnel thing that ran south toward the hospital. She had taken a left turn and that would put her in the basement of

David Wong

that smaller building behind the asylum. This would have been the administration building, with all of the offices and stuff.

Amy glanced around at the computer workstations and suddenly had a revelation that made her feel like Neo in *The Matrix*, the first time he realized he had gained the power to stop bullets.

This was the nerve center of the quarantine, before the government abandoned it. And they left their computers behind.

Figuring out which workstation she wanted was an easy choice—there was one that had three monitors attached to it. She held her breath and hit the power button. It came up, and she wondered how much electricity she had—the room had to have been running off of a generator, but the guys in charge of putting gas in it or whatever were gone. There was nothing to do for it, but to work fast.

The system booted and a network password box came up. At this point the question was how many passwords did this system require. There was a big difference between getting through one password and getting through three—getting through three would be much easier.

She was, after all, at the workstation—she wasn't trying to break in remotely (which she couldn't do, but she knew people who could) and in the world of computer security there is a threshold of just how many passwords a human can remember. Give them one, and they're fine. Two, they're probably still okay. But give them three—say, one for the workstation, another for the network, and a third for whatever application they use—and they're going to have to start writing them down. She started opening creaky desk drawers and found the big one in the middle contained nothing but a box of ballpoint pens and a single Post-it Note with a list of nonsense words and characters. The first would be the username, the rest would be passwords.

And just like that, she was in. She tried to make sense of what programs they had on their desktop, then noticed something that made her yelp with joy.

This computer has Internet access.

Holy crap. She didn't even know where to start.

She nervously checked both of the locked doors—still no sounds from the other side—and settled in at the workstation. The first task, she decided, would be to get a sense of the layout of the system, and what exactly she had available to her. She found what they were using for e-mail, and saw tons and tons of messages in the in-box with attachments—status reports and equipment requests and lots of other standardized forms. Bureaucratic spam. There were also long e-mail exchanges about sound—reports and experiment results about frequencies and modulation and terms she had never heard before, like "infrasound." The staff were sending audio clips back and forth, and huge walls of analytical text referring to them full of technical gibberish. She'd have to set all that aside for now, she could spend weeks trying to get through it all.

She next found a program that, when she clicked on it, took over all three screens, filling them with banks of various camera feeds. Absolutely nothing was going on in most of them—you wouldn't know they were live if not for the occasional bit of trash that would blow into view—but they were clearly of the exterior of the hospital quarantine.

She got out of that, and found a separate application that gave her a full aerial view of the hospital grounds, rotating slowly just like the gun-camera video Josh had shown her earlier. She was going to hit "Esc" to back out of it, but suddenly had the irrational fear that if she hit the wrong key, she'd see a missile come flying out of the bottom of the screen and blow everybody up. After a little more snooping she found out that the aerial drone thing was controlled elsewhere, which made sense. You wouldn't control something like that from a keyboard, you'd want a control stick and all that. She was just watching the feed as a spectator—

David.

She saw him, because the camera view swung around and focused on him. She had no control over that, whoever was operating the drone, wherever they were, had done it. The view blinked and zoomed in, then blinked and zoomed in again.

It was David, plain as day, in a standoff with a big guy who looked really mad. They were surrounded by a crowd, next to the huge bonfire Josh had said was some ceremonial thing (and no matter how she looked at it, it really did look like skulls and bones in there). There was radio chatter going back and forth in the video feed, but it was faint and Amy couldn't make it out word for word. What she was able to gather was that the guy flying the drone was asking for permission to fire from a superior, and then Amy realized that she wasn't just watching this through a camera, but a *gun* camera, and that the gun was pointing right at David.

"No! Don't shoot!" she said, stupidly, at the computer monitor. She had to have some ability to contact them, right? There were landline phones here. And she would say, what? That she was a random girl who sneaked into the REPER command center and that she didn't want them to shoot her zombie boyfriend? All that would do would alert them to the fact that they had an unauthorized person on their network and that they needed to remotely shut down everything.

On the video feed, the big guy raised a gun, pointing it right at David. The camera view shifted slightly, putting the big guy in the crosshairs.

"Yes! Shoot that guy!"

They didn't. She picked up enough of the radio chatter to get that the drone pilot (who she gathered went by the code name "Guardian") had been told to stand by and await further orders. Several excruciating minutes later, David was hauled away and taken inside the hospital building, and the camera view zoomed back out so that it could see the whole yard and, presumably, any zombies who tried to make a run for the fence. The next most likely one to make a run for the fence, however, was David, if she knew him at all. And David was not a zombie. This was not wishful thinking on her part—when David was talking to the big gun guy, he was gesturing and conversing exactly the way David had the last time she had talked to him. David was no more a zombie than he had been two weeks ago, and Amy had faith that the drone operator in fact did not know that. He had been sold the same B.S. that Josh believed, about murderous infected non-humans. Those things did exist—Amy just watched them eat the crew she had ridden down here with. One could burst in that tunnel at any second. But the people inside that fence were people.

And the military was about to bomb them all.

In the end, it took Amy an hour to make the connection. As a hacker, she was a novice, but she knew that by far the most effective way into any system was what hackers called "social engineering." The biggest weakness in any network is the human beings. It doesn't matter how many firewalls or passwords you set up, in the end the system was manned by people. Lazy, busy, harried people who when all was said and done, would take the path of least resistance.

Figuring out where the drone pilot was operating from was easy—a Google search told her that Unmanned Aerial Vehicle or UAV pilots operated from only one location—Creech Air Force Base, just outside of Las Vegas, Nevada. Next she went sifting through the e-mail system to see if she could somehow get so lucky as to find e-mails from dronepilotdude@ creechairforcebase.mil but there was no such luck. What she *did* find was a series of e-mails flying back and forth from the day before, with various people clarifying the "ROE" (which she figured out was Rules of Engagement) with the "Zulus" in the quarantine, as apparently the drone had shot a guy who was attempting to climb the fence and Amy gathered from reading fifty or so e-mails that they were supposed to wait until somebody actually got over the first fence before shooting. Somewhere buried in all of these forms she found an "Eyes Only" document that had been sent to the guy who manned this workstation, some kind of after action report on that incident that named the drone operator: a Captain Shane McInnis.

This was part of an e-mail thread that bounced back and forth between people with REPER e-mail addresses. The issue was the kid who had been shot, a twenty-two-year-old male they were referring to only as Patient 2027. She sifted through a bundle of scanned Eyes Only reports, until she found some kind of admission form they were using for the quarantine. Everything was expressed in jargon and acronyms but Amy was able to piece together that the kid had been held only because he was found in proximity to somebody else who was infected—the kid had killed that person with a baseball bat. But the relevant part of the report on the kid himself were these five words that ended the admission form:

"No signs of infection detected."

Patient 2027 was not a zombie. He was just a kid. And now he was dead.

One thing became clear when following the chain of e-mails on this subject: that particular fact had not been shared outside of a very small group of people in REPER.

Amy looked down at the clock. It was now 4 A.M., which would be two in the morning Nevada time. The shooting happened at 3 P.M. yesterday. Obviously it wasn't the same guy manning the drone all the time. Did they work some kind of regular shifts? If so, that meant Captain McInnis would be back behind the stick in the morning. It really didn't matter either way, that name was all she had.

All right. Start simple. Did Captain Shane McInnis have a Facebook page? She searched. Yes, he did. Set to private, which made sense for a guy in that line of work. She could break into that—Facebook's password reset request form was easy to fool—but she wasn't sure that'd get her what she wanted. Back to Google. She looked up the schools around where the air force base was located, and searched for anything on Google with the names of the schools and "McInnis" in the same article.

Boom. Nevaeh McInnis, point guard on the middle-school basketball team. Want to bet that's Captain McInnis's daughter? Thirteen years old—Amy *knew* she'd have a Facebook page. Ten seconds later, it was up on her screen. She had left everything public, her pics—including shots of her posing with Dad in a dress uniform—her friends list (there was Dad, listed under "family"). Nevaeh had 132 Facebook friends. Amy sent her a friend request, wondering what time Nevaeh would wake up in the morning to check it. But Nevaeh was apparently a night owl, because even at two in the morning her time, she was up to immediately accept a friend request from a total stranger ten years older than her.

Teenagers.

Five minutes later Amy was chatting with Nevaeh McInnis, and realizing that this was going to have to be handled with some delicacy.

Nevaeh McInnis: who is this?

    Amy Sullivan: Hi navaeh, this is going to sound really weird but this is kind of an emergency and we don't have much time.

    Nevaeh McInnis: Nevaeh

    Nevaeh McInnis: Not navaeh

    Amy Sullivan: Oh sorry

    Nevaeh McInnis: its heaven spelled backward

    Amy Sullivan: Right its very pretty

    Nevaeh McInnis: I cant sleep

    Nevaeh McInnis: Chatting with my friend in Taiwan

Amy Sullivan: Anyway this isn't a scam or anything, I'm not going to ask you for any money or account numbers ok

Nevaeh McInnis: k

Amy Sullivan: And no naked pictures or anything like that

Nevaeh McInnis: I have a friend named Taylor, she's only a year older than me, and this guy emailed her and offered her a modeling contract and then her mom drove her all the way to LA to have pictures taken, and do you know what happened then?

Amy Sullivan: Nevaeh, this is really important. I'm in [Undisclosed] right now. Do you know what that means?

Nevaeh McInnis: omg are you a zombie

Amy Sullivan: No! That's kind of the point.

Nevaeh McInnis: oh wow dont tell anybody but my dad is in the air force and he flies a robot plane shooting zombies

Amy Sullivan: I know

Amy Sullivan: That's why I contacted you

Amy Sullivan: I'm here on the ground and so is my boyfriend

Amy Sullivan: And we're not zombies

Amy Sullivan: But your dad doesn't know that

Nevaeh McInnis: hes in bed

Amy Sullivan: OK is he going to fly the robot tomorrow

Nevaeh McInnis: hes tired all the time

Nevaeh McInnis: i think so

Amy Sullivan: Nevaeh, I'm really scared

Amy Sullivan: We're all scared down here

Amy Sullivan: Because I think they're going to shoot all of us

Nevaeh McInnis: They won't do that

Amy Sullivan: I need you to make sure they don't

Amy Sullivan: I need you to talk to your dad

Nevaeh McInnis: I cant talk to him about his work

Nevaeh McInnis: hes not allowed to talk about it

Nevaeh McInnis: and he gets mad

Nevaeh McInnis: and he gets quiet

Nevaeh McInnis: hes tired all the time

Amy Sullivan: Then you have to let me talk to him

Nevaeh McInnis: hes in bed

Amy Sullivan: I just need his e-mail address.

———

There was a long, long pause without a response. This was the point where any caution young Nevaeh had developed about strangers on the Internet should have triggered her alarm bells. Amy tried to picture the girl on the other end, almost two thousand miles away. She imagined her simply closing her laptop and curling up in bed. Then she imagined her going into her father's room and trying to wake him up. Then she imagined her calling the police.

Finally, the chat window blinked to life again, and an e-mail address appeared.

It was as simple as pulling up the e-mail that had the attached form with the analysis of Patient 2027, and forwarding it to the personal e-mail account of UAV pilot Captain Shane McInnis. "No signs of infection detected." The body of Amy's e-mail was concise and to the point:

> Read this. The boy you shot was not a zombie. The people inside the quarantine are not infected. They are people. They are American citizens. You have been lied to.

There were a million things that could go wrong with this—it could wind up in his spam folder, he might not even check his e-mail in the morning before going on duty, he might dismiss it as a hoax. But she couldn't think of where else to go with it.

All right. What next? After the drones, the other layer of security around the fence was the unmanned gun things. Amy brought up the bank of video screens, which she had figured out were feeds from those guns. Still a whole lot of nothing going on outside the fence, a series of static scenes tinged night-vision green. She spent the next half hour poking around, trying to figure out how the guns worked. They were called Gladiators (long name: Gladiator Tactical Unmanned Ground Vehicles, or TUGVs). They had diesel engines that both turned the wheels when they needed to move and charged onboard generators to keep themselves powered up. Just as with the aerial drone, she hit a brick wall when she tried to find an application that would let her actually control one of them. That was too bad because she had this fantasy about taking one over and just rolling it around the fence, going on a robot shooting spree and taking out all of the others. But, again, she wasn't thinking—those machines were military, the room she was in was REPER. And no matter how hard she tried, she could not figure out who was operating them.

She was getting frustrated at this point, but she knew that wouldn't help. This was a system, one set up by people, and it had flaws. What was the flaw here?

Diesel.

The Gladiators (or TUGVs or whatever) needed fuel and that meant they needed people to fuel them. Even if the human operators were on a base in Japan, the refueling job had to be done by people here, on the ground, operating out of this very building. Which meant that there had to be some mechanism by which they could disarm the guns so they wouldn't get shot when they approached them with gas cans. She just needed to find it. And she would.

From the room behind her came the sound of metal scraping against floor.

Something was pushing the vending machine out of the way.

Amy sprang to her feet. She couldn't panic. She had a door on the opposite side of the room she could unlock and run through. Where it led, she didn't know, but she would get there as fast as her feet could carry her.

Molly ran over and faced the door standing between them and the intruder. She let out a low growl. The scraping continued. When it stopped, what replaced it was the sound of something stepping over the vending machine. Then, there was the crunching of glass, something stepping across the shards that had crashed out of the machine when Amy tipped it over.

Amy ran for the opposite door and cranked open the dead bolt. Molly did not move from her spot. Amy was about to call to her when she heard—

"Who's there?"

A tiny voice, from the room the intruder had entered. It sounded like a little girl, and Amy had the crazy thought that Nevaeh McInnis had somehow teleported in from Nevada.

The little voice said, "Can you unlock the door? Hello?"

Amy cautiously made her way over and said, "Who's there?"

The voice answered, but Amy couldn't hear. Then, louder, it said, "What's your name?"

"My name is Amy. Are you lost, little girl?"

"I'm not little, I'm eight."

"Who's with you?"

"It's just me. Can you let me in? I'm scared."

Amy glanced back at Molly, who looked as skeptical as a dog can look.

Amy unlocked the door, and opened it just a crack. "Uh, hello. Who are you?"

The little voice said, "Anna."

2 Hours Until the Aerial Bombing of Undisclosed

I ducked down and banged my head on the window crank on the Caddie's door. I anticipated the thunder of gunfire and the sound of lead punching holes in the Cadillac's door panels. Then I realized I may very well hear nothing at all, because John had *grossly* underestimated the caliber of the sentry guns. The twin barrels on that turret looked big enough to put my thumb into, ready to fire bullets that would effortlessly pierce the thin metal of the Cadillac's door panels, a microsecond later taking a nice leisurely path through my squishy internal organs.

But the guns did not fire.

John screamed, "Let's go! Let's go!"

"What? No!"

"We got 'em confused, we have to get out before they get their shit together and turn us into Swiss meat!"

He opened his door and dragged me out. He reached into the backseat and grabbed something—the green mystery box from my toolshed.

We ducked down, putting the Cadillac between us and the gun—not that there wasn't another, identical gun on the other side—and ran. We hurdled the concrete barrier and there, in front of us, were the woods.

Beyond it, a convenience store bathroom that would hopefully take us away from here.

Déjà vu.

Only there were no soldiers chasing us now. No, now there was a crowd of armed townspeople, carrying shotguns and hunting rifles and machetes, half of them running, half of them aiming their guns and drawing down on us. And, unlike the National Guardsmen in those disorganized early hours of the crisis, here were people who knew what a breach in that fence meant. I risked a look back and saw the gaping hole we'd torn in the fence. Red jumpsuits were gathered on the other side, everyone gawking out at the outside world, as if a hole had suddenly been ripped open in the sky.

And then I saw the gathering crowd, onlookers on the other side of the fence—every one of them armed—with the exact same expression on their face. Two sides of a mirror, the same ideas dawning on both sides.

The fence was broken.

The sentry guns were not working.

Everything had changed.

Shots were fired. We plunged into the darkness of the trees, we scrambled across the muddy ditch, we emerged from the other side and ran for BB's.

Assuming that BB's is even still there . . .

It was. And this time, we didn't even care where the magical shitter door spat us out, as long as it wasn't *here*. If the door wasn't working, if the network of interdimensional wormholes or whatever they were had been shut down by the shadowy fuckers in charge of all of this, then we were dead. We would be torn apart by the mob.

We tumbled into the bathroom and pulled the door closed. A gunshot punched a hole in the door right as the door did its thing and then, we were tumbling—

It was a baffling sensation. The whole world turned, like we were on an amusement park ride. I fell on top of John, both of us suddenly flat on our backs. The door that had been in front of us was now on top of us, we were looking up at it. I got a leg untangled from John and kicked the door. I was looking up at an overcast sky. I pulled myself out and realized

I was emerging from the ground, like a vampire rising from his coffin after sundown. Boards and bricks and broken glass covered the grass around me. I climbed out, and looming above me was the old Ffirth Asylum. There was a huge hole in the wall, the debris of which was scattered all around me. We had teleported less than half a mile away. We were alone for the moment, but could hear the shouts of the mob down the street.

I stumbled out onto the wreckage and John emerged behind me. He stared down at the hole we had come from, confused, and then closed the door I had thrown open. I saw that the door and its frame were in fact laying loose on the ground, flung aside when the blast destroyed the wall. When John picked up the door again, underneath was just dead grass.

John said, "Shit, I left my shotgun shells back at the Caddie."

I took a breath and said, "Look . . . you remember when we watched *Star Wars* with Amy? And she's like, 'Why is Princess Leia being such a bitch when those guys just rescued her?' Well I don't want to be the Leia in this situation and I completely appreciate what a sweet ramp job that was back there. But did you have *any* kind of a plan at all?"

"I'm working on it."

"Because time is running out here . . ."

John was looking up at the old building, staring hard at the mossy brick walls.

I said, "What?"

"I took some Soy Sauce earlier."

"You did?"

"Yeah. And I came by here."

"Okay . . ."

"And . . . there were shadows here."

I followed his gaze. The rows of windows in the moldy brick were boarded over with ancient, warped plywood. It kind of made it seem like the building had cataracts. I saw no shadow people.

I said, "Do you see any now?"

"No."

He turned and saw something else, though, and said, "Here," handing me the green mystery box. He jogged away from me, heading for the corner of the building. I spotted the ass of an RV parked there. I followed him. Faint shouts from the armed mob were growing louder.

"John! What are you—"

My words died at the sight of bloodstained grass surrounding the loose earth of a huge, freshly filled-in hole. Like a mass grave. John pulled out his ridiculous customized shotgun (he had it wedged down the back of his pants) and ducked into the RV. The windshield was busted out and when I followed John through the driver's-side door, I saw that the tan upholstery of the driver's seat was one big bloodstain.

Christ.

Leading with the shotgun, John quickly searched the inside. There were rows of hooks on the opposite wall that it took me a moment to realize were gun racks, all of which were now empty. John started throwing open foot lockers and found them stocked with at least four different types of ammunition.

"Bingo," he said, stuffing his pockets with shotgun shells. "See? Things have a way of working out. We needed shells, and here they are."

I looked around. On the floor was a busted laptop computer. At the very back, the floor was damp and it smelled like piss. There didn't seem to be anything of use here other than the bullets—

I froze.

"Oh, no. Oh, fuck no. No, no, no . . ."

John joined me and said, "What? I think these were . . ." but his words trailed off. He saw what I saw.

Two objects, that a man in denial could have dismissed as meaningless: a mostly empty tub of red licorice, and an orthopedic pillow designed for people with back problems.

Amy.

It really only told me what I already knew. She'd come for me, because that's who she was, and she'd find a way in, because she was too capable not to.

John glanced nervously out of a side window. The mob would wash in at any moment. He was saying, "Okay, we don't *know* this was hers. And even if it was, we do know that isn't her blood in the driver's seat. Amy can't drive . . ." but I was already jumping out of the RV. Outside, I immediately I saw another, smaller bloodstain, this one in the grass in front of an open basement window. Laying in it was a single empty shoe. A man's.

I said, "Amy got somebody to give her a ride in. So they pulled up, something nasty came flying out of that window down there, and they killed the shit out of it. Look—next to the window. Spent shotgun shell. Maybe it got the driver first. Then the rest of the posse in the RV, and Amy if she was with them, they bail out and go inside. Probably in there right now. Then a hobo came along and pissed in the RV."

"Dave, why would they—"

Ignoring him, I leaned my head down toward the basement window and yelled, "AMY! HEY! AMY? IT'S DAVE." Nothing. "ANYBODY? IS THERE ANYBODY IN THERE?"

A shot was fired. A bullet took a chip out of the wall. We ducked and John grabbed my sleeve, yanking me around the corner, toward the front door. Neither one of us had to debate the merits of getting down and crawling through that basement window. That violated two rules of living in Undisclosed: 1) never put yourself in a spot where you don't have an open, and *fast*, means of escape, and 2) don't go through any entrance that has a huge goddamned bloodstain in front of it.

We reached the front door and John said, "Plug your ears." He pointed the shotgun at the locks on the front door and blew a grapefruit-sized hole in the wood. We pushed our way inside.

105 Minutes Until the Aerial Bombing of Undisclosed

It appeared the feds left behind anything that would take more than five minutes to load onto a truck. Boxes of medical supplies and biohazard suits and filters for biohazard suits and every other thing lined the main hallway, abandoned in the evacuation. Halogen work lamps were set up on stands here and there, a few of them still on, blasting bluish beams through the shadows of the huge corpse of a building. We pushed the front door closed and dragged a huge metal cabinet in front of it.

Out of breath, I said, "We could have relocked that door but somebody blew a hole in it."

"I'm sorry, princess."

"And by the way, those shotgun shells in the RV? They weren't there waiting for us because a guardian angel dropped them from the sky because you needed help. They were there because somebody else, somebody who believed in being prepared, paid for them with their own money. Keep that in mind the next time you get yourself in a bind and somebody is there for you with bail money or a sofa to sleep on. It isn't providence. It's generous people who work hard jobs to buy things you can take."

We were jogging down a main hallway now, heading deeper into the building. John said, "Search one of these crates. See if you can find some fucking antidepressants."

"All right, all right—"

"Seriously, it's an emergency. I'll cram them down the barrel of the gun and blow them right into your brain."

We moved in silence for a moment and I said, "How did we screw this all up so badly, John?"

He shook his head. "We always find a way."

We had to stop to climb over a knocked-over pile of plastic storage bins in the hall. I said, "Damn, the feds left in a hurry. They got overrun? By infected?"

"Not exactly. I told you Falconer had to spring me out of here, we had to blow a huge hole in the wall to do it. They had us in like a big gymnasium and we saw a couple of liquid oxygen tanks along the wall and we're like, 'Let's blow that shit up and get the hell out of here.' It worked but I guess in the confusion a bunch of the infected they were holding here got loose and they decided to just leave town and let the situation sort itself out."

"Wait, you're the reason the feds abandoned ship? Jesus, John."

"Well I feel like it's their fault for trying to hold me. They should have known that shit comes with consequences."

John clicked three shells into his ridiculous tri-barreled shotgun, glancing nervously back toward the front doors. Nobody came crashing through. Wait, was the armed, angry mob scared to come in here? That couldn't be a good fucking sign.

"AMY? ANYBODY?"

Echoes bounced off moldy walls. The building seemed five times bigger on the inside. It had the tangled floor plan common to all hospitals, seemingly designed by someone who believed in the healing power of watching confused visitors aimlessly wander around hallways. It didn't help that all signage in the place had faded, or been stolen, or painted over with graffiti. We came to a "T" in the hall.

I said, "Which way?"

"When I was here earlier I—HEY!"

John took off running to his right. I followed, the heavy green mystery box banging off my legs as I ran. I considered dropping the stupid thing.

"What? What did you see? John!"

We skidded to a stop at the end of the hall.

"I saw somebody."

"Was it a . . . person?"

He shook his head, in a way that meant he didn't know.

"Are you sure you saw them?"

"Is that an elevator?" It was. Down at the end of the hall. The doors were closed. "Probably no power to it though, right?"

I said, "I think you might be wrong. I rode in it. They had me down in the basement for a while."

"They did? You didn't tell me that. What's down there? Surely nothing worth complaining about, or else you would have brought it up by now."

"Don't know. They had me knocked out the whole time and then put a bag on my head when they hauled me out to go to quarantine. I don't want to shake your faith in government but I'm thinking this REPER is kind of a shady operation. Find the stairs."

There was no need to debate getting on the elevator, thanks to rule number one I mentioned just a moment ago. You get on one of those things, and you're sealed up and somebody else is controlling where you go. All of these rules were learned from terrible experience.

John said, "Boom. Stairs. Right over there."

We jogged toward the stairwell door and at the exact moment John's hand grabbed the handle, the elevator dinged behind us. We heard the doors slide open.

From behind us, a tiny voice said, "Walt?"

90 Minutes Until the Aerial Bombing of Undisclosed

I very nearly pissed my pants. John saw the look on my face and spun around with the shotgun. He led the way, and we inched toward the now-open elevator. Inside was a little girl. Long, black, straight hair. She wore a filthy nightgown.

John said, "Holy shit. What are you doing here?"

I said, "John, back up . . ."

The little girl looked at me and said, "Don't be scared."

"Anna?"

She nodded.

John said, "You know her?"

"Don't lower the gun, John."

"Do you want to hold it? I'm not pointing a shotgun at a toddler."

Anna said, "Why are there so many holes on that gun?"

I said, "What do you want?"

"I can take you to see Amy."

"Is she here?"

Anna nodded, silently.

John and I exchanged a look.

Quietly, he said, "Okay, I admit she's pretty creepy."

I whispered, "Man, if this was a horror movie the audience would be screaming for us to get the fuck out of here."

"Well, they'd be thinking it. They wouldn't *scream* it unless they were bla—"

"She's downstairs," interrupted Anna. "Your dog is here, too. Get in."

John said, "Uh, no. If we go down, we take the stairs."

Anna shook her head. "There are no lights in the stairs. We should stay away from the dark."

I swallowed and said, "Because of the shadow man."

She nodded. John whispered, "Jesus Christ."

To John, I said, "I'm gonna leave it up to you."

He clearly had no idea. This was so obviously a trap. And we so obviously had nowhere else to go.

John asked Anna, "Where is she? What floor?"

"The second basement. Mr. Bear is down there, keeping a lookout."

"Okay, and is Mr. Bear a—"

"It's a stuffed bear," I said, answering for her.

"Right." John said to me, "We do it this way. You wait here. For two minutes. I'm taking the stairs. If there is something waiting for us, I'll find out how it likes buckshot. Then you head down on the elevator and I'll meet you there. Then if she, uh, attacks you, you only have to last for two floors. Against a toddler."

Anna said, "I think we should all ride together."

John was already heading to the stairs. I took a breath, steeled myself, and stepped into the elevator with Anna. I hovered my finger over the "B2" button, and counted to a hundred. I braced myself for the sound of shotgun blasts, or screams, or anything.

Nothing.

I hit the button.

The door closed.

Anna stood to my left, motionless, looking forward the way people do on elevators. The elevator rumbled and we were heading down, and down. A tiny, soft, warm hand curled around mine. I looked down at Anna and she smiled up at me.

We jolted to a stop.

The light went off.

The little fingers squeezed around mine. I slapped at the door and yelled, "JOHN! HEY!"

No answer. Anna's hand squeezed tighter. Strong. *Too* strong.

I punched buttons on the panel. Nothing. I kicked at the door. I tried to pull my hand away from Anna's grip and I couldn't.

The fingers changed. I felt them melt under my grip, fusing together, becoming something like a snake or a tentacle—

The light blinked on. I wheeled on Anna and she was just a little girl with little girl hands.

She said, "The lights do that sometimes."

I stared hard at her. Her eyes were the picture of innocence. The door opened, and John was there, aiming a shotgun at my face.

I said, "Don't shoot. The, uh, light went off. We all clear here?"

"Yeah."

Anna led the way out of the elevator, stopping to pick up a teddy bear that looked like it had been bought and sold in three different garage sales over twenty years. She clutched it and headed down the hall.

I recognized the corridor and the rust-pitted steel doors, and the smell of shit. I followed Anna and John followed me. He had the shotgun by his ear, aimed at the ceiling, trying to look in every direction at once.

We turned a corner, passing more doors. We reached the end of the hall and a bullet-riddled maintenance door that had been barricaded from this side, metal bars laid over it with fresh welds locking them in place. There were empty bags of cement and masonry tools scattered around the hall, and I wondered if on the other side of that door I would find a steam tunnel sealed with fresh brick and concrete.

Anna turned left, down another hall. Then it was through a doorway marked ANNEX, which opened to an impossibly long hallway that seemed too long for the building. We headed down, our footsteps echoing endlessly in both directions. The walls were covered with a faded mural, depicting huge, smiling faces that may have been clowns or mimes. Time and moisture had peeled the paint in patches, so that huge swaths of the colorful landscape were corroded and eaten away, the smiling inhabitants unaware that the very fabric of their world was crumbling. Graffiti artists had painted signatures and anarchy signs and cocks. Along the wall to my left, in huge letters, was the phrase:

THE END IS NOT NEAR

IT HAS ALREADY HAPPENED

WE JUST DIDN'T CARE

Anna looked back and me, and smiled. Invisible ants raced up my back.

I glanced back at John and saw on his face that he had already realized that what was up there, whatever it was, was not Amy. What was up there was bad news, and it was only a matter of how we would deal with it. We were not in control of the situation. We were never in control. The last of the working emergency lights was only halfway down the hall, and the light faded long before we reached the end. Our own echoes followed us down, and down, into the darkness. Anna slowed down and I once again felt the tiny, warm hand in mine. We walked together and at the end of the dark hall I could see a closed door, with light pouring from the bottom. Just like people describe in near-death experiences—the long passage with a door of light at the end.

"Amy is in there," whispered Anna. And in that moment, I decided that this was probably right, but not in a literal way. Whatever was waiting behind that door was, almost certainly, the quickest way to see Amy. Or at least, to join her, if there is no such thing as seeing in that place.

We reached the door. Anna let go of my hand and said, "It's locked. Only she can open it. Call for her."

I said, "Amy?" but thought it was too soft for even Anna to hear. I cleared my throat and said it louder.

In that moment, I realized I was smelling something, a scent totally out of place in this rotting, forgotten building. A scent I had smelled a hundred times before, one that was sparking memories that triggered a wave of sadness.

I heard the latch turning on the door.

70 Minutes Until the Aerial Bombing of Undisclosed

The smell was microwave popcorn.

The door opened and there was Amy, her handless left arm curled around said bag of popcorn. Her eyes got huge behind her glasses and then her arms were around me and we were crushing a popcorn bag between us. She was sobbing and pressing her face into my chest so hard her glasses had gone askew. I squeezed her and ran my hand through her hair and whispered to her that it was all right, that everything was all right.

I have no idea how long we stood there like that, or how long John and Anna stood there and waited. All I could think was how much I wished, for the second time, we could just freeze a moment and run credits over it.

John said, "Sorry that took so long. I had to ramp something."

Amy pulled away and wiped her eyes and said, "Oh my God you won't believe what I just did. I got hungry and I used a microwave to make this and it tripped a breaker that I guess runs out to the generator and if the computers had been on that same breaker we would have lost everything."

She gathered herself and said to John, "I never doubted you."

John said, "Now *there's* a lie. But I don't blame you."

I said, "Shit, I'm *still* doubting him."

Amy looked down at Anna and said, "You and Mr. Bear did good. We're all here. Even Molly's here."

She was. Curled up on the floor, under a desk. Holy shit did that dog get around.

"How did she—"

I was talking to Amy's back. She was scurrying across the room to a desk where she had set up no fewer than five computer monitors and three keyboards. There was a box of donuts and a pot of coffee going. It looked like she'd been working here for a week.

Amy said, "Okay, this setup looks ridiculous but I finally figured out they had different parts of the security set up on different workstations and there was no way to monitor them all without running back and forth across the room. I had to crawl around and reroute network cables and—anyway, all of the security robots around the quarantine are offline, they're in maintenance mode and as far as I know they can't be reset remotely, so that should be taken care of. The UAVs, the drone things, I think they're okay. It's—it'd take a long time to explain but I e-mailed a guy and got that taken care of. All that is the good news. The bad news is—wait, the good news is that I know how they're blocking the cell phone signals, it's not done through the provider level or anything, they have a jammer somewhere, probably outside of city limits, it's a big thing called a warlock jammer, a TRJ-89, it sits on the back of a truck. The bad news is that I can't shut it down from here. There's an actual crew manning it, that's why I think it's outside of town because

REPER pulled all of their staff out beyond city limits but they're still manning the jammer because it's really, really important that nobody in town be able to call out until they drop the bombs."

Amy stuffed a handful of popcorn in her mouth.

I said, "Right, they're going to bomb the quarantine at noon."

She shook her head so hard that her hair went slapping around her cheeks.

Around a mouthful of chewed popcorn she said, "Huh uh. They're going to bomb the whole town."

1 Hour Until the Aerial Bombing of Undisclosed

John said, "Even that Cuban sandwich place?"

She nodded. "An hour from now."

I said, "Bullshit. They can't get away with bombing an entire city. What are they gonna do, claim an asteroid fell on it?"

Amy looked surprised, and said, "David, you don't understand what it's been like out there, out in the real world. Everything has been just totally cut off from the town. Everything the world knows about what's going on in [Undisclosed] is based one hundred percent on what REPER has told them. They don't have to *claim* it's anything. The whole country is begging them to do it. Here. Look. This was twenty minutes ago."

She spun around to face one of her monitors and brought up a video clip, from one of the network news sites. It was a group of haggard-looking middle-aged men, facing a bank of microphones. And there, among them, was my shrink. Dr. Bob Tennet.

The first guy, introduced as the head of the outbreak task force, spoke and confirmed that they had in fact been given permission by the president of the United States to use military assets to "disinfect" the entirety of Outbreak Ground Zero, and that this would proceed as soon as it could be confirmed that all military and REPER personnel were clear of the area.

I pointed to Tennet standing in the back and said, "You see that guy back there, with the Caesar haircut? That's my therapist."

"But why would he be—"

"It was all part of the setup. He works for Them."

"Who? Oh, you mean capital 'T' Them."

John said, "He's talking."

On the video, Tennet strode up to the microphone, his title displayed as DR. TENNET, CONSULTANT, REPER.

"Thank you, Mr. Secretary, I'll be brief. You've all come to know me over these trying days, and I've found myself in the unexpected position of relaying to the public the serious nature of this threat with what I hope you appreciate as frankness, honesty and transparency, while trying to ensure that caution did not turn into panic. What I have been saying from day one continues to be just as true now, if not more so: fear is the most dangerous contagious disease.

"So with that, I want to address the question a moment ago about deaths resulting from the bombardment, that is, the thermobaric disinfection of the affected area that Secretary Fernandez just explained, which will, as he said, commence at noon local time. This needs to be made perfectly clear, for you here, for those watching this on the news, and for our children and grandchildren who will try to understand this act when it passes into the pages of history books. As far as we know, there is no one left alive in the city of [Undisclosed]. As you know, the National Guard and multiple agencies including the CDC, FEMA and REPER took decisive coordinated action to create a buffer around the city, a five-mile band that we referred to as the Yellow Zone but in the news media has been unfortunately redubbed the Dead Zone. In this, we were successful, and we may never know how many lives were saved by moving rapidly and decisively to isolate the infection zone.

"*However,* efforts to stop the spread of the contagion, which has colloquially become known as the Zulu Parasite, within the city itself have utterly failed. The infection rate within city limits is now at or near one hundred percent. This operation is about the disposal and disinfection of tens of thousands of highly—*highly*—infectious *corpses.* Now, I have worked very hard all week to shoot down the more outlandish rumors that have spread about the parasite, and I suspect I will spend the rest of my life doing the same. That is the nature of that contagion we call paranoia. But the situation is this. Whatever residents of [Undisclosed] are still walking and moving, are, for all intents and purposes, effectively dead. We have explained this *ad nauseum*; the parasite completely breaks down and effectively rewires the victim's brain tissue. The victims retain some basic motor control and become extremely, extremely violent as the parasite continues to corrupt the central nervous system. From then, until the victim is finally rendered immobile, they are *highly, highly* contagious. This stage of the disease is what has unfortunately led to some of the more sensationalist rumors of 'zombies' and the like. But I want to make it perfectly clear: these are nothing more than people who, after death, are able to remain mobile, dangerous and infectious."

John said, "Well, that should put everybody at ease."

I snorted.

Amy said, "I wasn't even paying attention, all I can picture is you having sex with him."

John said, *"What?"*

Tennet was still talking:

". . . which is what makes the situation so exceptionally dangerous if we don't completely eliminate the threat using all means available to us. The sights and the sounds of this terrible, but necessary, process, will be shocking. This is something none of us wanted to see happen in an American city. But let me make it clear now, and for all time: we are only disposing of the dead. Nothing more. Thank you."

John pointed at the screen and said, "You notice they even started using a 'Z' word to describe the parasite? Might as well have called it the 'Zombie Virus.'"

I shook my head. "Son of a bitch. Marconi was right. That panic is just going to ripple out, like splashing a rock in a pond."

John said, "What do we do?"

I said, "We get the hell out of town and find some other place to live. Man, I wonder if the insurance will pay for my house getting bombed . . ."

Amy said, "David, we can't let them do this."

"Babe, I don't think there's a choice. They set it up so that it would be the only option. If they don't scour this town off the face of the earth, then people will never be satisfied. People will be killing each other in the streets, a new panic set off every time a normal-looking person monsters out. It's shitty that they'll get what they want, but . . . this is kind of checkmate. They kill [Undisclosed], or the world kills itself."

John said, " 'They.' What a bunch of assholes."

Anna walked up beside Amy.

"Can I have some of your popcorn?"

"You can have the bag, honey. Sorry it kind of got squished."

"It's okay."

Damn, that was a creepy kid.

To Amy, John said, "You've got working e-mail there? Can't you send a message to the *New York Times* or somebody? Telling them what's going on?"

"Oh, I did. I also found out that the news channels and all the big papers were getting over a hundred thousand messages a day from zombie cranks and apocalypse crazies and everybody else. Mine will be one more in the pile. Maybe some intern will get to it six months from now. Maybe it'll mean something to the town they build on top of the ashes of this one."

I said, "Damn, girl, you got cynical in the last couple of weeks." She didn't smile. I read something in her face and said, "Wait a second. How did you get here? Did you come in on that RV?"

She nodded. "I came down with some guys. Hipsters who thought they were going to come down and shoot zombies and have future high schools named after them."

"They, uh, didn't make it, did they?"

She shook her head.

"Jesus, Amy. *Nobody* else made it?"

She shook her head again.

I went to her and hugged her again. "How the hell did you get away?"

She couldn't answer. Instead, she pulled away and said, "It really is perfect the way they set this up. It brought everybody's worst fears out of the woodwork, and every little thing the government said made it just a little bit worse. It was all there, David. Under the surface. They just came along and pricked everybody's balloon."

I said, "Well, it doesn't change anything. Our mission is to get the hell out of here. Then if, you know, they drop the bombs, that sucks, but all we can do is tell the world what we know."

Amy stood up and brushed a dozen pieces of dropped popcorn off her lap.

She said, "What are we waiting for?"

I gestured toward Anna and said, "What do we do with her? We don't have time to find—"

"Where'd she go?" John was looking around the room.

I said, "She was right he—"

The lights went out.

"Damn it! I knew she was a monster! John! Amy! Listen! *Guard your buttholes.*"

I heard John knocking objects off a nearby table, blindly grabbing for his shotgun.

From the pitch blackness, Amy said, "Calm down, it's probably just the generator. It probably just ran out of gas." She shouted, "Anna? Honey? Are you okay?"

I heard the click of a door lock.

Molly started barking.

"Somebody's leaving! Who's leaving? I heard the door!"

John said, "I got the shotgun. Somebody look for a flashlight."

"Anna? Are you in here? It's okay, honey, don't be afraid."

I said, "That's right, little girl. Everything is fine. Come . . . get in front of John's shotgun."

Something long and slim and warm slid into my palm. It had bumpy ridges, like an earthworm. It slipped through my hand and around my wrist and forearm.

I yelled and yanked my hand away but the thing—the Anna thing, in its true form—held fast. It slithered around my elbow and came to rest under my armpit. Then another tentacle was wrapping around my knee. I made panicked, cursing noises and stumbled backward.

"DAVE! HEY! WHERE ARE YOU?!"

I went to the floor. There was a crash in the darkness, presumably John tripping over a chair while blindly flailing to my rescue.

Amy screamed. "DAVID!"

"IT'S GOT ME! SHE'S GOT ME!"

I kicked and thrashed and the bundle of flexing tentacles slipped around my abdomen. And then, around my neck.

I threw myself to my feet, and tried to find a wall to slam into, to crush it. I wound up flinging myself through thin air, tripping over a box.

The monster was shrieking in my ear. I pulled at the limb around my neck but it was strong, so freaking strong.

Everybody was yelling, but I could hear nothing over the screeching that was turning into an ice pick in my ear. Then, there was a crash from the room next to us, metal and glass like something big and heavy had been knocked over. Amy screamed. Molly barked.

I got to my feet once more, wearing the Anna monster like a writhing backpack. I found a wall and slammed backward into it.

It didn't budge. Somebody was screaming my name.

I heard a door burst open.

"ANNA!"

This was a new voice, a man's voice, with an accent.

A blast of light flooded the room. Everyone froze.

Standing in the doorway was a Latino guy who I thought looked like Marc Anthony. I knew I had seen him before but in my state of panic, couldn't place where. He was holding a huge flashlight and he whipped it around the room, first finding Amy, who was still standing next to the dead computer and squinting at the sudden brightness. Then he spotlighted John, who was pointing his shotgun right at my face.

Then the light found me, and I felt the tentacle loosen from around my neck. The Anna thing slithered to the floor, and in the harsh shadows of the beam I saw a filthy nightgown tangled around a nightmare wad of tentacles that looked like they were made of knotted clumps of black hair. Somewhere in the center of it was a pair of eyes on either side of a sideways mouth and clicking mandibles.

The man with the flashlight said, "Anna. Are you okay?"

The tentacles started twisting and bundling together, fusing and melting and re-forming. In a few seconds, there was the little girl again. She straightened her nightgown and sniffled and started crying.

David Wong

The man said again, "Are you okay?"

Anna shook her head.

"No, you're all right."

In the shadows I could see John looking back and forth, between me, the guy, and Anna. He was still pointing the shotgun at me, he realized, and he pointed it at the floor instead.

To me, the guy said, "Are you all right? You're David, right?"

"She . . . turned into a . . . thing . . ."

"I know that. Did she hurt you?"

"The light went off and she got me around the neck . . ."

"Did she *hurt* you?"

"No."

Anna sobbed and said, "He hurt *me!*"

The guy said, "Now *Anna*, you scared him. You turned and you scared him."

"I didn't mean to! The lights went out and I c-couldn't h-help it . . ."

"Anna, you need to say you're sorry to David."

Anna did not agree with this.

"Anna . . ."

She defiantly said, "I'm *sorry.*"

To me, he said, "Do you accept her apology, as heartfelt as it clearly wasn't?"

I had no words. "I . . . she turned into a . . . thing . . ."

Anna started crying in earnest once more. Amy said, "Hey. David." I turned and out of the darkness, an object came hurtling toward me. I flinched, threw up my hands and squealed. A filthy, stuffed bear bounced off my gut.

I found it on the floor. Handling it like I was passing a piece of meat into a tiger cage, I kneeled and extended the bear toward Anna.

She flung herself toward me, utilizing her preternatural, little-girl speed. I had no time to react. She flew at me, and threw her arms around my neck. She pressed her wet face against mine and hugged me. She said, "I'm sorry I scared you, Walt."

"It's, uh, okay." I put an arm around her, and for the tenth time in a week felt like I had become numb to the ridiculous.

Anna pried herself away from me, plucked Mr. Bear from my hands

344

and navigated her way through the wrecked room, over to the flash-light man. He kneeled down to catch her, and gave her a kiss on the forehead.

I said, "I . . . don't understand. Is she . . ."

"This is my daughter, Anna. She's eight years old."

"And you are . . ."

"I'm Carlos."

50 Minutes Until the Aerial Bombing of Undisclosed

John, reading the expression on my face, said, "You two know each other?"

Carlos answered for me, saying, "We were over in quarantine to-gether."

I said, "And you are . . . you're like her? Right?"

"No. Not like her. What I mean is, she's not like me. She won't hurt you. She hasn't hurt anybody. Not like me."

"So, you are the one who—"

"Not in front of her. But yes."

"But you want us to believe that we're safe. From you, I mean."

"There is a lot about this situation that you do not understand. In quarantine, they were using you to sort the infected from uninfected, right? But you can't really do it. Not like I can. Me, I can see them, as easy as telling man from woman. I can see it at a glance."

"All right. But I don't under—"

"There isn't time. Let me just say that . . . I can tell you what I know, but you don't want to know it. About who is and isn't infected, I mean. And when I say you don't want to know, I'm not trying to up the sus-pense. I am saying that *you don't want to know*. It won't make doing what you need to do any easier. It won't make it easier for you to live in the world."

I started to ask a question, but stopped myself. I tried to absorb what he was saying. Finally, I said, "Dr. Marconi . . . he, uh, hinted to me that there may be more infected than everybody thinks."

"Let's say he's right. Let's say he's really, really right. Now we got to ask ourselves what that word means. 'Infected.' Infected like me? Or like my Anna here?"

I had no answer. I tried to weigh the implications of this, and couldn't begin to. Molly had joined Anna, and the little girl was scratching her behind the ears.

"Or infected like Dr. Bob Tennet."

"You mean he's—"

"He's something else altogether. When I look at him, you know what I see? A black cloud. I don't even see a man. Do you understand what I'm saying? He's not a man. And maybe neither am I and maybe that doesn't mean anything anymore. But I'm going to say this to you, David, and to your friends here—Tennet is more dangerous than a million of me. He and the people he works for, they figured out how to use a signal, inaudible sound waves, to affect people like me. Turn us, make us lose control. I'm telling you, when left to myself, I can control it. The parasite, it whispers in my ear but I can overcome it. You just got to have the will, to put that cockroach in its place."

I said, "So we're supposed to just turn our backs on you and walk out. Knowing all of the people who are—" I glanced down at Anna "—who are, uh, gone, because of you. I'm supposed to just let that go. And you're going to just, what, go back to work next week? Everything back the way it was?"

"I'm all she's got. Her mother is gone. And she has to deal with her . . . condition on top of that. Well, she's going to have a life, the life a little girl should have. And she's going to learn how to live with this. Who else is going to teach her? Who else will understand?"

He nodded at John and said, "So, what, you want your friend to shoot me with his sawed-off five-barrel shotgun? And then Anna either gets rounded up by the government and dissected in a laboratory, or torn to pieces by that mob out there? No, you won't do that to her. I know you won't."

I groaned and rubbed my forehead.

John said, "Okay, can somebody quickly just summarize for the shotgun department who it's okay and not okay to shoot?"

Carlos said, "The world doesn't make it that simple for us, friend."

I said, "Yeah, if somebody tries to make a video game based on this situation, I'm telling you right now I'm not fucking buying it."

Carlos stood, and took Anna's hand in his own.

I said, "And I still don't . . . I mean, I didn't think children could get infected."

"Dummy, she's not infected like the rest. She's been this way for years. This isn't new. How can you, of all people, not know that?"

"I . . . I guess I . . ."

John said, "Well, I'm lost."

I said, "Marconi. He had infected patients he was studying, but he had this theory that some of them would literally never turn, that the parasite could just . . . live there."

John said, "So, what, we just accept that? These invisible bugs multiplying inside people and we just shrug and move on? Knowing that any day any random person can just murder the shit out of a roomful of people?"

Carlos just shrugged and said, "That's been the situation for longer than you know. Way longer. And you need to ask yourself, are you even sure all of *you* are uninfected?"

Amy said, "We're sure."

"Are you? Your man there, he spent a lot of time in town, in quarantine, in the basement of this place. He can't even account for his own whereabouts for the last week or so. You a hundred percent sure he came out of all that clean?"

John shrugged and said, "Eh, he wasn't all that clean before. No offense, Dave."

"Fuck you, John."

To Amy, Carlos said, "I'm not joking, you know. How would you truly know—"

I said, "She knows what I am."

"But if you were infected you would deny it—"

"Carlos. *She knows what I am.*"

Silence. Then he nodded and said, "All right, then. Now are you going to let my Anna, and all the rest like her, get burned up in the hellfire they rain down on this place?"

Amy said, "We have to stop the bombs."

I rubbed my eyes and sighed. "How can that possibly be *our* responsibility?"

John said, "There's a way. Everything Tennet said in his press conference is bullshit. The streets out there aren't full of shambling hordes. They're full of all-American types carrying hunting rifles and protecting women and children. The reason Tennet had to lie is because he knew he'd never sell the public on those people being zombies. We just got to show them."

I said, "And then when those all-American Joes get out, and some of them fucking turn into monsters, what happens then?"

Amy said, "Then we will once again err on the side of not *letting people be murdered*. You take the choice in front of you. And then you keep picking the non-murder choice as long as you can."

I said, "And *that* is why I wanted you to stay home."

John said, "We have to shut down their cell phone jammer. Twenty-thousand cell phones and cameras and Internet connections will suddenly blink to life. Then people can call and e-mail and upload videos and that'll be that, the lid will be off their whole charade."

It took me a moment to figure out what John had said because he pronounced it "sha-rod."

Amy said, "Then the president will realize he can't bomb the town without losing a bunch of votes next election."

I said, "Setting aside the fact that we now have less than an hour to accomplish this, and that we'll be gunned down the moment we set foot outside this building, do you have any way to find out where the jammer even is?"

"Well, I think there's only one place it can be. It needs line of sight, right?"

"Okay."

"So it needs to be someplace high. The highest point they can get it."

"Where's that?"

"Well it'd be somewhere around the water tower, right? For the same reason."

"The water tower needs line of sight?"

"It needs to be at the highest point."

"Oh."

"Because the gravity pushes the water down and that's what makes the water come out of your faucet."

"Yes. Right. I absolutely knew that before right now."

John said, "Shit, we saw it. That big-ass black semi they had parked out there. They had it in place the first day. So, fine, let's go fuck that shit up."

To Carlos, Amy said, "Can you lead us out of here? We don't have a flashlight."

45 Minutes Until the Aerial Bombing of Undisclosed

We spilled out of the elevator onto the first floor. Carlos and Anna stayed behind, Carlos holding the door open.

I said, "I don't want this to come off as a lack of confidence on my part, but you might consider trying to get out of town. Just, you know, on the tiny chance that the three of us are unable to thwart the plans of the most powerful fighting force on the planet."

Carlos shook his head. "Got people I can't leave behind. We're all counting on you now. Including little Anna here."

Goddamnit.

We turned and headed for the front door. I noticed that Molly stayed behind with Anna. I wondered if she hadn't chosen the better team.

In the lobby, John said, "Stop." To Amy, he said, "We need you to open the box for us."

I said, "No. Oh, no."

"We got no choice, Dave."

"Absolutely not, John. I thought we were toting this around just to make sure the bad guys didn't get it. It would be irresponsible to—"

"To what? Risk *damaging* something? Dave, they're going to blow all this to hell. If there was ever a time to use . . . *it,* this is that time."

I reluctantly sat the green mystery box on the floor.

Outside, thunder rumbled.

To John, I said, "I can't see the latch. Can you?"

"Yeah, I can now."

I said before that there was no visible latch or lock on the box. That was true. But there was an *invisible* one. I stared at the front of the box, and focused. If I stared hard enough, a simple lever swam into view. It had been a long time since I'd taken Soy Sauce. I assumed John could see it clearly.

You may have heard about amputees feeling a "phantom limb" beyond their stump, the nervous system sending back false reports that gives the illusion that the appendage is still there. Well, if John looked at Amy's missing hand, he would see a literal phantom limb, a translucent hand. If she closed her eyes and concentrated on opening and closing the hand, and flexing the fingers, John—and anyone else under the influence of Soy Sauce—would see the fingers flex. Even though Amy herself would probably not. Amy's abilities came and went, she had never taken the Sauce but I think she caught some effects from me due to, uh, transfer of bodily fluids.

She squinted and said, "I can see the latch, but just barely. It's just a shimmer, like the Predator."

Amy had done the trick with the box lever once before. She leaned over and, to an outside observer, held the stump of her left wrist a few inches from the box. To John's eyes, her phantom hand grasped the hidden lever and pulled.

A click. The lid rose slowly, on its own.

Inside the box was what looked like a gray lump of fur the size of a football. It was actually metal, and the "fur" was thousands of rigid metal strands, thinner than needles, standing straight up. The first time I saw it, I said the thing looked like a steel porcupine. John said it looked like a wig for a robot. The only part of the device not covered by the metallic fur was the simple metal grip at the end, where it could be picked up. On the handle was a trigger.

It was a gun. What did it do? Well . . .

Back in the summer, after we lifted the box from the convoy, we had brought it home and spent several days figuring out the ghost latch. We then stared at the object inside for a bit, and debated what to do. John dubbed the thing the "furgun" because we had decided it was some kind of weapon and of course it had that metal fur on it.

Then, late one night, John and I had gotten good and drunk and taken the furgun out to a field to test fire it. John set up three green Heineken beer bottles on a log, then pointed the furry gun thing and squeezed the trigger.

The device made a sort of honking sound, like some people make when they blow their nose. There was a strange ripple in the air, like the heat-warped space above a fire. The beer bottle on the far right was suddenly five times bigger than it was before. John had cheered and whooped and declared the device to be an enlarging ray. He said he'd point it at cornfields and use it to cure world hunger. He fired it again, aiming at the next bottle. It stayed the same size, only turned white. When we approached it we realized the bottle had been turned into a bottle-shaped pile of mashed potatoes. John stated that he would still use it to cure world hunger, but more importantly, he pointed out that he had been thinking of mashed potatoes at the exact moment he had pulled the trigger, and speculated that the gun could react to your thoughts somehow. We fired it at the third bottle and it immediately turned into a double-ended dildo. A black one. John said this confirmed this theory.

He had then handed the furgun to me, and I fired at the first bottle.

That bottle, and the dildo, and the log, and the ground, all were consumed in a ball of fire so bright it looked like a miniature sun had landed in the middle of the field. The blast was so intense that John and I were blinded for half an hour after, and saw blue-white spots in front of our eyes for most of a day. When the fire subsided, there was a twenty-foot circle of earth in front of us that had been scorched into black glass. The papers said the light was reported by witnesses six miles away.

That next morning we had sat at my kitchen table, my head pounding, eating Amy's macaroni and cheese–filled omelets and staring at the green box in front of us.

John said, "I want to try it again tonight."

Amy shook her head. "Come on, somebody's going to get hurt."

I said, "Yeah, it clearly doesn't work."

John said, "We don't know that. We just have to learn how to use it."

I shook my head. "No. Remember the truck, and what happened to the guys guarding the thing. If They couldn't control it, and They built the damned thing . . . well, in our hands we might as well be cramming gunpowder and ball bearings up our assholes."

John said, "See, I got a different theory. I don't think They built it. I think They found it, and had no idea what to do with it. But here's the thing. At the moment when you were taking your piss turn off the tower, I was thinkin' back to the best birthday present I ever got. I was nine, and my uncle had gone to a garage sale and found, for ten bucks, a cardboard box of GI Joe action figures. Even had all their guns, backpacks, everything. There were more than thirty of them in there, somebody's entire collection. Then, well, you saw what happened to the men in the truck. *I* made that happen, Dave. With my mind. From a thousand feet away. We can master this thing. We just need practice."

Amy said, "You almost started a forest fire."

"*Dave* did. We'll be more careful next time."

Amy sat a plate in front of him and said, "Uh huh. *You* just turned a truck full of people into toys. But either way, good luck opening the box without me."

Needless to say, it was never opened again. Until today.

I reached in and took the furgun by the handle. John said, "Uh, no."

"What?"

"I actually agree that the gun isn't safe in *your* hands. Give it to me."

Amy said, "*I'll* take it."

She did. I said, "What am I supposed to use?"

John said, "We shouldn't have to *use* anything at all. We get to a door—you know, one of the wormhole doors—and we go right to the water tower. We break their jammer thing, everybody's phones work again, the world sees the city isn't full of zombies and the bad guys got no choice but to call off the bombing. Tennet goes to jail and we all go to Waffle House and have breakfast."

I nodded at the furgun and said to Amy, "We run into anybody, point and imagine something nonlethal. Just . . . imagine you're Dumbledore, casting that spell that knocks people's weapons out of their hand but doesn't hurt them."

She sighed and said, "You think I'm five."

John said, "All right, I'm thinking we can't use BB's, because there's probably a huge mob there by now and I'd prefer to not have to shotgun two dozen rednecks today. What's the next closest door?"

"No. Think, John. We went through a door and came out here—right where we needed to be. *You* made that happen. Because of the Soy Sauce, you have control. You can control the doors the way *They* do. We'll go back to the door we came in, the one out on the lawn. You're going to concentrate—and I know you can do this—you're going to concentrate on the water tower Porta-Potty and it's going to take us right there. Right?"

Thunder rumbled outside. The wind picked up and the arthritic old building creaked under the strain.

John nodded and said, "Right. This is going to work."

We ran to the front door. We dragged away the cabinet we'd used as a barricade. I took a deep breath, opened the front door and was immediately staring down a dozen gun barrels.

Armed townspeople were swarming the scene. Amy said, "Don't shoot!"

I put my hands in the air and, to the firing squad in front of me said, "I know you're all worked up, but listen to me. The feds aren't going to bomb the hospital. They're going to bomb *the whole town*. That means as of right now, we are all in the same boat. As far as the rest of the world is concerned, *all of us are infected*."

The guy nearest to me, a big black guy who was built like a linebacker, screamed, "DROP YOUR WEAPONS AND LAY FLAT ON THE GROUND. THIS IS THE ONLY WARNING YOU GET."

Then I noticed the earmuffs everyone was wearing. I took a deep breath and screamed, "THEY ARE GOING TO BOMB THE TOWN IN AN HOUR!" I tried to pantomime a plane dropping a huge bomb, but I think the motions conveyed that I was warning about a bird shitting on his head.

No response. To John and Amy, I muttered, "I'm thinking we need to go back inside."

Under his breath, John said, "One. Two. Three—"

We spun and ran back through the big wooden doors—

—and I ran gut-first into a rusting Ford sedan. Amy slammed into my back. I looked around and realized that we were not, in fact, inside the main hall of the asylum. Rows of broken cars grew in a field of yellow weeds all around us.

John cheered. "HA! It worked! Screw those guys!"

Amy said, "This is not the water tower."

It was, in fact, the junkyard south of town.

John and I spun around at the same time and saw the blue Porta-Potty standing in the weeds behind us.

"Damn it!" said John. "They moved the shitter. What is this, the junkyard? We're way the hell on the other side of town."

The first sprinkles of rain were coming down. I took a calming breath and said, "It's okay. You're going to concentrate, and we're going to go back into the Porta-Potty, and you're going to send us to the water tower. There has to be a door there we can come out of up there. You're going to send us to *that* door. Any door in the vicinity. You are *not* going to send us back to the asylum. Right?"

Something changed with the light, like a shadow was passing over-head. I looked up and, for the second time that day, saw that a car was flying toward me through the air.

We ran screaming in three directions as a rusting sedan flattened the Porta-Potty with a thunder of rending metal. I stumbled, fell and got a face full of dried weeds. I scrambled to my feet and screamed for Amy, found her crouching behind a hatchback.

John screamed, "There! There!" and we turned to see a shrunken, dried-up old man who looked about ninety. He was maybe twenty-five yards away, standing near a twenty-foot-tall faded fiberglass statue of a smiling man holding a slice of pizza. The old guy looked completely normal, other than the fact that he had a huge third arm growing from his groin, and had massive leathery wings.

The old man bent over and with his dick arm wrestled an old engine block out of the dirt. He shrieked and threw the engine at us underhand, like a softball. The four-hundred-pound hunk of metal turned in the air, little sprays of rainwater flying out of its cylinders. We dodged again, moments before the engine crushed the roof of the hatchback in a cloud of glass bits.

John's shotgun thundered next to me. It had absolutely no effect on the old man—I don't know if he missed or if the old guy was immune to bullets. John broke open the gun and fumbled with three more shells. Two of them fell into the weeds.

"AMY! SHOOT HIM!"

Amy turned, raised the furgun, closed her eyes and fired.

The alien gun made that low, foghorn honking sound. The air rippled. The old man recoiled, his hands flying to his face. When his hands came away I observed that he now had a thick, white wizard beard.

John screamed, "GODDAMNIT, AMY! YOU'VE GOT IT SET ON BEARD."

The man advanced. Amy fired again. The man's beard grew twice as long.

I yelled, "AMY! YOU CAN GO LETHAL ON THIS ONE!"

"I'M TRYING!"

The old man was running now, terrifyingly fast, arms pumping. Running right at us. We ran away. Amy tried to turn and fire the furgun. The shot went wild and suddenly the fiberglass pizza man had a huge beard.

I screamed, "GIVE IT TO ME!"

Amy tossed me the furgun. Before I could turn on the old man, I was sent sprawling with a blow to my back that knocked the air out of my lungs. I hit the weeds, gasping. I rolled over to see the old man ready to swing a car bumper at me a second time. I pointed the furgun up at the old fart. I squeezed the trigger.

The gun went off with a booming sound that shook the earth. There was a gut-wrenching impact, and the man was disintegrated into a fine, red mist. The grass burned in the spot where he had stood, the soil itself charred.

John walked up and said, "Jesus, Dave. Why don't you, uh, give that back to Amy."

Amy said, "The toilet! That car flattened the toilet!"

"We don't need it." I looked at John. "John just needs *to concentrate.*"

"Hey, it worked last time, they just moved the—"

"I know, I know. You're doing great. Now just find something we can go through. The doors aren't random, not for you. *You have the power to control them.*"

John jogged down the row of cars, rain plinking off of metal trunk lids. He arrived at a windowless van, took a moment to concentrate, then pulled open the doors.

John said, "I think I can see it. I can actually see where it goes . . ."

"Okay, great. Where?"

"I can't tell. But there's an army truck parked there."

"Perfect! Go."

We climbed through—

—and tumbled out of the back of a different van in the rear parking lot of some restaurant or other. It was certainly not the water tower.

40 Minutes Until the Aerial Bombing of Undisclosed

I punched the air and cried, "GODDAMNIT WHY ARE WE SUCH FUCKUPS?"

There were in fact two military trucks parked nearby, so he had that part right. No personnel in sight.

Amy said, "Go back—"

John said, "No, we have to find a different door. That'll just take us back to the junkyard."

John jogged toward the restaurant and went through an open EMPLOYEES ONLY door. We followed him into an empty kitchen—stainless appliances and grease-tanned walls. It smelled like detergent and vaporized animal fat. We passed into a main dining area full of small round tables. The building was silent, the restaurant closed—probably had been since the outbreak. We could hear the soft drumming of rain on the roof. Along one wall was a bar lined with bottles and two big-screen TVs that would be showing some kind of sporting event if it weren't early morning on a Monday during the apocalypse. The opposite wall was covered with a mural depicting a smiling cartoon buffalo, eating a burger.

"Oh. Buffalo burger," John said, unnecessarily. We had all eaten here before (yes, the burgers were made from buffalo meat) and we were apparently going to be incinerated here.

"Find a door, John. We—"

Glass shattered. We all ducked, and there was a chubby, balding guy in his fifties on the sidewalk out front, wearing earmuffs. He had bashed in the glass front door with the butt of a shotgun.

"SHIT!"

The guy ducked through the shattered glass and racked a shell into his shotgun.

"HEY! WE'RE UNARMED! WE'RE NOT INFECTED!"

The guy put the shotgun to his shoulder. He knew exactly who we were.

We dove behind the bar. A shotgun blast shattered three bottles, bringing a rain of liquor and glass. Amy blindly stuck the furgun up over the bar and squeezed the trigger. A small wheel of cheese landed softly on the bar and bounced to the floor.

"GODDAMNIT, AMY! LETHAL!"

A shotgun blast punched the bar, flinging chunks of particle board between us. Amy raised the furgun, squeezed her eyes in concentration, and fired.

The gun honked.

The air rippled.

A huge, black blur the size of a minivan flew through the air above us, a furry shape that bellowed with a sort of grunting moo. In the split second it was airborne I somehow registered what the object was: a buffalo. And I mean a real buffalo, huge and furry and trailing a stink like wet dog.

The buffalo hurtled toward the man, its dangling feet flailing as it soared through the air. It smashed into the bald guy, flinging him aside, then blew through the door behind him, wrenching it off its hinges.

"YEAH!" screamed John, triumphantly. "That's what you get! THAT'S WHAT YOU GET!"

The buffalo turned on us. It snorted, belched, farted, sneezed. It charged back into the restaurant, loping across the floor tiles, each hoof landing with a sledgehammer impact that I could feel in my gut. Amy screamed. The beast blasted a swath of carnage through the dining room, tossing aside tables and chairs like they were doll furniture. We scrambled to our feet and tried to run. I made it out from behind the bar, then tripped over a chair and fell, taking Amy with me. She rolled over, leveled the furgun at the beast, and fired.

The buffalo recoiled, stopping in its tracks. It suddenly had a thick beard, streaked with gray, as big as a man's torso.

"RUN!"

I don't remember who said it, but none of us needed to be told. We dodged and juked around tables, jumping over the unconscious bald guy, rounding the buffalo and heading for the street. It was trying to get turned around, knocking over six tables in the process.

We flew through the smashed doorway, emerging onto a sidewalk downtown. Rain hammered the street, soaking our clothes. Two seconds later the buffalo blew through the door behind us, tearing off another foot of door frame on every side.

We ran across the four lanes of street, looking for cover or, better yet, a door. I turned to Amy and screamed, "HERE! GIVE IT TO ME!"

I took the furgun. I squeezed the trigger, and for a second, nothing happened. The beast charged, hoofs drumming across pavement. Then, out of nowhere, the buffalo was hit by a semi. The truck splattered buffalo guts thirty feet in every direction as it plowed through the screaming beast. It finally skidded to a stop, scraping a half ton of buffalo meat along the pavement and leaving a crimson skid mark of blood and entrails that stretched for a block and a half.

We all stood and looked at this with disgust for a moment.

Amy said, "Gross."

John said, "Over here!"

He was running into the alley, toward a Dumpster. He stood up on a crate, took a moment to gather his energies, and threw open the lid.

"BOOM! That's it! I see water tower, bitches!"

John climbed in. I helped Amy up next.

I stepped up on the crate and looked down. I saw it. That is, instead of garbage, I saw open landscape. Patches of wet, green grass and mud puddles. It was dizzying, looking down and seeing the horizon at my feet. Rain was falling on the back of my neck, and falling perpendicular to that inside the universe of the Dumpster.

I threw my legs over and stepped through, and felt that roller coaster flutter in my guts as gravity changed and—

I stumbled forward as the ground rushed up at me, smacking my palms. I was suddenly on my hands and knees in mud, cold rain pounding down my back. I got to my feet, soaked from head to toe, mud caked on my knees and shoes. I squinted through the pouring rain. Thunder rumbled overhead.

The water tower was right in front of me. I looked around for the truck John described, and found it. A big, black semi tractor trailer. Next to it was a black military troop transport. Next to it was a black Humvee. Next to it was another. Then about three dozen more.

John said, "Ooooh, shit."

The water tower construction project was now the home to the makeshift REPER command center. Black military vehicles and mobile homes and tents stretched out as far as we could see. And, standing around us, were dozens and dozens of guys in black space suits, carrying assault rifles. All of them were currently screaming at us to drop our weapons and lay flat on the ground.

A man strode up in a white space suit, carrying a helmet under one arm. His gray hair was still somehow perfectly combed even under the bombardment of the rain.

Dr. Tennet glanced at his watch and said, "I was starting to think you wouldn't make it."

37 Minutes Until the Aerial Bombing of Undisclosed

We were hauled under a tent, an open one like you'd see at a county fair. There were two long folding tables and along the back of the tent, just outside of the rain, were a series of carts holding stainless-steel canisters.

There were two spacemen right behind us, holding some kind of weapons on us that I didn't recognize. They were bulky and ended in some kind of slanted lens thing. I kind of wanted to get shot with one just to see what it did. Then, fifty feet or so outside the tent, were a dozen gunmen with regular old military-grade assault rifles. I was one hundred percent sure that their instructions were that if we overpowered the two guards next to us, they were to turn everything—including the guards—into the finale of *Bonnie and Clyde*.

Tennet strode up from behind us, and handed Amy a towel. Not sure why John and I didn't get one.

Tennet said, "I have good news and bad news. The good news is that we are, of course, outside of the blast radius—though close enough that the noise will be very, very loud—unless someone at the Air Combat Command has made a grievous error in their calculations. A series of twenty-five thousand bombs will be dropped from the back of C-130 aircraft, starting from the center of town outward, in a series of concentric circles. The shock wave from each bomb can shatter ten city blocks, and liquefy any organism standing within a thousand feet in any direction. Once all of the structures have been blown into kindling, a second squadron of B-52 bombers will drop a series of thousand-pound CBU-97 incendiary cluster munitions, releasing a flammable aerosol that will ignite and raise the temperature at the center of town to a temperature hotter than the surface of the sun. The resulting conflagration will inhale so much surrounding oxygen that from here, we'll feel like we're in a monsoon—winds will reach fifty miles an hour. I'm told the noise of all the air rushing to feed the massive open-air furnace sounds like the world itself is howling in anguish. It should really be something."

John said, "And let me guess: you're going to jerk off while you're watching it. And *you're going to make us watch you*."

Amy was actually using the towel to dry her hair, and I felt like she should have just left it wet out of solidarity.

Ignoring John, Tennet said, "That's the good news. The bad news is that you are of course being charged for this session."

He went back to the row of steel canisters and examined them. "I kid, of course."

I said, "So how do you get into the supervillain business, anyway? Is it something that happens gradually or do you just wake up and decide to go for it?"

Tennet said, "I'm going to let you in on a little secret, and I apologize ahead of time because learning this will mark the end of your extended childhood. Nobody involved in a conflict thinks they're the villain.

And considering I'm on the verge of saving a couple of billion lives, I'm thinking I deserve hero status on this one. Even if you're too short-sighted to understand."

I said, "Uh huh. So who is the bad guy, then?"

"Everyone, depending on the day. In this case, I don't know who is responsible for the parasite. That is, I don't know their names. This is what you can't—or aren't willing to—understand. You found a cockroach in your hamburger. You want a two-word answer to the question of who put it there. Well, it's not that simple. Was it the kid working the grill, who didn't check the beef? Was it the franchise owner for buying beef from a shady supplier? Was it the slaughterhouse, for failing to adhere to contamination standards? Was it the government, for not funding FDA enforcement of those standards? Or was it you, the customer, for de-manding lower taxes that resulted in that funding being cut, and for participating in a consumer culture that rewards cutting corners? Well, in that scenario, think of me as the harried assistant manager who has to apologize to the unhappy customer and try to keep the restaurant from getting shut down. Only here the 'restaurant' is all of civilization."

I said, "Okay, I'm . . . wait, what does the hamburger represent again?"

"My point is, I have a job, just like you. I get a paycheck, I get memos. Just like you, I have superiors, and they have superiors who I am not allowed to speak to. Orders filter down from on high, arriving at my level stripped entirely of all context or rationale or justification. Orders do not come with an illustration of how they serve the overall goals of the organization. Same as any other job. Was the parasite released in-tentionally? And if so, for what purpose? It is not my job to know. All I know is that it is a near certainty that if it gets out, it will destabilize civilization as we know it. I have worked nonstop since the outbreak to contain this in a way that would let the world move on. And, I'm proud to say, I'm on the verge of succeeding."

Amy said, "By killing everyone."

"No. Not everyone. One medium-sized town. Some perspective helps here. Globally, a hundred and fifty thousand people die every day. From natural causes, accidents, war. The population of this town will be barely a blip in the worldwide dying that happens in an average month. So while you think you're being heroic in saving it, you are, right now, *in this situation*, the villains. I know you don't think you are. But you are."

I said, *"Then why are you the one giving the supervillain monologue?"*

He walked back to the silver canisters. He put his back to us and started messing with some mechanism in whatever mad scientist setup he had back there. I heard liquid running. We were not restrained in our chairs, but there were so many guns on us that if I scratched my nose, the shooting aftermath would look like somebody had just spilled a huge lasagna here. I looked at Amy, who was impassive, and then at John, who looked like he was mentally running through escape options just like I was. The furgun was still laying in the grass where we had landed when we arrived. They probably thought it was a hairbrush. I pictured John trying to wrestle away one of those futuristic-lens guns the two guards behind us were carrying. Then I pictured him squeezing the trigger and a cartoon boxing glove popping out of the end.

I watched Tennet work fluids from his steel canisters and wondered if we weren't choosing between quick death under a hail of bullets, or something much, much worse caused by whatever he was brewing up there. He turned back to us, striding calmly our way. He placed three small Styrofoam cups in front of us.

"We have sugar over there, but I'm afraid we're out of creamer."

Coffee. I left mine in front of me. Amy, without asking, had been given a cup of hot water and a tea bag. She dropped in the tea bag and asked Tennet if he had any honey.

She is terrible at this.

Tennet walked back to the coffee carts and returned with a container of honey shaped like a bear.

He said, "Think. Who allowed the outbreak to occur? Who failed to report the appearance of the parasite to any authorities? Who prevented any containment at your house? Who created the breach at the REPER command center? Who created the breach in the quarantine containment fence? Who has *single-handedly spread this infection?*"

John said, "We didn't do any of it on purpose. We're just . . . not very good at things."

"Or, it could be that just maybe, one can act on what one believes is his own agency, while in reality perfectly serving the purposes of another."

He held up the honey bear.

"Where do you think this comes from, hmm? Do you think the

bees toiled night and day to make this because they knew we were going to take it away from them and drip it into our tea? Of course not. Because we are a higher life form than they, we can make them serve our purposes, while letting them believe they are serving their own. You have been used like bees." He glanced at me. "This was all but explained to you before."

Another space suit walked in out of the rain, and went and got a cup of coffee from the coffee carts. I wondered how he was going to drink it.

Tennet continued, "Don't get me wrong, I know why you think what you think. I have sons in their twenties. I was there myself once, believe it or not. Because you have no responsibilities, you get to sit back, in school or at your inconsequential service job, and judge the grown-ups on the impossible choices we have to make. Of course, if you were in our position, *you'd* never go to war, or lay off a factory full of workers, or enlist the help of one murderous dictator to stop another one who's even worse. All moral choices seem easy when you *don't actually have to make them*."

Amy shook her head slowly and said, "You can't talk your way into this being anything other than mass murder. And people are going to know."

Tennet said, "What exactly do you think they're going to know?"

"That the people in the town are just people. That this isn't so clearcut. They're going to know."

"Even if someone decided that the infection rate down there was something less than one hundred percent, and if they could go to a mountaintop and shout it to the world, it wouldn't matter. Because the people *want* this. They want their neighbors to be monsters. It's why we lust over news stories of mothers murdering their children, and run after conspiracy theories about a government full of greedy sociopaths. If the monsters didn't come, we would have willed them into existence."

John nodded and said, "Just so they have an excuse to sue the burger place."

I said, "You're . . . several steps behind here."

Amy sipped her tea and said, "The people out there won't believe it if they don't have a choice. If they see it for themselves."

Tennet calmly said, "I know you came here to try to take out the warlock jammer. As the villains in this story, that's exactly what I expected you to do. This would be why we have an entire army protecting it."

David Wong

Amy said, "Speaking of which. The guys standing right behind us with the weird guns, do they know that you're going to have them killed, too? There's no way you can let all these people wandering around here in their space suits just go back home tomorrow, knowing what you did here. Somebody will talk, right? To their wife or their kids, or maybe they go online and blog about it. Maybe cash in on a book deal. Do they know you're going to orchestrate something for them, just like you did for the town?"

Tennet said, "I like you. I do. But think about all of the assumptions you just made. First, you assumed that the men behind you could hear you. Second, you assumed that the men behind you have ears at all. Third, you assumed that the men behind you are even men. Would you like to know what's under the hoods of these decontamination suits?"

The space suit back by the coffee turned toward us. He sat his coffee on the cart and approached our table. Tennet didn't turn to look at him. Whatever was inside the space suit reached up and started undoing clasps around the neck of its red-tinted face mask.

Then, it pulled open a zipper.

The gloved hands then raised and grabbed the sides of its helmet, and lifted.

30 Minutes Until the Aerial Bombing of Undisclosed

We barely had time to register the face we were seeing before the spaceman pulled out an enormous silver handgun, and pointed it at Tennet's head.

Detective Lance Falconer said, "Freeze, shitbird."

Tennet sighed and said, "And who are you?"

"Shut up. Call off the planes."

"Infecting the whole world to prevent you from putting a bullet through my skull would be an *incredibly* selfish move on my part."

Amy said, "Forget it, we don't need him."

John said, "He's right, we just need to turn off the cell phone jammer. Then he won't have a choice. It'll blow the lid off the whole sha-rod."

"STOP SAYING IT LIKE THAT."

Tennet looked right at me and said, "Is there something you want to say about this, David? Before this man splatters my brains? I've been reading it on your face."

I met Falconer's eyes, then Amy's.

I said, "I, uh, am not sure he isn't right."

Amy said, *"David . . ."*

I shook my head. "I don't like it. I don't. Amy, you know I don't. But . . . Marconi . . . he was right. The fuse is lit and this, right here, this is our chance to snuff it out. There has to be a sacrifice. He said that." I looked at John. "John, I'm telling you, he saw all this coming. Marconi knows his shit. And maybe if we'd been smarter, if we'd handled it better, we could have put a stop to it without anybody getting, you know, incinerated. But we just kept fucking up and . . . it has to end at some point. And preferably some point before an event that could be called an 'apocalypse.'" I made air quotes with my fingers. "Guys . . . we have to grow up and see this through. This is our chance, to save the world. From itself."

John looked at the ground resignedly, and I knew he agreed.

Falconer said, "Bullshit. They are *not* getting away with this."

John shook his head and said, "They are, detective. They really are. Try to put that guy on trial. You'll see. Your witnesses will disappear. Or maybe *you'll* disappear. Hell, your suspect there will disappear. He's just a pawn like the rest of us. Aren't you?"

Tennet didn't answer, but he didn't have to.

Amy wasn't listening to us. She was turned, looking over the town, as if to take it in for the last time. Thunder crashed. Rain drummed on the tent.

Amy walked out into the rain, looking up into the sky, her hands forming a visor over her eyes. A dozen gun barrels followed her.

I said, "Amy . . . you understand why we have to do this, right?"

She turned and said, "Do you mind if we continue this discussion under the table?"

"What?"

The spacemen outside the tent were suddenly alarmed. One of

them was looking up at the sky, and trying to get the attention of the others. Radios appeared in hands. Black figures started running. I looked past Amy, squinting into the gray sky. There was, up there, a speck, a shape that I mistook for a bird for the second time in two days. The speck grew in the sky, taking on the shape of a tiny, thin, pilotless plane.

Amy got down on her hand and knees and scurried under the table. It hadn't dawned on the rest of us what was happening. She said, "David! Get down!"

A pair of white streaks grew out of the bottom of the drone, zipping across the sky and down, rocketing off to our right. I turned just in time to see the black semi truck vanish into a cloud of smoke. The shock wave threw us to the grass, flinging me under the table on top of Amy. A huge piece of debris—I think it was a truck tire—whizzed past the tent, trailing black smoke like a contrail.

I was laying in the grass, my ears ringing, Amy's elbow in my face. Her tea had spilled on my shirt.

Amy scrambled to her feet, threw her arms in the air and said to the sky, "YAY! YOU RULE, SHANE! WOO!"

27 Minutes Until the Aerial Bombing of Undisclosed

Falconer wrestled Tennet back to his feet, his gun at his temple. Falconer said, "Well, that fucking settles that."

Amy looked down at me. "You *know* this is the right thing. Even if you don't know you know it."

John said, "Shit yeah, I'm on Team Amy now."

I said, "Who the fuck is Shane?"

Tennet said, "That accomplished nothing. That pilot will be convicted of treason. But before he can even be prosecuted, *They'll* get hold of him. There'll be nothing I can do about it. Do you have any idea what They can do? Maybe They'll inject him with Compound 66. That's a serum that will turn a man into a cannibal. Let him eat his own children before they arrest him."

Two dozen spacemen were on the scene now, guns raised, creeping forward. Falconer got an arm around Tennet's neck and was using him as a human shield.

Falconer said, "Call off the planes. It's over."

The word "call" triggered something in Amy's mind, and she dug into her pocket and pulled out her phone. "Hey! I've got bars!"

Tennet said, "You have absolutely no leverage here, detective. You shoot me, my men will cut you to pieces. The bombs will drop and nothing will change. I'm sorry your supercop fantasy isn't going to play out like you wanted. But you have no cards left to play here."

Falconer repeated his demand, but Tennet went silent. Falconer threatened him with creative bodily violence. Tennet gave no reaction. Minutes passed this way, and I sensed the time bleeding away from the bomber countdown. I glanced nervously at the sky, then back toward the town.

And then, in the distance, came the crackle of gunfire.

19 Minutes Until the Aerial Bombing of Undisclosed

We all rushed out, looking toward the sound. Down the hill and toward the highway, where the REPER barricades had stood since the morning of the outbreak. A pickup truck had crashed through the barriers and was laying on its side. REPER spacemen were filling it full of holes.

Then, a spaceman went down. And another. On the other side of the barricade was the Undisclosed angry mob. And they were armed.

Amy said, "I think *somebody* figured out that they are about to be bombed and remembered as zombies in their obituaries."

John said, "There! See? It's *over*. The word is out. You're not going to be able to cover this up, doctor. Call off the planes."

Tennet said, "You would be surprised what They can cover up."

I said, "You call off the planes, and he'll let you go. No charges. You get out of the country, change your name and go retire in Argentina like Hitler." I looked at Falconer and said, "Right?"

Falconer said, "Yep. Absolutely," in a way that did not convey an ounce of sincerity.

To the spacemen behind us, Tennet said, "On the count of three, if he does not release me, start shooting. If you can get him over my shoulder, that would be nice. But if you have to shoot through me, so be it. This is bigger than me."

Falconer withdrew his arm from around Tennet's neck, grabbed something small and black from a pocket and held it in front of Tennet's face.

"Do you know what this is, shitbird?"

I didn't, but Tennet nodded.

"And you know what happens if I push this button?"

Tennet didn't answer. But he knew, and didn't like it.

"Yeah, I know more than you fucking thought, don't I?"

To me, Falconer said, "Look to your right. See that big-ass monster truck thing with the huge wheels? We're all going for a ride."

Falconer put an arm around Tennet's neck and dragged him toward the vehicle that did in fact look like an armored monster truck. Amy and I followed. John took off the other direction, then came running back with the furgun. Through all of this, the spacemen kept their weapons trained on us, waiting for an order that never came.

To John, Falconer said, "Can you drive this thing?" and before he finished the word "thing" John was already behind the wheel. Falconer forced Tennet into the passenger seat at gunpoint, then took the backseat so he could keep his gun pressed to the back of Tennet's skull. I went around and slid in next to Falconer, Amy jumped in beside me and slammed the door. John made the engine of the monster truck rumble to life, and a hundred miles away a seismologist saw the needle on his machine twitch.

Amy mumbled, "I cannot imagine the penis of the guy who designed this thing."

John said, "Where to?"

Falconer answered, "Right down there, past the barricades. Inside the blast zone. Let's see if that motivates this asshole to pick up this radio and call off the planes."

With no hesitation, John rumbled down toward the area that was about to be bombed into scorched rubble. Somewhere, the ghost of Charles Darwin smiled and lit a cigar.

16 Minutes Until the Aerial Bombing of Undisclosed

There was a road. John did not take it. He tore diagonally across the cornfield, tearing through broken cornstalks toward the mass of angry humanity at the Highway 131 barricade.

The spacemen were winning. There were a lot of them, and they had taken cover behind their vehicles, rattling gunfire into the crowd. We rolled to a stop just short of the mayhem. I heard a stray bullet ping off the grill of the truck.

To me, Falconer said, "Watch this." He told John, "You see that button there, marked 'loudspeaker'? Punch that. Turn that volume knob all the way to the right."

John did. Falconer pulled the little black box from his pocket.

"Open the mic. Click the—yeah. Hold it there."

Falconer reached up toward the mic mounted on the console and pressed a button on his little gadget. I could *almost* hear the noise the little gadget made. In the cab of the monster truck it felt more like an irritating vibration, like if you pulled a long strip of crinkled aluminum foil between your teeth. I saw Amy wince.

But the effect on the spacemen was immediate. They flinched, or fell to a knee, or dropped their guns. Some collapsed entirely. The longer the tone played, the more debilitating the effects.

Several of them turned their guns on the truck and opened fire, bullets plinking off the armor and leaving white bird shit–like pockmarks in the bulletproof windshield. Then the spacemen charged the truck. One of them climbed the front bumper, and I realized he had found the loudspeaker on the roof. Others reached the doors and clawed at the handles. I flinched at the sound of something crashing against the window next to me, and saw a spaceman rearing back for another blow on the glass with the butt of his rifle. He slammed it again, and made a crack. Amy ducked.

Meanwhile, the guy on the hood was going after the loudspeaker, smacking it with the butt of his own rifle. But none of the men had a fraction of their usual strength. Falconer kept his thumb on the death buzzer, and the spaceman collapsed onto the hood, landing right in front of the windshield, his faceplate shattering with the impact.

Amy gasped.

Two open, dead eyes looked back at us. The eyes were different colors, one brown, one blue.

The rest of the face was gone. What was left was a skull, held together with pink tendons and ribbons of fraying, decaying muscle. Running all through the skull, twitching between the gaps in bone and sinew, were ropes of something that looked like spaghetti, twisting and pulling and, I was sure, reaching down through the ruined body of the former man inside, operating him like a puppet.

The spaceman outside my door had also collapsed—the ground around the truck was now littered with them. Falconer let off the buzzer. The battle had gone silent.

The mob on the other side of the barricade was frozen, baffled by what they were seeing. They weren't even celebrating. Even if it meant winning the battle, this was a group of people who absolutely did not feel like seeing any more weird bullshit today.

Amy opened her door and yelled to them, "We're the good guys! Don't shoot!"

John said, "Look! What the hell?"

Something was going on with the face of the dead spaceman on the hood of the truck. One of his eyes was twitching. Then the eye started pushing forward out of his skull, oozing out like a snake. The other eye did the same.

Amy said, "What? What is it?"

Out from the spaceman's dead skull crawled two spiders, each as thick as a bratwurst, each covered in tiny legs, each ending in a single, lidless, human eye.

From outside the truck, I heard glass breaking. Faceplates on dead spacemen were cracking and bursting open. Out from each crawled a pair of the eye spiders.

John yelled, "OH FUCK! TENNET TELL THEM TO BOMB THIS! RIGHT HERE! NOW! SHIT!"

The spiders raced through the grass, toward us. And there was Amy looking right at them, out of her *open* door, because she couldn't see them.

I lunged across her and pulled her door closed right as one of the spiders leaped, wedging itself into the gap at the last second before I could get it all the way closed. Amy screamed, because *now* she could see it, now that the thing was writhing in the gap of the partially closed door a foot away from her face. Its legs were thrashing as it frantically tried to press its way inside, the single, human eye twitching, looking all around the cabin of the truck.

The hood man's eye spiders had crawled onto the windshield. Others had joined them, the skittering parasites hopping onto the truck, running across the hood and windows. Soon a dozen disembodied human eyes were staring in at us, hungrily looking for new skulls to occupy.

They skittered over to Amy's door, toward that few inches of gap the first spider was holding open with its body. They crowded around and started forcing their way in, a mass of disembodied eyeballs on black parasite bodies. I pulled with all my strength, trying to crush the little bastards. But they were too well armored and I wasn't strong enough.

One finally pushed its way in, flipping onto Amy's lap. She shrieked. Another followed it. Then it was a torrent of the squirming creatures, pouring into the cab of the truck.

One leapt at John's face. He caught it, cursing.

Falconer, who couldn't see the invaders but who could easily guess what was happening, yelled, "OPEN THE MIC! OPEN THE MIC AGAIN!"

John, fighting with the parasite trying to burrow into his face with one hand, found the loudspeaker button with the other. Falconer pressed the button on his gadget. The hum filled the air. The spiders shrieked.

One by one, they exploded, splattering the interior in a spray of yellow goo.

Finally, the pained shrieks died, and all that was left was the soft drumming of the rain.

I wiped eyeball spider guts off my face.

John said, "Seriously, just, right here. All the bombs. Right here in this spot. We'll wait."

I said, "I agree." Amy was too traumatized to say anything at all. But to John, Falconer said, *"We're running out of time. Drive."* He did.

12 Minutes Until the Aerial Bombing of Undisclosed

John rolled over bodies of spacemen—going out of his way to do it, it seemed—and rolled past the carnage of the pitched battle that had been raging just minutes ago. He knocked aside REPER vehicles and pushed through the damaged barricades on the highway. The mob in front of us fell silent, parting as we rolled slowly into town, into the blast zone of the bombs that even now were riding in the bellies of planes just over the horizon.

"That's far enough."

John stopped, and Falconer yanked Tennet out of the truck. He reached back into the cab and grabbed the mic for its radio and pulled it as far as the little coiled wire would let it. Falconer put his gun to Tennet's head and said, "All right, shitbird. This is ground zero. They drop those bombs, you get flash fried just like the rest of us. Now get on this radio and tell them to *abort*."

Tennet looked at him with genuine disdain. "What you are threatening me with is the *best-case scenario* if I fail in my task. How are you failing to understand this?"

A huge, blue, extended-cab pickup truck emerged from the crowd in front of us. It had a wood chipper in the bed, and out from the driver's seat stepped a guy in a cowboy hat and absurdly tight pants. From the passenger seat emerged Owen, still in his quarantine-issued red jumpsuit. The cowboy had a shotgun, Owen had his pistol. They looked like the stars of an eighties' era show about loose cannon undercover cops. Called something like *O-Funk and the Cowboy*. From the backseat of the pickup stepped Dr. Marconi. I tried to imagine the conversation the three of them had on the way over and my brain just spat out error messages.

To me, Marconi said, "I managed to convince them that, despite their differences, they also have a great deal in common."

The Cowboy hurried over to Falconer and said, "Holy shit. You got the son of a bitch. I owe you a twelve-pack, detective."

"It's not over yet. The bombs are coming and this asshole won't call them off."

Owen spoke up and said, "Why don't we start feeding his feet into the fuckin' wood chipper, see if that changes his mind."

Tennet said, "All right, all right. Give me the mic."

Falconer handed it to him. Tennet yanked, ripping the wire out of the console, and tossed the mic onto the ground.

Falconer growled, smashed the butt of his gun into Tennet's face and threw the man to the ground. Falconer followed him down, straddling his chest, punching him over and over.

I said, "Should we, uh, stop him?"

John said, "Nope."

9 Minutes Until the Aerial Bombing of Undisclosed

Marconi walked up and said, "Why do I have the feeling I am not going to receive my consultant's fee for this project?"

I said, "Everybody is so freaking *droll* today. Jesus."

John said, "Well, what the hell do we do now?"

To Amy, Marconi said, "You have one of those fancy cell phones, correct? One that can capture video?"

She said, "Yep," and pulled it out.

"You have a signal, correct? And access to the Internet?"

"Sure, sure."

Somebody in the crowd said, "Look! There's a plane! To the north! They're coming!"

I turned. There was a speck in the sky, that even from this far away I could tell was not our friendly Predator drone coming back to rescue us somehow. Not sure what it would have done anyway. This was a big bastard, with propellers on the wings, one of the big cargo planes you always saw on the news hauling troops back and forth to the Middle East.

Marconi asked, "And you can stream video? Meaning you can capture video and upload it live?"

"Yeah. What am I recording?"

Marconi sighed and said, "Our deaths."

8 Minutes Until the Aerial Bombing of Undisclosed

I said, "What? *That's* your plan?"

He stuffed his hands in his pockets and gave me a sad look through the rain.

"What's that around your lady friend's neck?"

I didn't have to look at her to answer. It was always there.

"What, her necklace? The crucifix?"

"Think about it. What I said before, back at quarantine. The—"

"*The Babylonian Bureau.* Yes. Goddamnit we don't have time—"

"The sacrifice, David. That is how mankind overcomes the Babel Threshold. Our little tribal circles, bound by social contracts and selfish mutual need. Everyone working in their own greedy self-interests and huddling together with their tribe, at war with all those outside who they regard as barely human. What breaks a human mind out of that iron cage of mistrust, is a sacrifice. The martyr who gives up everything, who abandons all personal gain, who lays down his very life for the good of those *outside* his group. He becomes a symbol all can rally around. So instead of trying to make a selfish, violent primate somehow empathize with the whole world, which is impossible, you only need to get him to remember and love the martyr. As one is forgotten, another must replace it. Unfortunately, as I feared, today that is to be us."

The plane grew on the horizon. Two more appeared in the distance behind it. I could hear the ever-so-faint buzz of its engines. Appropriately enough, they sounded like bees. Just like Tennet had said. A swarm of bees, attacking a . . . hamburger I guess.

Amy was staring at me, eyes wide. Owen and Cowboy looked befuddled. Falconer was standing over an unconscious Tennet, his fists bloody, eyes defiant.

7 Minutes Until the Aerial Bombing of Undisclosed

John said, "*Fuck* that bullshit. Everybody in the truck, we're heading out."

Marconi said, "So we ride to safety, while the tens of thousands who remain in the city behind us burn? And then what? We drive out across the buffer zone outside those barricades, and a few miles later you will meet another, larger barricade, manned by the U.S. military. Martyrdom isn't something you choose. It is thrust upon you."

Amy said, "Oh! Wait! Ohmygod it's so simple. We just—okay, we just have to get to an open area. Between us and the plane, so he sees it—the cornfield! Everybody go to the cornfield!"

To John, she said, "Get on the, uh, the speaker thing in the truck! Tell everybody to go to the cornfield!"

We didn't need to tell anybody anything. Hundreds of people were flowing past us, through the ruined barricades, the city draining out through the highway like water.

We piled into the truck, managed to get it turned around without running over a dozen people, and rumbled off toward the cornfield.

On the way, Amy said, "The plane! Oh God I can't believe I didn't think of this! It's flying low, under the clouds! We can see it! So it can see us!"

"I don't understand how that—"

"The pilot thinks we're zombies. We just have to show him we're not."

5 Minutes Until the Aerial Bombing
of Undisclosed

We rumbled to a stop in the field, refugees of Undisclosed scattering past us, on foot and in trucks and on bicycles, heading off toward the second military cordon that I was pretty sure most of them didn't realize was there. What did they think they would find out there? Their out-of-town loved ones, waiting for them with a six-pack? The president, with an apology bouquet?

John took to the loudspeaker and said, "WE GOT ABOUT FIVE MINUTES TO PULL THIS SHIT OFF, SO LISTEN UP. GATHER AROUND. WE ARE GOING TO SPELL OUT A MESSAGE FOR THE PILOT OF THAT PLANE UP THERE. HE DOESN'T KNOW WHAT HE'S ABOUT TO BOMB. WE ARE GONNA SHOW HIS DUMB ASS."

We all bailed out of the truck. The pickup carrying Owen, the Cowboy and Marconi, which upon further reflection is totally a cop show I would watch, pulled up alongside.

I glanced nervously up at the plane and said, "Son of a bitch. We don't have time, we don't have time—"

John said, "It has to be something simple! Like 'HELP' or something!"

"WE DON'T HAVE TIME TO FORM FOUR FUCKING LETTERS, JOHN!"

Marconi said, "You don't need letters, David. You need a symbol. One that man up there is sure to recognize." Marconi nodded toward Amy.

John said, "Right! He's right!" John ran off, stopped a group of women and said, "Stand in a line! Right here! Hurry! You! Over there! Stand here! COME ON, GODDAMNIT, WE NEED AT LEAST A HUNDRED PEOPLE! MOVE!"

* TRANSCRIPT OF AN EXCHANGE BETWEEN CAPTAIN PABLO VASQUEZ (SPEARHEAD), PILOT OF AN MC-130H TALON II, LEAD AIRCRAFT IN OPERATION LEPPARD, AND COPILOT CAPTAIN LAWRENCE MCDONNEL (STALLION) AT 11:59, NOVEMBER 15TH *

Spearhead: Loadmaster, we are six-zero seconds from primary payload release. Prepare to open bay doors, on my mark—

Stallion: Hey, uh, take a look at the barricade area. On the road, the uh, highway—

Spearhead: I see it.

Stallion: We have a, uh, crowd forming, are those REPER?

Spearhead: Negative.

Stallion: Friendlies Evac should have been completed by—

Spearhead: Negative, those are not REPER.

Stallion: Jesus, are we looking at Zulus here?

Spearhead: Affirmative, I'm seeing overturned vehicles and debris, it looks like the barricade has been overrun.

Spearhead: Will the blast get them out there?

Spearhead: Affirmative. Loadmaster, we are now three-zero seconds from primary payload release. Opening bay doors now.

Stallion: Look. Down at the uh, that area to the east of the highway. In that field.

Spearhead: Copy that, there is a crowd forming in the field—

Stallion: Look. Look how they're standing.

Spearhead: Is that—

Stallion: Look at the rows, they're perfect rows—

Spearhead: They're almost forming the shape of—

Stallion: It's not almost. It's perfect, it's too perfect a shape— .

Spearhead: All right. This is—Uh, Command, this is Spearhead, do you read me? We, uh, I don't believe what I'm seeing here, but we are observing a crowd of Zulus less than a kilometer outside of the target area and they are standing, uh, they are standing in the shape of a human penis. I repeat, the Zulus have organized themselves into a perfect shape of a human penis in an open field below us. We are looking at this with our own eyes.

Stallion: They are not Zulus.

30 Seconds Until the Aerial Bombing of Undisclosed

We stood there, in the field, shivering in the rain, in the shape of the dick John had formed us into. Dr. Marconi was to one side of me, looking disapproving. Amy was in my arms, her eyes turned upward, rain bouncing off her glasses. She was praying.

The cargo plane growled toward us, swooping lower, so low that I wondered how the thing expected to escape its own explosion.

Amy closed her eyes and buried her face in my chest and said, "I love you."

"I love you, too."

"It's turning! Look!"

The hulking plane banked, making a gentle turn in the sky and veering away from the town. We nervously watched it humming off into the distance, making a wide circle to head back the way it came.

A cheer went up in the crowd around us. There were five planes in the formation, and we watched as one after another they peeled off and circled back.

Falconer walked up and said, "I just want to say right now that this is the stupidest shit I've ever been involved in."

John said, "Hey, you don't have to like our methods, but you can't argue with the result. Everything turned out okay, right?"

10 Seconds Until the Aerial Bombing of Undisclosed

Amy said, "Why isn't that plane turning back?"

The trailing plane in the formation was not, in fact, changing its course. It growled straight through the air, swooping right over us. The crowd all watched it glide into the distance, heading toward the part of town that had become home to the quarantine.

The plane swooped lower and lower in the sky, as if it was going to attempt a landing. Only it was not slowing down, it was speeding up. It released its payload, following the bombs down until both bombs and plane met the earth. A silent, black plume instantly appeared in the distance, the boom reaching us two full seconds later. The detonation would be heard two states away.

We were too far away to realize it at the time, but both buildings of the old Ffirth Asylum had been reduced to a crater full of thousands of tons of shattered concrete and brick. All of it was cooking in a furnace fueled by aviation fuel, floorboards, old furniture and tons of other flammable debris that would still be smoldering ten days later. Somewhere, at the bottom of it all, rooms full of malformed inmates were vaporized in a fraction of a second. In the old administrative building next door, a single basement room full of computers and gigabytes of incriminating data on hard drives, all melted into a bubbling, black stew.

The Soy Sauce, Redux

John said, "Now there's a shitty bomber pilot."

The rain was starting to let up. I took a deep breath of morning air and said, "The town is still there, Tennet. You played your hand, and you lost—wait, where is he?"

Falconer said, "Oh, son of a bitch!"

The blue pickup, which Tennet had apparently stolen while we were all standing in the shape of a dong and waiting to die, was barreling north up the highway.

I said, "Who cares? He's going to run smack into the Army's cordon. Hopefully they'll arrest his stupid ass."

But Falconer was already sprinting toward the monster truck. He was damned if he was going to let somebody else get his collar after all this. I was about to bid him good hunting, when John brushed past me and jumped into the passenger seat. And then Amy was running toward the truck and I realized that nobody else was going to be happy until they saw a proper end to this. I ran and jumped into the backseat, my shoe dragging on pavement as the truck almost took off without me.

The sight of the Army's airtight cordon operation instantly ruined every zombie movie for me. These people weren't stupid. Strategy was their *thing*. They assessed the enemy, and adjusted their plan accordingly. If it was zombies, so be it.

Thus, there was not a single soldier visible, not a single exposed face or neck available to be bitten and zombified. Instead, there was a row of armored vehicles full of soldiers—Bradley Fighting Vehicles, I would later learn—arranged in a formation that would give them clear shots from their gun ports and from the turrets mounted at the top of each vehicle. They sat well back from concrete barricades that would stop any suicide vehicles in their tracks. Coils of razor wire were strung along the ground on both sides of the barrier. A horde of five thousand zombies—even fast zombies—could rush the formation and they would be easily blown to pieces by a crisscross hail of large-caliber rounds. These men were told they were staring into the ravenous maw of a zombie outbreak, and they were prepared to mow that shit down like dead grass.

After having followed him the five miles across the Dead Zone, we thought Tennet's truck was going to just keep going and plow right into that green wall of death, at which point I assumed he would find his weight in lead rushing through his windshield at the speed of sound. Was this a suicide-by-armored-vehicle? For what, just to spite Falconer? Goddamn this guy was a dick.

Instead, Tennet's truck skidded to a stop short of the barbed wire. We stopped behind him, watching. Tennet jumped out, and walked toward the soldiers, waving his arms in the air. It wasn't like he was signaling surrender, it was more like he was waving them away, screaming and pointing and acting like a crazy person.

Then, he was tackled and ripped to pieces by a monster in a black space suit.

I said, "Well, that worked out."

We all watched Tennet's well-deserved and awesomely ironic death, when we heard the first thud of heavy machine guns erupt from the line of vehicles ahead.

To our right, descending down from the water tower construction site, was a nightmare horde of shambling, malformed, infected REPER personnel. They crawled and howled and shrieked and sprouted snapping appendages. Then it hit me that this was, in fact, Tennet's dying plan. Tennet had thrown his personal horde of infected at the army cordon, giving them their zombie apocalypse, and every reason in the world to unleash hell on the city beyond, regardless of what one airplane pilot claimed he saw.

I screamed, "GET US OUT OF HERE!"

The infected were washing in from our right, swarming toward us and the line of armored vehicles in front of us. More and more of the vehicles were going weapons free on the horde, the turrets and machine guns punching fire and lead into the air.

Falconer was already throwing the monster truck into reverse, cranking the wheel and getting us perpendicular to the highway, then cranking it the other way to get the big bastard of a vehicle heading the other direction. The roar of the big guns outside was like the finale of a fireworks display. I couldn't hear myself think.

The truck shook. Amy screamed. Something had hit us.

Falconer growled and fought with the wheel. We weren't moving. I smelled smoke. Another shell smacked the front of the truck, knocking the hood askew.

Flames flew up in front of the windshield.

"GET OUT! GET OUT AND GET FLAT!"

Falconer threw open his door and ducked out. John was messing with something in his lap. The furgun had fallen to the floorboard. I grabbed it, then climbed over Amy and threw open the door. The sound of monster shrieks and cannon fire filled the air. My shoes hit the pavement and I heard Falconer scream, "THE DITCH, GET TO THE DITCH."

I saw where he was going—the deep drainage ditch along the west side of the road, no more than ten feet in front of us. John spilled out behind me, all of us now using the burning truck as cover against the barrage of gunfire. Falconer sprinted forward, making himself as low to the ground as he could, and dove into the ditch.

Amy screamed, "JOHN!"

John wheeled around to see a big infected fucker loping toward him from behind, dragging the tattered remains of a black space suit.

I fumbled with the furgun but before I could even get it sitting properly in my hand, John hit the let's-just-call-it-a-zombie with three barrels of shotgun. Suddenly the monster was missing everything from the neck up.

To Amy, I yelled, "Stay low! As low as you can! GO!"

We ran from behind the truck and tumbled down into the drainage ditch. Bullets punched the dirt and pavement overhead. The truck exploded, sending flaming debris whirling through the air above us. It was the second time I'd almost been hit by a flaming truck part in the last half hour, a new personal record.

Amy screamed, "THEY'RE GOING TO KILL US!"

I said, "DOWN! GET YOUR HEAD DOWN!"

A spray of bullets raked across the water behind us, punching into the mud of the embankment.

She yelled, "WE HAVE TO STOP THEM!"

John was frantically trying to pull something out of his pocket—

shotgun shells, I assumed. Something whistled past my ear. Next to me, Falconer tumbled into the shallow water of the ditch. The stream under him ran red.

"FALCONER!"

"AMY! NO!"

I grabbed for her arm. She pulled away from me.

She scrambled up the embankment.

Right into the line of fire.

It seemed to happen in slow motion. She stood up, right into the storm of bullets, and started waving her arms in front of her, like she was trying to flag down an oncoming car. She was shouting something at them that not even I could hear over the hellstorm erupting all around her.

Time seemed to stop. I had this frozen, snapshot image of her, standing up there, silhouetted against the iron-gray sky, her pants soaking wet and splattered with mud, her skinny freckled arms up in front of her, pulling the tail of her shirt up to reveal two inches of pale, vulnerable skin. All these details, captured perfectly in my mind, in that endless moment.

And the moment was, in fact, endless, because time had stopped.

From behind me John said, "Finally. Jesus."

It was dead silent all around us. The water at my feet had frozen. A spray of bits of mud hung in the air in the embankment above me, where a bullet had struck a microsecond before.

I turned to John, who had the Soy Sauce container in his hand. I said, "What the—"

"Oh, Dave! You're here with me. I stopped time. I hope that's okay."

"You . . . you can do that now?"

"Yeah, ever since I took the Soy Sauce last night. I'm like Zach Morris in *Saved by the Bell*. The only catch is you can't actually accomplish anything while time is stopped. You can move yourself but it's, uh, mostly informational I guess."

I climbed up the embankment, taking in the frozen battle all around me, like some sort of huge, open air, incredibly fucked-up sculpture in a museum. I looked back at Amy, a statue frozen with her mouth open, exposing her crooked incisors.

I shrugged and said, "Well, it's actually not the weirdest thing that's happened on the Sauce."

John walked up behind me and said, "I wouldn't even put it in the top five. And I know what you're thinking, and no, we can't push her out of the way. Nothing can be moved. And I don't mean that in the sense that they tell you not to change anything when you go back in time, like it's a rule or something. I mean literally nothing can be moved. I tried."

I said, "I can move the furgun." I still had it in my hand.

"Right, and you're moving your pants when you walk. I think it's anything you were touching when everything stopped."

"How long does it stay like this?"

"I don't know. I've only done it once before. I couldn't intentionally make it start up again but . . . I got the sense that it lasts until you do what you need to do. Whether you know what you need to do or not. If that makes sense."

"What do we need to do?"

I stared over at the column of smoke frozen over the burning truck, the still flames looking like orange-blown glass sculptures. Then, from the still, black column, a whisp of smoke moved.

At the exact same moment I thought it, John said it out loud:

"Oooooh, shit."

The shadow men were here.

It started with that single, black shadow, hanging in midair. It was moving toward us.

Then I saw another one. And another. They grew out of the air, black shapes like holes burning in the white curtain of reality, revealing the darkness beyond. Three and four at a time they appeared, the darkness taking on the vague shapes of men. Each time my eyes focused on one spot, walking shadows would appear where I wasn't watching. It was like trying to count snowflakes as they landed on a windshield.

John and I backed away from them, then realized they were behind us, too, on the other side of the ditch.

We were an island in a black tide of them.

and I must emphasize that my encounters with the Shadow Men have been rare, in the sense that stepping in dog feces is rare. That is, the potential is always there, you never forget it when it happens, but you go just long enough between incidents to let your guard down. Yet, everyone has been in the presence of a Shadow Man, in the same way that everyone has been in the presence of electricity. It is all around you, invisible, tickling at the periphery of your perceptions. Then one day, you touch a bare wire . . .

These beings live in between moments and outside of time, across dimensions and perhaps never fully exist in any particular one. They have been called ghosts, and no doubt they wear the faces of the recently dead in the imagination of a person trying to reconcile what they saw in that dark corridor, or in the silence of their bedroom at three in the morning. For others, they will perhaps appear to be tiny, gray aliens. Centuries ago a Shadow Man would have been called a faerie, or succubus. That is how the human brain works, when it looks at a formless cloud, it tries to see a shape, or a face, or otherwise associate it with something that makes sense in some known cultural context, like the proverbial image of the Virgin Mary seen in the grain of a tree stump, or a slice of toast. But make no mistake—the observer supplies the face.

You have never heard of anyone being harmed or killed by a Shadow Person, in the sense that you have never met someone who failed to be born. Our unique, limited perception limits us to see only one possible outcome of an event. If we grow tiresome of a tedious conversation with a man, we cannot, say, simply switch to another quantum reality in which that man did not survive a bout of childhood pneumonia, winking him out of our thread of existence like turning the channel on a television. The Shadow Men can.

There are enthusiasts of the paranormal on the Internet and elsewhere who point to the tens of thousands of people who go missing worldwide each year and speculate that they have been taken by the Shadow Men. But I am prone to think that this is misunderstanding their methods. If the Shadow Men, say, invaded your home and took your wife, you would in that next moment have no recollection of ever having been married. At best, you would have only a terrible, gnawing sense of something missing. A hole in your life into which something should perfectly fit, something that should rightfully exist, but does not.

One young man I know, who has written about the incident in his own book, claims that he retains distinct memories of a friend who was lost in an encounter with the shadows. The parents of the friend still live in town. Yet, they do not recall a son. The rental records of his apartment show no person under that name ever resided there, the records of the public school system retain no mention of a student by that name. The difference between our reality and the reality that this young man remembers could be so close that only molecules separate them—a particular sperm that failed to fertilize a particular egg in one reality, but that was successful in another. Some speculate that we sense the ripples of these changes in the form of déjà vu, or those infuriating occasions when we insist we remember an event or a conversation with a group of friends that no one else in the group recollects. You hear of a prominent person passing away, and swear that you heard that same news years earlier.

But of course, the real power of the Shadow Men is that we do not perceive them at all.

The Bible II

John and I backed up. I raised the furgun, stupidly, having no idea what effect it would have on these beings. We retreated, slowly, bumping backward against the rigid Amy statue what was still standing there, frozen. Her arms were outstretched, her eyes wide, unwittingly putting herself in an absolutely perfect posture for the situation.

The shadow man closest to me was no more than ten feet away. I had the furgun on him because I had nothing else. Where there would be eyes on a man, burning coals of yellow and orange flared on the shadow man, like a pair of lit cigars floating in the blackness. And in that moment I knew that this wasn't just a shadow man, but was *the* shadow man, the one I had seen in my bathroom, the one that lurked in my cell in the basement of the old asylum, the one that now, in this moment, I sensed was actually never far from me. I could not bring myself to think, *What are you?* Instead, the feeling was more akin to, *It's you again.*

I . . . have spoken to it before . . .

The blackness closed in on us, no gap between the shadow men now, their cold intelligence, malice and cataclysmic lethality advancing as a solid black wave, like the artist who painted our reality had knocked over an ink bottle on it. We had no room to retreat, both of us pressed against the Amy monument.

"Dave . . ." John hissed. "Dave . . . shoot. Shoot them. Do something . . ."

But my eyes were fixed on the burning coals of the shadow man in front of me, and something was passing between us. There were no words, but we were communicating. The thoughts passed instantly, faster than words could have managed, like files instantly streamed between two computers. If I had to translate what the shadow man told me into words, it would be this:

What is a man? What do you think a man is? What do you think we are? What do you think your relationship is to us?

You believe in a spirit, or a soul. What do you think that is? It lives inside your flesh, but only your flesh can interact with the world, only your flesh can speak and eat and fight and fuck and reproduce, and ultimately the soul must obey the impulses of the flesh. What, then, is the soul but a prisoner of your flesh? An undying yet constrained energy, bound and enslaved within a shuffling, steadily rotting suit of tissue and savage needs? By virtue of your birth, you make a prisoner of a soul. An enslavement that multiplies as you multiply, breeding with grunts and stench and the spilling of squirming fluids.

You recoil in horror at the idea of the parasites, these creatures who against your will can commandeer your sensory interaction with the world, imprisoning your mind behind a repulsive monstrosity that can command your limbs and even your very thoughts, poisoning every aspect of your being with its own alien desires until it becomes impossible to distinguish your own personality from the urges of the squirming thing living invisibly inside your body. Until nothing that is truly you remains.

Now, you understand.

For us, man is the parasite.

Somehow, I could feel their hate, an energy that was too big and too cold to get the scope of it, the way that from the ground, the curvature of the earth just looks like a straight line. The shadow people moved in. So, so slowly. A dark tide creeping in on an island of mud and grass maybe ten feet in diameter and shrinking. All those glowing eyes, little pinpricks of light floating on dark, featureless faces.

John said, "Dave . . . do it. *Dave. Now.*"

"Do *what?*"

"Focus! Focus on the most powerful thing you can imagine and squeeze that trigger."

But that wasn't right. A nuclear explosion would not work here. Fire would not work. Violence would not work. That was the energy *they* were made of. Shadows aren't repelled by the dark, they're repelled by the light—

The shadow man—my shadow man—floated right up to me, right up to Amy. I found myself shrieking, "NO! NO! NOOO!" in short, barking bursts, the single word over and over again.

Amy's outstretched arms were beside me and the shadow man was on her now, drifting right into her left hand. My stomach turned as I watched her hand dissolve and vanish completely. All that was left was a stump, her left hand gone forever. But, no, that must have been the confusion of the moment because of course her left hand had always been gone, the accident and all that.

I raised the furgun, pointing it right at the "chest" of the shadow man. It was *in* his chest.

My mind was blank.

I reached out and grabbed Amy's other, frozen hand and squeezed. I closed my eyes.

I need to think like Amy.

In that one second before I squeezed the trigger, a face popped into my head. The face was the same one that would have come to probably 75 percent of Americans, if put in the same situation. A bearded face that was surely from the imagination of some long-lost Italian painter, a face that looked nothing like a Middle Eastern Jew. I suddenly remembered two dozen horrible kid shows my adoptive parents made me watch on VHS, where in the final scene the main character always turned toward the camera and said some variation of, "I know how we'll solve this problem! With *Christianity.*"

Well, their programming worked. When terror drove everything out of my mind, I fell back on the iconic face and all I could picture in my head was that painting, that shitty velvet Elvisey Jesus that had hung on my wall, that was still sitting in the trunk of John's Caddie for all I knew.

I squeezed the trigger.

A flash of white light poured forth from the device in my hand. The whiteness condensed down to a shape. Small. Square.

Suddenly, hovering there before us, in midair, was that stupid painting.

The painting swiveled, facing the dark hordes. The eyes on the face of Velvet Jesus burned with white fire. The mouth opened, and let loose an inhuman roar.

Velvet Jesus faced a shadow man to my left. Laser beams fired from his eyes.

The shadow man exploded.

The eyes lit up again, and fired. Another shadow man left the world. The painting turned in midair, we hit the dirt. Beams of white fired left, then right, clearing swaths through the shadows, piercing the blackness with a glare that was somehow equally terrible, a white-blue light that I knew would leave me blind if I looked too long. The terrible light chewed through the shadows with a sickening righteous energy that genuinely made me pity them. I suddenly knew how the scientists of the Manhattan Project felt the first time they saw a nuclear detonation, witnessing the power of what they had unleashed, the reflection of the light off of the surrounding sand bright enough to blind a man wearing dark glasses. Power so astonishing that it became hideous.

And then, there was only one shadow man left, my shadow man, the one in front of me that had taken Amy's hand, or made it so that her hand was already gone.

Velvet Jesus flew toward the shadow man, then circled behind him. The painting screeched like an animal and the mouth on the painting opened wide. The painting launched itself at the shadow man.

Velvet Jesus bit his head off.

The shadow man's body evaporated like a cloud of car exhaust.

Then there was a flash, so bright that I couldn't close my eyes to it because they were already closed, but the brightness penetrated to the back of my eyeballs, burning all through me. There was a thud in the ground, a shock wave that sent a ripple through reality. The painting disappeared. The furgun exploded in a miniature supernova of blue light.

I don't know how I ended up flat on my back, but I was staring up at the still, gray clouds and trying to blink spots out of my eyes. All was silent.

John appeared over me and said, "When they write the sequel to the Bible, that shit is *definitely* gonna be in there."

My ears were ringing. Somehow, *all* of my senses were ringing. Overload. Then John was pulling me to my feet and saying, "Look! Look at that one's face."

He was pointing to one of the still life–infected REPER men, one I didn't even know had been standing there when the world froze. It had been in the process of rounding the burning truck, running toward us. It would have reached Amy in about three seconds if John had not called his Soy Sauce time-out. I walked over to the infected spaceman. His eyes were a pair of road flares, sizzling and crackling and smoldering with white light.

The parasites were burning.

All of the parasites were burning—at least the ones around us. The white, crackling pinpricks of light were twinkling from the infected spacemen, the sizzle of the frying spiders filling the preternatural silence in that still world.

And then the lights blinked out, one by one, the sizzling of the flesh fading, as the last of the parasites in the field died. The men they had lived in would not suddenly wake up and find themselves cured—happy endings like that never happened in Undisclosed. When time sped up, they would collapse, dead. But they would be free. And they would be no threat to us.

In the stillness of the aftermath I said, "Man, I need a nap."

I looked around at the frozen battle, one that nobody involved in knew had just taken a radical turn in the infinity between ticks on the clock. "What happens now?"

John surveyed the landscape and said, "We just got to get out of the way, right? Time starts back up and the army realizes the zombies are all down and they'll stop shooting and then they'll give us all medals."

I said, "Amy is still out in the open. If I position myself so that I'm kind of pushing her over, when time starts back up we'll tumble down into the ditch, right?"

"Yeah, I guess so. Try not to break her neck."

"Go down there and get ready to catch us."

John jumped down into the ditch, looking over Falconer, who had been shot multiple times. He certainly looked dead because he wasn't moving, but nobody was moving so we couldn't know for sure. I walked toward Amy, her frozen arms outstretched toward me like she was trying to ward me off.

Something hit me in the chest.

Actually, I ran into something. Something hovering in midair, something small and sharp.

A bullet.

An inch long and as thick as a pencil. Fired from one of the many guns bristling out of the line of green vehicles behind me.

David Wong

There was no mistaking the trajectory. It was heading right for Amy. Specifically, right for Amy's heart. In the frantic fog of zombie combat some guy—who had probably enlisted to help pay for his college education—had taken a shot at the waving figure next to the ditch, and the shot was good. It was going to take her right out.

John saw me standing there, slackjawed, looking at this frozen projectile, this little copper-jacketed death warrant hanging in the air about eight feet away from Amy. He looked back and forth between the bullet and the frozen Amy and didn't need me to mutter, "Headed right for her," though I did it anyway.

He said, "Okay, okay. Let's think it through. What if we—"

"One of us has to die."

"Now, that's not true—"

"Either it tears through her heart, or one of us stands in front of her and lets it tear through ours."

"Bullshit. It doesn't have to be your heart. You can, like turn sideways to it, press your bicep against it, get that big bone in your arm in front of it."

"A bullet like this . . . John, this thing is traveling at half a mile per second. They design them to punch through military-grade helmets and body armor. It'll smash through the bone and rip through your lungs and take out your heart anyway."

"You don't know that—"

"I do, because, Marconi was right. I knew he was right. They still need their freaking sacrifice. Otherwise this thing won't end. It's a bill that needs to be paid. Somebody has to die."

"Fine. I'll do it."

"No, you won't."

"Dave . . ."

"If you don't understand the symmetry here, well, just think about it. It has to be me. It's right. It fits. You said yourself that time won't resume until we do what we're supposed to do. If you stand here, in front of this thing, you're going to be waiting forever. It won't go off pause until I do it."

He said, "Fine. Then leave it on pause. We'll go do, whatever. Whatever we want. Piss off the top of the Statue of Liberty. Walk across the ocean and screw with frozen tourists in Paris. We got all the time in the world. We'll use it. We'll tour the world, you and me."

I shook my head. "And leave her here, this thing hovering in front of her heart? Knowing things could suddenly snap into action at any second? No, I'd never be able to relax, knowing that. We're screwing around somewhere on the other side of the world and suddenly she takes a bullet and she dies here, alone? Calling for me, her last thought to wonder where I am? No. I spent my whole life putting off what I knew I needed to do. No more of that."

"Well fuck you, then."

"Yep. Fuck me."

"Wait! You can leave a note. Like, a final message to her."

"I don't have anything to write with."

"You have the contents of your own body. Smear the note onto the street. *With your shit.*"

I stared at him. "Yes, John, let's have that be Amy's last memory of me. I mean, once time starts again all of this is going to just be instantly in front of her. So from her point of view, she stood up, then in the blink of an eye suddenly I'm sprawled dead in front of her and I LOVE YOU BABE spontaneously appears onto the pavement, spelled out in smeared human feces."

"Oh my God, do it! You'll be a legend."

He laughed. I laughed.

I said to John, "Good-bye, man."

"Just . . . just wait, okay? There's no hurry. There's a whole list of things I need to say first—"

"No, there isn't. There really isn't. Whatever you think you need to say, I already know. Trust me. Just . . . if you make it out of here, don't . . ."

I thought, and shook my head.

"Just don't *waste* yourself. Do you understand?"

He nodded, almost imperceptibly.

I nodded toward Amy and said, "And take care of her."

"She takes care of herself, if you haven't noticed. I'll see you on the other side."

"Yeah." I didn't mean it. "You got your phone?"

"I got *your* phone. Want me to call somebody?"

"No. You're going to get video of this. Once things start up again, I mean."

I had a feeling time was going to whip back up to speed the moment I was in position. "Let's do this."

I took a deep breath, my last, I figured, and stood about a foot in front of the bullet, its shiny tip aimed right at my sternum. I had been shot before, and it hurt quite a bit. But I had a feeling I was never going to feel this one. I thought this bullet had a serious chance of passing through my breastbone and through the soft tissue behind it, through my spine and then out again. But by then the bullet would be badly off course, tumbling through the air, breaking into fragments. It should miss her easily.

I steeled myself, trying to make my body harder, as if that would make a difference. I stared down the projectile, waiting for time to resume. I started to get impatient, and made a twirling motion with my fingers. "Come on. Start the clock, damn it."

In the last second before time resumed and the bullet exploded forward, I registered an orange blur, bouncing along the ground. I turned—

Sacrifice

An explosion of noise crashed in on me from every direction. In an instant, the guns were barking and the wind was howling and the stink of smoke was burrowing into my nostrils.

The orange blur was right in front of me, kicking and thrashing through the air. And then there was a thud and a yelp and Molly was bleeding at my feet.

Amy was yelling "DON'T SHOO—" at the soldiers, finishing her sentence from before the Great Pause, her words choked off in confusion. In a blink, there I was, standing in the road in front of her—to her eyes, I had teleported there. And there, on the ground in front of me, was Molly.

I spun and dove and tackled Amy, pinning her to the ground, sending her glasses askew. The guns thundered behind us, and I craned my head around to see that Tennet's army of infected were, as I thought, simply collapsing dead where they stood, like marionettes whose strings had all simultaneously been cut. Their parasite puppeteers had been burned to ash.

Torturous minutes stretched out as we lay there and the gunfire continued over and around us, the amped-up soldiers getting their money's worth. Bullets skipped off pavement and whistled overhead. But slowly, finally, one gun after another got the cease fire command. The Zulus were down.

Amy squirmed out from under me, and goddamnit, she ran right out into the open again, and toward Molly.

She kneeled down over her, crying, pressing her face to the dog's.

I slowly stood, waving my arms at the soldiers, for all that good it had done Amy last time. Nearby I saw the shredded sleeve of one of the black space suits, and I grabbed it and waved it like a flag.

They didn't shoot.

I went over to Amy and Molly. The dog wasn't whimpering or howling, thank God, because I don't think either of us could have handled that. She was silent, her eyes closed, still. She never even felt it.

Molly had moved when the rest of the world was still, she had been able to navigate the paused world just like John and I had, and I doubted I would ever know how, beyond the fact that there were a lot of things about this animal that I didn't understand. When things had stopped, she ran, from wherever she was, and she ran as fast as her paws could take her, knowing where she needed to be and what she needed to do. And what she needed to do was to steal my goddamned hero moment.

We kneeled there in the cold, and finally somebody called out to us. It was a soldier, who I had a feeling was doing it against orders. He had emerged from a hatch at the top of one of the vehicles, and was yelling something at us. I couldn't hear what he was saying, so I just showed him my empty hands and said, "We're not armed."

If somehow the crying girl at my feet and I still looked like zombies, then John convinced him otherwise since he was performing the distinctly human—and distinctly non-zombie—activity of filming everything with a cell phone.

The soldier climbed out of his vehicle and jumped down, then crossed the barricades.

See, that's how you get eaten in a zombie movie, kid.

I heard cars approach from the highway behind us, refugees from

Undisclosed who had presumably been huddled down in the Dead Zone behind us, hearing World War III erupting up ahead. But now they came, in their pickup trucks and dirt bikes and ATVs, driving with an adherence to posted traffic laws that zombies so rarely display.

No one on the other side of the barricades panicked and opened fire. The spell had been broken. Amy was whispering to Molly, stroking her fur. I was standing over Amy, my hand on her shoulder, looking down at them. Boots appeared on the road next to me and my eyes tracked up past gray camo pants and black knee pads. A wicked-looking assault rifle was pointed at the ground, a gloved hand on the grip, the finger resting outside the trigger guard.

The soldier said, "Sir! Please identify yourself."

"My name is David Wong. I am not a zombie or infected with any kind of disease that creates zombie-like symptoms or whatever other bullshit you were told by your commanding officers."

The soldier gestured toward the approaching vehicles and said, "You've escaped the city? Are there other uninfected back there?"

I thought for a moment, studying Amy's face. I swallowed and said, "As far as I know, everybody in town is uninfected. The effects of this outbreak have been grossly exaggerated."

"STOP FILMING, SIR! SIR!"

John obeyed, stuffing the phone in his pocket. He said, "You can confiscate the phone if you want. A copy of the video is currently hosted on my Web site. And you can try to get that taken down I guess, but it's on a server based in the Ukraine. So good luck with that."

Other soldiers were approaching cautiously from behind the first guy, and in a zombie movie this is when Molly would spring back to life and bite one of them, and then everything would go to hell. But this was not a zombie movie, Molly stayed where she was, her blood turning cold on the pavement.

The cold rain started again. John took off his jacket and laid it over Molly, so she wouldn't lay there and get soaked. It was for Amy's benefit, I knew.

One of the soldiers behind the first guy, a medic apparently, said, "Is anyone in need of medical attention?"

John said, "No. We're fine."

Then a furious voice emerged from the ditch to my left, saying,

"UH, HELLO? I've got three bullet wounds down here and I'm laying in fucking freezing water. Somebody?"

We didn't realize at the time that we would have to basically ban ourselves from watching television in the aftermath. The video clip of the small, wet, redheaded girl weeping over her shot dog would be downloaded 18 million times from YouTube alone in the next month. It would air on CNN, Fox News, the BBC, Al Jazeera, all three broadcast networks and everywhere else. Amy couldn't stand to watch it, and for a long time, it was *everywhere*.

If it had been me laying there, nobody would have given a shit. A big, chubby guy in a green prison jumpsuit and a weird reputation? The factions who were still calling for blood afterward, who talked of undetectable infection and for internment—if not extermination—of the town, would maybe have still won out. Same if it had been John, or Falconer, or Owen. They could have dug up dirt on us, claimed the corpse was infected, claimed we had killed a dozen orphans just prior to taking the bullet. We'd have just been one more body in the street.

But no one could argue against a dog.

The loyal dog, sacrificing itself to save its owner, laying there bleeding in the rain. Then add in the tiny girl kneeling over her—the dog's owner that the bullet had been meant for—who couldn't have appeared more harmless if she'd been made of kittens. The image doused the world's bloodlust like a bucket of ice water. A perfect, undeniable symbol for the price the innocent pay for unchecked paranoia.

Eulogy

John wrapped up Molly in his jacket and laid her in the backseat of the pickup Tennet had driven out to this spot. A crowd was forming, and vehicles were now lined up bumper to bumper down the highway, an echo of the scene from the day of the outbreak. We were heading the other direction, though, back into town. In the distance, the column of smoke from the asylum inferno drifted into the sky. We passed one house where a guy was unloading suitcases from his trunk and glancing around in confusion, like he had just come back from a two-week vacation and was wondering what the fuck happened while he was gone.

We drove to my house, or the charred remnants of my house, anyway. Amy was pretty upset at the sight of it but John pointed out that we had in fact burned the place down ourselves.

I was exhausted down to my bones, but there was this last piece of business to take care of and no way to put it off. I grabbed the shovel laying in my yard and John and I took turns digging a grave for Molly, rain pelting our shoulders. The temperature dropped into the forties but Amy stood out in it the whole time, watching us, shivering.

I laid Molly in the ground and John volunteered to say the eulogy:

"This here is Molly. She was a good dog. And when I say 'good dog' I don't mean it the way other people mean it, when they're talking about a dog that never shit on the floor or bit their kids. No, I'm talking about a dog that died saving Amy's life. By my rough count, that's half a dozen times Molly saved one of our lives. How many dogs can say that? Hell, how many *people* can say that? One time, Dave was in a burning building, and Molly here rescued him by getting behind the wheel of his car and driving through the wall. You know that couldn't have been easy for her.

"Anyhow, Molly died in the way that all really good things die, fast and brutal and for no apparent reason. They say that even though it often appears that God just really, really doesn't give a shit about what happens down here, that that's just an illusion and He really does care after all, and it's all part of His great plan to make it appear that He doesn't care. Though what purpose that serves I can't possibly imagine. I think God probably just wanted Molly for Himself, and I guess I can't blame Him.

"Well, God, here's your dog back, I guess. We hereby commit Molly to doggy heaven, which is probably nicer than regular heaven, if you think about it. Amen."

Amy and I said, "Amen" and I noticed she was crying again and felt utterly helpless to stop it. She buried her face in my chest and I stroked her tangled, wet mess of red hair.

I said, "Let's find a roof."

She said, "Let's find a bed."

We walked away from the ruins of my former house and John said, "Wait, what if Tennet arranged all of this as some elaborate form of therapy?"

EPILOGUE

It was December 22nd, or Christmas Eve Eve Eve as John so irritatingly called it. I was alone, staring out of the kitchen window of a cheap, mostly empty mobile home supplied by the Federal Emergency Management Agency. There was a single Christmas card on the counter next to me, laying on top of its mutilated envelope.

The trailer had come with furniture, but the sofa smelled so bad we had dragged it out into the yard. I think the trailer had previously seen service in New Orleans after the hurricane and I think it got moldy. In the corner of the living room was our Christmas tree, a two-foot-tall plastic tree with huge googly eyes and a mechanical mouth. John had found it in a thrift store, it had a voice box on the bottom and I think originally it was supposed to do a humorous Christmas rap when somebody walked by. When we put batteries in it, the mouth locked in the wide-open position and it uttered a high-pitched, electronic scream of garbled feedback until we pried the batteries out again.

Under the tree sat John's gift, a wrapped object that was perfectly the shape of a crossbow.

I had a feeling it would take me years to piece together the whirlwind of lies that had obscured the incident the news media had finally decided to call the "Zulu Outbreak." The consensus seemed to be that fewer than 70 people were ever actually infected with the pathogen, which they decided was some kind of rare form of bovine spongiform encephalopathy, caused by the consumption of some kind of mutated protein from contaminated sausages. So the final death toll was, according to the final CDC reports, 68 dead from Zulu, 406 dead from the violence resulting from mass hysteria.

Plenty of people from in town came forward to dispute those reports. And plenty of other people came forward to dispute *those* reports. A hundred different versions came out and so the public just defaulted to what the guys in suits told them. In the end, They didn't need to cover up anything—They just drowned it out in a blizzard of conflicting stories. The world eventually gives up and moves on. Like the whole thing with the envelopes of anthrax after 9/11.

Well. Whatever. Now it was a matter of seeing if there would be another outbreak, maybe in another town. But nothing so far.

Snow was inching up the little wooden cross we had planted at Molly's grave. Every time I looked at it, I imagined replacing it with a little star and crescent, so my neighbors would think that somehow my dog had died a practicing Muslim. I was waiting for a call from Amy, but instead I got a knock at my door. I assumed it was a reporter, which kind of cheered me up because I was making a fulfilling hobby out of giving a completely different version of the story to each and every one of them I spoke to. Why let everybody else have all the fun?

But when I opened the door, there was Detective Lance Falconer, in a black turtleneck and looking cropped from a cover of *GQ*. It actually took me a second to notice the crutches.

Once inside my living room, I said to him, "You knocked. Usually you just let yourself in."

"I spent five weeks in the hospital, Wong. I'm in no mood."

"Merry Christmas Eve Eve Eve."

"*What?*"

"I got some frozen taquitos in the oven, you want one?"

"I don't even know what that is. Look, I'm not gonna waste your time. I just got off the phone with my agent and I'm talking about doing a book on the Zulu thing, and he informs me that there are no fewer than thirteen books on the subject in the pipeline."

"Yeah, I know. Marconi is writing one, his will be the best. Though I got to admit, the one I'm most looking forward to reading is Owen's."

"And you're writing one."

"Well, Amy actually. She's my ghost writer. They just put my name on the cover."

"My point is," he said, straining for patience, "is that they're fine with multiple books because they're from different angles. But yours and mine are basically the same. Because we kind of went through it together."

"Oh. I can see that."

"And they don't want mine, because they already have yours."

"Oh, right. I mean, you should have moved faster to make a deal."

"I was in the hospital recovering from getting sprayed with a fucking machine gun."

"Oh, right. Right."

"And I don't suppose I can change your mind?"

I said, "Detective, I want you to use your powers of deduction to detect the fact that I'm living in a goddamned FEMA trailer. The video store just opened back up two weeks ago. No paycheck, that whole time. I go back to work and the first customer I get is Jimmy DuPree, returning his copy of *Basic Instinct 2*. I'm like, you're payin' late charges on that. It wasn't in the deposit box when I got here this morning. He didn't like that."

"I thought there was some sort of victim's fund from the government . . ."

"There is, and maybe one of these days I'll actually get a check in the mail in return for the eight thousand forms I had to fill out. But they're going to sit on it until they see what I write in the book. They want to see how I tell the story, if you understand what I'm saying."

"And how are you going to tell the story?"

"I'm going to tell the most ridiculous possible version of it I can think of. People are going to close it and be like, 'What the fuck did I just read?'"

He nodded. "I have material that you won't have access to. I got transcripts of the radio chatter between the pilots. Some other stuff you won't be able to get."

"I'd love to have you on board."

"I'll cooperate on one condition. You portray the coolest version of me possible. I'm talking total action hero here. If you're making things up, then embellish me into a badass."

"I can do that."

"And give me a cool name. And make me good-looking."

"Sure."

"And say I drive a Porsche."

"What? Where are you gonna get a Porsche on a cop salary?"

"Because I'm awesome. Alex Cross drives one. So does Lucas Davenport."

"What, are those cops you know?"

He headed for the door, moving more smoothly on the crutches than I did on my own legs. On his way out he turned and said, "And don't put a bunch of bullshit in my mouth, or get cute and try to make me look stupid. Now if you'll excuse me, I have to go to the salon to have my pubic hair straightened and dyed white so that my dick looks like Santa Claus." He closed the door, farting loudly all the way to his car.

I went and pulled my taquitos from the oven. I let them cool and went back to my place at the kitchen window. Falconer's gleaming new Porsche was turning around in my yard, pulling through the snow and disappearing down the street. Actually, now that I looked at it I think it was a Ferrari. I ate a taquito.

As I chewed, the light changed behind me. A shadow grew over the surface of the kitchen counter.

I had time to notice the shadow had no left hand. It spoke.

"Hey!"

I spun, saw pale skin and freckles and red hair.

I said, "Oh! Hey! I was waiting for you to call."

"John picked me up at the bus station while you were out shopping."

"Merry—"

My words were interrupted by Amy throwing her arms around my ribs, squeezing like she was trying to deflate me.

She said, "I brought cupcakes! I left them by the—"

It was her turn to be interrupted, by me pulling her shirt over her head.

"—door. Can we go get Cuban coffee later?"

"Uh huh, sure, sure," I said, working the zipper on her pants.

"Oh my God, David, they will not stop calling me. I changed my number and the reporters found it like two days later. When does this end? When do things get back to normal?"

Who knows? We were both naked by the time she made it to the question mark.

I was half asleep, curled up against her in the bed, Amy in the sweats and T-shirt she wore as pajamas. She was reading the Christmas card that had been laying on my counter.

"When did it come?"

I mumbled, "Couple days ago."

The front was a festive Christmas scene over the words FELIZ NAVI-DAD. Inside, scrawled in red Magic Marker, were the words:

MERRY XMAS TO WALT AND AMY AND DOG

There was no return address.

"That is so cute! She's just as bad at names as you are."

"Mmm."

She said, "David?"

"Hmmmmm?"

"I don't know if I told you, but I'm seeing somebody."

"Mmm. Okay. Is he good-looking?"

"A counselor, I mean. For the post-traumatic stress and all that."

"Oh. Okay. Sure, that's good. Let me, uh, know if he's a supervillain."

I drifted off again.

"David?"

"Hmm? What? Is it morning?"

"Do you ever wish you didn't know any of this? Like if you could just erase it from your brain so you'd be like everybody else?"

"Sure. Actually . . . no. Because if somebody came along and offered me the chance, like if they told me if I took a pill I could make it all go away, I wouldn't do it. I'd be afraid the good stuff would go away, too. Like maybe I imagined all of it but then maybe I imagined you, too."

"I'm not saying you imagined it all, obviously."

"That's exactly what you would say, if you also were imaginary."

"All right, go to sleep."

"Hey, you started it."

Silence. I drifted off.

She said, "I was going back and reading Marconi's last book again, and there's this part that always gets me. He points out that the amount of the universe a human can experience is statistically, like, zero percent. You've got this huge universe, trillions of trillions of miles of empty space between galaxies, and all a human can perceive is a little tunnel a few feet wide and a few feet long in front of our eyes. So he says we don't really live in the universe at all, we live inside our brains. All we can see is like a blurry little pinhole in a blindfold, and the rest is filled in by our imagination. So whatever we think of the world, whether you think the world is cruel or good or cold or hot or wet or dry or big or small, that comes entirely from inside your head and nowhere else."

We laid in silence for a while. Finally, I said, "Wouldn't it be nice if that was true?"

Amy's answer was a soft snore.

ACKNOWLEDGMENTS

The character "John" is the invention of my "friend" and long-time "writing partner," popular Internet columnist Mack Leighty (pronounced least-ee, for the audio book narrator). Mack allowed me to use the character of John and demanded nothing more than at least one scene per book in which he "ramps something," along with a flat payment for each time I use the name in print (this is why I frequently construct sentences in a way that lets me avoid using the name completely). You can find Mack's columns on the subject of addiction, parenting, and his boner at comedy megasite Cracked.com under the username John Cheese. Unless, of course, you're reading a dusty copy of this book a hundred years after its writing, in which case I cannot say whether Cracked.com or the Internet in general still exists. All I know is that Mack and I and everyone else involved in the publication of this book will be long dead, and that the royalties will go to my ungrateful heirs, who will surely use the money to buy some kind of futuristic space drugs.

While on the subject, I should thank Jack O'Brien and Oren Katzeff and all of the rest of my bosses at Cracked who were accommodating to this project in every possible way and who, again, are naught but still bones in a forgotten grave here in the year 2112.

Also, here's to horror filmmaking legend Don Coscarelli, who somehow turned the first book in this series into a cult classic featuring Oscar-nominated Paul Giamatti, thus putting me and these books on the map and possibly saving me from ever having to work at a real job

David Wong

again. Do not blame him when I self-destruct a few years from now, that would have happened anyway.

And finally I should thank my wife, who is the only reason I ever do anything.

TURN THE PAGE FOR A SNEAK PEEK
AT DAVID WONG'S NEW NOVEL

FUTURISTIC VIOLENCE AND FANCY SUITS

AVAILABLE FALL 2015

THE NEAR FUTURE, SOMEWHERE IN RURAL COLORADO ...

If Zoey Ashe had known she was being stalked by a man who intended to kill her and then slowly eat her bones, she would have worried more about that and less about getting her cat off the roof.

Said cat was on said roof because it was terrified of the Santa Claus hologram in the front yard, a tacky Christmas decoration Zoey's mother had brought home from Walmart two weeks ago. Everybody else in the trailer park had them, so she apparently had felt pressured to demonstrate her Christmas spirit with this dead-eyed apparition that unenthusiastically said, "HO-HO-HO-MERRY-CHRISTMAS" in a flat robotic voice to anyone who approached. Zoey thought it was a little unsettling herself, but every time the cat saw it blink to life, he would hiss and go streaking off to some high place where he thought the translucent bearded devil couldn't reach him. So that's why on the evening of December 16 Zoey was standing in the snow trying to coax the cat off of the roof while just a block away, a man was waiting to abduct her and stream her slow mutilation to half a million viewers.

ONE

For eight hours, Zoey's pursuer had been staking out the trailer where the twenty-two-year-old lived with her mother, waiting for the most dramatic moment to make his appearance. Catching Zoey in bed or the shower would be optimal, but he got the sense that this particular young woman had no rigid schedule for doing either of those things. All day he had been watching her through a dirty bay window that put their trailer's whole, sad living room on display. Zoey had begun her day promptly at one p.m. by waking up on the sofa and initiating a "morning" routine that involved going to the bathroom, returning to the sofa and then staring blankly at the ceiling for an hour. Then she read for a bit, ate a bowl of cereal, and did something with her hair that involved wrapping part of it in tin foil while a nature documentary about pack hunters played on the TV behind her. Now the sun had gone down and Zoey, still in her pajamas, was standing in her yard and yelling up at a cat that had jumped onto the roof. Her stalker had intended to send the news media a video of his entire pursuit of the girl, but he knew now that this part would have to be edited way down.

He was out of patience. He resolved to move in for the kill and even switched on the tiny camera he kept pinned to his lapel, so his fans could watch. But then he had second thoughts. The man called himself "The Jackal," but had decided an hour ago to switch to "The Hyena" after watching them tear apart a moose during the documentary that had played on Zoey's television earlier. He thought it was fitting—hyenas were wild, unpredictable predators and had the most powerful jaws in the animal kingdom (that last part was what had really sold him on it).

But then again, the documentary seemed to show them only hunting in groups (whereas he was definitely a loner) and, unless he misunderstood, the female hyenas had penises, and even gave birth through them. That was a problem—when he became famous and the press started speculating on why he chose that moniker, he didn't want pundits throwing around a bunch of wild theories about his genitals. But if he amended his manifesto to address the issue, or included photographic evidence that he had a normal penis, then that would just make *him* seem like the weirdo for bringing it up. Maybe "The Wolf" was a better name. Or "The Shark."

As he sat in his rental car and wrestled with this decision, Zoey went inside the trailer, then returned dragging a kitchen chair through the door. She tried to use it as a step stool to reach the cat on the roof, at which point she immediately overbalanced and fell off, landing hard in the snow. She gathered herself, brushed snow off her butt, mounted the chair again, and searched in vain for a cat that, unbeknownst to her, had already jumped down the other side of the trailer. This went on for a very long time, before Zoey finally noticed the cat was not on the roof but rather lying in the snow under the very chair she was standing on. Exasperated, the girl trudged back inside cradling the cat with one arm and dragging the chair with the other. The Shark (The Piranha?) decided he would wait for her to get settled again, then make his move.

Instead, Zoey reappeared at the door and headed for the old and busted Toyota Furia in her driveway. Her stalker wasn't worried about losing her if she left—the advantage of self-driving cars for a man in The Piranha's line of work was that their navigation systems were very easy to latch onto. He could just set his own to follow the same route and the car would do the tailing for him—he could literally stalk the girl while relaxing and playing a game on his phone. He watched as Zoey scraped frost from the Toyota's windshield with what appeared to be a spatula, and then pulled out of her driveway, leaving behind a dark square in the snow as if the car had forgotten to take is shadow with it. The Piranha gave her a ten-second head start, and then told his rental car to follow. He tried to picture the headlines that would tick along the bottom of the news feeds next week, like, "The Piranha Claims His Sixth Victim." Hmmm, maybe "The Leopard" would be better. It needed to be some kind of biting animal, otherwise the surgery would have been a waste.

He rubbed the itchy line of stitches that ran from one temple to the other, looping under his jawbone like a chinstrap. He'd had his entire lower jaw and upper teeth augmented with a motorized black market implant consisting of a graphene lattice frame and titanium chompers that could bite through metal. As soon as he had gotten home from the surgery, he had turned on his camera and announced himself to the world by biting through a hunk of copper pipe. He thought it made for an ominous demonstration of his new abilities, even if he'd had to quickly turn off the camera at that point because he had cut up his tongue pretty badly. No matter—the jaws worked, and his next test would be on Zoey Ashe's fingers. Then he'd just chew his way up from there.

She made a left turn, then another. Circling the block. Did she suspect she was being followed? The Leopard would have to be careful—prey animals were weak, but alert and wary. The girl surely could sense the malevolent predator that lurked behind her in the darkness.

TWO

Zoey Ashe had forgotten to tell the Toyota's navigation to stop for food, so she had already missed the turn by the time she was able to convince it to deviate from its route by screaming repeatedly at the windshield. The car reluctantly circled the block and pulled into a food distribution center that people in the future call "the Wendy's drive-thru." Her Toyota's heater had stopped working weeks ago, which was bad news in a Colorado winter, so she needed something hot inside her. Zoey pulled up to the window and ordered a small container of a semisolid, protein-rich foodstuff that the people in her time call "chili," in hopes it would warm her up a couple of degrees (at least before the heat left her body a few minutes later in the form of several dozen hot farts). She urged the lethargic compact car back onto the deserted streets, where the autopilot took over once more. The Toyota whined its way through the darkness, heading directly toward the Zombie Quarantine Zone, which was the name of the topless bar where Zoey's mother worked.

The radio had stopped working years ago, and so Zoey made up for it by singing a hit pop song from her time called "Butt Show (and I Don't Charge Admission)" while she plugged in the strand of Christmas lights she had tacked around the top of the car's interior. She peeled the lid off her chili, watched steam waft into the frigid air and decided that things really could be worse. Zoey tried to appreciate the little things in life, like the fact that just a generation ago you couldn't devote both hands to eating a bowl of fast-food chili while the car drove itself (how did people use to eat car chili? With a straw?). She had also recently upgraded her phone to one that displayed a little holographic image of the caller, but so far she had found this feature was only useful for ter-rifying her holophobic cat, which hardly justified the cost of the up-grade. However, that feature did allow her to see that the call that saved her life came from a man who was fond of wearing fancy suits.

When her phone rang, Zoey was only a few blocks away from the trashy, zombie-themed bar where she was supposed to pick up her mother at the end of her shift, aka, the point in the evening when the younger girls were rotated in for the lucrative night crowd. When the phone's hologram blinked to life it startled the crap out of her, as she had for-gotten the phone was in her lap and for one terrified moment thought a ghost had emerged from her crotch. Zoey flinched, cursed, and splat-tered chili everywhere before she figured out that she was not in fact going to have to undergo an incredibly awkward and invasive exorcism. She groaned and tried to scoop hot chili off her jeans with her fingers, and panicked when she saw she had also gotten it all over her new phone. She licked chili off the screen and, in the process, accidentally swiped the "Answer" slider with her tongue.

The little hologram man floating above the phone looked puzzled and said, "Hello? Is this Zoey Ashe?"

"Hold on. I got chili all over my car."

"I—are you there? What's that sound?"

"It's the sound of me eating chili off my phone. Who's this?"

"Zoey, my name is Will Blackwater. You are the—I'm sorry, are you still there?"

"Yes, I'm listening. Are you actually wearing that suit or do you just have your phone set to display you wearing it?"

"Please listen. You are the daughter of Arthur Livingston, correct?"

"No. I mean, yeah he is my biological father but we have nothing to do with each other. Is he in jail again? Are you his lawyer? Is that why you're all dressed up?"

"No. Listen to me, Zoey. A man is coming to abduct you. Right now. His car is one block behind you."

"Wait. What? Who is this again?"

"I'm going to take control of your car. Don't touch the wheel or the pedals, or do anything else to disengage the self-drive. Do you under-stand?"

"Wait? You can do that?"

"Please buckle your seat belt."

Headlights loomed in her rearview mirror. Zoey, her hands shaking, tried to latch the seat belt as the Toyota abruptly lurched to the left, jumped the curb, flattened a row of shrubs, and plowed across a lawn.

"WHAT? HEY! JESUS CHRIST!"

Zoey grabbed the dash and held on for dear life as her car smashed through two fences and a swing set before it thumped over another curb and turned left onto a residential street.

The hologram man on her phone, Will, said, "I apologize for that, I'm not driving the car. My associate Andre has the controls and I'm afraid he's had several drinks." From somewhere in the background she heard another voice in the phone say, "Hey, I drive better when I got a few in me."

Zoey was thrown against the door as the Toyota went power sliding around a turn. She twisted around in her seat and saw the headlights of her pursuer streak through the yard they had just left, sweeping onto the road behind them. The Toyota abruptly turned into a too-narrow alley, missing a brick wall and a dumpster by half an inch on either side. Her side-view mirror exploded when the car clipped the corner on the way out.

The man on the phone said, "I'm terribly sorry to tell you this, but your father was killed. It happened earlier this week."

"So? I didn't even know him! I assumed he died years ago. Who are these people?!"

"Hold on."

The Toyota jumped off the road again and plunged into a grove of pine trees, branches raking the doors with a noise like frantic predators clawing to get in.

Over the phone, Zoey faintly heard Will say, "Cut the lights."

The headlights blinked out, along with all of the dashboard lights and the navigation overlay on the windshield. Zoey was now hurtling through the darkness of the trees, completely blind.

She screamed.

The little hologram man on her phone, which was now located somewhere on the back floorboard, told her to calm down. The car emerged from the trees onto a lawn, fishtailed in the snow-covered grass, then shattered somebody's solar panel array with an explosion of sparks.

Another hard left turn, and they were on a paved street once more. Exactly four seconds later, the tailing sedan was behind them again.

Will said, "Don't let this question alarm you, but do you have any weapons in the vehicle?"

"No! Why would I—wait, I have a spatula . . ."

"Well, we have no indication your pursuer is a pancake, so we'll abandon that angle for the moment. Now I will need you to stay calm. We can't outrun him in this vehicle. I'm going to have you get out."

"How is that possibly going to help?"

"But we need to pick a spot where he'll be forced to follow on foot. Otherwise he could simply run you over with his car, obviously."

"Obviously. Who is he again?"

"It's a hired thug. You don't know him."

"Hired by *who?* What does he want?"

"I can explain later, I can assure you that knowing the fine details won't enhance your survivability and it certainly will do nothing to ease your panic. Let me just say that this particular thug took the contract for a reason, which is that he likes when the targets are women. And he likes to take his time. He's calling himself The Hyena, according to his feed."

"Does he give birth through his penis?"

"What? Zoey, listen to me—our map shows a pond about two hundred yards ahead, but does not show us if it's frozen over. Is that a safe bet this time of year, where you are?"

"It . . . I don't know! I don't go ice-skating! I know the kiddie pool our neighbors left out in their yard is frozen, but—"

Zoey was thrown against the door again. Another hard right that was taking them off the road, this time through a pasture. They swerved to miss a single cow that was lazily grazing in their path. It mooed at them, probably telling them they should turn their headlights on.

Will said, "It's our only option. Hang on."

"What's our only option? What are you going to—"

Zoey was thrown forward against her seat belt as the Toyota slammed on its brakes, skidding across the rough carpet of frozen grass.

Will said, "Go! Get out onto the ice! It will support you but not his car, if he wants to follow he'll have to get out on foot."

"But then wha—"

"GO! NOW!"

Zoey grabbed the phone, threw open the door and ran toward the frozen pond. Before her was a moonlit sheet of snow that Zoey thought was like the thin frosting on a cake made of filthy water and dead fish, because the bitter wind had frozen the part of her brain that thought up metaphors. She didn't even know she had made it to the ice until her sneakers slipped and sent her down to her knees, the surface below her crackling and popping a warning in response.

As Zoey climbed to her feet, her shadow suddenly stretched across the ice—headlights looming behind her. She tried to move quickly but gingerly, but after three steps, she slipped again and this time fell hard on her butt. She heard a car door close behind her. She risked a look back and saw only a silhouette backlit by the twin bluish shafts of headlights. Zoey pushed herself up once more, her hands swiping aside fresh snow to reveal black ice underneath, her stumbling path across the pond leaving a row of haphazard streaks behind her like Chinese calligraphy. Two more steps—now the ice was making wheezing complaints like a squeaky door hinge each time she lowered her foot. She thought she could hear liquid water sloshing up ahead—she had no idea how thick the ice beneath her was, but knew that not far up, that thickness became "zero."

She had stuffed her phone into her coat pocket at some point and from inside, she heard Will say, "Are you still there?"

Zoey dug out the phone with numb fingers and whispered, "He's coming. He's coming and I can't go any further. What do I do?"

"Let me do all the talking. Just hold out your phone."

Through the wind, Zoey could barely hear her pursuer say, "I've reached the edge of the pond." Then after a dramatic pause, he declared, "She has nowhere left to run."

Zoey asked Will, "Who is he talking to?"

"He's streaming this live, he has a Blink camera pinned to his jacket. You don't want to know how many people are watching. Let me talk to him."

Zoey held her phone out toward the menacing shadow in the headlights. The foot-tall holographic ghost of Will Blackwater said, "Stay on the shore, Lawrence, the ice isn't thick enough to support the weight of both of you. You're a beefy guy and you'll notice Zoey here is not what one would call 'willowy.' "

David Wong

The shadow took a few strides onto the pond and said, "Come back off the ice, sweetie. You're going to come with me one way or the other, and you won't like 'the other.'"

Will's hologram replied, "Talk to me, not to her. We both want Zoey for the same reason, with the minor difference that I do not also want to eat her flesh on a live video feed. Your advantage is that she is worth more to us than she is to you. Our advantage is financial. It appears this leads to easy compromise—we're happy to more than compensate you for what you lose by foregoing the contract on Zoey here. No authorities will be notified. You know my word is good, Lawrence."

"Call me by my true name." He paused, as if thinking. "The . . . Bite . . . Master. And, you left out several important points. First of all, there is the fact that I'm here in person, while you appear to still be in the city, six hundred miles away. Second, there is the fact that you and I both know the girl is worth much more than that contract. And third, as you mentioned, I have a *personal* use for her afterward, which means more to me than any financial reward."

"I am actually aware of all of those factors. I am, however, still confident that an arrangement can be reached. Mr. Livingston had substantial resources, as you well know, and again we're more than willing to ameliorate whatever perceived losses you may incur by turning Zoey over to us. As for your . . . personal predilections, surely some dollar amount could be assigned to the loss of visceral pleasure. Perhaps, even, we could offer a substitute for Ms. Ashe here. We daresay we could produce a subject you would find even more satisfactory."

The man laughed. *A fake laugh*, Zoey thought. For the camera.

"You are a piece of work, Will. But let me ask you—if you were to take a gazelle from the jaws of a lion, could you satisfy it by substituting a hundred and fifty pounds of Cat Chow? No, because as an apex predator, the lion doesn't just want to eat. It wants *the prize it won in the hunt*. That is why you are to call me 'The Lion,' from now on."

Will, appearing completely unperturbed by this conversation with a serial killer, said, "I understand perfectly, and I see no reason we should permanently deprive you of your prize. We only need Ms. Ashe's services for about forty-eight hours. And after all, is there no greater pleasure than that sweetened by delayed gratification?"

Zoey tried to process what Will had just offered the man, but the

422

howling, frozen wind and the sound of ice clicking and wheezing under the stress of her weight made it difficult to think of anything but a sudden splash followed by endless darkness and paralyzing cold.

The silhouette in the headlights said, "If I was amenable to such an arrangement, I would of course need guarantees that my property would be returned to me at the agreed-upon time. And I would need compensation immediately to make up for *delaying* my gratification."

Will said, "I would suggest nothing less. How about a nice used Toyota Furia?"

Zoey's driverless car came flying onto the ice, smashing into the man and throwing him onto the hood. A split second later, man and car went crashing through the ice, sinking into the frigid pond so close to Zoey that the splash threw freezing droplets of water onto her stunned face.

Will said, "RUN!"

Zoey did not need those instructions. She took off in the opposite direction of the car-sized hole behind her, praying there was a path of solid ice between her and the bank of snowy dead grass that marked the shore. She took a step, fell, crawled, stumbled to her feet, nearly fell again, then slid and skidded her way incrementally forward. She made frustratingly slow progress, like one of those nightmares where you run and run but the light at the end of the hall just stretches farther and farther away. She was about ten feet from the shore when she heard the ice below her shatter once and for all.

She was in freefall, the world gone beneath her feet. It happened in slow motion—first she felt the stabbing freeze of the ice water swallowing her feet, then her calves, then her knees. Then the bitter, frigid depths engulfed her knees, and then her . . . knees. This was when Zoey realized the water this close to shore was only knee-deep. She sloshed through the broken ice and climbed onto dry land, and only then turned back to see her poor Toyota gurgling as it pushed its nose deeper into the depths, taking the psychopath with it.

From the phone in her hand, Will said, "Are you all right?" Zoey faintly heard the other voice in the background, the man remotely operating the car, say, "I can't believe that shit worked."

Zoey said, "I'm hanging up. You offered to let that guy eat me to death."

David Wong

Will said, "That wasn't a real offer, it was a delaying tactic. Half of negotiation is about dealing with people on their level. Speaking of which, we need to have a word."

"I'm not *negotiating* with you."

"Right, overcoming resistance to negotiation is the other half of negotiation. Can you get somewhere where we can talk?"

"I'm freezing and I'm stranded. I have no idea where I even am."

"Circle around the pond and take The Hyena's car. It's still running, and he won't be needing it."

THREE

Zoey sat shivering in the serial killer's Changfeng sedan, a cheap rental that nonetheless had a wonderful working heater that was pure bliss against her soaked jeans. She had driven away from the pond and parked in the shadowy rear of a building downtown that was marked as a real estate office but by its shape had clearly once been a Pizza Hut. Zoey shivered, put her head in her hands, breathed slowly, and tried to gather herself. The hologram man in her phone was now sipping from a glass of scotch, while under him scrolled a notification that her mother had tried to call.

Zoey said to her phone, "All right. Who are you again?"

"Will Blackwater. I worked for you father."

"Right, and he's dead? Did I hear you say that?"

"Yes. In an accident. There was . . . an explosion."

"What, was it a meth lab or something?"

"No, nothing like that. Or maybe it was, no one is quite sure. I'm terribly sorry for your loss. He was . . . a great man."

"Mr. Blackwater, I only met that man like two times in my entire life. The first time I ever saw him was when I was eight. It was my birthday. He gave me a football, because somebody told him I was a tomboy. The last time I was sixteen, so it's been . . . like five years at least. He was a total stranger to me. So, why would him getting exploded to death cause people to come after me?"

"It's just a misunderstanding. But there is a contract out on you and you'll be in danger until we clear it up."

"A contract? As in, whoever kills me gets paid a bunch of money?"

"They actually need you alive."

"Oh, well at least there's that."

"But the contract specifies that after you've served your purpose, they can have their way with you. It's difficult to explain and also moot, as long as we're both in agreement we don't want you falling into their hands. Zoey, we need you to come to the city. Have you ever been to Tabula Rasa?"

The actual spelling of the city's name was Tabula Ra$a, with a dollar sign instead of an "S," because that's what happens when a bunch of rich douchebags build a brand-new city in the desert and reserve the right to name it themselves.

"I've never been, and I'm not going now. I'm going to the police. And then I'm going to bed."

"That would be a mistake. We've already made plans for accommodations here, we already have a car on the way, it will be there in a few hours. We'll give you a location and a limousine will—"

"Wait, a limo? How many drugs did Arthur Livingston have to sell to afford one of those?" She was never going to refer to the man as her "dad," since the connection was genetic only and she would disavow even that if she could.

"Listen, Zoey, this must be done quickly, for everyone's sake. There could be other bad guys en route right now."

"I . . . I'll think about it. I have to talk to my mom."

"It's dangerous to involve her. You shouldn't even go back home."

"I'd need to pack a bag. And I have to tell her *something*."

"Tell her that your father unexpectedly passed and that his estate has requested that you make an emergency trip to his estate to meet with his associates. Tell her you were so stunned by this news that you drove your car into a pond. Tell her that to compensate you for the inconvenience, the estate is prepared to pay you fifty thousand dollars. That last part is true, by the way." He paused, to let that sink in, then added, "That should cover the damage to your car plus pay you the equivalent of a year's salary in addition."

Zoey had a solid line of reasoning in her brain that demonstrated with perfect clarity why she should refuse, but it was quickly obscured behind a chorus line of dancing dollar signs. Fifty thousand was actually way more than one year's salary—she worked at a coffee bar, after all. It was the kind of money that could get her and her mom both out of the trailer park, or to a nicer trailer park, anyway. It could get her back into school. She could get a degree in some lucrative field, like nanotechnology. Then she could open a quaint little nanotechnology boutique in Fort Drayton, next to the bait shop. Still, Arthur Livingston was a criminal, which meant this man who "worked" for him was also a criminal, regardless of what kind of fancy little suit he wore in his holograms. That meant the chase that had just occurred was really between two factions of bad guys—he had, after all, just told her not to go to the police.

She asked, "If I leave, how do I know more bad guys won't come after my mom while I'm gone?"

"If you leave, they'll have no reason to. The contract is on you, not her. But if you stay, then *I guarantee you that more of them will come*, which means that just by delaying, you're putting both you and your mother in danger. Making this trip is literally the only safe option."

Zoey remembered the psycho's soft call of *Come back off the ice, sweetie*, and shuddered.

She said, "All right, how do I know you're not just more bad guys trying to collect on this 'contract' yourselves?"

"Honestly? We don't need the money. And if we meant you harm, couldn't we have just driven your car into an abutment earlier?"

That made sense, she supposed. Still, she wasn't getting into a car with any of these people. Even if she decided to make the trip to Tabula Ra$a—which on some level she knew would be incredibly stupid and reckless—she'd find her own way there.

Will said, "Are you still there?"

"Prove the money offer is real."

"Hold on. All right, check your account. I just sent you five hundred dollars." Zoey logged into her bank account and found he wasn't lying— she now had a total of five hundred and seventeen dollars in her savings. Zoey sucked in a breath and thought, *we can get the refrigerator fixed.* Will said, "The rest I can put into an escrow account, give me twenty minutes and I'll set it up. If you agree to make the trip."

"I'll think about it. But don't bother with the car, if I go I'll take the train."

"Ms. Ashe, I would strongly, strongly advise you *not* to—"

She hung up.

It was seven p.m., if she took the train out of Denver, she could be in Tabula Ra$a by midnight. She pulled into traffic, not realizing that a tiny camera The Hyena kept on his dash had recorded her entire conversation, or that more than 1.5 million people were watching.

FOUR

Zoey didn't want to be paranoid, but there was something about the man in the loincloth made of charred doll heads that made her nervous.

He was at the opposite end of the train car, standing in the aisle muttering to himself, his only other item of clothing a pair of blacked-out welder's goggles that made him look like he had bug eyes. When he had boarded at Salt Lake City, Zoey had immediately assumed he was another crazy who had come for her, but then he had just silently taken a standing spot at the other end of the car and she felt bad for prejudging him. Still, Zoey studiously avoided looking his direction, as any mass transit commuter can tell you that the only way to counter the dark powers of the mentally ill is to avoid eye contact. She gazed out of the window at the scrub brush blurring past at 250 miles an hour. She wondered if her head would go flying off if she stuck it out the window. Her cat meowed a complaint from inside the plastic carrier on her lap.

Zoey's nerves were eating her alive. For the tenth time she pulled out her phone and logged into the escrow account, mostly just because she liked seeing the $49,500.00 displayed on the screen. She dropped her phone back into her purse and nervously started scraping black polish off her thumbnail with her bottom teeth. It was her first time on the high-speed rail and for about five minutes she had been awed by the speed, and then she had quickly gotten bored and started to notice how much this particular car smelled like pee. She had bought her ticket at the gate and the only open seat was this one at the very rear of the car, next to the restroom. Whoever designed the train had put the seat about three inches too close to the restroom door, so it bumped her seat every time somebody went in or out. It had happened exactly nineteen times so far and what was worse was that each person who did it would stop and look down at her like, *whose idea was it to put this weird* girl *in the way?*

Someone said, "What's your cat's name?"

Zoey gave a start, because for a moment she thought the male voice was the crazy homeless guy with the doll heads on his crotch. But it wasn't, it was the stranger in the seat next to her, a fancy young man in an old-fashioned suit who had been checking his email constantly for the last couple of hours via a pair of wired-up eyeglasses. She looked him over and got the sense that this kid had taken vacations that cost more than she made in a year.

Zoey forced what she hoped was a friendly smile and said, "Excuse me?"

"Your cat. What's his name?"

"Stench Machine."

"Really? That's mean." He grinned, flashing perfect teeth.

"Have you smelled him?"

"No, but still."

Zoey finger-petted Stench Machine through a slot in the crate. He was a Persian, white except for his face and chest, which were black fading to brown (he looked like somebody had thrown a cup of coffee in his face, and the fur around his mouth gave it a downturned expression that made it look like he wasn't at all happy about it). He wore a black leather collar encircled with silver spikes. It made him look like a punk rock cat, Zoey thought.

Jacob asked, "Does he answer to that name?"

"Cats don't answer to anything."

"My name is Jacob, by the way."

"Good to meet you." Zoey realized she was supposed to give him her name at that point, but even when she wasn't a target for abduction, she didn't go trusting train strangers that easily.

Jacob asked, "Is this your first trip to Tabula Rasa?"

"Yes, and I'm already a little freaked out. I grew up in Colorado, a tiny place called Fort Drayton. It's way out in the boonies. Just to give you an idea, at the entrance of the—" She almost said "trailer park" but caught herself in time. "—uh, subdivision where we live, there's this big statue of an elk, made of concrete. And the whole thing is chipped with bullet holes where over the years drunken hunters have shot it by mistake."

Jacob laughed, showing those perfect teeth. Zoey squashed the jealousy she always felt toward people whose parents had actually taken them to the dentist as a kid. She was missing a lower canine due to a skateboarding accident when she was eleven, and had a chipped incisor due to an encounter with a drunken stepdad. She suddenly wished she had more than just the one amusing anecdote about Fort Drayton to share with Jacob. She could tell him about that time the high school basketball team made it to the state finals and one of the players got diarrhea during the game. . . .

Another person shuffled down the aisle toward the restroom, and this person *also* glanced down at her, an act that was starting to seem intentional—Zoey swore everyone who passed was doing it. Did she still have chili stuck to her face? This time it was a black teenage girl with wired-up glasses like the ones Jacob was wearing, which meant for all Zoey knew the girl had the built-in camera on and was broadcasting a feed, maybe one called something like *The Worst Hair Dye Jobs on Mass Transit Daily* (today's episode: "The Cat Girl in the Back Row with Cyan Bangs").

Jacob said, "Well, you're about to enter a whole new world out here. How much do you know about it?"

"I know it didn't exist twenty years ago, it was just an empty patch of desert in Utah. Then a bunch of rich people started putting up skyscrapers and suddenly there's a city there. There's no government, right? That's all I know. Oh and every picture I see of Tabula Rasa looks like the Blade Runner universe is holding a Mardi Gras parade."

Jacob laughed again. "Yeah I'd say you're in for a bit of culture shock. There is no place like it on earth. Your phone will never die, though, there's wireless power coils under everything. Charges the cars as they drive."

"Great, maybe I'll get cancer while I'm there."

Zoey glanced at the doll head man again, and thought she had caught him staring at her—it was hard to tell behind his bug-eye goggles. She watched as the man stuck a filterless cigarette between cracked lips. He then casually lifted his hand, touched the end of the cigarette with his finger, and lit it. *With his finger.*

Jacob said, "There's construction everywhere. After dark, it looks like the half-finished buildings are full of fireflies, all the crews in there working through the night, welding the metalwork—"

"Did you see that? What that man just did?"

Jacob glanced toward the doll head man. "Yeah there's no smoking on these trains. You want to tell him or should I?"

"No, he . . . never mind." Zoey decided the guy must have had a match hidden in his palm, or something.

Jacob stared at the guy in amusement and asked, "Are those tiny heads glued to his crotch?"

"You know what the scariest part is about people like him? Everything he's doing makes perfect sense in his own mind."

"Ha! Though I guess that's true of all of us."

No one else had noticed the doll head guy doing his cigarette trick. Yet, just in the time Zoey was looking that direction, two other passengers had craned their heads around to look at *her.* She knew she wasn't just being paranoid now—one at a time they would glace around their seat or raise up a bit to see over, peer back, then quickly turn around again when they saw she was meeting their gaze. The bathroom door bumped Zoey's seat. The black girl shuffled past and she made a point to look down at Zoey *again.* She felt to see if there was something in her hair, but then remembered she was still wearing the knit cap she had pulled down over her ears during the ride to Denver. Were they making fun of the hat? Or maybe they were looking at Jacob? Was he a celebrity?

"Anyway," Jacob said, "it's amazing how fast they can build them now. You leave for vacation, and when you come back a week later there's one less gap in the skyline, you have to stare at it for a minute to figure out what they added. They're amazing to watch, the way they work. They never stop."

" 'They?' What, like robots?"

"No, Mexicans. All of the crews are immigrants on work visas. Great workers, though."

"Oh . . . that's kind of racist, isn't it?"

"Is it? I mean, I guess some of them are probably bad workers. Anyway it's kind of mesmerizing to watch them go, they have these huge fabricators right there on the job site, like big 3-D printers that just ride up the side of the building and stamp out whole sections of wall, ready to assemble." Zoey tried to figure out if Jacob was hitting on her or if he was just bored from the train ride. She imagined the scary doll guy coming back and pulling a weapon or something, and Jacob punching him out like one of those old-timey boxers. Jacob continued, "One Friday on the way home from work, I made an offhand comment to my friend about how I wished we had a Falafel Fusion joint in our neighborhood. Then when I was on my way home from work Monday evening, there it was! They had built it over the weekend, almost like they had heard me say that. It went from vacant lot to open business in less than seventy-two hours. That's Tabula Rasa in a nutshell—you blink and the landscape changes around you. It's like an American Dubai, back when Dubai was Dubai."

Zoey mumbled, "Yeah, that's weird," and she knew Jacob picked up on the fact that she wasn't really paying attention. He fell silent. Thinking desperately of something to fill the lull in the conversation, Zoey said, "Do you like your glasses? My ex-boyfriend couldn't live without his, but they always give me a headache when he let me put them on."

Occasionally Jacob's eyes would dart up and to the right and she knew he was refreshing an inbox that was only visible to him, otherwise she had no idea what he was actually seeing out of the glasses. They made games where you could bounce a little rubber ball off the faces of the people in the room (the ball was only visible to you, of course) or that would obscure everything with a fantasy world and leave you blind to your surroundings, which if you did it on the bus, was a good way to get your purse stolen. But either way, any time you talked to a person who was wearing the glasses, you never knew if they were actually seeing you.

Jacob said, "You get used to them. They leave kind of an afterimage when you take them off, and you find yourself constantly looking around for your notifications."

"My boyfriend downloaded an app that would superimpose a cartoon mustache on anyone he was talking to. He'd laugh and laugh. The glasses got broken when he got hit in the face with a football and I was kind of glad." She realized she was now talking about her ex-boyfriend a little too much, and in fact had forgotten to add the "ex" just then. She quickly added, "He was stupid. We broke up two months ago."

That was pretty subtle, right?

Jacob said, "If you're free over the weekend I'll show you around the city. There's tons to do." Huh. So he was probably another serial killer. Still, this was Thursday night; she wondered if she could lose twenty-five pounds or gain four inches in height by Saturday. Then she realized that, while she was thinking about it, she had neglected to actually answer his offer and had created an awkward moment by leaving him hanging. Jacob, trying to cover for it, said, "So what brings you into the big city, Zoey?"

"My father—my *biological* father—died." Wait—when had she told Jacob her name?

"Oh, I'm sorry. When's the funeral?"

"I'm, uh, not sure. They said they needed me for some other stuff, legal paperwork or something. It's pretty weird."

"What happened? He couldn't have been very old, you're only—"

"Twenty-two. It was an accident. I don't know anything yet. They said something blew up."

"Wait, was it that warehouse explosion?"

"Yeah, I guess so. Unless there was more than one. You heard about it?"

"Everybody did, it was big news. So you're Arthur Livingston's daughter? I'm so sorry for your loss."

"Was he famous?"

"Around the city, yeah. Probably could have run for mayor, if the city had a mayor."

"Well, good for him."

Jacob picked up on her cold tone and went quiet, creating Zoey's second awkward silence of her five-minute relationship with Jacob. She pictured bringing him home to her trailer in Fort Drayton, this kid in his three-piece tweed suit with the silk tie and dainty gold pocket watch chain dangling across his vest. She imagined him pulling up in a restored classic car that rolled in silently on battery power, then getting out with a walking stick and striding to the door. Then Zoey would invite him to sit on a sofa that was covered in cigarette burns and frayed wounds inflicted by cat claws. At that point she pictured him either running for his life, or staying and offering to rescue her from the squalor. She didn't know which would be worse.

Zoey noticed a tiny pinprick of blue light at the corner of his glasses near the hinge, and said, "Oh, is that on? Were we live this whole time?"

The wired glasses all came with forward-facing video cameras that could be left on around the clock, broadcasting everything you did. If you didn't want to wear the glasses but still wanted to livestream your life to the world, you were in luck—you could get those tiny cameras in any accessory you could imagine—pocket watches, necklaces, earrings, tie clips, hats, little copper dragonflies that teenage girls clipped to their hair, whatever. You didn't need a viewfinder, the camera captured a panoramic view of everything in front of you, with software that automatically zoomed and focused on faces and other points of interest—you just turned it on and it recorded your life. The kids these days (and ever since she got out of high school, Zoey had thought of everyone under twenty as a "kid") never left the house without a live feed running.

So who was watching their broadcasts? Nobody, or everybody—if they left the feed public, anyone could jump in and watch. The cumulative cloud of all of these millions of connected camera feeds was referred to as the Blink network, or just "Blink." As in, "Did you see the fight between Ayden and Madison at Isaac's party?" "No, but I saw the Blink." Occasionally you'd hear someone use it in past tense, saying they "Blunked" their whole vacation and that you should totally watch it. If you obstructed their feed they'd say you "Blanked" them, and they'd refer to their Blink followers as their "Blinkers," at which point Zoey usually felt the urge to stab them. The point was, that little blue light on Jacob's glasses meant a thousand people could have been listening in on their conversation this whole time. She tried to remember if she had said anything embarrassing.

Jacob put a hand to his glasses and said, "Oh, yeah, I'm so sorry. Jesus, I should have told you it was on. I don't even think about it. Don't worry, I don't have any followers, and lately it's just my mom and a couple of guys from Pakistan who want to see what America is like. The only people watching right now is an old couple who jumped in when I boarded, they're planning a trip and wanted to see how clean the train was."

"Oh. Did you tell them it smells like pee?"

"I did not, but I assume they heard you say it just now."

He tapped his glasses and the little blue light blinked off. The light was mandated by law, so pervs couldn't sneak them into locker rooms without everybody knowing they were part of a live broadcast. But Zoey didn't think the light was near prominent enough, considering she hadn't noticed it until just now. Her eyes drifted toward the window again. The scrub brush and occasional mountains had been replaced by a dirt field growing rows of wood frames that would eventually bloom into housing developments. Black ribbons of newly paved roads undulated between them in gentle curves, sometimes ending abruptly where they met an empty space that would probably be another development a year from now. Zoey noticed that as they got closer to the city, the houses became more finished and had less motion blur—the train was slowing down. She looked around for the doll head guy. He had moved a few rows closer, where he had finished his cigarette and was now smashing the butt under a bare foot, grinding it into the carpet.

Eager to restart the conversation with Jacob, Zoey said, "So what's it's like, living in Tabula Rasa?"

He thought for a moment and said, "Overload."

"What does that mean?"

"You'll see. The population sign comes with an epilepsy warning. Oh, and you can fight a bear, if you want."

"You can what a what?"

"You can pay twenty bucks and a guy will let you fight a bear. In the park, there's a roped off area and you get five minutes to fight a grizzly bear."

"How is that legal?"

He shrugged. "Everything's legal when there's nobody to enforce the law. Three months ago half the cops went to jail in this big bribery scandal. Most of the rest walked off the job. Paychecks were bouncing, it's a huge mess. They've got such a backlog that nothing gets prosecuted."

"Wait, really? Who do you call if a psychopath breaks into your—"

"Look."

He was nodding toward her window. Zoey looked and thought, *overload*.

On the horizon was a cylindrical skyscraper with a gigantic serpent curling around it. The snake writhed and twisted and turned menacing red eyes toward the train. It opened its mouth and hissed. Below it appeared the words, "COMING DECEMBER 23." The building, Zoey realized, was wrapped in crystal clear video screens from roof to foundation, every single window flashing one continuous animation—an ad for a movie. The huge, computer-animated snake snapped around and writhed off *onto the building next to it,* twisting its massive emerald body around letters five stories high that said, "JADEN SMITH IN . . ." The serpent slithered along the skyline, and Zoey realized that every structure in downtown Tabula Ra$a was synced to carry a continuous video along every inch of its surface, the snake sliding smoothly from one building to the next, the ad playing to the people on the arriving train. The serpent then crawled onto the front of the domed roof of the train station they were about to pull into, wrapping its body around red block letters that spelled, "JADEN SMITH FIGHTS A GIANT SNAKE."

Jacob said, "I like how literal they are with the titles now, you know exactly what you're getting."

The animated snake then *burst out of the ceiling of the station,* climbing into the night sky—Zoey gasped, startled for a moment before she realized it was just a hologram set up on the roof of the building, positioned to give the illusion the snake had broken free of the screen. A couple of the people on the train gasped and laughed and took pictures. Zoey noticed Jacob had a big stupid grin on his face. He had seen her jump. She elbowed him and told him to shut up, but she knew she was smiling, too, and had to remind herself to keep her lips closed as not to show off her substandard teeth. And then the train slipped between skyscrapers and suddenly downtown Tabula Ra$a was puking gaudy colors all over her window.

Looming over them was a crystal canyon of towers in various stages of construction—they passed a hotel that blasted a Sony ad into the heavens, then a building that was just a darkened framework of girders topped with cranes that stuck out like a spiky haircut. Zoey looked down and saw that below the rail was a gleaming, blinking river of cars. Swimming in the slow current of cabs and fleet vehicles were the flamboyant, tricked-out rides of the kind of people who were (a) rich enough to drive and park in the city and (b) hadn't been rich long enough to develop any taste. There was a bright red motorcycle whose body had been molded in the shape of a dragon, the rider an Asian guy in a green suit with a six-inch-tall pompadour wig. Hulking in the next lane was a monster truck on tires as tall as a man, a jet of blue flames pouring out of completely unnecessary chrome pipes. Behind it was a Ferrari from the 2020s with an LED paint job flashing undulating colors that rippled across its body in beautiful psychedelic patterns. Behind it, a massive retrofitted 1960s Cadillac convertible, sporting a white leather interior and a huge black man in a white cowboy hat.

Just off the pavement on one side of the street was a deep trench where work crews in orange vests were laying some kind of underground cable. Their project was slicing right through a construction site where someone else was trying to dig out a foundation for yet another building, pallets of brick and bags of cement scattered like islands in the dirt, a flow of tire tracks swirling around every obstacle where forklifts and Bobcats had scurried to and fro.

And swarming over all of this were the people. With no finished sidewalks to speak of, pedestrians leaked out into the gridlocked traffic, shuffling between bumpers. There were drunk girls in tiny dresses and fake hair giggling and leaning on each other, packs of burly guys off to construction jobs, Japanese kids in sunglasses and glue-on sideburns, Indian families with double-digit packs of kids. Every fifth person wore one of those irritating blinking shirts, fabric that flashed brand logos or obscene sayings or cartoon characters performing the same looping animation over and over. Flickering, pulsing torsos floating around taillights, everyone screaming for attention in a cloud of light and noise. Zoey had to remind herself that this is what the city was like at eleven p.m., *on a Thursday.*

Zoey asked Jacob, "Do you *like* it here?"

He laughed. "That's a complicated question. All I know is that now I can't tolerate living anywhere else."

The train was gently penetrating the station now, brakes whining against the rail. They passed a parking garage bearing glowing signs promoting all of the standard car rental franchises. Standing on each side of the entrance were men in black suits and ties, which Zoey thought brought a nice touch of class to a parking garage, until she noticed they were carrying machine guns.

Zoey said, "Tell me those guys are cops."

Jacob leaned over to see out her window, casually pressing his body against hers, and said, "Private security. Those guys are probably Co-Op, you can tell by the suits. A bunch of the bigger companies pooled their money to fund their own security when it became clear the city's police were worthless. It's a good thing, you call the cops here, you get voice mail telling you to leave a message."

"Oh, wow. So you get in trouble, you call those guys instead?"

"You probably can't afford those particular guys, Co-Op is more for corporate customers. But yes, private security is who you call. There's a big board online where you can post jobs and they bid on them. It gets kind of crazy, half of the guys are freelancers who either got their private security licenses by taking a five-day gun safety class, or by paying forty bucks for a fake one. It's a little bit Wild West out here. That's what I was saying, somebody like you shouldn't walk around alone."

Jacob was still leaning against her and she smelled aftershave and hair gel. He let out a breath that Zoey felt on her neck and settled back into his seat. He reached into an inside pocket and pulled out a sterling silver flask, and took a sip.

He held it out to Zoey and said, "It's going to be cold out there, this'll warm you up."

As far as she knew, she had never in her life drank from an unmarked container from a stranger. She didn't like germs and she didn't like getting slipped date rape drugs, but how often do you meet a rich, handsome stranger on a train? She took a drink and felt lava ooze down her throat. Whiskey. She coughed and they both laughed, and she felt like she was in some dumb movie. They were in the station now, a half-finished geodesic dome that Zoey thought when completed would be absolutely stunning, or the ugliest building in America—it was too early to tell. The finished parts were all glass arches with art deco flourishes, alternately futuristic and old-fashioned. The rest was a tangled mess of exposed steel skeleton and bundles of wiring that dangled like innards, as if the building had been in a knife fight.

Just off the platform, behind the hundreds of waiting travelers, was a row of fast-food and -drink franchises Zoey had never seen before. She was a little ashamed of how excited they made her, but Fort Drayton only had five places to eat and one of them was a gas station. Tabula

Ra$a's train station alone had twice that many. Just from her seat she spotted an AwesomeChanga franchise, where according to the ads you could get just about anything as long as it could be wrapped in a thick tortilla and deep fried to a crisp. Next to it was a Waffle Burger, which is just what it sounds like, and then a Go-Juice bar serving a long line of exhausted passengers waiting to pay nine dollars for a mixed fountain drink containing four hundred milligrams of caffeine and twelve percent alcohol. Next to it was a From-the-Oven cookie stand with a clear glass oven under the counter where you could watch them bake chocolate chip cookies right in front of you. Then they'd pull them out and shove them into your hand, still warm, the chips melting all over the wax paper. Zoey decided after she got off the train she would stand over there and just smell that place for half an hour. At the end there was a beverage joint called Spiked Ice, selling sugary fruit smoothies that, according to their sign, were laced with "fuel shots" that sounded illegal as hell—Codeine, Lithium, Hash Oil, DXM, Modafinil. She half wondered how such a place could just operate in the open, cops or no cops, but mostly she just wondered how much the drinks cost and which one she would get. The line in front of it was the longest of all.

Stench Machine meowed and stuck a paw through a slot in the crate, getting restless. He had never been put in an enclosed space for this long and he was probably wondering where the stink was coming from. The train finally bumped to a stop and Zoey heard the passengers up by the door stand and start wrestling carry-on bags out of the overhead bins . . . and easily half a dozen of the passengers glanced back at her as they did it. And yes, they were looking at her, not Jacob. She had an urge to stand up and ask them what they were staring at, but decided she was being silly. She needed to find her hotel, and was about to ask Jacob for a ride but right as she opened her mouth a new voice said, "You know what's the difference between you and me?"

It was the doll head man, shouldering his way through the departing passengers. Looking right at her.

"You," he said, to Zoey. "With the blue streaks in your hair. Do you know what's the difference between you and me?"

He edged up until he was looming over them in the aisle. The rest of the passengers were shuffling away behind him, grateful to be on the other side of the crazy man's attention.

Jacob said, "Come on."

He made as if to stand and bring Zoey along with him, but Doll Head put a hand on Jacob's shoulder and pushed him firmly back into his seat. The man was not huge, but had a body like leather stretched over bundles of steel cable.

Jacob said, "Buddy, we don't want any trouble, just move along or we're gonna have to call the—"

"Shut up. I'm talking to her." He rested his hands on a pair of seat backs, arms and torso forming a bridge across the aisle. He squeezed the seat cushions and veins throbbed under his biceps. Zoey saw her own pale face reflected in the man's pitch-black goggles. "And I asked her a question. Do you know what's the difference between you and me?"

Exasperated, Zoey said, "I don't know. What?"

Doll head man smiled. "The difference," he whispered, "is that *I* would never have let a stranger intimidate me into answering such a question."

Jacob said, "Now you listen here—"

The doll head man, without looking at him, raised his right hand to Jacob's face. He snapped his fingers and there was a crackle and a piercing flash of bluish white light, like the man had just spawned a tiny lightning bolt from his fingertips. Stench Machine hissed and thrashed inside the crate.

Jacob recoiled and said, "What the—"

The man shushed him. "I am *talking to her.* There is a long, long line waiting to feed off this chubby little piglet. Please *wait your turn.*"

Yep, her first instinct had been right. This psychopath was here to finish the job that had been left undone by the last psychopath, both presumably sent by someone who had an endless ready supply of them. And here she thought she was being open-minded. It hit Zoey all at once that she had just traded a gruesome death for fifty thousand dollars—not even enough for her mom to buy a nice car later, even if Livingston's people followed through with payment, which they almost certainly wouldn't.

Zoey peered around the man to see if there was a guard, or conductor, or burly passenger, or *anyone* paying any attention to what was happening in the back of the train. But no one in uniform appeared, and none of the shuffling passengers wanted any part of whatever was going on with the crazy naked hobo and the young couple he was tormenting. This man, Zoey realized, now had absolute power in this tiny corner of the world.

She was going to die on this train.

"Do you know what these are?" He gestured toward the doll heads. Zoey didn't answer. He said, "It is rude not to answer direct questions."

"They look like doll heads that you've melted with a lighter or a blowtorch. Because you thought they would make you look scary."

The man grinned. "They are souls. Each represents a soul I have taken. I am the Soul Collector. They will serve me in eternity."

Before Zoey could even begin to formulate a reply, a bored but authoritative voice said, "You need to clear out the car, pal . . ."

Finally. All three of them looked up to where a balding man in a gray uniform was leaning in the sliding door. His eyes met Doll Head's inhuman black goggles and all of the color drained from his face.

"N-now we don't want any trouble here. Whatever business you got with those folks, just clear out and take care of it elsewhere, all right? No need to hold up the train."

Zoey glared at him. "Are you kidding me? Call the cops!"

Doll Head turned away from the uniform, facing his hostages again. He smiled and said, "I agree with the blue-haired piglet completely. Call the police. Call Co-Op. Call the black vests. Call the LOB. Tell them all that the Soul Collector has Arthur Livingston's daughter. If anyone tries to enter this train, or if she does not give me what I want, I will add her to my collection."

FIVE

The platform was now crowded with onlookers recording the scene from dozens of tiny cameras, people probably watching their viewer counts skyrocket as word spread that someone was about to be lightninged to death by an escaped mental patient. No one made to intervene, they just watched in dull curiosity as if Zoey, Jacob, and Homeless Zeus were behind the glass at a zoo enclosure. Doll Head stalked up and down the aisle of the train car, glaring out of the windows at the crowd. Zoey realized he wasn't trying to scare the onlookers away, but was making sure all their cameras had a chance to get a clear shot of him. At one point he stood in the open doorway, raised his hand, and with a crackle that made the whole crowd flinch, did that lightning trick with his fingers. The audience was impressed. Zoey wondered if she had lost her freaking mind.

Something else that was weird, which had almost gone unnoticed by Zoey due to the other, weirder things happening in her life at the moment, was that there were *a lot* of armed people in that crowd. Scattered among the gray-jumpsuited rail staff, white-shirted security guards, and hundreds of gawkers, Zoey could see half a dozen of the Co-Op guys in their black suits and ties, looking like Secret Service agents with their little machine guns pointed at the air. Then she counted at least five more men and women in black vests full of pockets, wearing amber wraparound shades and black backward baseball caps, clutching assault rifles with fingerless gloves. And then there were the armed loners—the odd man or woman who didn't seem to be part of any team. There was one guy in a tank top with two pistols in shoulder holsters, beside him was a bald Japanese guy in a leather jacket with a katana on his back, then a woman with pink hair and a short double-barreled shotgun strapped to each thigh. They hadn't shown up in response to the developing hostage situation—they hadn't had time. They must have been waiting there, but why?

"I have to say," thundered Doll Head, striding up the aisle, "they were wise to hide you on the train. But I found you, as was my destiny. Now you have seen the power inside me. You know what I can do to you."

Zoey replied, "Okay, don't, uh, go into a psychotic rage here or anything, because I'm more than happy to cooperate. But right now *I have no idea what you're talking about.* Okay? I know there's some kind of contract. But here's the thing—I don't know who wants me, or what they want me for, or anything else. And I *don't want to know.*"

Doll Head grinned. "You are truly Arthur Livingston's daughter. I should have expected nothing less."

"Did he owe you guys money? Is that what this is about? Did he screw you on a drug deal or something? Whatever it is, I don't care—if you want me to call the guy I talked to earlier and tell him to pay, I'll do it. But I *didn't know Arthur Livingston.* He tried to give me a car for my sixteenth birthday, I gave it back. His money was dirty, I wanted no part of it."

"Good. So you will open his vault for me."

"I would absolutely do that, if I knew where it was, or *what* it was, or how to get into it. But I swear, this is the first I'm hearing of it."

"I want you to know that I am not surprised, nor disappointed. In fact, I should have been disappointed in anything less. After all, you have no reason to respect me. Like all who have power, you only respect others who have it. You need me to demonstrate my power to you. So that you can respect me, and deal with me as an equal."

"No, no, you really don't—"

Doll Head reached out with his left hand and grabbed Jacob by the throat.

Jacob thrashed and tried to twist out of the man's grip. His perfect hair tumbled down into his eyes as he choked out the words, "Hey! No! What are you—let go!" Doll Head was not choking him. Just keeping him in place. "Zoey!" hissed Jacob, tendons straining in his neck, face turning red with panic and exertion. "Just do . . . what he says . . ."

Doll Head said, "Shhhhhhhh" and, continuing to pin Jacob to the seat with his left hand, reached out and laid the other hand gently on Jacob's forehead. He held his palm against Jacob's brow, pressing his thumb against one temple and his middle finger against the other, gripping his skull like a bowling ball.

"Zoey . . . tell him . . . how to . . ."

"Shhhhhhhhh."

"*Please.*"

"Shhhhhhhhh. The only human destiny is to succumb to one stronger."

There was a pop, and a sizzle, and smoke. Jacob's body went rigid, his hands clenched and flew to his chest, his feet kicked the seat in front of him. One shoe flew off. There was a stink like steamed broccoli. Zoey's cat howled and hissed and tried to claw his way out of the crate. Doll Head withdrew his hand and Jacob slumped back, his eyes open but blank, his mouth hanging slack. A low gurgle escaped from deep in his throat, a line of drool ran from his mouth, a pool of urine spread across his lap. In Jacob's temple was a smoking hole made by the electrical current that had fried his brain.

Zoey screamed. "WHAT DID YOU DO? WHAT DID YOU DO?!?!"

"I have freed him from that weak husk. He has joined me, become part of something far more powerful. Only the limp vessel remains. I have added him to my collection."

It was chaos out on the platform. A TV camera crew was now covering the situation live, and Zoey heard the soft drumming of helicopters outside the station. The big screen that ran along the rear wall had flipped away from the local weather report and switched to live coverage of the scene. The headline that crawled along the bottom was not, as Zoey expected, "Crazy man holds up train" or "Hobo harnesses the power of lightning." No, what it said was:

LIVINGSTON DAUGHTER HELD HOSTAGE

Zoey clenched her teeth and wondered how many times she was going to have to pay for her mom having chosen a scumbag for a sperm donor. Jacob, his half-closed eyes twitching aimlessly around the cabin but seeing nothing, slumped over against her. Zoey pushed him off and screamed through her window at the people on the platform.

"HELP ME! HE'S GOING TO KILL ME!"

Once more, they just stared. Up until that point in her life, Zoey had lived every moment with the unspoken assumption there was always *somebody* she could call if things went to hell. Her mom, a teacher, the police, God. But now she was trapped in this giant steel tube—just her, and this man, and death. Maybe everyone feels like this at the end. The ice breaks under your feet and you realize that there had never been anything below you but cold and darkness. It was the point at which things could not get worse.

There was a stir in the crowd. People started to turn, to look back at the main entrance of the station. Then the crowd parted, slowly, as if a wild animal had wandered in and no one wanted to startle it with sudden movements. From the split in the crowd emerged first a huge black man, with a perfectly bald, polished head Zoey thought looked like a Whopper, the chocolate candy. She didn't know if that was racist or not, but all of the progressive attitudes in the world wouldn't change the fact that his head looked exactly like a Whopper. Behind him was a stunning but stern-looking Chinese woman, walking with the gait of someone whose skirt is too tight to be practical, but who is quite used to it. Behind her was a man in a cowboy hat with bushy eyebrows and a red nose who looked like he had popped out of a cartoon. Looming behind them was one more man she couldn't see clearly. But the crowd knew who he was, who they all were, and wanted no part of them. No one in the group was visibly armed, but not even the men with machine guns would make eye contact with them. Everyone just stood down.

The Soul Collector reached out a hand and pressed it against Zoey's brow, digging finger and thumb into her temples.

He whispered, "I can take your treasure, or I can take your soul. I desire no outcome over the other. You choose. You have three seconds. One."

"No! Listen!"

"Two."

"PLEASE! I'LL TAKE YOU TO THE SAFE OR WHATEVER IT IS WE'LL FIGURE IT OUT I'LL DO WHATEVER YOU—"

"STOP. I'm here."

At the door stood a striking, pale man in an overcoat and fedora. He had cold blue eyes and sharp cheekbones. His suit jacket, vest, shirt, and tie were all shades of gray and silver—Zoey thought it made him look like a robot. Nothing wrinkled when he walked, as if the clothes were the skin he was born with. She had seen this man once before, projected through her phone. The Soul Collector turned to face the man, arms loose at his sides, blocking the aisle with his body, putting himself between the silver suit and his prey.

Will Blackwater glanced around the train car as if assessing the situation, then calmly said, "First things first—are you all right?"

Zoey was about to answer when she realized Will was asking that of the Soul Collector, not her.

He smiled and said, "I wondered when you would arrive, Will."

Will stopped where he was and removed his hat. His hair was a black helmet that looked ready to withstand a hurricane.

"How are you doing, Brandon? Are you still taking your medication? You're not, are you?"

"I'm free of all of that now. Thanks to Molech, I have become my destiny. I am the Soul Collector."

"Yes, I can see that. The boy in the back there, is he dead?"

"His soul is with me now."

Will nodded, considering, as if doing some minor math in his head. "All right. That complicates things. I can get you out of here. But we have to go *now*. The girl looks unharmed. Is that correct?"

"Yes."

"All right. That's good. I'm sure you've noticed we've drawn quite a crowd here."

The Soul Collector cast a scornful glance toward the platform. "I possess a power that can reduce all of them to ashes."

"Well, I don't want to get ashes all over my suit, so let's go ahead and do this as cleanly as possible. We have a car outside and we can get you through this crowd without incident if we move *soon*." He looked past the Soul Collector and said to Zoey, "You're coming with us. We're taking you to your father's estate. That's where his vault is. Do I need to tell you that your best—and only—course of action is to comply?"

Zoey glanced at the brain-dead man slumped next to her, thin tendrils of smoke still drifting out of the burn holes in his temples, stinking like piss. She said, "Please. Just . . . let me go. Whatever shady business

Arthur Livingston was into, whatever money he had, the vault, I don't care about *any of that.*"

"It doesn't matter. You're involved because your father involved you, and now you're a hunk of meat in a kennel. If you don't do what I say, things will get bad in ways you cannot comprehend." Will stood straight, placed his hat back on his black helmet of hair, straightened his sleeves, and addressed them both. "Now, the situation is this. You see what's happening out on the platform. In the absence of an actual organized police department in this city, what we have instead is a gaggle of grossly unqualified and often mentally unstable hired guns. Every single one of them knows Livingston's daughter is here, each of them thinks they can get a payday out of this. It's a lot of very stupid people, pumped up on adrenaline, who know their every move is being broadcast to a live audience. We have to make it clear to them, and to everyone who may be laying in wait between here and our destination, that we are in charge of this situation. Now, I'm going to walk out that door first. Zoey, you'll be next. The Soul Collector will be right behind you. The moment we step out, we will be swarmed. Zoey is going to address the nearest camera and say the following. Listen carefully. Are you listening?"

Zoey nodded. Beside her, Jacob let out a guttural sound while his cloudy, unblinking eyes shifted aimlessly around the car. In a flash, a whole alternate future played in her head, one in which Zoey and Jacob arrive at the station without incident, the two of them shuffling off the train together. . . .

He carries her bag for her. On the platform, she gives him her cell number. They agree to meet on Saturday night. The day comes and Jacob picks her up at her hotel. Her handsome stranger has a convertible and even though it's December they put the top down and cruise through the chill air, the fifty-story video screens flashing ads and brand logos overhead. They go to a fancy restaurant, maybe one at the top of a tall hotel that looks out over the new city, and there's a long line but of course Jacob can get right in because he knows people. And afterward, they're waiting for the valet to bring the car around and the night air is cold and she's a little bit drunk and Jacob drapes his coat over her shoulders. . . .

Zoey said, "I'm listening."

"You're going to say, 'My name is Zoey Ashe. I am Arthur Livingston's daughter, and I am being held hostage. I have—"

"Held hostage by the Soul Collector," said the Soul Collector.

"Right. 'I am being held hostage by the Soul Collector. I have been told that if anyone tries to intervene, he will kill me. Please do not interfere with this process. All other bounties have been rescinded.' Got it? It doesn't have to be those exact words but the idea has to come across. Everything is under control, there is no money to be made if they interfere."

Zoey nodded. She stuck a finger into the cat crate and scratched Stench Machine's head. "Let's get out of here."

She stood, and realized Jacob's silver flask had fallen into her lap. It was wrong to take it, she barely knew the guy. But she took it anyway, and stuffed it into her purse. Something to remember him by, if she lived through this. The moment Zoey stood, a buzz went through the crowd outside, everyone trying to muscle into position, to get a shot of the hostage and captor emerging from the train. Will wrestled her carry-on from the overhead bin and stood by the door. Zoey followed as instructed, carrying Stench Machine's crate by her side.

Zoey felt a hand on her back, and flinched. Even through her jacket she thought she could feel a buzz from the Soul Collector's fingers, a jittery vibration like ants crawling between her shoulder blades. The door slid open and the noise hit her like a wall—reporters crowding around and screaming questions, gray uniforms trying to shove back the rubberneckers. All of the screens on the back wall were now tuned to the local news, and the local news was showing the three of them. Zoey watched their situation play out on the monitors five seconds after it occurred in real time—the tall man in the overcoat and fedora, followed by all five feet two inches of Zoey, looking pale and frazzled with black and blue bangs dangling out of her wool cap. Behind her, the strapping savage in the loincloth. The crowd backed off at the sight of him.

The trio edged out onto the platform, into the massive unfinished building that Zoey had only glimpsed from inside the train. She saw another train on the next platform over, the line to Las Vegas. All roads lead to Tabula Ra$a, a place that didn't even exist when she was born. A TV news crew rushed up, and then another. She was famous. It sucked.

Behind them, the guys in black vests and sunglasses prowled into position. The Co-Op men in suits with their little machine guns edged toward the door, to block the path. Will glanced back at Zoey and nodded. There were cameras all around now—hell, even the random onlookers were essentially walking cameras—so Zoey didn't look at any particular one.

"Um, can everyone be quiet? I'm supposed to say something."

She gave the commotion a moment to die down. She glanced back at the train car and saw paramedics rushing inside, to tend to Jacob. She wondered if his family was here in the crowd, or if they even lived in town.

"Okay, um, listen. I am being held hostage, by—" She couldn't bring herself to say his stupid name. "—the scary-looking man behind me. He has told me that if anyone tries to interfere, he will kill me."

A stir went through the crowd. Gasps. What the hell did they think was going on here? Zoey looked back at the TV screens again and saw the cameras had zoomed in on the Soul Collector's face. He was baring his yellow teeth, inscrutable eyes behind the bug-eye goggles, TV monitors along the back wall reflecting back his own face in their pure black lenses. He was soaking up the attention. Zoey realized she was watching the greatest moment of this man's life. She bit her lip so hard it bled.

Zoey cleared her throat and continued, "His name is the Soul Collector. He has magic powers."

Zoey turned to face the man and said, "Show them." She held up her thumb and forefinger. "Show them the trick with the lightning. So they know you're serious."

The Soul Collector thought this was a fantastic idea. He bared his teeth again and raised the hand, letting all cameras focus in. Zoey, feeling like now would be the perfect time for some liquid courage, unscrewed the cap on Jacob's flask and tipped the rest of its contents into her mouth. The Soul Collector leered at her, held his hand in front of her face, fingers spread, and let the piercing arc of blue electricity leap from thumb to forefinger.

Zoey spat half a flask of whisky at him, the mist flying through the arc and igniting into a fireball. She had aimed at his face, but the ball of fire instead descended and engulfed his crotch. The Soul Collector shrieked like a man whose nuts were on fire, and fell hard on his ass. Zoey grabbed Stench Machine's crate and sprinted through the crowd.